InSignificantly
UNIQUE

Bethel Bates

iUniverse, Inc.
Bloomington

InSignificantly Unique

This is a work of fiction. All of the characters, names, incidents, organizations, and dialogue in this novel are either the products of the author's imagination or are used fictitiously.

iUniverse books may be ordered through booksellers or by contacting:

iUniverse
1663 Liberty Drive
Bloomington, IN 47403
www.iuniverse.com
1-800-Authors (1-800-288-4677)

Because of the dynamic nature of the Internet, any web addresses or links contained in this book may have changed since publication and may no longer be valid. The views expressed in this work are solely those of the author and do not necessarily reflect the views of the publisher, and the publisher hereby disclaims any responsibility for them.

Any people depicted in stock imagery provided by Thinkstock are models, and such images are being used for illustrative purposes only.

Certain stock imagery © Thinkstock.

ISBN: 978-1-4759-1929-5 (sc)
ISBN: 978-1-4759-1930-1 (e)

Printed in the United States of America

iUniverse rev. date: 5/29/2012

Introduction

I don't know why we were born to die or why grass grows green and there is blue in the sky. I don't know why the sun is so bright, why day becomes night, or how wrongs become rights. And I don't know why the strong prey on the weak, why there's war instead of peace, or why my parents have forsaken me.........I don't know why.

Dedication

This book is dedicated to the motherless and fatherless children alike all over the world. It's dedicated to the adult who never had the opportunity to be a child. And to those who struggled with coming to terms with abandonment and questions that were never answered.

InSignificantly UNIQUE

BETHEL BATES

While most little girls lay safely snug in their beds with an occasional sugar plum dancing about their heads. They have ponytails and bows, polished nails and manicured toes. They play dress up and hop scotch, enjoying ice cream and lollipops. With their heads floating high, their dreams nestled safely in the clouds. They feel secured, loved, and adored, with food on their tables, locked window and locked doors

But my story was a little different......

CHAPTER ONE

The heat of the day blistered with a thickness in the air that made it difficult to breath. I had a final paper that was due in just a few days and I thought I'd get an early start before the burning heat of the day rose to an unbearable temperature. My professor had already given the class a courtesy by allowing a three day extension, and so I was running out of excuses. But at already 9:45 in the am the temperature was soaring at a sizzling eighty-five degrees.

I came out onto the porch with my school books in hand, ready to proceed with the task that lie before me, when nostalgia began to have its way, taking me back some eight years earlier to a time that seemed almost unforgiving.

It was report card day and I had just gotten in from school. I came in and placed my report card on the kitchen table in our small and reserved one bedroom apartment. I went over to the refrigerator, opened the door, and wasn't surprised to see that it was practically empty, aside from two cans of Old English and a bowl of something that had lost its solidity and become liquified; giving off a horrendous stench that would fill the entire house the very second the refrigerator door opened.

I took the foul substance and poured most of what I could down the drain of the kitchen sink. And what was left of it, I placed in a doubled Shoprite plastic bag and sat it outside in the dumpster. My disgust was not only with the condition of my surroundings but it was also with the dismal outlook on my family's mere existence that almost brought me to tears, yet again.

My thoughts were abruptly disrupted by the ravenous cries of my lil' brother Ice, who had always looked to me for all the answers.

"What we gonna' eat Uni, I'm hungry?" he said.

"Is she here?" I asked as I surveyed the room and saw proof of her presence.

Ice pointed towards the bedroom with apprehension. I took a deep breath and began to walk in the direction of the bedroom that I shared with my Mother. I opened the door and there she was, completely held captive by that which she manifested daily; her insecurities, her skepticisms, her discontentment, and a host of other demons that plagued her.

It had been two weeks since we had seen our Mother. She had a bit of a tendency to disappear whenever life would overwhelm her, which seemed to be constantly.

"Why couldn't she love herself?" I asked myself. "Why was she only strong when he was around? Why couldn't she be strong for us?"

"Lola. Lola wake up" I called out to her as I shook her from her near graven sleep. There's nothing to eat Lola, wake up," I almost pleaded.

"Take my watch to the pawn shop. See what Mr. Pete can give us for it," she moaned with her eyelids still shut.

"I took your watch to Mr. Pete two weeks ago, right before you left.

"It ain't been two weeks", she screeched. "It was just a couple of days ago", she insisted. "It ain't been two weeks."

"It has been two weeks, Lola. It was two weeks ago that you sent me down to Mr. Pete's with the watch. Remember? He gave me twenty dollars for it. You took ten and gave me the other ten to buy milk, cheese, and bread – and then you left. Don't you remember?" I asked.

"Whatever", she said smugly. "Well go down the street and ask Miss Bertha if we could borrow a couple of pieces of bread and some lunch meat. Tell her I'll set her straight at the first of the month when I get my check, plus I'll give her extra for her troubles," she quickly said.

I walked out and slammed the bedroom door behind me.

"Slam it again and see if I won't raise up and knock a couple of inches off your ba-lack ass," she yelled.

"I'm sick of this shit," I mumbled to myself.

"Where you goin'?" Ice asked as he ran after me beggin' me not to go.

Ice, whose Christian name was Isaac Jefferson, was almost four years behind me and had some abandonment issues that were more than justifiable. And so, I did understand perfectly well why he was so afraid that I would leave one day and never come back.

"You leaving again?" he asked.

"I'll be back in a half hour, I promise," I always had to assure him.

"That don't mean nothing around here," he said with anger as he looked into my eyes as if he wanted me to give him some sort of guarantee that I was really coming back .

Ice was always so happy to see Lola after she would return from wherever she had been. But he was also so disappointed in the fact that her disappearing acts would cause him great anxieties. I knew that he really didn't understand why she did the things that she did. And I wasn't able to explain something that I really didn't understand myself. And so we didn't speak much on it.

"Have I ever lied to you?" I asked Ice. "Look at me. Have I?
I stood there and waited for his response.
"I said I'll be back, Okay," I repeated as he looked away with an expressionless face.

I left and returned about two hours later with a happy meal order of chicken strips, a large order of french fries, a bacon double cheese burger and two vanilla shakes. I also had a couple of bags that contained a gallon of milk, two loaves of bread, peanut butter and jelly, margarine, a dozen of eggs, a box of Alphabet Cereal, and some orange crème popsicles – Ice's favorite.
My hands were pleasingly filled, disallowing me to grab hold of the door knob to the front door of the apartment and so I began to kick the door, signaling Ice to come and open the door for me.

"Who is it?" Ice asked.
"It's me, open the door."
"You went shopping?" he exclaimed as soon as he saw my bag filled arms.
"Here, take this", I said as I handed him the McDonald's bag with the chicken strips and fries.

"Mickey D's - yes. Thanks Uni," he exclaimed as he wrapped his arms around my waist with gratitude and appreciation.

"Go ahead with that'," I modestly responded as I tried to act as though his thankfulness and affection didn't matter much to me. But the real truth was that it meant everything to me.

Our mother wasn't able to be there for us like I've seen other mother's be there for their children. Ice has never known our mother to be a mother in that way. But I knew her when she was different. I knew her when she was a beautiful, almost nurturing and caring person.

Most people tell me that I look just like her. They say I'm the spitting image of her. They tell me that our eyes are the same and the texture of our hair is the same. They tell me that we have the same smile.

There was a time when she would have never left us alone on our own to fend for ourselves. But once she started riding the white horse, the white horse became her primary purpose in life.

She began to change shortly after our father was murdered. Ice doesn't remember like I do because he was just three years old when it happened. I remember it like it was yesterday. It was one week before my seventh birthday. It was gonna' be one of the happiest days of my life because I had never had a birthday party before. But instead, it turned out to be the worst day ever.

"We have money, Uni?" Ice questioned.

"We have some, but not much" I responded.

"But where did it come from?" he asked.

"That's for me to know," I said as I gave him a sisterly pop on top of his head.

"Sit down and eat and stop askin' so many questions."

I put the well needed groceries away and sat down with Ice and we ate our first real meal in weeks. Then there was a knock at the door. I licked my fingers, wiped them with a napkin, and got up suspiciously. I looked into the peep hole of our apartment door and saw that it was a strange lady of European descent that looked as if she were a bill collector.

"Yeah?" I asked through the door.

"Yes, Hello, I'd like to speak to the parent or guardian of Unique Jefferson", the lady said.

"In reference to what?" I asked like I was taught to do.

"Are you Unique?" she asked.

I stood there for a moment as I studied this chic through the small visual.

"What if I am?" I asked.

"Is your parent or guardian at home?" she asked

"No, what is it that you want?" I started to get agitated.

"My name is Christina Jameson and I'm a representative with the National Junior Honor Society. It seems you, or Unique Jefferson, was recommended by a staff member at her school to be a part of a special program that our organization offers to youth like yourself or her," she explained.

"Youth like me?" I asked. "Like me how?" I gave up my identity.

"May I please come in for a second? This won't take long,"

I opened the door just enough for her to slip through.

"As I was saying, is there someone, an adult perhaps, that I could speak to regarding this matter?" she asked.

"You can speak to me. My mom's not home at the moment," I lied.

"Well our organization has a special program that aides gifted youth like yourself who did exceptionally well on the Taranova and PSSA test in the areas of math and science; and who also resides in a single parent home with an annual income that is slightly challenging," the strange lady went on to explain. "The program will be incorporated directly into your school's agenda and you will meet with the other candidates twice a week. Once you have completed the program successfully, at the end of your senior year, you will be given a full scholarship and recommended to a college that best suits you and your aspirations.

Our records show that a package with all the information that I just mentioned was mailed out to your home some time ago to be signed and mailed back. So far, we have yet to receive the signed permission slip. We've sent the package several times. But I do happen to have with me today, an identical package that I was hoping could be signed by your Parent or Guardian today," she said.

"Well, like I said, my Mom's not here right now, but if you give me the package I can make sure that she gets it," I said as I observed her stature, long legs, her freshly done hair and nails, the sand colored Dolce & Gabbana bag on her shoulder, shoes colored the same, and the tailor made suit that was on her back. I remember looking at her wondering; how could someone like me achieve that?"

"Do you always make house calls?" I asked sarcastically.

"No, only when there's something important enough to warrant it. Here is the package and also my card with my name and number on it in case there are any questions that you or your Mother may have about filling out the application. It was very nice meeting you Unique. I hope to see you during our candle light ceremony later this month.

"Good-bye," she said.

"Good-bye," I responded.

I closed the door and stared at the card and the packet for a moment and then threw them both in the trash just as I'd done with the other packets that came through the mail.

"Who was that?" Ice asked.

"Nobody," I answered.

While eating the last morsels of our McDonalds, I started to daydream about flying. My mind wondered away from me as I sat and thought about my life and how dreams were called dreams for a reason. They're a series of thoughts, images, and sensations that develop mysteriously in a realm deep, deep inside our brains.

I thought about the bad dreams that occur at night while we are sleeping; why some are called nightmares. And then there are the dreams that we have while we're wide awake - day dreams. The day dreams are usually more pleasant and you can make better sense of them. I've often wondered, what if any, is the purpose of a dream? Dreams offer false hopes and fake expectations with reaches that are unobtainable.

But even in all of their deceitfulness we cling to them because they encourage us to look forward to happier times and they help us to live another day.

Once I finished cleaning up I settled in and took out my Jane Austen novel and continued where I left off.

CHAPTER TWO

The next day moved at a speed that was slower than the day before. I decided to go down to the cave to see what was poppin'. The cave was the hang out for the teenagers and young adults; some not so young, that lived in the neighborhood. It was also a place where a great deal of rift raft did their business and their dirt, which was all one in the same.

The cave came fully equipped with a couple of pool tables, a mini arcade, a picture booth, and a dine in section. It was known city-wide for its ribs and wings. The cave was where Bailey and a few other associates of hers hung out on a day to day basis. I myself didn't make it my business to frequent the cave, because if you weren't careful, something not so good might just rub off on you.

"Hey, what's your pleasure Ma? I thought you didn't hang out in places like this?" Jeremy said.

"I don't," I responded.

Jeremy was complicated, a bit like myself. We grew up in the same neighborhood and knew all of the same people. He's been kicked out of school more times then I can count. His life, like many of ours, wasn't something that we would have ever chosen, given the option, but rather something that was grievously thrusted upon us. And so we did the best that we could do with it.

"Yo, what up girl? Whachoo doin' here?" Bailey asked.

"Lookin' for you - what else. I didn't see you last night. I just wanted to make sure you were okay," I expressed.

"As you can see I'm fine," she responded.

Bailey was my closest friend. She was a lot rougher than me. She was true to the game; a real warrior. She was feminine in a lot of ways. But in a lot of ways she wasn't. The both of us were always told that we were pretty. And people would always compare her beauty to mine. But her tom boyish rough exterior would always stir the male persuasion in my direction, just like she intended.

I don't know who's life was worse - hers or mine. She crashed at my house at least twice a week, dreading to go home. It wasn't really safe for her to stay in her own house and so she would come pass my crib mostly after one o'clock am.; on any given night, no questions asked.

She'd crash at my crib, get up and shower the next morning, get dressed, and then she'd leave. She was always on the move, never steady like me. Lola was never aware of her presence in the house because Lola was never really there. And even when she was there in body she was stoned out of her mind, and so she never even knew the difference.

Although my house wasn't anything to brag about, it was clear that Bailey felt safe right there with Ice and me. There were no restrictions and no threats. With Ice and me she was out of harms way.

"I need a job real bad," I told Bailey. "But nobody will hire me. They all say you have to be at least sixteen and have workin' papers,"

I confided in Bailey. "I can't wait two years. I need a job now. My mom is getting worse. She's not even payin' the rent. We never have any food in the house anymore and I'm tired of beggin' for it. And if I don't get a job or something soon, I'm scared we gonna' be out on the street. I went down to see Mr. Lloyd to ask him if he could give me a loan," I said.

"What?" Bailey exclaimed. You went down where to ask who for what? Uni, how did you even know to do that?" Bailey asked.

"I heard Lola and Miss Irene talkin' about it one day. They said Lloyd lends money to people in the neighborhood when they fall on hard times. All you gotta' do is pay'em back with a little extra."

"How much did you get from him?"

"Fifty"

"Un huh. And where you gonna' get the money to pay him back?"

I hunched my shoulders as I wondered the exact same thing.

"I don't know," I said. "I'll figure it out. I guess I'll have to cross that bridge when I get to it."

"I betchoo Mr. Lloyd can't wait for you to figure it out," Bailey said. "I bet he's hoping that you can't pay him back. And then he's gottchoo.

Bailey had a lotta' streets smarts because she's been practically takin' care of herself since she was about nine years old. That's how long she's been runnin' away from home. She ran away from home so much that nobody even comes lookin' for her anymore.

"How long did he give you?" she asked me.

"A week," I answered.

"That gives us a little time to think of something. Don't worry," she assured me.

And from that moment on I didn't worry.

Just then Brick, a twenty somethin' year old slanger who was known for movin' a lot of weight came in. He was buff and everything, but he really didn't do anything for me. It was just something about him that didn't set right in my spirit, especially the fact that he was a grown man and liked girls just fresh out of elementary and middle school.

He walked over to Bails and me, slightly touching the side of my leg in passing.

"When you goin' let me take you out – get your nails or your hair done for you?" he asked.

"Never," I said.

"Damn! It's like that? You just goin' cut a brother straight smooth," he said.

Bailey couldn't stand Brick. I always believed that something happened between those two, but I couldn't prove it. She had a way of always tryin' to protect me from some of the bad experiences that she had and I loved her for that.

"Come on girl. Let's get outta here. It's getting' crowded," she said as she tapped me on my knee. So I got up and began to follow her out.

"Oh! It's like dat huh?" Brick asked. "But look, that's ok. If you ever need anything lil' sista, you come see me," Brick hollered after me.

I turned around slightly as I was leaving. My eyes met his eyes as we stared at one another for about three seconds. Ask me; I don't know what that was about but it was strange.

I hadn't been to school in about a week or so. I had other things on my mind – like eatin'. When you're hungry it's hard to concentrate on anything except those hunger pangs. But I decided to go to school the next day since I was able to buy a few things to put in the fridge.

I needed a break from worryin' about Lola, Ice, and keepin' a roof over our heads. If anybody cared to know, school is where I'd rather be any day of the week. It was where I felt most at home. It's what calmed me. Unlike most kids, school was something that I felt I could do forever.

"Well, Miss Jefferson. So happy that you decided to grace us with your presence today," said Ms. Malone.

I had Ms. Malone for first period math and advisory. She was very Afro-centric and proud of who she was and where she came from. She wore soulful jewelry and clothing that spoke of an ethnic flair. Her hair was naturally locked and her demeanor and method of teaching resembled a minister preaching a sermon on a Sunday morning.

She didn't know it, but she was definitely my favorite teacher. I think one of the reasons she was my favorite is because I truly believed she loved what she did. She had a crazy passion for books and shared that passion with every kid that crossed her path.

Every week she would share with us a book that she had read; bursting at the seams to disclose the message of the book and how she felt the message was beneficial to us all as a whole.

It was clear that she was not only proud of who she was but she wanted us to be proud of who we were, as well. She would always remind us to be mindful of our surroundings and of how we spoke and pronounced our words in public. She wasn't a great fan of ebonics, but she understood that we had our own way of saying things and that America would always down play the very things that they really couldn't understand or relate to.

And so taking that into consideration, I spoke according to what my environment dictated. I had a habit of speaking one way when I was around my family members, just being me. And then I spoke another way when I was around those who didn't know me and judged me.

Ms. Malone was an absolute advocate and a great fan of African American Literature. She wasn't even my English teacher, she taught math. But she loved the writings of such people as Phillis Wheately, the first African American Poet and the first African American Women whose writings were published.

Ms. Malone introduced our class to Olauda Equano aka Gustavas Vassa, who was one of the most prominent Africans who reached early high points with the Harlem Renaissance and was involved with the British movement for the abolition of slave trade in 1807.

She encouraged us to read written works by Walter Mosely, Toni Morrison, Langston Hughes, Maya Angelou, Booker T. Washington, and W.E. B. Du Bois. But not only did she promote African American writers, she promoted great writers in general. She was adamant about being versatile and well rounded in our readings. She instilled in us the value of knowing our own history first before we could learn about the history of others. She encouraged us to read Macbeth and Hamlet, written by English poet and playwright, Williams Shakespear. She implored us to examine A Tale of Two Cities and Great Expectations by English Novelist, Charles Dickens. But that's not all. There was Ernest Hemingway, Mark Twain, Edgar Allan Poe, Virginia Woolf, Homer, and D(avid).H(erbert) Lawrence.

Ms. Malone treated everyone in her class as though they were her very own children and wanted nothing but the very best for them. I believe deep down in her heart she felt she had a parental responsibility to us and intended on honoring it.

She truly believed that it took a village to raise a child, although she didn't have any children of her own. But rumor had it that she used to have a son who became very ill with some rare disease and died some years back. And so I believe that she transfers all the love that she gave to him when he was alive, over to us.

"Cameron", Ms Malone said as she removed the hat from his head. "A gentleman always removes his hat before entering a room, especially in the presence of a lady" she said as she physically removed the hat from his head.

"Awl, come on Ms. Malone, can I get my hat back?" he begged.

"Sure you can. I'll hold it for you until the end of the school year. Maybe by then you'll know how to wear it" she said.

"Man, you can't be serious, what am I gonna' tell my Mom?" he asked.

"I don't know what you're gonna' tell your Mom. I guess that would be you're problem and not mine? If you want your hat back before the end of the school year, your mother will have to come up here in person to pick it up" she said.

"Awl, that's wack. Why you gotta' be that way?" he asked.

"The same reason you have to come into my classroom day in and day out with that funky hat on your bean head, when I've spoken to you about it multiple times. I am not a recorder and so I will not be repeating myself" she stated. "Now that is the end of that conversation. Everyone be seated and clear off your desk ."She said firmly. "People, people, calm down, and clear your desk of everything except a writing utensil." Ms. Malone instructed.

"You're kiddin' me. You givin' us a test on a Tuesday?" asked Jose Torres

"I'll test you on whatever day I feel like giving you a test, Mr. Torres". Ms Malone said with conviction.

"Yo, she went there on you man," Lance Cunningham exploded.

"Settle down people," Ms. Malone said. "You have twenty minutes to complete this quiz. When the timer goes off, even if you have not finished yet, you must stop, put your pencils down, turn your paper face down, and fold your hands in front of you. You will keep your eyes on your own paper. There will be no talking, no chewing, absolutely no movement of lips at all. If you get caught doing any of these things, it will result in an automatic zero. Do you understand?" she affirmed.

"Yeees Ms. Malone," the whole class said in unison.

"Does anyone have any questions?" she asked.

There was complete silence. She then commenced to passing out the test. After twenty minutes the alarm went off and Ms. Malone called time. She collected the test and we were dismissed.

"See everybody tomorrow and have a great day," she said as she dismissed us.

CHAPTER THREE

The Carnival was in town and it was one of the biggest annual events that occurred in our community. It was a real big deal for somebody like me who's never been outside of the neighborhood or the Detroit area. It got bored pretty quickly around the way and that may have been one of the reasons it was easy to get into stuff. It was just nice to do something a little different from time to time. The Carnival gave everybody an opportunity to socialize and have fun. It would only be in town for a week or so. And just like Christmas, you would wait for it forever, and that time would come and go before you even knew it.

Lola was M.I.A. again. It had been a couple of days since the last time I'd seen her. I remember when I used to lose my mind worrying about her. Sometimes I'd sit up all night cryin' myself into a frenzy, hoping that she was alright and that she would come home soon. But it's become such a frequent and tiresome routine, and with it my tears have all but dried up.

Now, I don't sit up all night crying, waiting, and worrying, although I still hoped that she was okay. But I realized a long time ago that my tears would never be enough to bring her back home to us for good. Besides, there's Ice to worry about now.

He's young and very easily swayed. And my concern was only for him.

It was about three thirty in the afternoon on Sunday and I only had about five dollars toward my debt to Lloyd. I had no idea how I was goin' get the rest of the money I owed him and I really hadn't thought on it. I sat out on the front stoop for about an hour or so as I watched Ice play stick ball with his friends, when Jonesy walked up.

"Where you on your way to?" I asked her as she came over and sat next to me on the stoop.

"I'm trying to find somebody to go to the Carnival with. Big Mike said that things are about to jump off over there," she replied. "You seen Addy?" she asked.

"Nope," I answered. "I ain't really seen nobody today. I just came out."

"Well she's probably over there already," Jonesy said. "You goin' walk me over there to see what's goin' on or what?" she asked.

"I can't right now I gotta' stay here and watch Ice," I responded.

"Girl, he old enough to play by hisself ain't he? You baby that boy too much. I keep tellin' you dat'. You ain't his momma. Well why can't he come wif' us?" she asked.

"First of all, I don't baby him too much. I'm just careful with him. And I know I'm not his Mother. But I'm gonna' make sure that he doesn't end up like the rest of these knuckle heads around here. And plus, it cost money to go to the Carnival, Jonesy. And Ice is gonna' want all kinds of things that I can't buy," I explained. "And I don't feel like all the drama."

"Well I'm leakin' too. Everybody's leakin'. But I gotta' couple of dollars that I don't mind sharing," she said.

"Thanks. But I'm ok. I guess it ain't goin' hurt to go around there for a little while." I said. "Just let me run inside and get my bag,"

I went inside and got my bag and came back outside.

"Ice, come on," I yelled.

"Where we going?" he bellowed back.

"We gonna' walk over to the Carnival for a lil' while. Get your stuff and put it in the house,"

"Yo, I'll catch y'all later," Ice said to his friends.

He put his things in the house, locked up, and we were on our way.

As soon as we got to the entrance of the Carnival, I recognized a lot of people from school and from around the way. We pretty much lived in a fairly mixed neighborhood, and so it was on the eastside of Detroit.

As we approached the speed ball game, I ran into some guy named Javier. Javier was a cuttie, he was. And he was sweet too. He had a fair pale Mediterranean complexion with dark brown hair, hazel eyes, and a strong, tight body structure, with a set of perfect lips and a chip in one of his front teeth.

When he spoke he made sure that everything he said rhymed. It was just his way. He was a jokester, always trying to make somebody laugh. He got on most peoples nerves with all of that. But I can say that it really didn't bother me. I found him to be quite humorous and it was for that reason that I could never take Javier serious.

"There she is, fine as wine, definitely one of a kind. Would it be possible for me to get a little bit of your time," he serenaded Jonsey.

"Boy, if you don't get outta' my face with that corney mess," she said.

"Oh! really? Corney?" he asked.

"Yes, corney," she confirmed

"That's because you don't know real poetry when you hear it, girl. What about you?" he turned to look at me. "You think I'm corney too, I suppose?" he asked.

"It was ok," I said.

"Was it ok, ok, or was it just ok?" he asked.

"I mean it was cool," I said.

"Was it real cool, or was it just regular cool?" he asked

"Javier!" I snapped as he began to annoy me.

"Okay, Okay, I'm satisfied with that," he stated. "So y'all here by y'allselves?" he asked.

"Yeah," I responded.

"Mind if I hang out with y'all?" he asked.

"Yes, we mind," Jonsey blurted out.

"I don't care," I said as I tried to smooth things over,"

Right at that moment we were approaching the water gun game and we stopped right in front of it.

"Ooh can we play?" Ice pleaded.

"No, you're not gonna' play every game you see. I don't have it like that right now, maybe later," I responded.

Javier looked at me and pulled out three dollars from his left pocket.

"Can I, Uni?" Ice asked me again as he looked at Javier and waited for me to say that it was alright for him to accept the money. I hunched my shoulders at Javier as if to say, "if that's what you wanna' do."

"Here you go lil' man," Javier said.

"Thanx," Ice replied as the two of them gave each other a pound.

I stood back and watched the transaction between Ice and Javier. It was scary to see those two interact and how mature Ice was becoming. Seconds later, Addison appeared, Addy for short.

"Hey now. What's going on?"

"How long you been up here?" Jonsey asked.

"I've been up here since around two," Addy answered.

"We just got here a few minutes ago," Jonsey said. "Where you on your way to?" Jonsey inquired.

"No where in particular. I'm trynna' find my sista. She is supposed to be up here some where. She's holdin' on to my money and I need to find her."

"Oh, okay, we saw her near the gate when we were comin' in," I said to her.

"Yeah," Jonsey cosigned. "We did see her near the gate. Come on I'll help you catch up to her."

"Okay," Addy said.

"I'ma catch up with you later Unique," Jonsey said.

"Okay then," I replied as Jonsey and Addy walked off.

It was just me, Ice, and Javier.

"So what you wanna' do next?" Javier asked.

"I don't know."

"We can go get a couple of hot dogs if you're hungry. It's my treat," he stressed.

I looked at Javier for a minute and saw that it would probably mean more to him then to me, if I took him up on his offer. It was clear that he wanted to show kindness towards me. And so I let him. By this time I looked around and realized that I had lost track of Ice.

"Alright, but I need to find Ice first," I said. "He's around here somewhere."

I turned toward the direction of the skee ball game where I last saw Ice. But I didn't see him. So I began to walk around slowly.

"Where did he git' to? You can't leave that boy alone for one second. Shhhii," I sighed in frustration.

"Where is he?" I spoke under my breath.

"Calm down. He can't be but so far. I'm sure he's around here somewhere," Javier assured me. "I was his age once. I remember how it was. He's probably…" but before Javier could finish his sentence, I spotted Ice across the way in front of the fun house.

"There he is," I said as I began to move swiftly through the crowd of people, as I couldn't get to him fast enough.

"What do you think you're doing?" I asked as I walked up on Ice and found him in a squatting position shootin' dice with four other juvenile delinquents who looked to be my age or older.

"Get your little ass up right now," I swore.

"Look Uni. Look, I'm winning," he responded.

"No, you're not, now come on," I insisted as I pulled the back of his shirt.

"Come on Ma'. You gotta' give us a chance to win our money back," one of the guys yelled out as I pulled on Ice."

"Oh I do! Okay watch this then," I said as I turned with Ice gripped up in my grasp, and we began to walk away.

"Damn, that little nigga' got me for a duce," I heard one of them say as we were leaving.

"He got me for fifteen," another one yelled out.

"If this ain't about a bitch!" another one said. "He got me for a duce too.

"Uni, what's the matter?" Ice asked. "Why did you do dat'? I can make my own money you know. I wanna' start helping you pay for stuff for the house. I wanna' get my own money and carry my own weight," Ice cried.

"Listen," I stopped him dead in his tracks and looked him in the face. "I know what you trynna' do. But when you get money that way, there's always consequences and repercussions to it. I don't know why, it just is. Bad habits always come wit' a price. And even when you win you lose. Do you understand what I'm sayin' to you?" I asked.

"I need you to hear me," I said.

"I hear you," he said reluctantly. "But I'm the man of the house and you keep holdin' me back,"

Although he was only ten and he was the only male in the house. I didn't wanna' burst his bubble and tell him, "No, you are not a man and you are far from it. You are still a little boy." But I couldn't because I did feel where he was comin' from and I knew where his heart was.

"Yes," I said. "And so as the man of this house you will do what no man in this family has ever done before. You will concentrate on your school work. You won't be slangin' and you won't be bangin'. You won't be shootin' no dice or playing no pool for money. And you won't be goin' to jail like all these other guys out here. You goin' go to school and live to grow up to be somebody. So don't worry so much about being a man right now. You have plenty of time for that. You let me worry about how we livin', you hear me?"

When I turned from Ice, I looked over at Javier and noticed that he had a look of embarrassment on his face, like he was embarrassed for me that he over heard what I expressed to Ice. We started walking toward the hot dog booth. Javier ordered the hot dogs and fires for the three of us. Things had calmed down and we began to eat when Javier spoke.

"If you don't mind me askin', who lives with you and your brother?"

"I do mind," I responded defensively.

"Are you always like this?" he asked. "I'm just sayin' that for a minute there you sounded more like a motha than a sista. I mean,

I heard and I dug everything that you said to him. It was real. I'm just sayin'. It was real grown up to say those things.

I got quiet for a minute – for a long minute. And then I became rational and apologized.

"I apologize if I came off wrong. It's just that, that subject is always a little touchy for me. I just prefer not to talk about it if you don't mind" I said.

"Cool, yeah that's – that's cool. I understand" he responded.

"So where do you get your money from – If you don't mind me askin?" I kicked it right back at him'.

"You don't wanna' know," he said.

"Yeah I do," I said. "Never mind. I already know," I quickly concluded.

"Naw. It's not even like that. See, I know exactly how your brother feels. I never woulda considered doing what I do in a million years - until one day I did.

My Mom got laid off from a job that she had for about seven years. She always worked and provided for me and my sista. And then all of a sudden, no more job; and we were ass out. My Mom was strugglin' to pay the rent with the unemployment checks that she received because they were a lot less money than what she was used to getting'.

She could barely buy food. All the utilities started to get shut off in our house. We had no water and no gas. We were basically drowning. And I saw what it was doing to my Mom. She would worry like everyday that we were goin' get evicted.

I knew I couldn't let that happen. And that's when I started doin' this. I made enough money to pay everything, you know. I took the money down to the utilities company myself, and one by one I paid them all.

My mom was shocked. She couldn't believe it. She was so happy. But when she found out what I was doing to get the money, she cold flipped. She told me that I had to stop and that it wasn't worth getting killed over or goin' to jail for. But I couldn't stop. Because I knew that if I did we would end up right back in the same situation.

But just recently my Mom found another job – a pretty good one. And I've been meaning to stop. I'm thinking about it all the time," he continued. "It's just hard, you know, needing things and…I just don't want to have to ask my Mom for anything. I like taking care of myself. But I know I gotta' stop one day soon because I'm not trynna' to go to jail and I'm not trynna' die out here doing this. It's getting' dangerous out here too, yo."

"Yeah and every day you wake up you're given a choice," I reminded him.

"And you know what, you're right," he admitted. "Today is as good a day as any," he said to me. And as far as I know he retired that very day.

"Well, I'm gonna' take Ice and head back up the way. Thanks for everything," I said with gratitude.

"Sure, whatever I can do." Javier said with a big ole cheese cake smile. "But let me walk you home to make sure, you know, that you get in OK," he said. "Besides, I'm goin' that way too.

He didn't even wait for a response, he just started to walk along side me.

As soon as we got outside the front gate, there was Brick.

"My, my, what do we have here?" he asked.

He had a big stuffed animal in his hand.

"Here you go sweetness, I won this just for you," he said wit' his fast talkin' ass.

"You can't do no better than that?" I asked with a tongue that was as sharp as a blade.

"You tryin' to chump me huh? Every day you amaze me?" he went on. "Oh baby girl, that cut a brother real deep. I thought I was sayin' sumpthin''"

"I know you bet you did," I came back.

"Can't you see my sista' don't like your ugly self," Ice came to my aid like he was my big brother.

Brick pushed the stuffed animal in Ice's face.

"Then this is for you, shorty," he said. "You take it"

Javier felt compelled to say or do something. He pushed the stuffed animal outta' my brother's face and back towards Brick.

"Yo! man, get a grip. Whatchoo doin'?" Javier jumped in and asked Brick. Come on Ice, we need to be going," he stated as he gave Brick a cold stare. Brick stared back and laughed.

"Damn girl! What you got the Gestopo out wit' you today? That's real cute though," Brick laughed.

"Uni, look," Ice exclaimed.

"Look what?" I asked.

"Look in that car over there," he instructed me.

Quickly, I looked over and noticed a silver Buick Lesabre with shinny new rims as it was stopped at the light. It was Lola and some strange guy. Javier had never seen Lola before but Brick knew of her and knew what she was into.

"You know that lady in that car?" Brick asked me sarcastically.

He knew damn well that was my Mother.

"What a crazy resemblance," he said as he looked at me and then looked over at Lola and shook his head with a smirk on his face. "Well I'ma let you go and be on you're way. I know you got things to do and I don't wanna' hold you up," he said as he put a card with his number on it and a twenty dollar bill inside my jacket pocket."You keep it tight "G", he said to Javier. "You too, lil' man," he said to Ice.

Javier walked us home and we said our good-byes at the door.

"I guess I'll see you tomorrow," I said.
"It's a bet," Javier responded.

I hadn't seen Bailey in a day or two. I was sure that I would run into her at the carnival. But who knows where she might be?

Chapter Four

It was Monday morning again. And it was one of those grey; rainy, gloomy and cool days. I turned on all the pilots on the top of our kitchen range to take the chill off the house. Ice and I were scrambling for our school things, trying to get out of the house on time for once. I was in my first year at Nat Turner High and Ice was in his first year at Martin Luther Middle School.

Martin Luther was just a few blocks from Nat Turner, and so I was able to walk Ice to school on most mornings, even on the days that I chose not to go to school. And there were a lotta' days like that. But even on those days I would still walk him to school, turn back around, and walk back home. Truth be told, when I first started skipping school, most times I wouldn't go to school because I would be waiting around hoping that Lola would come back.

But on this particular day I got to school on time and went straight to my locker to get my Math book. I had Geometry for my first period class and Ms. Malone would have a fit if you showed up to her class unprepared. As I was closing my locker, Bailey crept up on me.

"Girl, you got some serious issues. You scared me. Where you been? How come I didn't see you at the carnival yesterday?" I asked.

"The carnival? That's for youngins. I'm workin' now. I got a job. I'm doin' some adult things," she elaborated.

"Mmm huh," I mumbled.

"Mmm huh is right. You betta worry about getting' Lloyd's money." she said. "How much you got?"

"All but twenty," I answered.

"Well check this out," she said as she pulled out about a hundred dollars at least from her pocket.

"Where did you get that? And who in their right mind gave it to you?" I asked.

"Aha, wouldn't you like to know. Meet me at the Cave after school and I'll tell you all about it," she said as the bell rang. We hurried to class.

It was about the last fifteen minutes of class when Ms. Malone put a problem up on the board.

"Who would like to come up here and solve for X?" she asked as she looked around the room. "Lailean," she called out. "How about you"?

Lailean dragged herself up to the chalk board. Lailean was Asian American. Her father was Black and her mother was Asian. She was a very shy and reserved person and hated to be called upon to participate in any classroom activities. Most of us hated to be called on for fear that we would mess up and be laughed at. Lailean was up there for about a good five minutes.

"Take your time and remember your steps," Ms. Malone encouraged her.

But Lailean was just plain stuck. She was up to step three but couldn't go any further.

"That's ok, let's give her a hand for all of her effort," Ms. Malone said. "You can have a seat," she told Lailean. "Who else wants to come up and try? Javier, how about you?" she asked.

Javier shook his head no.

"No," Ms. Malone answered for him. "Okay, Miss Jefferson, how about you?" she asked as she motioned me with her hand to go up to the board. I dropped my head for a second but then I held it up again. I was so bashful. All I wanted was for it to be over and so I walked up to the board quickly and erased the work that Lailean had done and in two minutes I had solved for X. I returned to my seat and watched as Ms. Malone went over to the board and reviewed the problem.

"She skipped a few steps and took a short cut, but the conclusion is absolutely correct. I'm impressed. Great job Unique. Maybe you would like to explain to the class tomorrow how you solved this problem and explain the short cut that you took," she said as the bell rang. "I'll leave it up on the board until tomorrow."

And then the bell rang.

"If you could hang around for just a few minutes, Miss Jefferson. I would like to have a word with you," Ms. Malone said as I was scooping up my books from my desk.
"Oh my God, what did she want with me now?" I asked myself.

I knew that I wasn't up to hearing another lecture. But still, I waited for everyone to leave and then I approached her desk.

"Yes, Ms Malone?" I responded to her request.

"Are you aware that you've missed ten days out of this quarter alone – all unexcused absences? You haven't turned in any homework or classroom assignments since this quarter began. But somehow you show up to my class, take every test and manage to do exceptionally well on them all.

You did that problem today in less than two minutes. I don't have to tell you how very gifted you are young lady. I just don't have the words. But unfortunately, it is not enough for you to just show up once a week and pass my tests. You have to be consistent in coming to class and you have to turn in your assignments. I implore you. Don't waste the gift that God has given you. Is everything alright at home, Unique?" she threw a curve ball.

"Yes," I said. I was gettin' pretty good at lying.

"Well what is it then child?" she asked. "I endorsed your membership with the National Junior Honor Society months ago because you are the perfect candidate. And since that time your attendance has dropped drastically and your class participation is non-existent. You're a bright and outstanding child. I just want to help, whatever it is. Tell me what it is I can do and let me help. I just don't want to see someone with your potential fall through the cracks like so many others I've seen," she stated.

I stood there with nothin' to say. I should have known that she was behind that lady coming over to my house.

"Well you feel free to come talk to me about anything, Ok? And remember, my door is always open," she confirmed her open door policy.

I wanted so bad to tell her everything that was going on in my shitty life. She spoke to me with so much kindness and with so much concern. I just wanted to tell her everything. I often had dreams about what it would be like if Ms. Malone were my fill in Mom. I know that it is kinda pathetic. But I know that if she were, she would come to all of my dance recitals. She would bake cookies for Ice and me. And we would go to the movies together, read lots of books, play word games, and take long vacations together. She would be my Mom until Lola felt up to it.

"Whatever it is, it can be worked out, I promise you" she finished.
"Is that all?" I asked.
"Excuse me?" Ms. Monroe responded.
"Can I go now?" I inquired.

Ms. Malone gave me a heart felt look; probably wondering if I had even heard one word that she said. She looked as though she was truly saddened and that she wanted desperately to help but did not know what else she could do.

"Sure," she responded disappointedly.
"Thank You Ms. Malone," I said respectfully as I left.

On my way home I ran into Ice after school and we walked home together. Once we got home and got situated, I looked up at the clock and saw that it was already five o'clock. Ice dropped his book bag in the middle of the floor, kicked his shoes off and started messing with the T.V.

"Here Uni," he said as he handed me an envelope.
"What's this?" I asked.
"It's the money that I won at the carnival. I want you to take it down to the cable people and get us some cable," he said.
"Boy," I squealed at him. "We got more things to worry about then some damn cable," I said with conviction.

"Unique, please?"

It was funny to hear him call me Unique. He never called me Unique unless it was truly a serious matter. And I guess for a ten year old, cable was a serious matter. So I felt I needed to do what he asked.

"Okay, give it here then. I'll try to go down there tomorrow," I said. "But in the mean time, pick your stuff up from off the floor, turn the T.V. off, and do your homework".

"How come I never see you doing any homework?" Ice inquired.

"You're not me are you?" I answered while he just looked at me. "I didn't think so; now shut it off," I said to him.

I looked around at our humble abode. There was the couch that we had been sittin' and sleepin' on for the past three years that was given' to us by my Uncle Blaze. Somebody had thrown it out into the trash and when he saw it he thought of us. We were always ending up with somebody else's trash.

Uncle Blaze was Lola's twin. When he found it, he put the couch onto his pickup truck and brought it home to us. The cushions had already shown signs of deterioration as they began to sink down into the foundation of the couch. So he placed a long piece of ply wood underneath the cushions to make the couch firm again.

Uncle Blaze helped me clean the couch with a scrub brush and soap water. We didn't sit on it for two days while it dried. Along with the couch we had a beat up recliner, two crates that we used as chairs, and a second hand two chair dinette set where we ate most of our meals. There was also the wobbly table stand that was used for our thirteen inch television set that was barely operable without cable

Our apartment vaguely resembled the two bedroom apartment that James and Florida Evans had on Good Times, except ours was a one bedroom apartment. I must say that when my brother and I stepped outside those four walls we looked just as good as everyone else outside. You couldn't tell us from those who had and those who had not.

Uncle Blaze came over every couple of weeks with a pair of clippers, so Ice always had a fresh cut. He came about every four to five months with bags of clothes that his children had outgrown, so we always had something to wear. And the clothes were in pretty good shape.

Uncle Blaze and My aunt Tamika had seven kids of their own. That was the main reason why we could never go stay with them. They lived in a very small three bedroom house. The three girls shared a room. The four boys shared a room. And my aunt and uncle shared the smallest room in the house.

Lola, Ice, and me lived in a Section Eight apartment where Lola was only required to pay twenty one dollars each month towards the rent and the state picked up the rest of the tab.

Although the rent was more than modest, Lola still had difficulties paying it. She hadn't paid rent in about five months to date; which violated the terms of agreement set forth by the Detroit Housing Authority. And once you get thrown out of the program, Section Eight would no longer help you pay your rent. And then we would become directly responsible to our Landlord for the full amount.

I knew it would be just a matter of time before it happened. And so it did. We were no longer a part of the Section Eight Program and Lola was now responsible for the entire amount of six hundred eighty dollars monthly for our rent. We received a notice about two weeks previously that said we had up until the seventh of the month to come up with all the back rent or we would be evicted. It is now the thirteenth of the month.

I hadn't told Uncle Blaze about any of this yet because I was extremely tired of burdening him with our troubles. For once, I would like to try and figure it out on my own. I was tired of always being needy and dependent on the family. We were the ones that everybody in the family talked about and pitied. I was tired of second and third hand clothes and the empty refrigerator. I wanted to know how it would feel to walk in a pair of shoes that had never been worn by anyone before me.

CHAPTER FIVE

I t was time for me to be on my way out to meet Bailey down at the Cave.

"I'll be back in a bit. Don't leave this apartment and don't answer the door for anybody, okay," I instructed Ice. "Okay," I reinforced.

"Okay," he responded.

It was about five fifteen when I got down to the Cave. I went inside but didn't see Bailey. Then from amongst the crowd came a familiar and unpleasant face. It was Brick. I guess when I looked at him he didn't look all that bad. I heard he did graduate from high school. He spoke semi intelligently, but that still didn't explain the mentality that would have him to choose drugs over a legitimate career, or a girl instead of a woman. But what did I know. In my mind he would qualify as a definite child molester; always chasing girls half his age.

"Hey! sweet thing. This must be fate. I've seen you about three times in one week. Are you stalking me or something?" he said jokingly.

"Don't play yourself," I said. "That will never happen."

"What's all this about? You hangin' out here now?" I have never seen you in here this much not even in a years' time let alone a week, he commented.

He continued to ask me a million and one questions. It all fell on deaf ears though, and he knew it.

"Oh, okay. I see. I've been calling you every delicious name I could think of because I don't know what your real name is."

He kept trying but got no where with that one either.'

"Oh you not goin' let me know your name?" he asked.

"Unique," I responded.

"What's Unique?" he asked bewildered.

"That's my name. My name is Unique." I clarified.

"Right. That's different. That's a new one," he commented.

"Is it really?" I questioned.

"Yeah, and it suits you. You don't think so?"

"No, not really. I hate my name. I mean there's a thousand ique's out there; you have Monique, Dominque, Boutique, Rafique, Tarique and the list goes on. Like where's the originality?" I asked.

"Like?" Brick broke out in a laugh.

"Oh that's funny?" I asked

"Yeah, you are. I think you're being pretty hard on your Mom. What if that was the only word she could think of to describe you the first time she saw you? Then would it be so terrible? If you had any say in it, what would you have called yourself?" he asked.

"Emma or maybe Josephine." I responded.

"You're kiddin' me right?" he asked.

I shook my head no as he looked at me in amazement.

"Now why would you go name yourself somethin' so common as that?" he asked.

"Those are common names. And I feel common", I answered.

"You must read a lot," he said.

"Why do you say that?" I asked.

"'Cause of the way you think and talk. Who around here thinks that way? And I don't know nobody around here who would name their child Emma or Josephine on purpose. Your Mom named you Unique because that's what she felt in heart about you. And really that should be all there is to it. I like your name and you should learn to love it." He finished.

Just then we were interrupted.

"Hey girl", Bailey interrupted.

"Hey, I'm sorry I was late," I said as she looked at me and then looked at Brick. She pulled me over to the side for a minute.

"What was that all about?" she questioned.

"What?"

"You know what. What you talkin' to him about?" she interrogated.

"Nothin," I responded.

"Well you make nothin' look like somethin'. Make sure you remember who he is," she warned.

"You asked me to meet you down here because you had something to tell me; like where you got the money from," I changed the subject.

"It's a long story," she said.

"Well make it short," I added.

"You know Big Tommy right? Well, while I was down at the pizza parlor. He asked me if I would do him a small favor. He told me that it would be worth my while. He asked me to go over to the room #17 of the Dudley Street Hotel and knock three times. He told me a man would answer and I was to keep him company. He said that I didn't have to have sex with him unless I wanted to. And all I had to do was let him touch me a little bit. And I get paid thirty dollars each time.

"Each time?" I asked.

"Yeah, I did it only a few times. It was nothing. Most of the men are old. They're just lonely," she justified.

"Bailey, this is way over the top, even for you. Are we talking about prostitution?" I asked.

"We? That's what you're talking about. I'm talking about makin' some legitimate money."

"But it's prostitution, Bailey," I insisted.

"Prostitution? It is not," she denied.

"It is and Big Tommy is your pimp," I proclaimed.

"No, now see…that's why I don't like to tell you nothin' because you are so dramatic about everything. You blow everything out of proportion," she said.

"No, you're not dramatic enough," I said.

"No girl, this is an escort service." What I did for Tommy was just for those few times. Now I'm working for myself," she tried to explain.

"An escort service that exploits children. Bailey, you're fourteen,"

"I know how old I am. But I will be fifteen in a couple of months," she tried to defend herself.

"Right, and that makes it so much better I guess. It's nothing short of child molestation," I said mockingly.

"Now really, that's sick. I'm not being molested and I'm not being raped. It's none of dat'goin' on," she said in frustration.

"Well, whether you know what you're doing or not, it's wrong and you and Big Tommy could go to jail.

"You're unbelievable, you know that?" she said in disappointment. "I find a way to make some money, money that I need, and all you can do is beat me down over it."

"I'm not beatin' you down. I'm just sayin'. I just don't think it's safe is all. There has to be another way," I said.

"Well, you let me know if you find out what it is. I gotta' go. Let me know if you change your mind," she said.

"You coming over tonight. right?" I asked

"I don't know. I'll let you know. Big Tommy said I can use the room as long as I give him a percentage," she answered.

And then she left.

CHAPTER SIX

At this point I really began to worry about Bailey and the dangers that she was surely about to get herself into. But she would always straddle the fence when it came to boundaries. That was who she was. Everything was about business with her. It didn't matter how risky it was. Everything was about survival to her.

As I was leaving the cave I ran into sleazy Lloyd. Lloyd was an older man - old enough to be my father. He was about an inch or two away from being six feet. He had silver streaks in his hair and beard and you could tell that he was a pretty boy back in the day because he still possessed a lot of those qualities, plus he kept himself groomed. But it was clear as water that some of the gleam that he once had was fading away slowly.

"I'll be expecting you to come by to see me tomorrow," he said.

"I know you're not really gonna' harass me over that lil' fifty dollars?" I asked.

"It's nothin' personal, it's business," he said.

He used Bailey's favorite line.

"And It's not harassment. I'm inquiring," he said. "I have an interest to look after," he corrected me. "And it's not fifty dollars, it's seventy five," he reminded me.

"Awl, here comes the bull shit," I said to myself. "I knew it. "Seventy-five, what are you talking about, seventy-five? I borrowed fifty dollars from you,"

"Yeah, but you forgot the fifty percent interest," he said.

"Fifty percent Interest?

"Oh! my God. Are you for real. I'ma child. Where would I get all of that from?.

"Look, I'ma equal employer opportunist. I don't discriminate. You was old enough to come to me and ask for a loan and you goin' be old enough to pay it back to me like everybody else," he cheesed. You can always get it from that Uncle of yours that's always coming pass bringing you things," he suggested. "And if that don't work, maybe we can work out some other arrangements"

I knew exactly what he meant when he said that. And I knew it wasn't goin' go down like that unless hell froze over, as my nanna' would say.

"No, that's all right," I responded. "I'll have your money tomorrow don't worry," I assured him.

"Alright then Missy, I guess I'll be seein' you tomorrow then," Lloyd said.

"Yeah, Ok," I said with plenty of attitude as I walked away.

A few blocks over, Javier appeared out of the darkness of night without a warning as I walked home.

"Wooo shoot, I gasped. "What are you doing sneekin' up behind people like that?" I asked Javier.

"Following you," he boldly answered.

"Are you serious?" I countered.

"As a heart attack," he stated.

"But why? What are you following me for?"

"I don't know. I was just thinking about you. For some reason I was worried about you," he responded.

"Well don't. I can take care of myself," I declared.

When I saw the seriousness in his eyes I calmed my role just a little. Because I realized that he wasn't rhyming or joking.

"When did you start worrying about me?" I asked.

"Since the other day," he said.

"Thank you, but seriously Javier, I'm fine," I reassured him.

"Are you?" he questioned.

"Yes, I am," I answered as if I didn't appreciate the doubt that he displayed.

"I saw you talking to Lloyd. Why are you dealing with Lloyd? I'm sure you know what and who he is, a loan shark. And once you're in debt to someone like him, he'll somehow manage to keep you there.

"Not me. I'm gonna' pay him back his fifty dollars, well seventy-five now,"

"So you're into him for seventy five dollars? So do you have his money?"Javier pressed.

"Not all of it. But I'm working on it"

"How short are you?"

"Why are you drilling me like this? About fifty, ok"

Javier looked down and shook his head.

"Do you have any idea what you're doing?" he asked

"I'll manage," I answered.

He reached in his pocket and pulled out the cash he had in it. He peeled me off fifty dollars and handed it to me.

"I can't take that from you," I said.

"You can't or you won't? You mean you can take money from somebody like Lloyd, but you can't take it from me, somebody who cares about you?" he asked.

I hesitated as I tried to find the words that would satisfy his question.

"I didn't know you cared. And besides, Lloyd didn't give me anything. It was a loan"

"Well, I do care. And if it makes you feel any better, than you can consider this a loan too"

"It's hard to know if you're serious when you're always joking," I explained.

"Does it look like I'm joking? For some reason I don't feel like joking when I'm around you. I feel different."

Silence claimed the air we breathed for about ten seconds before I finally spoke.

"Well when should I pay you back?"

He grabbed my hand and placed the money inside my palm.

"Whenever you feel like it,....whenever," he stated as he gazed into my eyes.

"Well thanks," I said as I accepted the loan.

We began to walk until we were in front of my door.

"I'll see you tomorrow?" he said in an asking way.

I nodded my head yes as I turned the key in the door let myself in. Ice had already fallen off to sleep. I laid the money that I was going to pay Lloyd on the dresser. I showered and read a couple of chapters before I dozed off.

CHAPTER SEVEN

The next morning I awoke, got dressed and was on my way down to pay Lloyd when I looked on my bedroom dresser and immediately noticed that the money I had was missing.

"Ice, Ice, I called out frantically,"
"Whaaat," he dragged his words out as he tried to wake himself.
"Where's the money that I put on this dresser last night?" I asked.
"What money?" he asked me back.
"The money that I put on the dresser when I went to bed last night. It was right here.
"I don't know. I'm sleepy," he responded.

It was clear that Ice didn't know anything about the money. He had no idea what I talking about.

"Oh my God, well get up and help me find it. Come on," I demanded.
"Awl man," he stated.
"Awl man nothin'. Get up dammit'," I ordered.

We turned the apartment inside out, but no money. In all the drama I happened to look over and noticed an empty bottle of Jamaica Red Stripe on the kitchen counter. It was the brand of beer that Lola drinks.

"Dammit', dammit', dammit'," I shouted. Damn you Lola. She got us again," I went on as I shook my head no.

"Are you gonna get the cable turned back on today, Uni?" Ice asked.

I looked at him and for a second I was about to respond to him in anger. And then I forgot that I had put the money that he had given me in the medicine cabinet in an empty band aid box. I got myself composed for my brother's sake and realized that he wouldn't understand the impact of what Lola did. He wouldn't comprehend the consequences of her actions. And so I decided to go about my day as I normally did, unsure of what the night would bring. I cleaned up the mess that we made while searching for the money I owed Lloyd and then I made a trip down to the cable company to get the cable restored.

I didn't know what I was going to do about getting' the money back that Lola took, but my only concern at that moment was putting a smile on my brother's face. And the only way I could do that was to make sure that he would be able to watch Sponge Bob when he got home from school.

When I came back from the cable company, I somehow ended up at the Cave - again. I was reminded that somebody told me that if you keep hangin' around a place like that, you goin get what you lookin' for.

Bailey was standing out front with a couple of chicks that I wasn't really familiar with. Since she started working, the class of people she surrounded herself with changed. Some of the ladies she associated with were a lot older than she was. But I guess it didn't matter when you're all getting paid for doing the same thing.

"Can I talk to you for a minute?" I said to her.

"I'll catch up with y'all later," she told her associates.

"What's up?" she asked.

"You know the money that I owed Lloyd?"

"Yeah," Bailey answered.

"Well, I had all of it right; that is until Lola came home last night and took it and left again," I explained.

"That's a damn shame," Bailey expressed. You goin' have to start lockin' your stuff up," she said.

"Yeah I know. I should've known better. It's almost as if she knows when I have something worth taking and then she shows up right at that moment. It's like she has radar or something. I just wasn't thinking. Now Lloyd is going to be looking for me to square up tonight. If I don't pay him, every night after he gonna' tack on more"

"What!" Bailey exclaimed.

"Just what I said," Yup, that's what he told me.

"Damn. Well I have, let me see," as she reached into her pocket to pull out her money.

"No, you can keep that. I came down here to talk business with you. I thought maybe I could come out with you tonight," I said.

"Huh? Come out with me where and do what?" Bailey asked.

"You know. Whatever you do?" I said.

"Well no. I don't think that's a good idea at all," she stressed.

"Why not? It'll just be this one time. If it's as easy as you say, then why you actin' like this?" I asked.

"Well for one thing, I don't recall ever sayin' it was easy. I mean have you thought about askin' your uncle or how about your grandma?" she questioned.

"I would if I thought they had it. But then again, maybe I wouldn't. Maybe I want to try and do things on my own. I just can't keep goin' to him for everything. It's just not right. And besides, me and my brother are not his responsibility," I explained.

Bailey nodded like she understood where I was coming from and the predicament that I found myself in.

"I do understand what you're sayin'. But what I am sayin' is that this is not for you. You not like me. Once you start mixin' it like this it changes you. And I don't want to see you change. You beautiful just like you are," she spoke from her heart.

"Why you getting' like this? You know I wouldn't even be coming to you if it wasn't that deep. But I need this. I need to get that money back so I keep Lloyd off my back and my ass. Ice is gettin' wise to this street game. He's already shootin' dice and playing cards. It's only goin' be a matter of time before he figures out how to do other things. And I don't want that to happen. So I have to make sure he has what he needs.

"Well what's the difference between you doin' this and Lloyd wanting you to do that? You might as well go head and give Lloyd some."

"Are you crazy?" I asked Bailey. "The difference is, I'm doing it on my terms. I'm not goin' allow no man to have me over a barrel."

"Do you always have to be so deep? Alright then. I guess you can roll with me tonight. I'm supposed to be down on Dudley in about fifteen minutes. If you sure you wanna' do this – be there" Bailey said.

"I'm sure," I said with certainty.

"Ok then," she responded.

CHAPTER EIGHT

N eedless to say, fifteen minutes came faster than it ever did. There we were, as we arrived at room seventeen of the Dudley St. Hotel. Bailey took a key from her purse and unlocked the door. She opened the door and we went in. It was my first time even in a hotel room and it really wasn't a big deal. The room was fairly small with a bed, a lamp that was atop a night stand, a table and chair, and a bathroom. There was a closet that had about a dozen or so pieces of Bailey's lingerie in it.

The lingerie was very small and revealing. It reminded me of the ones that Lola has in her closet. I always wanted to wear lingerie like Lola's but I don't know if I quite pictured wearing it under these circumstances. Some of the pieces were satin hot top and bottom type and others were completely lace with spaghetti straps or some had no straps at all. They were the see through kind with the matching panty thong.

"Pick one and put it on. You can change in the bathroom and place your stuff in the bottom of the drawer," Bailey said.

I went into the bathroom and changed. I came out, stood in the middle of the floor.

"Now what?" I asked Bailey.

"Now you wait," she replied.

"Wait for what?"

"Wait for the clients to show up. The clients know the room numbers to all the rooms that belong to Big Tommy. Sometimes they be watching these rooms to see who goes in and that's how they know which room they want to go to.

"You mean some strange man coulda' been watchin' me when I came in here?" I asked.

"That's what I'm sayin'"

"Do you always come to this room?" I asked.

"No," she answered.

"Big Tommy rents this room along with about five others in this hotel on a monthly basis. The clients set their appointment with Big Tommy and Big Tommy schedules them for me in half hour increments," she clarified. That way the clients won't over lap each other. And if the clients want more time then they'll have to pay extra. Everybody thinks that Big Tommy is my pimp and I like it that way because they'll think twice before they try anything.

Bailey had way more street smarts then me. She was only nine months older than I was. She was the only girl in her family. She had three brothers, two of which lived with their fathers and the baby her mom just had with her psychotic boyfriend named Felix.

Her mom works two jobs and is always tired. So she never really bothered to notice the nights when Felix would disappear from their bedroom and end up in Bailey's. Bailey says that Felix always wants to pretend like she is her Mom.

Felix is very abusive and controlling where her Mother is

concerned. He works odd jobs in the neighborhood but never anything steady. He is known around the way for his womanizing. And it seems that he is never worried about Baileys Mom catching him. Because her Mom has caught him a few times before but never did anything about it. She has questioned him about it but he never seems to give an answer. His response is always, "you think what you want", and then he leaves it at that.

Felix always kept Bailey's Mom in her place with the power of his two fist. Bailey's Mom hated her life and did nothin' really to fight to change it. Bailey said that she would always curse the day she ever had children and believed that if she hadn't had children, maybe she would have more luck with decent men.

And so this is one of the reasons that prompted Bailey to stay away from her house as much as she did. She told me that in the last year or so, Felix has been making more bolder advances towards her. She said she couldn't even use the bathroom without him barging in on her every chance he gets hoping to catch her with her clothes off and in the shower. So she'll only use the bathroom when he is not at home. He purposely broke the lock on of the bathroom door so that the door can't be locked. He told Bailey's mother that the lock would be fixed as soon as he had the time. But it's already been three months.

"Please get out and close the door behind you, you crazy ass psycho!" Bailey screamed at Felix to get out of the bathroom after he came in to assault her.

Bailey said that when she did that, he would laugh so hard that it would make her sick to her stomach. She said he laughed because the whole thing was nothing but a big joke to him and he loved to torment her.

It was around that time that I noticed Bailey starting to wear loose fitting clothes because she didn't want the new curves on her body to show through; the curves that every man with a lustful perversion for young girls paid attention to. She took on a style of dress that would prove to be less attractive than that of her previous self.

"I'll be in room nineteen," she told me. "Here take this," she said as she handed me a can of pepper spray. "Don't be afraid to spray one of those bitches either and don't let them do anything to you that you don't want them to do, ok? "Just scream or dial this extension if you need me" she stressed. "We'll meet downstairs at nine o'clock to give Big Tommy his money.

Nervous didn't describe how I was feeling. I just couldn't believe that it had come down to this. "I mean, what was I doing there?" I thought to myself as my mind began racing a mile a minute. My palms and underarms where wet with perspiration and my hands were so unsteady.

I began to pace the floor, back and forth from the door to the closet. I looked in, and then looked away. And then I did it all over again. And then it became real when I heard a knock at the door. And then there was a second, third, and fourth knock. I was paralyzed with fear and couldn't move. Finally, I convinced my feet to move forward towards the sound of the knocks. I placed my sweaty palm on the knob of the door, turned it, and pulled slowly. I opened the door just wide enough to see a man standing with a brown paper bag in his hand.

"For a minute there, I didn't think anybody was home," the man on the other side of the door proclaimed. "You mind if I come in?" he asked as I stared him down.

So I opened the door wider and turned and walked away. I sat at the small table that was next to the window. The strange man who smelled like old socks walked in.

"You mind if I have a seat?" he asked.

Barely making eye contact, I hunched my shoulders in an uncaring motion.

"Thanks. I've never seen you before. You new?" he asked.

I continued to stare off into nothingness.

"Ok, um, it's alright if you don't wanna' talk. I can appreciate that. "You mind?" he asked as he referred to the brown bag that was in his hand.

Again, I just looked on expressionless, not knowing what to expect. He reached into the bag and pulled out a bottle of brown liquor and two glasses. He opened the bottle and began to fill one of the glasses. He stopped midway and he looked up at me.

"Can I get you one?" he asked

I shook my head no.

He then screwed the top back on and brought the glass up to his mouth and began to drink. I finally got up the courage to really look at him. He was dressed in an old faded gray suit with a skinny tie, a white shirt, and a pair of easy walker shoes. His hair was silver at the temples and he looked to be of Hispanic decent.

He got up and went over to where the television was and turned it on. He played with the antenna until he was able to get the picture to come in. He came back over and sat across from me on the edge of the bed.

"Wanna' come over and watch a little TV? Come on," he said before I could even answer yes or no.

I got up and slowly came over to the bed and sat down beside him, yet keeping my distance. Not that it mattered to me at all, but he introduced himself.

"I'm sorry for being so rude. My name is Enrico. You got a Name?"
"Unique," I answered. "I didn't have enough sense to give an aka."
"Oh yeah, I can see that," he said.

He reached over and touched the charm on my necklace. I was extremely hesitant as I pulled back.

"So, you like sea shells huh?" he said. "I'm not gonna' hurt you", he said. You don't have to worry about that," he assured me.

I was confused by the fact that he was almost nice to me. But then again, why wouldn't he be?

"You remind me of somebody I care a lot for," he said. But I don't see her very much. Matter of fact I don't see her at all," he went on as he began to stroke my hair. I nervously began to pull back. "This is your first time?" he asked.

I nodded yes. And then he drew his hand back and reached over, got the bottle of brown liquor and the other glass. He began to pour.

"Here, this will help to relax you. I was nervous my first time too. Don't worry it's not a drug," he said. "I don't believe in drugs. This will calm you," he insisted.

He held the glass out toward me and surprising I reached for it and began to drink slowly while keeping my eyes stayed on him. I held my breath as I drank but I could feel the brown liquor burn the lining of my esophagus as it traveled down my throat. I caught myself gagging as he helped hold the glass up to my mouth to ensure that I drank all the liquor from the glass.

"It's Okay, it only burns for a little while," he said. "You Okay?" he asked as though he really cared about me.
"Yeah," I shook my head.

He continued on with his small talk for about twenty more minutes. By that time the brown liquor began to take its effect.

"I think I could go for another one," he said as he poured himself another drink. "A young lady should never drink alone," he established. And with that he poured us both another drink and we drank.

The TV had a blank screen and so he got up to fix it.

"Anything in particular you wanna' watch?" he asked.

My mind really wasn't on watching the television. So I could care less what was on.

"No," I said as I started to feel my muscles relax.

He came back over and sat next to me.

"Where did you get that?" he asked as he touched the scar on my arm.

I wonder what made him feel like he could even touch me like that? I guess the liquor told him that it was OK.

"My brother did it," I answered.

"Your brother? Well how many brothers and sisters do you have?" he asked as he began to rub the scar on my arm.

"I'd rather not say," I responded.

He was just trynna' get too personal as far as I was concerned.

"Well that's ok. He's lucky to have a sister like you. I hope he knows how lucky he is," he said as he moved in to kiss my nose, and then my right cheek, and then my neck.

As he began to slide my satin robe down from off my shoulders I felt myself getting light headed as he continued to pull the robe down off my arms. He then began to kiss and rub my shoulders. I had a mind to say, "no, I can't do this." But the words never came out. But why didn't they? Why didn't I leave at that very moment? It was like I was somebody else.

As he continued to undress me he started to lay me down. I turned towards the window and looked at the gleam of sunlight that peeked through the curtain and made myself go to another place. It was somewhere very far away.

I went to a place where I could see my dad and it was my birthday. There was a giant birthday cake and a brown and white pony. It was the birthday party that I was promised but never got the chance to have because life happened.

The pillow that I rested my head on became soaked with the quiet tears that had filtered down from my eyes as I day dreamed about all the wonderful places that I had read about in magazines.

I dreamed about toasting marshmallows on the flat crescent shaped beaches of the Nicobar Islands of Bengal. And I dreamed about drinking glassses of Vino from the finest vineyards in Italy, savoring the finest cheeses while touring the Riviera.

The pain and the thrusting back and forth brought me back to the current time as Enrico released himself into my virgin womb. One last grunt and he collapsed, laying on top of me breathing heavily. With no emotion at all, I pushed him off of me and with the entire sheet in my hand, I quickly got up and slowly began to walk in the direction of the bathroom. A sticky clear substance containing blood crept down the inside of my thigh and sent chills up my spine.

I walked with my legs far apart from one another so as not to mesh the disgusting fluids between my thighs. I closed the bathroom door quickly behind me and jumped into the dingy walled shower and turned the water up as hot as I could bear it and I washed… and washed….and washed. Then finally, I came out into the room and Enrico was still there.

"I'd like for you to leave now," I said.
"Oh ok," he said.

Enrico got up and put his boxers on top of his unclean manly tool of perversion, slipped his pants on, and then his shirt and tie. He buckled his belt and slicked his hair back with his hands. He pulled out a wallet from his pant pocket and pulled out five ten dollar bills.

"If you need anything, school clothes, lunch money – you know, anything like that, here's my number," he said as he laid a card with his phone number on it, down on the dresser along with the money.

"Unique, it was very nice meeting you," He said as he exited the room. "And thank you for a lovely time. I hope that we can do this again sometimes.

He left a half empty bottle of the brown liquor on the night stand. With a tenacity and an emotionless face, I stared into the mirror that hung above the bureau as I filled my glass yet again with the brown liquor.

My stomach soured at the thought of me selling away my virginity for a measly fifty bucks. It was suppose to have been for somebody special; somebody worthy – someone I loved and cared about. It was supposed to have been for someone who loved me back. But instead, it was given away to a total stranger; a man who was as old as my father would be had he lived.

As I poured me another glass there came another knock at the door. It was another client. And there were three other clients that followed him. Once my virginity was lost I knew that I could never get it back again. And so I felt like "why stop now?" I was determined to make it all count for something.

It was twelve midnight and I was completely out of it. And to be truthful, I preferred it that way. I could barely remember the clients that came and went that night and their faces were a blur. But what I do remember is that by the end of the night there were three empty pint bottles of various types of liquor that sat atop the dresser and an open package of yellow pills. I had quite a bit of money stashed inside the pillow case when I looked right before I passed completely out.

CHAPTER NINE

I went home about eleven thirty that night and paid Lloyd the money that I owed him. I had his money and plenty to spare. The refrigerator was empty again and Ice's birthday was in one week. He will be eleven years old. And on top of that the rent was way past due and Lola was no where to be found. I had a pretty good idea on how to find her if I really wanted to but what would be the purpose. The streets had a hold on her and either she was too weak to break free from it or she just didn't want to. It really didn't matter much even when Lola was at home with us physically because her mind would always be out there somewhere.

But given all of that, I would never be able to change the fact that she was still our mother. And I felt that if she could just pull herself away from that life just long enough for her to be able to clear her thoughts maybe she could see that Ice and I really needed her. I wished with all my heart that she could find the strength and courage that I knew she had deep within her to fight to come back to us.

Was I dreaming? Maybe, but I couldn't give up hope. And so I decided to go out and look for her. I just wanted her to know that we still loved her and needed her even if she didn't love us anymore.

After the night that I had, I felt I had lost a giant piece of myself. I wondered if this is what it was like for Lola. I was afraid of what would come next in my life. Would it resemble her life? Would my life turn out like hers? I would never let that happen. I would never disappoint my brother the way she disappointed us.

So, I went down to the Motorcycle club where Lola was known to hang out. My father had been dead for seven years now, but it seemed like an eternity. When he was alive biking was everything to him. And Lola loved being the wife of a biker. My dad had a reputation of being one of the fastest around these parts. Nobody from here to the East Coast could touch him; he was King.

He was given the name Speed as a teenager. And because of his reputation there were those who envied him and wanted the title that he was given. A guy named Wolf was one of those guys who despised my father just because he wanted to be him. And he was every bit of what his name suggested; highly aggressive, destructive, unpredictable, and untrustworthy. He preyed on the weak and waited, lurking in the shadows for the right opportunity to strike his enemies.

It was common knowledge that Wolf always had a thing for Lola; he along with all the other bikers at the club. Lola was beautiful and all the guys at the motor club would haggle for her affection. They acted as if Lola was a Goddess. She had an Egyptian skin tone that complemented her copper colored shoulder length hair that always held soft silky waves. Her measurements were featured on the famous Commodores song, Brick House; thirty six, twenty four, thirty six. Her eyes were and still are the color of walnuts, big, bright, and sultry. She was so full of life and had a smile that would melt any man's heart who laid eyes on her.

Remembering back, I woke up many nights to the angry voices of Speed and Lola, fighting over something Lola did or didn't do. Speed was convinced that Wolf was deliberately trying to come between the two of them and he thought that Lola was encouraging him. Speed knew that Lola was a bit of a flirt and thought that Lola was showing Wolf way too much attention, giving him the wrong impression and sending him mixed signals.

Wolf had even gone so far as to publicly announce around all of their common friends in the motorcycle club that whenever Lola was ready and willing to be taken care of by a real man that he would be equipped in all aspects of the word to meet that challenge. And when he made that announcement Speed was infuriated.

Wolf knew that Lola's heart belonged to only one man; and that man was Speed. And that mere fact made Wolfe's blood boil. Before Speed came on to the scene, Wolf was the main center of attraction. He was number uno and he was used to having things his way. But then Speed came along and stole the spot light right from under him and won the affection of the only woman that ever rejected Wolf; Lola. And Wolf didn't take rejection well at all.

The night that Speed was murdered was foggy to me. I don't know what parts were real and what parts I dreamed. Lola said that Speed was on his way down to the club to negotiate a price for a big race that was coming up. There was a ten thousand dollar purse at stake and all bets were on. Everybody in the club knew that Speed ran laps down by the old abandoned paint factory in the industrial district. And he went there practically every night to get some laps in. And that's where he was when he was gunned down. He was shot in the heart with a high powered rifle from some forty feet away.

It was obvious to everyone including the police that it was a hit. Whoever killed my father didn't take any of his belongings. Not one thing. Whoever killed my father had something personal against him. And the first name that was given to detectives by almost everybody was Wolf's.

The investigation went on for about six months and then it went cold. The detectives couldn't find any evidence that would link Wolf to the scene of the crime that night and he was the only suspect that they had.

As soon as the investigation dried up, Wolf began to come around our house to see Lola. He was there almost every day. He would come over pretending to console and care about Lola. He claimed he wanted to be there for her. And Lola was so blinded by her grief that she couldn't see what he really wanted. Ice was only three years old at the time and so he really doesn't remember any of it. But it was something about Wolf that I didn't like but I couldn't put my finger on it. I had a bad feeling about him. Every time he came around I felt creepy crawly things all over my body.

After Speed was murdered, Lola started to confide in Wolf about everything. She started to trust him. She allowed him to help collect money for a fund that the motor cycle club had established in Speeds honor. I noticed that Lola had become so dependent on Wolf that she almost couldn't do anything without him. And on most days when Wolf was around, Lola's mannerism changed. She seemed to almost be in a trans.

One night I got up to go to the bathroom and the door to my mother's room was pushed to but it wasn't completely closed. As I approached the door I could see the shadow of light from the lamp escaping through the bottom of the door. I peeped in and saw that there were pills emptied out onto the nightstand next to her bed along with some sort of needle.

Wolf was on top of my mom and she seemed to be non-responsive. He heard me and looked back at the door where I was standing and saw that I was looking in. And in that second, he picked up a small statue that my Nana had given my Mom and threw it at the door. I was scared to death at that point and my heart almost jumped out of my chest as I almost went to the bathroom right then and there.

In my mind, I could see the horns coming out of his head. I ran back down the hall as fast as I knew how, jumped in my bed and got under the covers with my head buried in a teddy bear that my dad had given me when I was about two or three. Oh how I wished he was here and that his death was all a dream.

About a week after I had been traumatized by Wolf, the Sheriff's Department came to our house and put all our belonging onto the sidewalk and padlocked our doors. That was the very first time we had ever been evicted. Lola had nobody to go to and so she went to the motor cycle club to see Wolf and explained the situation and asked if he could help her out with the rent.

She saw that he was preoccupied with some other female named Swan. The rumor was that Swan got her name by swan diving on the joy sticks of her male counterparts, sinfully bringing them to their climaxes in less than a minute flat by her seductive ways.

When Lola walked into the club everyone stopped what they were doing to witness what was about to go down. Everybody in the club knew that Lola had been victimized by Wolf as so many others were. They knew that he preyed upon her during the most vulnerable time in her life and most of them didn't like it. They also knew that it was never really about Lola, but it was all about Speed.

Wolf was never able to get near Lola when Speed was alive. And it wasn't enough that Speed was dead. He knew that the one thing that would hurt Speed, even in death, would be him hooking up with Lola. So he purposely set out to bring Lola down, hoping and praying that Speed was watching from wherever he was and that he would finally know how it felt to be defeated.

Lola eagerly approached him with all confidence, even in her poor state. She didn't quite look like she looked six months prior to that day but everyone was sympathetic towards her because they knew that she was going through a rough time and Speeds death had obviously taken a great toll on her physically.

"I need to talk to you for a minute," Lola approached Wolf.

"I'm in the middle of a game right now," he responded with his back turned.

"I wouldn't be here if it wasn't important," she stated.

Wolf didn't even bother to turn from his game to look at Lola.

"I'll talk to you when I'm through," he replied with a cold brush off.

Lola was enraged as she reached out and smacked the cards right out of Wolfs hands.

"You'll talk to me now," she insisted.

"Damnit'," Wolf growled as he got up from the table, grabbed Lola by the arm and pulled her into the next room and closed the door.

Jackson, an old friend of both my parents, walked over to the door of the room that Wolf and Lola were occupying. He could hear everything and so could everyone else.

"I'm being evicted. The Sheriffs Department came by and put all my stuff out on the street. I have no where to go," she said.

"Well you can't stay with me," he made clear.

"I'm not askin' to stay with you. I need you to front me the money so that I can pay the landlord what I owe," she said.

"I can't even pay my own rent. I'm strapped," he responded.

"So that's it?" she asked.

"What more is there?" he asked

"I should have known," Lola began to become incensed. You were around jus' long enough for me to cash that insurance check weren't you? How's the new bike running? You looking pretty good these days. Pretty fly," she stated.

"Did I ask you for that motor cycle? You insisted that I get a new bike. You wanted me to look good. Remember? Isn't that what you told me? And I'm not the only one that had their hand in the cookie jar. And let's not forget that a great deal of that money went into your veins," he finished.

Lola was steamin'. She reached back and with all of her might and tried to slap every taste bud off Wolf's tongue. He retaliated and slapped her back. Lola rubbed the cheek that Wolf hit in disbelief. She looked at him with rage and started swinging. Wolf drew his fist back in an attempt to punch Lola when Jackson barged in and stepped in between the two of them, grabbing and squeezing both of Wolf's hands with all his might. Jackson looked Wolf in his eyes and said,

"You've done enough."

Jackson continued to hold Wolf's hands in mid air, letting him know that he was stronger than him. Then Jackson pushed Wolf back into the wall with great force.

"That's it. It's over," Jackson said. He turned towards Lola whom he respected despite her disposition.

"You alright?"

Lola nodded and said, "yes, thank you".

"Look, I got a little bit saved up. You're welcome to......,"

Lola cut him off in mid sentence.

"Thank you, but no thank you. I'll be fine," she said with pride.

When Ice and me came home that day and found that we were locked out, we sat on our couch that was in the middle of the sidewalk until Lola got home. I remember that day well.

"Did you find him Mama?" I asked. "Is Mr. Wolf gonna' give us the money?"

"No, I think we've seen the last of Mr. Wolf," Lola stated.

Lola went down to the corner and made a couple of phone calls. She called her only brother, Uncle Blaze. Uncle Blaze came to pick up the little bit of furniture that we had and put it into storage. He and my Mom had a few ugly words before Lola was about to storm off. They were always fighting.

"Where you goin'?" Uncle Blaze called out.

"I don't know yet," she answered.

"Well why don't you leave the kids with me until you find out?" he asked.

"No," she stated. "They're my kids and they go where I go."

"That's what I'm afraid of," Uncle Blaze commented.

"And what's that suppose to mean?" Lola asked.

"It just means that they need to be in a stable environment. They need stability Lola and you're having a hard time with that right now. It's been less than a year since Speed died and it's been hard on you. Word on the street is that you been using," he confronted her.

"Is that what this is about, huh? I'm fine, and I can take care of my own god damn kids. Don't you do this to me; not now," she went off.

Lola took me and my brother by the hand and began to walk extremely fast. Our legs could hardly keep up with her. I looked back and saw Uncle Blaze still standing there. Once he saw me looking back he began to wave at me and signaled me to call him. Lola took us to a shelter that night and every night after that for about two months. Then finally we were offered public housing through the Detroit Housing Authority. And it's been downhill ever since.

CHAPTER TEN

So there I was inside the motorcycle club. I looked around to see if I could recognize any faces but they all looked strange to me. After a few moments had gone by a man with a seemingly familiar face came over to me. His eyes were soft and his expression was gentle. His skin was as brown as Hershey's milk chocolate. He had a robust jaw bone with a perfectly sculpted mustache that rested upon semi full lips.

"Can I help you with something beautiful?" he asked.

"Uh, yes, I'm looking for..."

"You're Lola's girl," he cut in.

"Uh, yes sir," I confirmed.

"I thought so. There's no denying that. But I bet you get that a lot," he commented.

"Yes sir. Have you seen her?" I asked.

"Who Lola? Uh, no, I haven't. Let me see. The last time I saw Lola was about a week or so ago," he said.

"You know where she might be?" I asked.

He looked into my eyes and saw the concern that they displayed.

"Why don't you have a seat for a minute. Can I get you anything?" he asked.

"No thank you," I said.

"When's the last time you saw your mother?" he asked.

"It's been a couple of weeks," I answered.

"A couple of weeks," he said in disbelief.

When he heard that - I could see he began to show great signs of distress.

"I knew your father," he began to divulge.

"You did?" I inquired.

"Yes I did. As a matter of fact he was a good friend of mine. He was an excellent rider, you know. As a matter of fact he was one of the best; the best I'd ever seen. But what I can remember most about him is that he loved his family. He always talked about you and your brother all the time," he said. By the way, I'm Jackson," he said as he introduced himself.

"I'm Unique," I responded – remembering him from the story Lola told me

"How appropriate," he said. "Your mother always had a flare for the dramatics."

It would be the first time that I had any positive feelings about the name my mother gave me.

"How well do you know my mother?" I asked.

"I know her well enough. At one time I had such a crazy crush on her. But she would look at me every day but she would never see me. Everybody knew that she only had eyes for your father. And I respected that. When he died I tried to be there for her...you know... support and all. But um...I just never knew how.

I'd like to say somethin' if I could on your Mother's behalf. You know sometimes things that you can never in a million years foresee happening, happens just tha' same. Now your mother loved your father as much as any woman could probably love a man. And 'till this day it seems she's still having a hard time with just trynna' figure out a way to live without him. It takes some people longer than others to handle their grief. But I believe in all that she is goin' through in her life, she loves you. So whatever you may think about her it's important that you remember that.

"So have you seen her?" I got right to the point.

"Well like I said, I haven't seen her in about a week. But I have a good idea of where she might be. You could probably find her over there on Franklin Street. But I wouldn't advise you to go over there alone. It's no place for a young lady like yourself. If you like I could go with you.

"Alright," I agreed.

So Jackson went with me over to Franklin Street where he thought Lola might be. He took me to an apartment building on the corner that was about ten stories high. We went inside the tattered, decrepit building that had a distinct smell of urine and bug spray. There was an out of order sign on the elevator so we took the stairs. We went up five flights of stairs and arrived at apartment five twenty.

"Stand over there near the stairs until I see if she's in there," Jackson instructed me as he gently pushed me out of sight.

He knocked on the door and took two steps back, looked over at where I was, turned back again, and waited for someone to answer. After about ten seconds someone opened the door. All I could see was a really light skinned man with a bald head.

"Yeah what do you want?" asked the light skinned bald headed man from behind the door.

"I'm lookin' for Lola," Jackson stated.

"Lola who?" the light skinned man asked.

"Look, I know she spends a lot of time here. If you could just tell her to come to the door," Jackson said. "I would appreciate it."

"What are you, DPD?" he asked.

"Naw, man. I ain't no police. I'm just a friend," Jackson replied.

"Look, I told you I don't know nobody wit' 'dat name," the high yellow dude insisted.

"Well I got somebody out here that needs to speak to her. It's a personal matter," Jackson continued.

The man opened the door a little. He looked at me and looked at Jackson and called out.

"Hey Lola, Lola. It's somebody here to see you," he stated.

"What the hell you callin' my name out like that for so the whole building can hear you?" Lola's voice screamed out.

"Somebody here to see you," the man said to her.

After about five minutes she finally came to the door. And she wasn't too happy once she laid eyes on Jackson.

"What do you want Jackson?"Lola asked.

Jackson stepped out of the way so that Lola could have a clear view of me standing under the stairway. She had on a one piece see through nightie with no panties and you could see that she didn't have anything on underneath. Her hair was mused and her lip stick was dry and cracked. Her makeup was tired and her concealer wasn't doing the job it was suppose to do because you could still see the darkness and broken veins under her eyes.

"What is this huh?" she asked Jackson. "What are you tryin' to do to me Jackson?" she responded angrily.

"Look, she was worried about you. She came pass the club lookin' for you. She would have found you sooner or later. I just came along with her because I didn't want her comin' over here by herself.

"And so you thought you'd do the decent thing and help her by bringing her over here to see me like this. How noble," Lola lashed out and began to speak over Jackson. It was clear that this wasn't the first time that he had concerned himself with her.

"How many times do I have to tell you that I want to be left alone, huh Jackson? How many times? I want to be left alone. Do you understand me? And leave my children outta' this. This ain't got nothin' to do with them. This is my life, you got that? You stay out of my business.

"It has everything to do with your children. Listen to yourself. You call this livin'?" he asked in a last attempt to make her see. "Your children are worried about you. They need you. Why can't you see that?"

"Oh! who you spose to be, huh? You judging me now?. You promised that you would never do dat'".

"Lola, you know I'd be the last one to judge you. I'm not here for that. I just want to help. Let me help you."

"You a lyin' son of a bitch. And you can go straight to hell. You just like everybody else with your hypocritical ass sittin' so high up on your shoulders. You don't know me. Why you comin' round here acting like you know me, huh Jackson?" she asked as she became extremely irate.

"Look, I'm sorry. I'm sorry," Jackson began to apologize. I just thought that maybe if you…." he tried to explain.

"Well whatever you thought you're wrong. You hear me," she screamed. You're wrong ok. I don't need you or nobody else thinkin' for me. You got that? I got everything I need right here," she said as she pushed the door open to show Jackson the drug infested table with liquor bottles, syringes, and little blue packets with the words dynamite on them.

"Close the door. Damn. You lettin' all the heat out, the light skinned man from inside the apartment called out.

And then Lola looked straight at me, then at Jackson, and then slammed the door. She didn't say hello or anything. Both Jackson and me stood there for a few minutes trying to understand what just happened. We both were messed up for a minute over that. You could tell that Jackson felt bad for me. But the funny thing was I felt bad for him too. We both turned slowly and began to walk down the stair well. I knew in my heart that it was gonna' be a waste of time going over there. But I felt I had to take a chance. Well now I knew for sure didn't I?

"I know you don't really understand any of this. I mean sometimes it's even hard for me to understand. But she's in a bad place right now. Somehow she got lost in all of this," he tried to smooth it over for Lola.

"I always felt that she only loved us because Speed did. And now that he was dead … she no longer had to," I said as I approached the bottom of the stairs.

Jackson was speechless. You could tell he really wanted to say something, but just didn't know what to say.

"Listen, you need anything?" he began to stutter as I witnessed him reaching into his pocket.

I acted as if I didn't even hear him and began to walk faster. I didn't want his help or anyone's help. It was clear to me that Ice and me were alone in all of this. It was us against everything and everybody. My brother was the only thing that mattered to me at this point.

"If you need anything you know where to find me," Jackson called out to me from a half a block away. And after that day, some anonymous person would leave a box a groceries at our door and an envelope with twenty or thirty dollars in our mail slot every week.

CHAPTER ELEVEN

Day in and out all I could think about was Ice. I really didn't have much concern about what happened to me because at that point I felt worthless. But I wanted Ice to have what he needed in life in order to accomplish what was required of him to successfully become a man. But would I succeed at making sure that he had whatever he needed without me losing myself?

Every day when I stepped outside my door I saw the kind of men that this neighborhood had produced and it frightened me. Most of the men were down trotted, beaten down, doin' a bid uptown, or dead in the grave. Most of them didn't make good daddy's because they never had a daddy around to show them how to be that. And they would never make good husbands until a real man showed them how to love, and how to respect the nature of women.

I wanted him to grow up knowing that we are responsible for each other and that nobody can make it out here alone. I didn't want Ice to grow up without a sense of who he was, having his child hood thoughts be distorted by memories of the life that we were living.

After coming back from seeing Lola I couldn't wait to get home.

But on my way I stopped by Ice's favorite place, Mickey "D's". When I got back to the house I went inside and saw him sitting in front of the television watching videos. I knew that it wasn't right that he had to spend so much time by himself. I did feel guilty about it but what was I gonna' do? He understood that whenever I was not at home I was out trying to get us some of the things that we needed. He definitely was a trooper throughout all of it.

"Where you been all day?" Ice asked. "I was worried."

"Look what I got," I said as I pulled a Happy Meal from behind my back.

"Thanks," he said.

Ice was eleven now and I began to notice that he didn't get as "happy" as he used to get when I brought home Happy Meals from Mickey "D's". He wasn't as excited to play with the toy that was inside the box. And so it was clear that he was getting older and outgrowing the Happy Meal.

"I'm sorry I'm home late. I'll make it up to you. The Incredibles is coming out on Friday. We haven't been to the movies in a while. Maybe I'll take you to see it next week.

"We have movie money? Where did you get movie money from?" he asked.

"Things are gonna' be different for us now. I found me a job baby sittin'. So I'm not gonna' be home that much. But I need you to keep this under wraps. I don't want anybody to know that you're here by yourself because people talk. If I'm gonna' be working I need you to take care of things around here when I'm gone. You think you can do that?" I asked.

"Sure Uni," he responded. "I'm the man of the house."

"Yes you are," I agreed. "We have to work as a team. Who knows, maybe you can get that Playstation you been wantin' to get," I said.

"Really!" he exclaimed. "You make that much baby sittin'?" he asked.

"I could. I would have to put in a lot of hours though," I replied.

"Well you work as many hours as you want. You won't have no trouble outta me.

"Thanks, I needed to hear that" I responded. "Listen, It's gonna' be day light savings time soon so it'll be getting' dark about an hour earlier now. You come inside. You do your homework and shower. Make sure you keep the curtains closed and I'll leave you something to eat in frige everyday Okay." I said.

Yes, he nodded.

"Say you understand," I demanded.
"I understand," he responded.
"Good."

CHAPTER TWELVE

It had been all of five months since I had my first client. I was making anywhere from two hundred to three hundred a night just with my regulars. I made enough on the weekends and was able to take off at least twice a week; usually Monday and Tuesday. None of the other girls including Bailey was pullin' in even half of what I was making. But I was on a mission.

I had almost become content with making money laying on my back. I realized that this predicament wasn't any of my choosing. It wasn't what I wanted but it was what I was given. I was only trying to take an already messed up situation and make it at least stand for something. And I was determined to make it work. It was business.

Christmas was on its way and it would be the first time I'd ever purchased a real live Christmas Tree. Ice was happier than I had ever seen him. I was able to get him everything I knew he wanted and that was all I needed for Christmas.

I finally got him the Playstion he wanted with an additional two games. I brought him a brand new bicycle so he no longer had to beg his friends to ride theirs. I brought him a brand new coat and a pair boots that nobody else had ever worn before him.

I didn't really get anything for myself. Christmas, the tree, the decorations, the presents; they were all for Ice. Besides, I brought us both quite a few pairs of jeans, tops, underwear, and socks over the previous months. I really didn't need anything. I was just fine. I was just happy to see my brother enjoying his life. I gave him a weekly allowance and so he always had money in his pocket.

Doing the type of work that I did made it extremely hard for me to go to school everyday. Even though I was a kid I felt like a grown up. I would have four to five clients a night and every night I had plenty of drink up in me along with pills and whatever else I could get my hands on. I could feel myself almost becoming dependent on those things in order to help numb me.

Sometimes I would have so much drink and narcotics on any given night that I would just pass out and wouldn't make it home until the next day. I tried my best to make it home on most evenings because Ice expected me to. I was almost sixteen and my responsibilities greatly surpassed my age.

The rent hadn't been late in six months thanks to my Johns. I was paid up on all the utilities, the refrigerator was full, and the bags of clothes that Uncle Blaze brought over would now make its way down to the Salvation Army for people who really needed them. I felt good about the fact that we no longer needed them. But somehow I felt like a pasture of dry weeds that desperately needed watering; like a barren tree in autumn.

In all honesty I had been without a mother figure in my life for so long that at times my heart did ache. I tried to deny the pain and there were moments that I was successful in blocking it all out. But then there were times when I just wasn't able to. I was doing the best I could to fill some of that void for Ice. But for me, it was really hard because no one was there to help fill mine.

Resentment began to stir inside me. I didn't know why but I began to really dislike Lola. Maybe it wasn't her fault that she was week and selfish. But it wasn't my fault either. I needed a mother but I figured I wasn't worthy of one or she would be here.

At every turn I would run into Javier. I thought he was nice but I knew he wouldn't be able to handle the truth about what I had become, and who would blame him. I had trouble with it myself. It seemed as if the more I tried to avoid him, the more I couldn't get away from him. I couldn't lie, I liked him. And if I was in a different place in my life I might have given him a chance.

I was coming out of the Dominican store on the Avenue and there he was.

"Hey beautiful, where you been"? he called out.
"Around," I answered.

He stopped and took a good look at me and got real serious on me.

"For real though, how you been Ma? I'm getting' the feelin' you been tryna' avoid me," he said. I came by the crib several times and ain't get no answer. You good?"

"Yeah, I've been great. Busy though. I've got a part-time job baby sittin'," I said as I started to believe my own lie.

"Oh yeah, for who?" he asked.
"Nobody you know," I replied.
"Well, what you do drop outta' school? I don't see you no more. But you lookin' good though. You're hair is fly; besides the fact that you look a little tired," he stated.

"Yeah, the long hours and all, you know," I responded.

"How's the Ice Man doing?" he asked.

"Who Ice? He's great," I commented with a smile on face.

"Maybe I could come past and get the two of you so we could go out and do pizza or something," he suggested.

"Sounds like fun. Um let me um, let me get back to you," I said hesitantly.

"Sure," he paused. "You uh, you get back to me," he stuttered. "Listen my birthday is next month and my Mom's is throwing me a pool party at the "Y" on Saturday. I'd really like for you to be there," he stated.

"What time?" I asked.

"It starts at seven," he said.

"I'll try and make it" I said.

"I'll see you then," he said.

"Ok," I shook my head in agreement.

And then we said good-bye. I looked at my watch and saw that I was late for a client. He was a referral, but what's a girl to do? I didn't really trust referrals but why sweat it. The money was all green.

When the referral showed up at room seventeen I was a little bit skeptical because he looked a little bit on the rough side. He had a scar across his nose that looked like it came from a razor. And he had a tooth missing from his upper front row teeth. He looked to be about twenty five years old or so with a lot of experience in gang bangin'. When he took off his shirt he revealed the battle wounds and the tattoo that were present on his body. And once I saw them I began to feel a little uncomfortable.

"You drinkin'?" I asked him as I poured myself a much needed drink.

"No, I don't drink," he responded as he continued to take off his clothes.

That was a bit of a shock when he said no because he damn sure looked like the type that could drink one hundred percent rubbing alcohol without blinking an eye. I guess looks are really deceiving.

"I need to be paid up front, if you don't mind," I stipulated in a calm voice.
"Sure thing. How much is it again?" he asked.

He took two twenty's from his front pocket and tossed it on the bed.

"I hope you're worth every penny of it," he said in a strange tone.

He walked over to me, and without warning, he licked the side of my face. An uneasy sensation crawled up my back. I gathered my composure and stepped back and reached for the money that he threw on the bed.

"Mr, I'm sorry. I don't think we can do this today. Here's your money back," I said cautiously as I handed him back his money.
"What, my money not good enough for you?" he asked.
"It's not that. I just don't….think…..," I began to explain.
"Awl, come on now. I promise you - this won't hurt a bit," he stated.

I backed up as he began to inch toward me. And with a tongue of a lizard, he quickly grabbed me by the arm and turned me around and pulled me in close so that my backside was firmly against the protruding bulge in his pants that poked me from behind. He put his arms tightly around my waist and began to lick and slobber my neck.

"Mr., Please, don't," I tried to discourage him. I gave you your money back.

"Yes you did. But I'm not leaving until I get what I came here for, little Miss."

"Someone will be coming past in a few minutes to check on me," I said.

"Really now. Well let'em come. The more the merrier, don't you think" he stated. But I suggest they hurry up for they miss the highlight of the evening.

"Please, Mr. Stop." I begged.

"You're gonna' give it to me and you're gonna' enjoy every minute of it," he insisted.

"No, please," I begged as he tore my one piece almost to shreds and violently placed himself inside my rectum. I began to move in a vicious attempt to escape his clutches with no success. My whimpers became full blown screams as I cried out.

"Help me! Somebody Help!" I cried.

"Shut up bitch," he barked as he started punching me in my head. He went crazy on me, pounding me in the stomach and in my back until he had finally beaten the screams out of me as I became fearful for my life.

He forced himself on me violently for the next five minutes, which seemed like an eternity. And with each and every thrust I became numb to the forceful plunges that were cutting me inside out like a jagged knife. My head was pounding as I felt myself going in and out of consciousness. And then all of a sudden he stopped. He got up from off of me and wiped himself off with the bed sheet and

I collapsed to the floor. He then proceeded to put on his underwear, pants, and shirt.

"Yeah, you were worth every penny" he said. "Maybe we can get together and do this again sometime," he commented cynically.

He combed his hair, left the forty dollars on the bed and left. After about twenty minutes, I managed to drag myself to the phone and called Bailey. She wasn't working at the moment but she was down on the first floor with Big Tommy. The both of them charged upstairs in a minute flat. They rushed in and were in complete distress when they saw the condition I was in; not to mention the room. It was a bloody mess.

"Oh God," I vaguely heard Bailey say through my busted eardrums. My eyes were almost swollen shut and I was bleeding from almost every hole on my body.
"What kinda sick son of a bitch....?" Big Tommy began to question.
"Come on let's get her up on the bed," Big Tommy told Bailey. "Cover her up."

Once they got me onto the bed, Bailey quickly phoned the paramedics.

"Don't worry," she assured me. You're good. Everything is goin' be fine. I'm right here girl.
"You know her family?" I heard Big Tommy asked Bailey.
"Yeah, I'm her family," she answered. "I know she's got a Uncle somewhere around here," she continued. "I'll ask around."

The paramedics arrived about fifteen minutes later. I couldn't remember everything because I was in and out of consciousness.

When I got to the hospital, they tried to get all my personal information they could from Bailey. She told the people at the front desk that I had been raped and beaten and that's all they should be concerned about. She found Uncle Blaze and he came right away. He got there right before the police showed up. As soon as he arrived he was questioned by child services and the police about why I was found in a hotel that was under investigation for prostitution and drug trafficking and who was my guardian?

Uncle Blaze did an excellent job of convincing the police and child services that whatever went on that night in that hotel, that he knew without a shadow of a doubt that I had no involvement in it whatsoever. He told them that I was a very naïve child and had no street smarts at all and just was in the wrong place at the wrong time. He told them that Lola was out of town on a family emergency and that Ice and me were staying with him until she returned in a week or so.

Meanwhile, I had suffered a cracked skull, two broken ribs, a busted eardrum, cornea damage to my left eye, a chipped jaw bone, and a loose tooth. The doctor had to repair some of the tissue to one of my eyes as it was slightly torn from its socket. And I received twenty stitches from my anus to my vagina.

I was engorged everywhere. It seemed like every part of my body was inflated. My face blew up like a balloon. I remember a lot of people coming in and out. Bailey came to the hospital I think maybe twice. She had a real problem seeing me like that. I guess it put a lot of things into perspective for her in knowing that what happened to me could happen to her.

She informed me that Big Tommy sent a few of his associates out to locate the man who did that to me. Three days later some kids came across a man fitting the description of the rapist. He was found naked from the waist down and tied to a tree with bob wire up in Beaumont. I was told that he couldn't even be identified by his face because it had been eaten all the way to the bone by battery acid. The police didn't have any suspects or any leads. And that was a good thing.

Bailey and I never entertained the thought of paying for protection like a lot of girls who worked those parts. With Big Tommy around who needed protection. Everybody continued to think that Big Tommy was our pimp but they were wrong. He did look after us but big Tommy wasn't anybody's pimp. The only thing that Big Tommy ever asked us for was a fee for the rooms. We thought that was more than fair. He had a daughter our age and he didn't believe in puttin' his hands on women or exploiting them.

Ice wanted to stay with me but the doctors wouldn't allow it. So he went home every day with Uncle Blaze. Javier came up to the hospital every day after school. He never once asked me about what happened but he was really quiet during the first couple of visits that I could remember. They say I had swelling on my brain and I was unconscious for the first couple of days. I was in the hospital for almost two weeks before I was released into the custody of my Uncle. Uncle Blaze took me over to his house to finish recuperating.

My Uncle and Aunt gave up their bedroom while they slept in the living room on the couch. Ice only knew bits and pieces of what happened like everybody else. When he looked at me you could tell that he was really hurt over how everything went down. He really couldn't understand how something like that could've happened. And for the days that followed he was by my side both day and night. I loved him too.

It wasn't long before I began to feel a lot better. My headache was almost completely gone and my face was back to its normal size and it didn't hurt so much to walk. After about a week after I moved in with my Uncle and Aunt, Uncle Blaze came into the room with a misplaced look on his face.

"You comfortable?" he asked.

"Yes," I responded.

"Look, I need to ask you a few questions about what happened," he began. "What exactly were you doing at that place?" he asked forth right. "Why were you even at that hotel that night and where have you been getting all the money you been spending on all the new things you been buying lately, and I don't wanna' hear nothin' about you baby sittin' because it ain't that much baby sittin' in the world?" he said with a seemingly wounded heart. "What is goin' on Unique?" he asked firmly.

He was askin' me so many questions, one after another, that there was no way I could process them all. And I knew that Ice and my Uncle would really be hurt if they knew the truth. And so I chose to lie yet again.

"I was there to meet somebody, I told you," I said.

"Yeah, I know what you told me, but I'm askin' for the truth," he continued to press.

So tell me again, why were you at that hotel?" he grilled me like suspect.

"I told you," I began to cry under the pressure. "It was just supposed to be a meeting with somebody I just met, that's all, just a meeting,"

"Well what are their names?" he asked

"I don't know."

"Where did you meet them?"

"I can't remember."

"You don't know or you can't remember? You hangin' out with people whose names you don't even know. How much sense does that make?

"I don't know."

I knew he didn't believe a word that I said. But what was I supposed to do tell him the truth?

"Blaze," my Aunt Mika said as she barged in. "What are you doing?" she asked as Ice looked on."Leave that child alone. She needs her rest now." she stated.

"Now Mika, I'm goin' get to the bottom of this if it's the last thing I do," Uncle Blaze assured her.

"I know Blaze, but today is not the day for all of that. She needs her rest. Now come on from outta there and let her alone," she demanded.

So Uncle Blaze respectfully but reluctantly backed off.

Ice and I was there for about another week when I felt strong enough. We packed up our things, thanked my Aunt and Uncle for their hospitality, and we went home. I was almost a month since the rape. When I got home I went to the nearest pharmacy to get my prescription filled. I was still experiencing back and jaw pain and needed my pain pills as soon as possible.

CHAPTER THIRTEEN

My first day home Javier came over right after school to see me. I hadn't seen him in two days. When I heard the knock at the door I felt a bit anxious. Ice answered and let him in. I sat on the couch as he stood there and looked around for a minute.

"Wow! It looks a lot different then what I remember. Way different than I remember." He said.

He pulled a chair up and sat down. There was complete silence in the room for a minute or so. Javier just looked at me. Nobody really knew what to say and it was obvious that Javier had a lot on his mind, but what?

"There's been a lot of rumors goin' around school and the neighborhood," he started.

I looked into Javier's eyes and knew that this was gonna' be one of those conversations and I knew exactly what it was about.

"Ice, go outside and play for a while," I said.

Ice looked at me, unsure of whether he should leave me or not.

"Go ahead, go play," I instructed him.

Ice picked up his new baseball mitt that I had recently brought him and left, but he didn't go far.

"The new furniture, the new clothes...where's the money coming from?" he came bold with it.

"Did you come over here to ask me of somethin' or are you accussin' me of somethin'?" I asked.

"I wanna' know what happened," he said. I wanna' know about Dudley St. Everybody knows what kind of girls hang out there," he stated.

"Oh! Really? What kind?" I asked sarcastically. And who do you think you are that you can come over here with all these questions and accusations? I mean what the hell Javier? I know you think you know me. A lot of people do. But you don't. And I don't give a damn. This is my house. And on no uncertain terms can you come up in my house and start judging me. In case you didn't know, my father is dead. I ain't got no daddy," I got emotional.

"On no uncertain terms, wow, ok, you're going deep on me. First of all, I'm not here for none of that. I just wanna' know what the hell is going on. I'm asking you," he explained.

"Askin' me what?"

"What have you been doin'? Have you been sellin' yourself for money?"

"What?" I asked when I was shocked to hear him actually ask me that. I mean to actually hear the words. "You tell me." I responded.

"I don't know that's why I'm here askin' you,"

"Did you know that this past year was the first year in a long time since my father has been dead that my brother and me didn't have to go to nobody to ask them for anything, I mean nothin'. I haven't had to go inside a gas station's bathroom to steal toilet tissue or burn candles because the light bill wasn't paid.

This was the first year that my brother and I haven't gone hungry for days at a time. I'm sixteen years old Javier. And even if I could find me a part-time job making five or six dollars an hour, it wouldn't be enough," I said.

Javier began to shake his head in disbelief at what I was saying. He began to back up a away from me.

"I know that this is not what you want to hear. And I know that you're disappointed in me because I'm not what you thought I was. But I'm not gonna' sit here and apologize to you or anybody else for not letting me and my brother go hungry. This is about me and him. We are in this world alone. It's about me doin' what I gotta' do."

"So it's true then?" he said.

"Yeah, but this is my truth, not yours."

"There's gotta' be another way. You don't have to do this," he tried to appeal to me.

"Then you tell me what it is," I said. You think I like doin' what I do? You think this is something that I'm proud of. You think this is easy for me? If there was something else I could do I would do it. If somebody woulda' told me a few years ago that this would be my life right now I would have laughed in their face. But I don't hear anybody laughin'."

"There has got to be somethin'," he repeated as he shook his head in disbelief.

"No there isn't. And it's not your problem anyway. Why are you so worried about it? Why do you even care? Why? You have your own life. Be concerned with that and stop worrying about what I'm doing."

"Look," he said. "I care about you and I am concerned. I've been diggin' you since fifth grade. You just never took the time to notice. And no, I don't understand how any of this could have happened. But what if I could get the money that you need to cover your monthly expenses? Would that be good for you? I mean, would that be a reason for you to stop?

"What are you sayin'?"

"Would you stop doing what you're doing if I could get the money?"

"No Javier, You don't need to try and do that for me. I can take care of myself," I said.

"Yeah, I see how you're takin' care of yourself. And you didn't answer my question. Would you stop?"

"But where would you get the money from?" I asked.

"You let me worry about that. Would you stop?" he asked again.

"I guess I would," I answered.

"Okay then it's done," he said. "Don't forget about my party. I want you to be there. I'll be by to pick you and the Ice man up around two O'clock so be ready," he said as he stood up and towered over me.

"You tellin' me?" I asked.

"I'm askin' you," he responded.

"Okay," I said reluctantly.

"I'll see you then," he said. And then he stole a kiss from my cheek.

CHAPTER FOURTEEN

J ust as Javier said, when Saturday came, he was at my door at two O'clock sharp to pick up Ice and me. The weather was appropriate. It was typical of a August day. I'll admit I was a bit hesitant about this Javier thing. And I knew that people were talkin' about me and I knew what they thought about me. I wasn't sure if I wanted to expose myself to all the ridicule. But one thing that Lola taught me was not to care about what other people thought. They were going to think whatever they wanted regardless.

Javier surprised me with a new bathing suit and a wrap skirt. I thought that was truly sweet of him. And now I had the perfect bathing suit. All I needed now was a fly pair of sunglasses to match. I went into my room and found the perfect pair like I knew I would. Ice had a couple of pairs swim shorts to choose from that I brought him at the beginning of the summer.

We arrived at the "Y" about a half hour after Javier picked us up. I spoke to Bailey early on in the week and she assured me that she would be there. As we approached the lower level of the pool area all eyes were on us. I never knew that Javier had so many gentlemen qualities. I was really startin' to dig on him because of it. He took my hand and led me out to a table that was reserved just for us. We sat there for a while and just chilled.

Everything was going just fine. Javier kept me laughin' the entire time and Ice was having the time of his life in a pool filled with girls my age.

"Don't hide behind those glasses," Javier said. "Take them off so I can see those beautiful eyes.

I'll give it to him. He had a knack for knowing the right thing to say at the right time. I sat there as long as I could until I couldn't sit no more. I got up and began to look around for a minute.

"Everything Ok?" Javier asked.

"Yeah," I responded. "I just need to know where the bathroom is.

"Hold up. Let me show you where it is," he said as he directed me towards the bathroom. "Go up the steps and make a right. Take the hallway all the way back and it'll be on your left," he said.

I found the bathroom just fine. But on the way back I ran into Shardae and a couple of her friends. Shardae was some uppity girl from the other side of town and she was always pretending to be more than what she was. Her Mom worked for the city and they had good benefits. She snubbed her nose at anybody who received public assistance.

"Excuse me," I said as I tried to get through the hallway where Shardae and her friends were blocking.

They all continued to talk and laugh as though they didn't hear me.

"Excuse me," I said even louder.

"Oh, I guess you trynna' get by," Shardae responded with plenty of attitude.

We stared each other down for a good five seconds.

"Oh, you said excuse me, oh okay. My bad," she mockingly added.

As I began to walk pass, someone threw an empty soda can at me from behind and hit me in the back of my head. I turned around to see if I could identify who might have done it. But I couldn't tell because everyone was laughing and trynna' play it off. So I turned around and began to continue to walk.

"Hooka," someone called out.

My first mind told me to keep walking, but my second mind just wouldn't allow me to do it. And so I slowly turned back around.

"If anyone of you cowardly bitches have something to say to my face feel free to say it now. I dare you," I challenged them.

I started looking around to see what vibe I could pick up in case they tried to jump me.

I started to turn again when I heard a voice from the crowd.

"Here you go Unique," Shardae said as she pulled out something from her bag.

"What's that?" I asked as I took the piece of paper from Shardae's hand.

"It's my Uncle's phone number. He and his friends are always looking for somebody to service them; you know, help them relieve some of that tension buildup. I heard you are real good at that.

"What?" I responded.

"You heard me. Did I stutter?" she asked.

At that moment, Bailey came from out of nowhere behind me.

"Well actually she does more than relieve tension. But she really don't have time to explain that to you. But you can ask Corey. I'm sure he'll be able to give you a full account - stroke by stroke about just how good of a tension reliever she is," Bailey said to Shardae.

"What did you say trick?" Shardae asked as she started to walk up to Bailey.

Bailey didn't even think before she responded. She grabbed Shardae by her Yacky ponytail and began punching her out ungodly. Shardae's friend Beverly attempted to help her, when I quickly pounced on her as soon as she tried to leap and I started gettin' it in. All of a sudden me and Beverly fell back onto one of the tables. Beverly was a lot bigger than I was but I was faster. I immediately rolled from under her, got up, picked up the folded chair that was next to me and started whalin' on dat ass.

Beverly kept tryin' to get up but I kept knocking her right back down. After about twenty seconds – which is a long time when you're fighting; she managed to get up, at which point I continued to wail on dat' ass about a half dozen more times before she lost her footing and fell over the railing and onto the deck below. If it wasn't such a short drop she would've definitely broken something.

Once Beverly fell over the rail, she got the attention from everybody on the lower level who had no idea what was going on up top. And when she fell people started screamin'. Then everybody from downstairs jumped up and started running upstairs to witness the fight, including Javier and Ice.

I really couldn't see a lot of what was goin' on around me. But when the people from downstairs ran upstairs they started jumpin' in the fight. I didn't know who was on who's side so I just started swinging at whoever came near me. By this time I was getting' winded.

The security guards called the police for backup as they tried to break up the fight but it proved to be more than they could handle. All I was thinking at that time was that I was so glad that I had a one piece bathing suit on. The crowd of people started to disperse when somebody yelled, "police." I saw the cops running towards everybody, swoopin' up whoever they could get their hands on.

"Javier," Javiers mother called out to him."Get your stuff and get out of here," she told him.

I was trying to take a beach umbrella from out of Ice's hand as he stood up on a table whacking anybody who looked like they were on the other side when Javier grabbed us both up and led us through the crowd.

"Bailey come on," I called out to Bailey as she was gettin' her last kicks and punches in. I looked around and saw clumps of hair, broken fingernails, and bikini tops all on the ground.

"I see right now I can't take ya'll now where," Javier said to Ice, Bailey, and me with a smile on his face as we exited the building.

We all looked a hot mess as we made our way home painted with ketchup, mustard, and other condiments. We began checking ourselves over to make sure that none of us were cut and bleeding.

My hair was saturated with soda pop and Bailey had a couple of tracks pulled from her hair. Ice and Javier were totally just as they were. We went back to my house, got cleaned up, and sat back and continued the party as we recounted everything that happened as everyone gave their own version of it. It was a humorous time.

CHAPTER FIFTEEN

The next two years passed quickly. As I promised Javier, I did stop tricking and I didn't miss one minute of it. I made a conscious decision to go back to school and we were one month into a new school year. I spent most of my days reading new books that I had purchased from the bookstore and doing mine and Javier's homework. He was too busy getting' money and didn't have a lot of time on his hands for school work. We would be graduating at the end of the year and so walking down the aisle depended on the two of us meeting all of our school obligations. Javier repeated ninth grade and so was one year older than me.

Everybody in the neighborhood knew that Javier and I were exclusive. We did everything together. I loved him and trusted him with my life and I watched as he and Ice formed a bond that was stronger than brothers. Javier was only five years older than Ice and he did things for him that a father would do. He went to all of his games. He took him shopping and to the Barber Shop. He always made sure Ice had money in his pocket and he stayed on him about his school work. They even balled together. I could tell that Ice respected Javier because he would always listen to what he had to say and would go to him for advice.

Javier was over our house almost every day. He practically lived there. Sometimes, if he was too tired to go home he would just stay over. Out of all the guys that I've ever known, Javier was the only one that had never tried to be with me intimately. We would kiss and embraced a lot; showing much love for one another, and nothing more.

I did question him about it once before and asked why didn't he want me like that. And he said that it was because I had expected him too. He told me that love was a deep emotion. It was an expression of the most highly regarded respect and admiration you can have for a person. It was truth. And that sex, in the mind of many men, did not necessarily have anything to do with love, but only the satisfaction of a physical need.

He told me that he never wanted to cheapen our relationship and that he wanted me to know that he was different then all the other men that had touched me. He told me that he wanted me to know how much he loved me inside and out and that his desire for me was with every breath that he took and that he would have me on our wedding day.

I couldn't believe how deeply he felt about love and how he was able to explain it to me like poetry. I never thought of him as a romantic, but he was. I knew how Javier was getting' his money and I remembered back to the day when we were at the carnival, almost three years ago when I told him he could stop slangin' anytime he felt like it.

But now I know better than anyone that when a person's back is pushed up against the wall you sometimes do things that is totally out of your character. We didn't discuss how he made his money. I didn't judge him like he didn't judge me. And I knew that it wasn't who he really was and that he was doing it for me. We were planning for our future together and all of this was just temporary. Javier made me feel safe for the first time in my life since my Dad died. I didn't know why he loved me. And I didn't know why he cared. All I knew is that I was glad that he did.

We were on our way back from seeing a new movie that everybody was buzzin' about; "Hot Buttered Biscuits And Jam" The Memoirs Of Seven, and we were agreeing that we had to go see the movie again because it was of a powerful nature. We were engulfed in a conversation when we looked up and there was Lola.

"Uni, look. It's Mom," Ice said.

We stopped dead in our tracks and looked directly across the street and there she was in action. Javier looked in surprise. It was his first time ever seeing our Mother in action.

She was dressed in a black booty high dress that was cut very low in the front down to her navel, revealing everything except the nipples on her breast. She had on pink fish nets and a pair of five inch black stilettos; a brunette wig with pink highlights, as she batted her two inch eye lashes and threw kisses at the passing cars with lips that had several layers of pink lipstick covering them.

She approached a car that had just pulled up when Ice instinctively began to head across the street towards her. He hadn't seen his Mother in almost three years and was very sensitive about that.

"Mom," he called out as he got closer to her.

"Twenty straight, anything else will cost you ten extra," Lola was runnin' it down to the potential client who pulled up to her.

"Mom," Ice called her again.

Lola looked up and saw that it was Ice and that he was talking to her.

"Is he talking to you?" the potential asked.

"No, not at all," Lola responded as she looked back at Ice.

"Mom," Ice repeated.

"Excuse me for a minute," Lola said to the man. "Are you crazy?" she turned around and asked Ice. "Can't you see that I'm working? You're a smart boy so act like it," she says as she begins to flare her arms in frustration as her potential client drives away. "He's gone, damnit'," she exclaims. "See what you did? You cost me twenty dollars. Do you have twenty dollars to pay me for my loss? Do You?" Lola yelled.

Ice took a couple of steps backwards and looked to be mortified at Lola's reaction.

"I have fifteen," Ice said as he pulled the money from his pocket.
"Give it here," Lola said as she snatched the money from his hand.
"You owe me another five you understand," she said to him as though she had no connection to him at all.

"I'm sorry Mom," I just....
"I told you and your sister not to call me that, now didn't I?"
"I miss you Lola," Ice expressed.
"You look good." Lola said as she calmed down like nothing ever happened. You been Okay?" she asked as if she cared.
"When you coming home?" Ice asked.
"Y'all don't need me around no more. Look at you. Y'all big now. Look at you all grown up. You seem to be just fine without me. I knew you would" she stated.

"Don't you miss us?"

"I've never been cut out to be nothin' but what I am and I'm cool with that. And you and your sista have to understand that. Hey baby," she immediately called out as she turned away from Ice and started to chase after another car.

Ice stood there in the middle of the street with the look of mistrust and defeat on his face. He always hoped more than anything that Lola would change her life and want to be a Mother to us. He often talked about how it would be when we would all be a family again. And for the first time, Ice came to realize what I realized long ago – that Lola cared only about Lola and it would always be that way.

Javier looked on with a deep sense of sadness I'd never really seen him display except when he found out I was hookin'.

"Come on ya'll. Let's go get a Pizza and some Ice Cream," Javier said as he tried to steer Ice away from his disappointment.

CHAPTER SIXTEEN

Soon after that incident I was celebrating my seventeenth birthday. Javier came by the house with a bouquet of Yellow Tulips and a picnic basket with a bag of groceries, and a birthday cake. I remember it was a perfect day. The atmosphere was warm, the sky was clear and it was the prettiest blue I'd ever seen.

"Come on let's go to the park and celebrate," Javier suggested.
"Ice isn't home yet," I reminded Javier.
"I know where he is." Javier responded. He's shootin' hoops with Donnie and Chris.
We'll pick him up on the way," he said.

Javier had recently purchased a white, Ford Escalade and he loved it. He used to talk about buying a Jeep for as long as I can remember, and now he finally had one. I was happy for him
We swung by the playground and picked up Ice and then we headed for the park for a special celebration. Javier had all our favorites. He had ribs from Famous Daves, a bucket of Popeye's Chicken, Shrimps, and Biscuits, Cole Slaw, Corn on the cob, pineapple soda, sparkling cider, and a small triple chocolate

cake that he purchased from Therese's For The Love Of Cakes
bakery.

Once we got to the park Javier laid a giant red blanket across
the ground and we organized everything on the blanket just right.
He pulled out three Champagne glassed from the bag and began
pouring the cider into each one.

"Let's make a toast," Javier said.

"To what?" Ice asked.

"To my soon to be wife," he said.

"What?" I asked.

"Unique Jefferson, will you marry me?" Javier asked as he pulled
a small box from his shirt pocket and opened it.

"Yo, that's a ring," Ice exclaimed. "Is it real?"

"It better be," Javier said. "As much as it set me back."

"But we're still in school," I said. "And I'm going to college."

"I know. We'll wait til' we graduate. We have less than a year.
We can do it right after prom," Javier said. "By then I'll have enough
money saved to buy us a house; a real house. You can still go to the
college of your choice. Your SAT's were high enough. And maybe, I
don't know, maybe I'll start a small business or something. Maybe
that's something we can do that together. Just say yes." He said.

It didn't take me long at all to give him my answer.

"Yes," I answered.

"Yes" Ice answered as well.

"Yes?" Javier asked in disbelief.

"Yes," I confirmed.

Javier and I began kissin' and huggin' and Ice wrapped his arms
around both of us. Javier then took my hand and placed the ring on

my finger. And it was settled. We would be married in about seven months. I enjoyed every second of that day. It was the best birthday I ever had. We ate until our stomachs were about to explode.

The year had come and gone. Business in the streets had really picked up for Javier. We didn't have any money problems. But in the process of doing good, Javier made some enemies. But it was understood that it came with the territory and that's just how it was.

Everybody knew how we were livin'. Javier was very popular in the neighborhood with certain people because his product was slammin'. But then he was popular because he simply had a very pleasing personality. People thought of him as a pretty nice guy, aside from what he did.

The guys who were from the same part of town as we were and in the same type business as Javier were a bit jealous of him because they knew that Javier was clockin' the dollars. He had a very large clientele. His nick name on the streets was "Pretty Boy". He hated that name because he was modest about his looks.

The girls from the neighborhood envied me for taggin' Javier. But those very same girls thought Javier was corney just a few years ago and wouldn't give him the time of day. Now when they see him they throw themselves at him and then have a nerve to cop a tude when he doesn't respond to them. They main reason they had a problem with him was because he was loyal to me. Most guys in his business had multiple women and children scattered all over the place.

At the end of every night Javier would bring the money that he made home and stash it. He wasn't really a flashy type guy and I liked that about him. He was very humble. Clothes really didn't interest him like that. The only love that he had outside of me was his ride. I've never seen him spend a lot of money on clothes or jewelry for himself but he spared no expense when it came to his ride and Ice and me.

I respected the fact that he was quite generous with his Mom and his sister as well. I was glad that his Mom and me really clicked, even from the beginning. That meant a lot to him. His Mom was real cool. She never interfered in our relationship. She treated me like a daughter from the start. She would always come by and pick me up and the two of us, along with her daughter, Pedra, would go shopping and do major damage in those stores. We had even started to look for the material for both my prom and wedding dresses.

Javier's Mom wasn't really keen on Javier and me getting married right out of high school. She stated many times that she would have preferred we waited a couple of more years. But she knew her son and she knew that he had a determined mind to marry me with or without anybody's approval. And so she gave in to the idea and said that she was just happy to know that we weren't gettin' married because I was pregnant or anything like that.

I already knew that I didn't want a big wedding because I didn't have much family and I expressed that to Javier. And it wasn't necessary to spend a lot of money. I would have been happy with a Justice Of The Peace wedding.

Javier expressed it to his family but they were not having it. Javier's Mother came from a big Catholic family and they loved to celebrate everything. And in her mind this was major. Javier was her only son and she wanted the occasion to be a memorable one.

I thought that Blacks were a little off the hook at times but Latino's were just crazy. But his family was really funny to be around. They were so dramatic and animated. I always looked forward to seeing them. But what was wild is the fact that they said the same thing about Ice and me. We all had so much in common that we meshed really well. And so that was a good thing.

I was excited. I had been accepted into Howard University; one of the most prestigious Universities in the U.S. It would be three hundred and ninety five miles from here to Washington DC and I didn't want to leave. But Javier wouldn't have it any other way. He knew that this was important to me and so it was important to him. He was making arrangements to get me down there and he and Ice would follow soon after.

CHAPTER SEVENTEEN

It was prom night. Our colors were egg plant and gold. Javier took care of everything from the tickets to the beautiful corsage that he placed on my wrist. We didn't bother ourselves to get a Limo because we were going to have a fully loaded Limousine for the wedding and so we wanted that experience to be special. Javier detailed the explorer and put some rims on it and we drove that. It was like riding in a brand new vehicle. Bailey came over to Javier's house to see us off like everybody else. She didn't get to go because she didn't have enough credits to graduate.

The night was magical. I knew without a doubt that I would share my life with Javier forever. The prom was held at the Night n'Gale Ball Room. It showcased its majestic high gold leaf ceiling that hung above a five hundred square foot stage that had gold and sequenced embroidered curtains, huge spotlights, and a seven hundred square foot dance floor. Its array of orange and gold's made me feel so warm and bubbly inside.

After four and a half glorious hours our beautiful prom night was nearing its end. It was almost one o'clock in the morning when we decided to leave. But as we were leaving there was a guy in a sea foam colored Hugo Boss seersucker two button suit that yelled out at Javier while he and I were exiting the building.

"Yo! money, nice set of wheels dog."

"Who is that?" I whispered to Javier as we got into the Ford Explorer.

"I don't know," he responded. He's been showing up out of no where lately actin' like he knows me."

"And you don't know him?" I asked. "You never had any dealings with him at all?" I questioned.

"Naw, never," he answered.

"Wow! That's creepy," I said.

"Yeah, tell me about it," he replied.

We started towards home when Javier got a call from a girl named Lisa. Lisa was a friend of Javier's sister Pedra. Lisa called in frantic mode explaining to Javier that Pedra was at her house and had way too much to drink. She told him that she was passed out on her couch and that she wanted Javier to come over and get her before her Mom came home. Reluctantly, Javier told Lisa that he was on his way. We pulled up in front of my house so Javier could drop me off.

"You want me to go with you?" I asked.

"No, I'm good. Look, I'm really sorry about all of this. But as soon as I go over and get Pedra I'll be back so we can finish out this evening appropriately, Okay wife?" he said.

He had been calling me his wife ever since we got engaged. I couldn't wait to make it official.

"Okay," I responded as he pulled me towards him and kissed me ever so gently on my lips.

He was only going to be gone for about an hour, but even that would seem to be too long.

"What is Pedra doing over Lisa's house anyway?" I asked Javier as I stepped out onto the curb and shut the door to the jeep. "I thought those two didn't deal with each other anymore?" I questioned.

"Yeah. Me too. But you know how y'all females are.

"No, I don't," I said in a playful manner. "How are we?"

"You know. Y'all are crazy. One day you're friends, the next you're not, and then you're friends again," Javier commented.

"Un huh. Well Pedra told me a couple of weeks ago that the reason she's no longer cool with Lisa is because Lisa tried to pull Emillio. You know she has a thing about goin' after somebody else's man. I heard she tried you. And when she couldn't, she threatened to turn you in. Is that true?"

"It might be. But I don't sweat the small stuff and I don't entertain threats. You know that. And that's all you need to know," he made clear. "Listen, the only thing that is on my mind right now is this wedding. We are definitely going to make that happen. So don't worry about none of that. It's nothin'. I'll call you when I'm on my way back," he said as he drove off.

I came in the house and got out of my dress because I didn't want to get anything on it. I went all night without gettin' so much as a drop of anything on my dress. And I wasn't goin' risk it now. Time had begun to pass. By now it was two-thirty and Ice was sound asleep. It had been well over an hour since Javier left. Lisa only lived about ten minutes away from me if you're driving. And to get to Javier's house from there was about fifteen minutes. So I couldn't imagine what was taking him so long to come back.

I phoned him a couple of times and he didn't pick up. It wasn't like him not to answer his phone, especially when he knows that it's me. Ice heard me fumbling around and woke up to inquire about the evening's events. I expressed to him what a lovely time that we had at prom and then I began to tell him about Pedra. He listened and then he fell asleep on the couch while I continued to try to get in contact with Javier. About twenty minutes later, Ice woke up again.

"He still didn't call yet?" Ice asked.

I just shook my head no. Twenty minutes later Pedra called me.

"Hello. What? Y'all can't call and let nobody know how everything went tonite?" Pedra asked.

"What?" I said. Where is your brother?

"What you mean where is he? I thought he was with you," she responded.

"No, he's not. He left here almost two hours ago to go pick you up supposedly, from Lisa's house," I said. "Where are you?" I asked.

"I'm home," she replied.

"You're home?" I repeated in disbelief. "Well how long you been there?" I asked.

"I been here all night,"

"Really? Well about two hours ago your girlfriend Lisa called Javier and said that you were over her house passed out drunk on her couch and she needed him to come over there and to get you before her Mother came home.

"What?" Pedra exclaimed.

"Yes, that's exactly what she said. I knew something didn't sound right as soon as I heard it. She's been trying to pull Javier ever since she

found out we were together. She probably found out that we're gettin'
married and now she's really desperate. Look Pedra, I gotta go.

"What are you goin' do?" Pedra asked.

"You know where I'm going. I'm on my way over to Lisa's."

"Well don't go no where until I get there. I'm going wit' you."

"Well you better hurry up because I don't know how much longer
I can wait here," I told her and then I hung up and phoned Bailey.
She and Pedra both got to my house in about fifteen minutes.

"Where is she?" Bailey asked Pedra when she came in.

Pedra pointed to the bathroom.

"Unique," Bailey called out.

"Alright, I'm coming," I said as I finished tying my sneakers.

"You hear anything?" Bailey asked me as we were on our way
out the door.

"No. Ice you stay here in case Javier calls," I instructed him.
"The plan is for y'all to watch my back while I whip this bitch's ass,"
I said.

"Oh! You know that's right up my alley." Bailey responded.

Lisa lived about seven or eight blocks away. Pedra had her Mom's
car so we got a ride. My adrenaline was flowing'. It wasn't the fact
that I was jealous because I wasn't the jealous type at all. I was secure
in myself and my man. But it was the principal of the thing and the
lack of respect that this girl had for me and Javier's relationship.

A few blocks ahead of us, there was a big traffic jam and so it was
taking us longer to get there than we anticipated. I was going crazy.
It must have been a pretty bad accident because there were lights
and sirens passing by; police cars and paramedics. At that point, I
couldn't take it any longer and so I got out and started walking.

"Wait for me," Bailey called out after me because I was moving.

Pedra pulled out of traffic and parked the car real quick and caught up with us. We were about two blocks away from Lisa's house. And we began to slow down as we realized that the flashing lights, sirens, police cars, and ambulance, were stopped at the corner of the apartment complex where Lisa lived. We saw the police cars blocking the entrance to the street at both ends and there was crime scene tape everywhere.

"What in the hell....is going on?" I asked.

Somehow Pedra, Bailey, and I got separated. I couldn't see anything through all of the people that were out there. I really started to get nervous as I cautiously proceeded. The cops were out there asking people all kinds questions. And then all of a sudden I could hear somebody screamin' out. When I got close enough I saw the cops restraining Pedra.

"No, No," she cried out in agony. "Why? They didn't have to do him like that," she cried.
"Oh my God," I said out loud. And then I started to hyperventilate. I became nauseous as I began to slowly call Javier's name under my breath. And then I called him louder and louder.

"Javier," I called out frantically as I pushed my way through the crowd. Bailey was right behind me.
"Ma'am, I'm sorry, you can't go pass this line I heard the officer tell Pedra.
"That's my brother," I heard Pedra cry out," as she was just ahead of me. That's... my... brother," she said again with even more conviction.

I walked up and immediately called out to Pedra.

"Pedra," I called.

"Unique," she called as she turned towards me and stumbled into my arms as Bailey tried to help me hold her up.

"Unique," Oh my god, they shot him; they shot him down like a dog," she cried out.

At this point I felt my whole entire body just go limp as I tried to form my lips to ask the question;

"Is he…..?" I tried to ask.
"They won't tell me nothin'."

I looked over and saw his escalade parked across the street. But I still wasn't able to formulate what Pedra said happened. My brain still wouldn't let me process anything.

"Are you any relations to the victim ma'am?" one of the officer's asked me.
"This is his wife," Pedra answered with a trembled voice.

"His wife," the officer responded in disbelief.
"Yes, he's my husband," I managed to say in agreement with Pedra.
"And how about you ma'am?" the officer asked Bailey.
"I'm her sister, Bailey responded referring to me.
"Very well," the officer replied. "I can tell you that they're about to transfer him over to Mercy University Hospital if you want to get in your cars and meet us over there, we'll be leaving in a few minutes" he stated.

Everything began to go in slow motion as I heard a distinct voice in my ear. It was Lisa. She was talking to one of the officer's as she was being questioned.

"You did this," I accused her as I slowly turned my head in her direction and without reservations, went straight for her throat. Bailey and the officer grabbed a hold of me almost instantly before I could do any damage.

"What did you do?" I asked Lisa. "What did you do?"

I was so numb that I couldn't even cry. As we walked over to the car, Bailey looked over at Lisa and simulated pulling the trigger of a gun. And Lisa just looked away and acted as if she didn't see her.

Pedra was making all kinds of phone calls, sobbing as she told the accounts of event over and over to different family members and friends.

"Why would anyone want to do this to him? He's never done anything to anybody," Pedra stated over and over as she continued to sob.

Bailey drove us to the hospital even though she didn't have a driver's license because Pedro was in no condition to and I was in a daze. I felt like I wanted to cry but for some reason I couldn't. When we arrived at the hospital; there was already an entourage of people in the waiting area of the emergency room; Javier's Mom, Grand Mom, Aunts, Uncles, and cousins.

"Don't worry. If Lisa had anything to do with this, she will get got," Bailey assured me with vengeance in her voice as we waited.

Then After about five hours of waiting the doctor finally came out to speak to the family. There was complete silence as the doctor gave a description on Javier's condition.

"There were multiple gunshot wounds. He sustained injury to the neck and torso. We managed to remove three projectiles from the torso and one from the neck, which caused massive bleeding. The heart muscle was deprived of oxygen which caused him to go into cardiac arrest. We attempted to revive him several times but there was just too much damage and blood lost.

And then he said those words.

"I'm sorry.......we did everything we could."
"What does that mean?" his mother began to ask frantically; knowing full well that it meant exactly what she thought it did. But she just couldn't believe that the doctor was saying it to her.

"Ms. Acosta, I'm very sorry for your lost," the doctor reiterated so that it would be no mistake in what he meant.

The family began to react to what the doctor was telling them as the words began to sink in. They went absolutely crazy. The weeping and wailing bounced off of the hospital walls like hi tech frequency sounds, filling the halls and the corridors. The sobbing and the cries out to God became muffled as I totally shut down and was unable to hear anything except the very loud beating of my heart as I sat there almost comatose. Bailey called my name several times as she tried to reach me and pull me from the depths within me.

"Uni, are you Okay?" I heard her ask me over and over again. "Are you Okay?"

I could hear her vaguely but I couldn't answer her as I was taken aback, remembering when my father, Caleb, aka "Speed" Jefferson was murdered; and how I felt when Lola told me. I sat at that moment wondering the same thing I wondered then. How could I ever survive this?

People call out to God when they are in crisis or when they are desperately seeking answers to the reasons why. But the question is does he hear you? Or better yet, is he even listening? I wanted to know what I had done to deserve any of this? I knew that crying would never bring anybody back that I loved and so I decided against it. I wanted so badly to scream out from the depths of my soul but the coldness that surrounded my heart like a fortress would not allow it. Everyone around me had broken down in anguish and was brought hysterically to tears….. but not me.

CHAPTER EIGHTEEN

B ailey brought me home that night but I don't even remember the ride at all. All I could remember was Ice screaming at the top of his lungs askin' me about what happened. Bailey tried to explain to him as she sat him down and tried to comfort him because I didn't have the strength to.

"He was supposed to be my husband," I mumbled over and over again under my breath. "He was supposed to be my husband."

The day of the funeral came and it was all such a big haze. His family mentioned me as his fiancé in the obituary. It meant a lot to me that his family recognized my relationship with Javier. On that frightful day I was robotic in my every move and every action I made on that day; only saying, thank you and nothing else to everyone that had a kind word to give me. Javier was so handsome even as he lay there in death. He was prepared beautifully. He looked as though he was asleep and at anytime he would wake up and say something to me like;

"Come on Uni. Let's go. We have places to go and people to see. Or let's go to Joe's Seafood place on South St. to get some of those soft shell crabs you like.

But he would never, ever again get up and say those things to me.

And after the funeral we took him to his final resting place at Linwood Gardens. It was a beautiful and serene place. But what did beautiful and serene matter? What did anything matter?

After we left his final resting place everyone went over to Javier's house; everyone except Ice and me. I just couldn't take another moment of it. I just didn't feel like hearing another "I'm sorry" or saying anymore "thank you's". I was tired and I felt as though I was fighting to even take in oxygen to breath. I needed to be home - alone with my memories and my thoughts of Javier.

Once we got home Ice took off the suit that I brought for him last year when we had to attend the funeral of one of his classmates that had been struck by a stray bullet. Javier's family was Catholic and his mother never missed Communion, and so she made me promise her that Ice and I were gonna' go with her one Sunday morning. It seemed to mean so much to her. But I knew that Sunday morning would never come.

Ice changed into his ball shorts and flip flops and stood in the middle of the floor staring at me. He was waiting for a reaction from me. He was waiting for me to say something to him.

He looked at me and asked, "Uni, why haven't you cried? I know you want to. It's okay."

I stared blankly out into space and said nothing, only thinking to myself;

"I cry for you, and you, and you.
I even cried a lot for me.
I cry when there is no one around;
where no one but you can see.
My hopes are not those that I had before.
The sky was once blue but not anymore.
My husband, my friend, now so far away.
Long gone is tomorrow and I am alone today.
pins of grey and stripes of gloom.
It is inside that I cry for you."

One week later, still in a state of shock, as I sat down in the living room, literally oblivious to my surroundings. I found myself starring off into nothingness. I was aware of the television that was directly in front of me but still I couldn't make out the picture. I looked at the huge plant that Javier brought home one day last year and grew it to three times the size that it was. And I was reminded of how he took so much pride in nurturing and watering that plant.

It had only been a week since Javier's death and the plant began to show signs that it too was grieving. That last time that Javier watered the plant was right before he got dressed for prom. He only watered the plant once a week, so why was the plant wilting? It was as though it could sense what had happened. Just last week it resembled a strong, firm, Tropical Brazilian Dumb Cane plant with thriving green leaves. But almost overnight it had become limp, yellow in color, and spotty.

I got up from the couch and went over to the plant and noticed that the plant was no longer secure in the soil and was loose and wavering. And so I began to lift it, turning the soil, and repositioning it so that it would stand tall in a firm foundation and be sure that it would be cared for; even in the absence of Javier.

I continued with the plant for about five minutes, when I felt some debris fall onto my shoulder from over head. I looked up and saw that the one of the panels in the dropped ceiling was about to fall down. I got a chair and stood up right under the panel and began to try and maneuver the piece back into place. There was a coolness that brushed across my neck and then a sudden warmth came over me. I felt the supernatural presence of Javier all about me. It was him guiding me and steering me. It was him touching me and holding me.

There I stood in total shock when a plastic bag full of money had fallen from the ceiling and onto the floor. I gasped and began to feel flustered as I stepped down and extended my hand in back of me, stumbling as I reached for the couch that was two feet behind me.

I sat for a few minutes and then got up, picked the bag of money up, and took the bag of money into the bedroom and dumped it out onto the bed. I stared at it for about a half hour before I began to count with trembling hands. I counted it seven times. And seven times I came up with the same exact number; thirty two thousand, eight hundred, seventy two dollars.

It was the money that Javier was saving for our wedding and the down payment on our new home. I decided not to think too much on it because it would change nothing….absolutely nothing. What good would it do to dwell on any of it? Would it bring Javier back to me? Would it give me a chance to tell him how much I loved him and needed him? No.

I would no longer be able to prepare for a wedding but I could make sure that Ice and me lived in a house that we owned. And so I took seventeen thousand dollars of the money and purchased a small two bedroom house for Ice and me. The house was being foreclosed on and so we got it for a really good price. The move was pretty easy. The neighborhood wasn't too far from where we lived. It wasn't the best neighborhood but it wasn't the worst and it was a bit of a step up for us. Paying rent was one thing that I didn't have to worry about anymore, thanks to Javier.

I took fifteen hundred dollars and brought us a modest living room set, a dining room set and television. I opened up a bank account with the other thirteen fifty which seemed like a lot. But when you're living off of it with no other income coming in, it dwindles away at a steady rate. And so every month I would withdraw money from the account to pay for food and utilities, or just to give Ice a couple of dollars to walk around with like Javier would have wanted.

As I withdrew money from the account I began to withdraw myself little by little from the outside world. In the beginning I would go out to run errands and go shopping a couple of times a week. And then it became every two weeks. And then it was maybe once a month. Subtly I became reclusive. I had absolutely no desire to leave the house at all.

A year had gone pass and I hadn't seen the outside in three months. I began to purchase everything over the phone from food to clothes. I had our groceries delivered and I ordered clothes from the gazillions of catalogues that came to the house. Ice was on an allowance and at fifteen years of age he was able to do most everything on his own. So he didn't need much from me.

Bailey would come over every three or four days, sometimes once a month. It was difficult for her to see me in the state that I was in. She was still trickin' and doing whatever she felt she had to do to live. School was never a priority for her because she didn't really understand the importance of an education. Although she spoke about gettin her GED and a legitimate job one day, she seemed awful content with doing what she was doing at the moment.

The last time that she came over it was clear that she felt helpless in regards to helping me get over Javier. She had never been in love before and so couldn't relate to losing a love. But she felt bad for me because I had. It was really apparent on her last visit.

"Hey Peanut," she greeted Ice with the pet peeve name that she'd given him some years ago. What's goin' on?" she asked him.

"Nothing'," Ice responded.

"Hey," Bailey said to me as she flopped down on the couch beside me. "You read any good books lately?" she asked.

"No," I replied.

"Listen, I have an idea. Why don't you let me treat you to the salon today? We can go down to the shop like we used to and shoot the breeze with the girls and just chill. It's a nice day to get your doo and nails done. Come on Unique," she pleaded. "My treat."

"Not today," I responded.

"Why not?" she asked. You've been saying not today for about four months now. How long are you gonna' let this thing beat you down like this? I'm trying to understand but I'm getting' real impatient. You know this is not what Javier would've wanted for you."

"How would you know?" I snapped.

"Because he loved you that's how I know. He wouldn't and you know he wouldn't.

Nobody can help you Unique unless you let them. I mean do you want to be like this? I'm starting to believe that you do. I believe that you think you're keeping him alive by being like this, laying around feelin' sorry for yourself.

"Shut up," I began to get stirred up.

"You like all of this self pity shit so people can say look at poor little Unique," she became harsh.

"I told you to shut the hell up," I hollered out as Ice looked on as if he understood Bailey's frustration.

Why should I?" Bailey asked. "It's the truth."

There was quiet for a few seconds before Bailey leaned over and placed both her arms around my neck and hugged me for about four or five seconds.

"I'm sorry. I just miss you girl. I miss us," she said. "I may not understand all of this because I can't get inside your head. I don't know how it is for you. But I want you to know that however long it takes I'll be here for you."

She kissed me on my cheek and then left. I looked up just in time to see Ice quickly wipe a tear away from his eye. I understood their frustration. But I was frustrated with myself. I tried to feel differently. I tried to bring myself to talk to Bailey on several occasions about all of it. I wanted to tell her what I was really feeling inside but I didn't think she would understand me or hear me. I wanted to tell her how I wasn't able to feel good no matter how hard I tried. And I was trying so hard to feel normal again but I couldn't. All I wanted to do was cry and I couldn't do that either. What was wrong with me?

I knew I needed a job quickly if I wanted to sustain this household. It took about twelve hundred dollars a month to run the house with the food, gas, electric, telephone, and cable. Not to mention what I spent on Ice and on miscellaneous items.

Ice was in his sophomore year. He was aware of my depression and he would always try and encourage me to go out, if only for a walk in the park. Sometimes he would ask me to go out with him to sit outdoors on the stoop. But I only wanted to be inside with my pajamas on.

One day after the school he came home and sat down beside me. I could tell that he was worried because he had no get up and go. When he did go out he didn't go far from the house because he really didn't want to leave me.

I found myself falling deeper and deeper, down into the trenches of despair and I could see that I was draggin' my lil' brother down with me. I hadn't been eating properly for some time now and so I began to lose a lot of weight. I went from a size eight to a size two. And I knew that it was killin' Ice to watch me fade away like that, but it was killin' me too, to know what was happening to me and not know how to stop it.

Ice came home on some days and would even cook for me my favorite things to eat; French Toast sprinkled with powdered sugar, eggs over easy, and scrapple. But I couldn't muster up an appetite for it and I felt bad about that. I was becoming so weak and the hallucinations were getting out of control. I missed Javier and wanted nothing more than to see him again. Ice was desperate and felt he had done all he could and so as a last result he reached out to Uncle Blaze for help. And Uncle Blaze came as soon as he called.

"Seems your brother is real concerned about you and so am I and the rest of the family," Uncle Blaze started as he looked over at my frail body.

"Unique. I didn't know Javier very well. But he must have been somebody real special to you. And I know that it must hurt. I know I'm not you and I'm not walking in your shoes but I know about love and when it's lost in any degree it hurts.

I can imagine how tough it's been for you and your brother. And I want you to know that if I can help you in anyway come to terms with everything that has happened to you in this past year, then I will. Whatever it takes. Even if it means you gettin' professional help. There are a lot of places that can help you with this.

I know that right now you can't see this situation getting' any better. But I promise you that it will get better with time. I'm just afraid that you won't be around to see better times if you don't start taking better care of yourself. You have got to eat Unique. You're committing suicide. And we are not gonna just let you lay here and do that. We love you; your Brother and me both. And you have to gather the strength that you need to find your way back to us.

I sat up as Ice brought me a plate of breakfast food.

"Uni, please," Ice pleaded as he looked down on me with nervousness in his eyes.

I took the plate and looked at the food and began to push it around the plate about twenty times with my fork. I began to will myself to eat if only for their sake. I picked up a small piece of French Toast as I twirled it around and around in the Syrup. And then I slowly brought the French Toast up and into mouth and began to chew with my eyes closed. It was painful and nauseating. I opened my eyes and looked up to see Ice and Uncle Blaze as they watched in anticipation.

"How is it?" Ice asked. "Is it good?"
"It's good. It's real good," I responded.

Chapter Nineteen

Well, needless to say, Ice cooked for me every day and every day I ate. I went up three dress sizes in no time. Although I appeared to be physically better nobody knew about the violent war that was going on inside of me and I had nobody to confide in. Although I was eating I hadn't been sleepin' very well. It was like every time I tried to sleep I would have nightmares. And they would be about Javier.

In the days to come I would be up and dressed by the time Ice would get home from school every day. I would even cook and have a plate ready for him by six o'clock. He was doing so well in school. I was really proud of him. It was the third report period of the year and he made honor roll. I couldn't believe it. It surprised me that he took such and interest in his school work. I really thought that I would have problems with him in that area but I was glad to be wrong.

I wanted to do something special for him to let him know that I appreciated him being my brother and that it was awesome that he was on honor roll. And so I decided to make him a pan of banana pudding- one of his favorites. I went into the kitchen to see if I had the necessary ingredients. Unfortunately I didn't have any vanilla flavoring or wafers and so it was off to the store.

It was five o'clock by the time that I left out to run my errands. It really felt strange to be outside. Everything looked to be so big. The store was only three blocks away and I had only one block left to walk. Suddenly, as I continued to walk I became flush. My body was hot all over. I was breathing heavy and my heart began to race. With every step I took the block seemed to get longer and longer. I finally made it to the store but once inside I was so bewildered and confused that I was having a hard time gathering my thoughts.

"Can I help you with something?" a man's voice echoed from behind the counter.

I heard him but I didn't answer.

"Can I help you with anything Miss?" he asked again.

I felt dizzy as I turned to my right, lost my balance, and backed up into a display of chips and pretzels. Embarrassed, I then turned around and tripped over my own feet. My breathing became heavy and my heart was pounding so loud that I just knew everyone in the store was able to hear it.

I needed air and I needed air right at that moment. I reached out towards the door and I made my way outside, feeling as if my life depended upon it. I started walking towards the traffic light when I looked down for just a second only to see Javier staring back at me. He was standing there in his prom clothes shot full of holes and the blood was everywhere. He was reaching out to me and calling my name.

I froze instantly. My feet became cemented into the ground. Everything around me had disappeared. The cars, the people, and the houses all started to vanish. There was nobody out there but the two of us. He just kept reaching for me. I wanted to go to him and comfort him so badly as I reached out hoping to touch his hand. There were voices whispering in my ear.

"What's wrong with her?" somebody said.

"She ain't been right every since that day," someone else said.

And then I heard a familiar voice.

"Unique," the voice called out. "Yo!, Unique, you alright?" the familiar voice asked as I felt something hold on to my arm.

"Unique," the voice called me again.

I began to break free of whatever had a hold on me.

"Yeah," I responded to the voice that was calling my name without really being able to focus on the face. As I became more aware of my surroundings I looked over to see Brick, along with about four other faces staring into mine.

"Hey, where you on your way to? You alright?" he asked.

"Yeah, Yeah. "I'm going home," I managed to answer as I continued to try and shake the spirits that haunted me.

"Damn girl, how you livin'?" he asked.

"I'm tired," I blurted out. "I haven't been sleepin'".

"Not sleepin'?" he asked as if he were concerned about my well being. "Well that's definitely no good; no good at all."

"No," I shook my head as I began to ramble on deliriously.

"Look, why don't you let me help you? Let me do this for you," he said. "This will help you get a good night sleep and it will keep the boogie man away – trust me," he said as he pulled me aside, reaching into his leather jacket and taking out two bottles. One of the bottles had pills in it that he referred to as pancakes. And the other was a small bottle filled with a purple liquid and he called that syrup; or its technical names, valium and codeine. He handed the items to me.

"Well how much is it?" I asked as I took the items.

"It's from me to you," he said. "Don't worry about it. Just let me know how it works out for you"

"Thanks," I said.

"You good to go home by yourself?" he asked.

"Yeah, I think I can manage," I responded as I began to feel like myself again.

"I told you a long time ago that if you ever needed me for anything, all you had to do was ask," he reminded me.

I managed to make my way back to the house and I couldn't have been more relieved. Finally, I felt safe again. I don't know what the hell just happened but I never wanted to go through that ever again. Ice was home waiting for me to bring back the ingredients for the banana pudding.

"Where is it?" Ice asked.

"Where's what?" I asked when it had completely slipped my mind.

"The wafers and the other stuff. You didn't get it?"

"No. I'm sorry. The store was too crowded. I have to go back later.

"Damn," he responded in disappointment.

"What did I tell you about that mouth?" I asked.

"Sorry about that," he replied.

I took the bottle of pills out my jacket pocket, went over to the kitchen sink and tried one. After about a half hour I was semi relaxed. While Ice was doing his homework I went back to the store but this time without any problems. He finished up his homework and played a few video games while I made his Banana Pudding. He ate two bowls of it before he went into his room for the rest of the evening.

I stayed out in the living room watching television and trying to wind down. I started to flip through the channels looking for something to watch when I came across the movie Jason's Lyric on TV One. So I started watching it. It was at that part where Jason made arrangements to get an empty bus so he could take Lyric on a special picnic he planned for just the two of them. The whole thing was so romantic.

It reminded me of the beautiful picnic that Javier planned for me in the park on my birthday; the day that he asked me to marry him. I still had my ring. I wore it everyday and I would never take it off. It would remain on my finger to remind me everyday of how much he loved me.

"How would I ever find anyone else in this ugly world to love me the way Javier did?" I thought as my breathing became erratic as I continued to think back on how different my life would be if Javier were still here.

I started to feel the same way I felt when I walked to the store the first time. I started to get hot again. And before I let myself have a full blown episode I reached in my pocket and took out the pills and the purple liquid that Brick gave to me. I took another pill and a swig of the purple liquid. I laid back on the couch and tried to relax and just take it all in. And within fifteen minutes melancholy had set in as I began to feel its affects.

My heart stopped racing and I began to breathe with ease as I found myself stepping outside of myself floating almost as I had a euphoric experience. Every thing was so calm and so complacent. I heard soft music playing and I could see a beautiful house across a lovely meadow where Javier sat on the porch in the tailored made suit that he wore on prom night and there were no blood stains. He was happy and smiling as he played the violin; something he said he always wanted to do; serenading me as I walked over and sat on the porch in a white rocker beside him, wearing a cool white sun dress. We got up and began to dance. It was the most beautiful music that I had ever danced to. And then I awoke and it was morning.

CHAPTER TWENTY

I t was the best sleep that I had since before Javier passed. Brick
had supplied me with enough to last me about a week. The next
day it seemed as though I had a lot more confidence in myself then
I did the day before and I felt like living. I got up and got dressed
early, went out to run errands, came back, tidied up the house, did
the laundry, and cooked.

It was Friday and so I fried up some whiting, made some coleslaw
and cornbread; the first meal I cooked in over a year. When Ice came
home from school he was just beside himself with joy. From the grin
on his face you could tell that he was more than pleased with the
tasty aroma that filled the air.

"It's good to see you feelin' better," he said as he came into the
kitchen to take a glance at what was simmering in the pan that was
on the stove. And without a word I turned around and kissed him
lightly on the cheek. He smiled caringly, tore off a small piece of
whiting, placed it in his mouth, and walked out of the kitchen.

After we ate Ice cleared the table. I washed the dishes, dried, and
put them away. We watched a movie that I had just brought earlier
that day and I took pleasure in the time that we spent together.

The both of us fell asleep and did not get a chance to finish the movie. It had been a long time since we had night like that. And it was later in the evening when Ice woke up and went to bed while I remained on the sofa in front of the television. I got up around four o'clock in the morning to go to the bathroom but had a difficult time getting back to sleep. I just couldn't seem to get comfortable.

I tossed and turned trying to situate myself in the right position. At first I thought it was because I was just too full with all that I had eaten. And then it just started feelin' like dejeveau all over again. I decided to stop fidgeting around and just be still. It seemed to be all I needed to do. And after about twenty minutes or so, I felt myself relax just enough so that I could drift off into a rem state of sleep.

The sound of fire crackers were goin' off and startled me out of my sleep. I was able to drift back off and then all at once I heard the fire crackers again. Except this time it sounded more like gun fire. I heard voices and people running outside my door and so I decided to get up and see what was going on.

Once I got outside there was a lot of commotion. I saw a couple of people who ran frantically around to the back of my house and so I walked around the corner to the back alley to see where they went when I observed a trail of blood on the ground that led me to the far end of the back of my house. I slowed down as I felt a need to proceed with caution. Once I got to the end of the alley I saw a male figure standing in the corner of the alley with his back turned to me.

"Are you Okay?" I asked the stranger as I witnessed blood coming from his left side. "I'll be right back. I need to call someone for help," I said.

"Don't leave me," the man said, still with his back turned.

"Don't worry I'll be right back. I'm just going around the corner real quick to make a phone call and I'll be right back," I assured him.

"Please," he said. "Don't go," he pleaded as he turned around and began to stagger towards me.

I rushed in closer to help him remain on his feet as he began to topple over towards me.

"Don't ever leave me," he said as he fell up against me.

"Huh?" I questioned as I tried to push him off of me so that I could go get the help that he needed.

But the stranger grabbed hold of my wrist and wouldn't let me go. As I looked down at the hand that held on to my wrist I saw that it was covered in blood. I then looked up into the face of the stranger and realized that he wasn't a stranger at all. It was Javier.

"Please Uni," he said. "Don't go," he pleaded over and over again as he held on tighter and tighter. "Don't ever leave me." he continued.

"No, please. Please let me go. Please," I begged as I became fearful. "No," I started to scream out in panic. No."

"What is it?" Ice rushed in when he heard the screams. "Uni, what's wrong?"

I had trouble explaining to Ice the dream that I had. And I knew that it would haunt me for many nights to come .

"I'm ok," I responded as I started to get my bearings, realizing that it was all just a really bad dream. "Everything is fine. Go back to bed. I'm fine. I was just dreaming." I said.

I got up and went into the bathroom and splashed water on my face, stared into the mirror and all I could feel was Javier holding on to my wrist. I missed him; his face, his smile, and the way he called me Mommie. I did want to see Javier again. There was nothin' that I wanted more than to have his arms wrapped around me again.

But to see him come to me in my dreams like that was crazy

weird. I mean, I couldn't understand why I was having those kinds of dreams? I would have them in the daytime and night time. It made me wonder whether Javier was at peace or not. What was he trying to tell me? Oh! God, this was freaking me out.

I went back into the living room where I had been sleeping since we moved into the new house. My bedroom was great but for some reason I didn't want to sleep in there. I couldn't explain why because Javier had never been in this house before. Perhaps it was the bed; a bed that we had never shared in a sexual manner, but shared just the same. I felt that we had been more intimate than any two people could have ever been. We spent many nights lying next to one another, taking naps together, holding and caressing each other.

I knew that after that dream there was no way I was going to be able to get back to sleep after. So I sat there on the sofa for a minute or two and then decided to take one of the pills that Brick gave me and a swig of the purple liquid just to take the edge off. I was really anxious to erase any traces of my previous dream state. I reached into my purse and took out my antidote for the evening and I'm glad to say that it didn't disappoint me not one little bit. It proved to be my savior that night; rescuing me from the dreadful images and thoughts that were in my head.

I didn't have to contemplate whether to take my night cap the evenings that followed because I knew without a doubt that I would. And it was that way for next three consecutive nights. But on the fifth night it came to my attention that I had taken my last dose. And so I would have to try to make another attempt to go it alone.

A darker and more haunting night approached. It was the darkest night yet. Mostly, because I was afraid to sleep without my medicine. I did make an attempt to close my eyes in hopes of a calming night without an episode. But the night would only try to have its way with me again with the sounds of ambulance sirens and police cars ringing loudly in my ears.

The walls in the house began to cry out with blood streaming down them with Javier's name written in it like some horror movie. I could no longer stay inside. I had to get up and get out. I was suffocating and I needed some air. Thank goodness it wasn't a cold night because I don't recall grabbing my coat or shoes on the way out. I found myself outside on the sidewalk in my stocking feet looking everywhere for Brick. Finally, I went to the same area where I saw him before and there he was.

"Baby girl. Whachoo you doin' out here this time of night. And where are your shoes. You alright?" he asked.

He knew damn well everything wasn't alright or I wouldn't have been out there like I was. But I knew it was all part of the game. And right at that moment he had the upper hand.

"Look," I said to Brick. "I like what you gave me. And I'm gonna' need some more of it – just a lil' bit; just until I can get over this insomnia thing, you know," I tried to explain.

"That's what I'm here for – to serve.

And without any question, he reached into his bag of tricks and pulled out my new found friends.

"Here you go princess," he said as he handed me the package.
"How much?" I asked as I waited for a response. But there was none.
"Is this enough?" I asked as I gave him a twenty.
"This is fine," he responded.
"Thanks," I said and left quickly.

Months had passed and my addiction grew stronger and took on a life of its own. I really didn't care to keep up with what day it was or even the time because nothing really mattered except making sure I had my medicine. But somehow I couldn't forget the date that Javier came into this world or the date that he left it. It had been two years since he was killed and it would be the first time that I'd gotten up the nerve to visit his grave site. And there was no way that I could have gone alone.

I took some flowers, my medicine, and a bottle of bourbon, along with me for company. I sat down and Javier and I talked for a good amount of time. I talked and it felt like he was real eager to hear what I had to say.

"Hi baby," I said as I began to lightly trace the letters on his headstone with my finger. I had taken a couple of pills and drank a good portion of the bourbon and by this time, I was stoned. "I know that I should have come out here sooner but it's been so hard you know. It's been real hard." I confessed.

"I miss you so much. I just never thought that this could ever happen. What happened baby? Why? I wish you were here because there are so many things that I need to tell you; things that nobody else would ever understand. I believe that Ice would. But I can't burden him with any of this.

I'm tryin' so hard to be strong – I am. But I'm afraid I'm not doing a good job of it. And you know what? I don't really care to. I wish you hadn't gone that night. I wish you would have just said no and then everything would be different. Now I'll never know what our babies would've looked like or even what they would've grown up to be. Or what it would've been like to grow old with you.

I wish I could hear you tell me that you'll be back and mean it. I didn't leave you. You left me. Why did you have to go? I need you to tell me what to do," I sobbed. "I need you to tell me that everything will be okay."

Hours later I awoke to the grounds keeper shaking me into consciousness.

"Miss, are you alright?" he asked.
"Huh?" I asked.
"Are you alright? It's late. Do you live around here?"

I woke up in a dazed and managed to fix my eyes on Javier's headstone, reminding myself where I was.

"No, I'm ok though." I responded as I began to remember the conversation that I had with him.

I got up and brushed the grass and dirt residue from my clothes and picked up the empty bottle of bourbon and put it in my pocket book and staggered off.

On my way back I started to think about the fact that I needed a source of income. Even though I didn't owe anything on my house I needed money to keep the utilities on and to by food and other necessities because we were almost out of money.

I came home later that day to find Ice waiting for me. I kept the jeep that Javier was so fond of. There were only two payments left on it so I paid it off .

"Where you been?" Ice asked with authority.

He would be seventeen in two weeks and he sounded almost like Speed. I knew that he had to have heard things about me in the street - hurtful things. And most of them were probably true. But I knew that he still loved me. That's one thing that I could count on and knew for sure. Ice loved me unconditionally.

"Nowhere," I answered. "It's not even important. What's wrong with your face? Have you been fightin' again I asked him? How many times has Javier told you that you are better than that, huh?" I asked him.

"Yeah, well that's what I'm tellin' you Uni," he started in on me. "For once you need to hear what I'm sayin' to you because you are not hearing me. You better than this right here," he said to me."You know why I'm fighting everyday? Do you really wanna' know. I fight everyday 'cause I'm tired of people calling my sista' a cake head. I'm tired of everybody talkin' about you like you ain't nothin'. I miss him too Uni. I loved him too. He was my brother. But he wouldn't want you to use his memory to tear yourself down. I'll fight for you every day if I have to. I don't mind. But am I by myself? I'm getting' tired of fighting for you if you ain't fightin' for you.

Wow! It was clear that Ice wasn't a baby anymore. And it was also clear that I was letting him down in a big way.

"You don't know what its like to be me," I tried to come back with justification for my actions. Nobody knows. I thought you of all people would understand.

"I do understand. But you don't know what it's like to be me either." He came back. You had a chance to know both Mom and Dad. You had the best part of them. But I don't remember what it was like to have either one of them in my life. I never was given that opportunity.

But I came to terms with it because at least I had you. You have been everything to me; both Mother and my Father. And what is it that you use tell me, huh? What did you use to beat me down with everyday? You told me that you refuse to lose me to these streets. You said that you would die first before you let that happened. And now I'm tellin' you the same thing. He said as he got up and started looking for my stash.

"Where is it?" he asked. "Where did you put it?"

"Where is what?" I questioned him.

"You know what I'm talking about, Uni." He said as he began looking through the draws and under the chair cushions.

"What is the matter with you? Stoppit' Ice," I yelled as he went into the kitchen and got warmer and then hot.

"Ice give it to me." I yelled as I witnessed him open the empty tea canister on the kitchen counter and begin dumping my stash down the sink.

"What are you doing?" I screamed as I tried to stop him, hitting him and smacking him, but he kept pushing me away.

"What gives you the right to do that, huh?" I cried out at him. "What gives you the right?"

"I give me the right." He looked at me sternly and said. "I love you. And every time I find you bringin' that shit in this house, the same thing's gonna' happen again and again." He made it clear before he stormed out.

CHAPTER TWENTY-ONE

After Ice left, I had the rest of the evening to think about what he said. The crazy thing about it was that I heard and felt everything that he said to me. And I knew that he spoke the truth. But I was helpless to do anything about it. I knew that I couldn't control what I was experiencing in my life and so I decided to surrender to it. I continued to bring my stash into the house and I made sure that Ice would never figure out where I kept it.

I hadn't seen Bailey in about a month. She knew that I had a serious problem and it was killing her that she wasn't able to help me fix this one. She was using too. But she would never let herself be as bad off as I was. Because unlike me, Bailey was in control over whatever she did. She wasn't dependent on anything. She could take it or leave it, stop whenever she felt like it.

But I still had to figure out how to get my hands on some money. And I only knew one way to get a lot of money in a short period of time; where I could work my way up from the bottom quickly, make my own hours and bring in a decent cash flow. So I went to the Cave tryin' to catch up with Bailey. But instead, who do I run into? Brick.

"You lookin' for your girl or you looking for me," Brick said sarcastically.

Needless to say I gave him the, "kiss my ass look and that was that"

"She over on Dudley Street," he said. She left here about an hour ago. You know the room number don't you?"

With no response, I turned around and was out.

"Can I come?" he said.

I turned around, stared at him, and kept it moving."

I found myself back in familiar surroundings as I knocked on the door of room seventeen but nobody answered. I knocked and tried the knob and the door fell open. I walked in on Bailey having a two for one discount as I found her asleep, along side two faceless half dressed men.

"Damn Uni, can't you knock?" Bailey squealed as she felt my presence standing over her and awoke from her drunken stupor.
"I did," I responded. "Get up, I need to talk to you," I said, dismissing her clients.
"Can't it wait?" she asked.
"No, not really. Put your clothes on. I'll be outside," I said.
It was all but five minutes when her clients made their exits and left the door wide open behind them.

"What is so urgent?" she asked.
"You into double time now huh?" I asked.

"I'm sure that's not what you came over here to ask me," she switched the conversation.

"I'm messin' up – bad," I came clean. "I only have a couple dollars to my name and I need money.

"Well, I have some put away. You know you can have it," Bailey said.

"I know. But I'm not even trynna' hit you up for what I need. I need a steady flow of cash.

"Well, what do you want me to do?" she asked

"I'm thinking about comin' back to work," I said.

"Are you serious?" she responded.

"Yeah, I don't see that I have a choice. I need money fast and on a regular or I'm gonna' lose my house."

"It's been a few years. You sure you thought about this?"

"Yeah," I shook my head in response.

"Well if that's what you want you goin' have to work that out with Big Tommy?" she said.

"I know. That's why I need you to talk to him for me." I explained.

"Talk to him? I don't know. How you doin' wit' that problem?" she asked.

"I'm cool," I lied.

"You sure, because if Big Tommy finds out that you lettin' that get the best of you….

"I said I'm good," I jumped in.

"Okay," she agreed. I'll talk to him.

"You been over there to see your Mom lately?" I asked her.

"I was pass there a couple of weeks ago. We talked.

"Yeah? I asked in disbelief.

"Yeah. I finally felt comfortable enough to tell her some of things I've been holdin' back from her," she started to explain.

"Un huh," I mumbled, letting her know that I was listening to her.

"It started off pretty good but as the details came out she shut me down like I knew she would. But it's cool. I just needed to get it off my chest no matter what her reaction was. I needed her to know. You know she had a nerve to suggest that I may have misunderstood his intentions," she said with tears in her eyes. "And then when she realized that she could no longer manipulate me or the situation she did a three sixty and turned everything around on me." she said with a burdened heart. "But I'm not mad at her. She's doin' what she gotta' do to make it. And I'm over it now anyway. It is what it is," she said.

"Yeah, life is a bitch ain't it?" I said.

"Yeah. So let's go down and talk to Big "T", Bailey suggested. "You know he always had a soft spot for you girl. He treated you better than me and I'm the one who introduced y'all. That's some shit," she said as we both broke out in laughter.

"Girl, stop.

"You know I ain't lyin'," we continued to laugh.

"Well come on. He's downstairs right now.

We stood outside of Big Tommy's office and knocked.

"Who is it?" he asked in his James Earl Jones voice.

"It's me Bailey," she said. "I brought somebody to see you.

"Well come the hell in. What you standin' out there for?"

Tommy had a couple of kids out there in the world that he was estranged from and he often spoke about his regrets and how he wished he had the chance to live his life over again just for the opportunity to be a better father.

And although he was not what you would call a role model by any means, I do believe that he legitimately cared about Bailey and me. He had reminded us on numerous occasions that we were the same age as his daughter.

Tommy knew what kinda' world we lived in and he accepted that. And he didn't really condone the way we chose to get paid but he didn't look down on us because of it either. He was easy like that; like a Sunday morning.

"Well, look who's here," he said.

"Hey Tommy." I responded.

"Hey Tommy? Is that all I get from you is hi Tommy? I bet you better get over here and hug my neck," he said with a smile on his face.

I walked over and gave him the longest hug ever.

"Sunshine, where you been? Sit down, sit down, here have a seat," he said.

We all sat down for a few minutes.

"Let me just say," he started. "I heard about the hand you was dealt," he became serious referring to Javier.

"Yeah well," I said. "Shit happens."

"Yeah, yeah. So how you been holdin' up?" he asked.

"I'm makin' it," I responded.

"Yeah, well I heard you was out there on that shit," he got straight to the point.

"I'm not goin' lie. I dabbled a lil' bit but I got that under control. It's like a pill here and there, you know. no big deal – really," I explained.

"Un huh, really?" he said suspiciously.

"Really," I tried to assure him.

"Well I hope that's the case. I really do. Because I've seen some pretty ones just like you and Bailey lose all their beauty, their hair, and their looks, everything, messin' wit' that narcotic," he said.

"That's not even goin' be me," I said trying to convince my own self.

"You know that do you?" he asked.

"Yeah, I do. I guarantee it," I said.

"You guarantee what? How you goin' guarantee anything? You ain't in the position of guaranteeing nothin'." he started preaching. The only thing in this world that you can guarantee is death 'cause that's eminent. You understand?" he asked.

"Yes Big Tommy," I responded like I was ten years old.

"Now why you here?" he went on.

"Well she needs some work," Bailey butted in. "Just until she can get back on her feet.

"I didn't hear her say that," Tommy said. "she gotta' mouth don't she?"

"I need to get back to work Big "T". I got myself in a bit of a jam."

"And you want your old room back, is that right?"

"Yeah."

"What makes you think I'd just let you go back up in there like that. I'm kinda thinkin' you should be in school some where; in college, studying to be a doctor or somethin' like that," he said in his tough mannerism. "I don't really think this is where you need to be."

"I need this Tommy. It's not goin' be forever. It's only gonna' be for a little while; just til' I can raise some capital"

"Un huh, well at the moment, Bailey is occupying that room. But you can have eighteen. There's somebody in there but I was gonna' evict them anyway. She'll be gone by tomorrow. You can have it then. Work there as long as you need to," he said.

"Thanks big pappa," I said as I gave him another hug around the neck.

"Go head now 'fore I change my mind." He blushed.

CHAPTER TWENTY-TWO

I began to get re-familiarized with the game quickly. But this time was a little different. The first time around I had no idea about what love between a man and a woman symbolized. I had experienced a love between a father and a daughter and a love between a brother and a sister. But I had never known the love between a man and a woman until I met Javier.

Javier made sure that I knew the depth of his love without me ever having to compromise my body. He showed me that love was so powerful that it would make a person lay down his life as a testimony of that devotion. Javier had a lyrical soul that loved me even when I was at my worst. I wished it was him that I was laying with.

They say, "it's better to have loved and lost then to have never loved at all." But I don't know if I quite agree with that because I know you can never miss what you've never had. And right now I knew what I was missin'.

Re-introducing myself to that game was something that I knew I would probably live to regret one day. My mind told me that I resorted back to it for survival purposes. But in my heart I knew that it was something more. I was over the age of eighteen and so the courts didn't have a legal right to take Ice from me any longer because I was old enough to be his guardian. But they could take him from me for other reasons; like for being unfit or not being able to provide a good and stable home for him. So why would I risk that?

The truth is, I could have put in a few job applications because I did have my high school diploma. I could have even attempted to go to college at least part-time to try and get a degree. I really didn't know why I chose to go back. And so I found myself picking up at the very place were Javier had rescued me from five years earlier. I was right back where I left off. Something deep inside me knew that Javier would still be here if it weren't for me. He stayed in that life so I would stop trickin'. And I think that's what hurts me most of all.

My clientele had changed somewhat. All the johns were practically new. I got three of the originals back from when I first started. But it didn't take me long to get my numbers back up. And before I knew it I had more clients than I could handle.

Most of the johns thought that I was the most beautiful thing that ever walked the face of the earth. But that was far from the perception I had of myself. When I looked into the mirror it was hard for me to believe that there was anything at all beautiful about me.

I always thought that Bailey was the beautiful one. But she thought that her beauty was a curse that attracted perverts and child molesters like a magnet. She said that when you have everyone wanting to be with you because of what they see on the outside; men and women alike – it's hard to tell which ones have a genuine love for you and for what you have on the inside.

I did manage to keep up my outwardly appearance even amidst the men and the drugs. I made it a point to keep my hair and nails done at all times and my makeup was tight. It was business and I worked it like that.

I brought every tantalizing erotic outfit you could imagine to keep my clients hungry. Role playing was a favorite of mine because I could be anybody I wanted to be. It was important for me to be anybody else except who I really was.

I practiced dominatrix and other sexually requested performances at a price that my clients were more than happy to pay. I never set many rules for myself in this game but I was firm with the ones that I did set. One rule that I did hold to was to never service married men. I never wanted to have anything to do with the demise of a marriage.

I catered to all my johns. I learned what their drink and drug of choice was and I made sure that I had it available when they came. Most times I wore a mask or a veil. Ironically speaking, Brick turned out to be one of my regulars. We had a crazy relationship because he was my supplier and my John. He had been chasing after me ever since I was a young girl. And I just decided to slow down and let him catch me. Besides, it was an even exchange for goods and services. He knew that I wasn't attractive to him physically and he was cool with that.

I made it clear to him that I could never return the feelings that he had for me. But twice a week like clockwork he would show up and we would exchange drugs for sex. He brought me a supply of volume, codeine, and a couple of dots of acid as a bonus for letting him taste the sweet nectar of my loins. And he would practically lose his mind when he saw me in costume. I was a lot different from the girl he used to know; scrawny, and flat chested with pig tails. He knew that he couldn't have me as his lady and so he wanted me any way he could get me.

My relationship with Ice became strained. He noticed a lot of things in me that he didn't like. He could see the change in me. I was high everyday and he hated it. I continued to support him in everything even though I spent a lot of time away from the house. I made sure that he didn't want for anything.

I made my choice and it was a choice that I knew that Ice would never accept. And the last thing that I ever wanted to do was alienate myself from my brother. He spent a lot of time at the playground taking his frustrations out on the ball. That was the one thing that remained constant in his life, his love for basketball.

Despite everything else that was goin' on, Ice managed to keep his grades up. And I was proud of him for that. My life hadn't amounted to much of nothin' but Ice showed me how strong he was in his character and in his will and how determined he was not to let anything hold him back – including me. And that's all I really ever wanted for him.

But one breezy March day while he was outside at the play ground shootin' a game of hoops with a couple of his friends he had an interesting conversation.

"Guess who's sponsoring the jump off this year?" Art asked Ice.

"Who?" he asked.

"That dude named Brick". You know him right?" his friend asked him.

"I mean I know of him. I don't know him, know him like that. But I see him around. He's always tryin' to know me for some reason. He's always askin' me if I'm straight or not. It's weird," Ice said.

"Well not to bring nothin' down on you, but word on the street is that he's the one that had that dude popped." Art said.

"What dude?" Ice responded as he started dribbling his ball a lil' slower as he turned his attention to Art.

"Yeah, that dude Javier, your sister's boyfriend or somethin' like that?"

"Yeah?" Ice responded.

"Yeah, well, supposedly Brick had a contract put out on him

and that girl Lisa… they said she was just a decoy the night he was killed," Art went on.

Ice was hesitant to answer.

"You sure about that?" Ice asked.

"Yeah, real sure.

"And sumpthin' else. You know that he's the one supplying your sista," Art revealed.

"Supplyin' my sista," Ice repeated as he stopped dribbling the ball altogether and stepped towards Art. "Whatchoo mean?"

"Yo man," Art began to explain. No disrespect against you or your sista man. I'm just sayin' It's just sumpin' I thought you should know. I know your sista's been goin' through a lil' sumpin', and I was just sayin'- maybe Brick is the reason for all of that.

"How do you know all of this?" Ice asked him.

"My cousin Manny; he deals for em'." And initially Brick came to Manny and offered him like five G's to take that job on Javier. But Manny turned him down.

Ice began to dribble his ball fiercely, pounding the concrete.

"And you're sure about all this?" Ice asked.

"no doubt," Art replied.

"You know where he be at?" Ice asked.

"Yeah, we could go check out the Cave. That's one of his main hangouts," Art assured me.

"Since when have you been hangin' out at the Cave?" Ice asked.

Ice and Art left the courts to make their way over to the Cave to look for Brick. They got there only to find that he was nowhere to be found.

"Check Dudley St Hotels, room seventeen or eighteen," some strange unknown dude called out to Ice as he walked pass him.

"Thanks," Ice nodded as he walked way.

"So what are you goin' do when you find em'?" Art asked.

"I don't know man. I just need to ask him for myself. I just need to know," Ice responded.

They reached room eighteen first as Ice and Art stood outside the door for a few minutes contemplating how he wanted to approach the situation. He wanted to have some sort of control of the situation as he considered himself a calm and reasonable person.

He began to bounce his basket ball when suddenly the door to room number seventeen opened and some crazy looking freak like dude with a bad eye and a missing front tooth came out and shut the door behind him.

"Yo, can you kill all dat' noise?" the guy said, referring to Ice bouncing his ball. "Me and my lady trynna' enjoy a movie and we can't hear nothin' wit' all dat' damn noise goin' on out here," the dude with the jacked up eye continued.

Ice bounced the ball one last time and then held the ball under my right arm.

"You seen Brick?" Ice asked the guy with the jacked up eye.

"I don't know nobody wit' dat' name," the dude responded, then turned and went back inside.

Ice started to bounce the ball again until the door opened once more. This time there was a female at the door in a robe.

"Bailey?" Ice said in disbelief. What are you doing here?

"Hey peanut," she greeted him. What are you doing here?

Ice was baffled. His instincts told him what was going on but his heart wouldn't let him go there. So he dismissed his feelings.

"You know Brick don't you?" Ice asked Bailey.

Bailey hesitated as she wondered why he was askin' about Brick. She became nervous at the thought of Ice adding things up and knew that it wouldn't end on a good note.

"You know em' or not?" he asked aggressively.

"No, I don't think I do," she responded carefully.

"Okay, that's how you wann' play it?" Ice asked as he starred into a set of eyes that he knew was lying to him.

"You tellin' me you don't know nobody named Brick?" Ice pressed. "Everybody knows him. How come you don't?" he asked sarcastically.

"That's what I said ain't it?" Bailey became agitated.

"Yo, she might be tellin' the truth," Art said. "Remember the guy said it was either room seventeen or eighteen. Eighteen is upstairs. Come on let's go upstairs and check it out."

"Um," Bailey became nervous. "Peanut," she called out. I do think I know him. If it's the guy I think you're talkin' about he came through earlier but he's gone now. But when I see him I'll tell him you wanna' holler at em'.

Ice turned around and looked at Bailey with suspicion and then turned back around and proceeded without acknowledging anything that she had just said.

"Where you goin"? Didn't you hear what I just said. He left earlier," she hollered.

"Awl shit," she said as she ran behind Ice and Art with hardly any clothes on. "Listen lil' boy. Where do you think you're goin'? Didn't you hear what I said? He's not here," she practically screamed.

"I heard exactly what you said but I don't believe you. So I'm goin' to see for myself," Ice responded. "You should go and put some clothes on."

Bailey really became uneasy which made Ice all the more curious as the three of them proceeded to room eighteen. Bailey began to move quickly as she managed to get herself ahead of Ice and tried to persuade him not to go to that room. They had arrived at the room when Bailey jumped in front of the door and refused to allow Ice to knock.

Ice forcefully move Bailey from in front of the door and began to knock loudly. Bailey had no idea that he was that strong. All of a sudden a dark skinned dude with no shirt on, a gold chain around his neck, an earring in his left ear, and tattoos on both arms, his neck, and across his chest, wearing a pair of pants that were unfastened, came to the door with a cigarette in his mouth.

"What the hell is goin' on out here?" he asked.

"Nothing," Bailey said quickly. "It ain't nothing," she tried to assure him.

Ice and Art was starring right into the eyes of the guy that the whole neighborhood knew as Brick. Brick looked at Ice and recognized him also.

"Young blood," Brick said. "What you doin' here?' he asked.

"I need to talk to you about something," Ice said.

"Me? Well, it can't wait until tomorrow? I'm kinda in the middle of something."

"Naw," this not goin' be able to wait," Ice stressed.

"What you need something? You in some kinda trouble?" Brick asked.

"Naw. I'm lookin' for my sista', you seen her?"

"Look, let me grab my stuff and we can go somewhere and talk. It'll only take a second," Brick said when he realized that Ice was there to confront him. "Why don't you and your friend meet me downstairs over by the vending machines," Brick suggested. And then he slightly opened the door and eased himself inside.

After a few minutes, Ice placed his hand on the knob and began to turn slowly.

"Ice", Bailey called out.

Brick came back to the door.

"Yo, lil' man. I told you to go downstairs and wait for me over by the vending machines and I would be with you in a minute." Brick said with more bass in his throat.

"You never answered my question," Ice said without showing signs of intimidation.

"What question?" Brick asked.

"I asked you if you knew where my sista' was," Ice pressed.

"No I don't," Brick answered. "Yo, what did I say man? If I see her I'll tell her that you're lookin' for her," Brick responded with attitude.

Ice looked over and saw that the door was slightly opened and Ice reached pass Brick and pushed it open so that he could get a better view of what was goin' on inside.

"Look man, what the hell are you doin?" Brick asked.

Ice looked in and observed a semi conscious and partially nude female with a sheet over her and a night stand covered with drug paraphernalia and a revolver. Ice immediately rushed in.

"Unique," he called out. Unique, get up"

I awoke to the sound of my brother's voice from out of a drug induced sleep to see my him standing over me with angry hurt eyes.

"What are you doin' here?" I asked him.

He quickly reached for my clothes that were in the chair across the room and threw them at me.

"Get up now and get dressed," Ice ordered with a tone that I had never heard from him.

"Wait a minute. What's the matter?" I asked

"What's the matter?" he repeated the question. "Do you even have to ask? All of this shit stops here - right now – today – that's what's the matter?" he said sounding like my father.

"Uni, I'm sorry. He wouldn't listen," Bailey tried to explain. I tried to stop him.

"Hurry up," Ice demanded. This all you think you good for is laying on your back? He questioned me with tears in his eyes. This is all you think you're worth?

"Just calm down lil' man," Brick instigated.

"What?" Ice challenged him. Yo, man, mind your business. Just shut the hell up and mind your business.

"We can keep this thing civil is all I'm sayin', Brick tried to reason;

"You trynna' play me nigga'? You standin' there talkin' that civil shit when you up in here takin' advantage of my sista' like this? Fuck civil"

Art was really getting nervous about what was taking place. He could see that things were not going well at all.

"Come on man forget him. Let's go. Let's get out of here,' Art said.

"Naw, I ain't goin' no where without my Sista. You know who you layin' wit'. Huh Unique?" Ice asked. "You don't know nothin' about this bitch ass nigga'?" Ice said.

"Yo, man lets jet," Art insisted as he felt the temperature rising in the room.

"What are you talkin' about?" I asked.

"Tell her Brick," Ice said.

"Tell me what?" I inquired. "What's he talkin' about?" I asked as I turned to Brick.

"Look, I have no idea what he's talkin' about," Brick responded.

"He set em' up," Ice spilled.

"Set who up?" I asked in confusion as I continued to get dressed.

"Go head and tell her how you set Javier up," Ice coaxed Brick.

"What?" I said sobering up quickly."

"Tell her about that night. Tell her how you felt threatened because Javier was taking all your clientele and how you were losing business. Tell her Brick," Ice insisted.

"Oh my God," Bailey said as she and Art looked on.

"It was you?" I asked Brick in disbelief.

"Unique. Yo," Brick started to try and clean it up. "I don't know where your brother is gitten' his information. But…

"You look me in my eyes and tell me you didn't have anything to do with Javier's death," I asked him as I stepped towards him and looked him directly into his eyes.

"You believe what you want," Brick said as he made it clear that he didn't care what I thought.

"You did it didn't you?," I asked as I looked into his eyes and saw the truth for the first time.

"Come on Unique. Ice said as he grabbed my hand and began to pull me towards the door.

"No," I said as I snatched away from Ice and came back towards Brick. "You played me."

"Come on now. Go head wit' dat'."

"You used me," I said. Imma kill you.

And with all my might and with all that he had cost me, I drew my fist back as far as I could and with all power in my hands I unleashed a flurry of punches up and down the side of Bricks face that he wouldn't soon forget.

Once Bailey saw me in action she jumped in and began to help me tear fire to his ass. Ice and Art began to try and separate us. All at once Brick slapped Bailey in the face and she hit her head against the door. Then he picked me up and threw me up against the wall and that's when Ice went crazy.

Ice and Brick started to fight and they were all over that room in a cyclone of motion. Ice was giving Brick a very hard way to go but Brick was bigger and stronger than him. Against his better judgment, Art tried to help Ice but was knocked out with the first blow that Brick landed on him.

Brick began to bash my brother's head into the floor and started to pummel him into unconsciousness. I somehow found the strength to get up and jump onto Brick's back and reaching my hands around to the front of his face and digging my finger nails as deep into his eye sockets as I possibly could while Bailey ran over to help Ice up off of the floor.

Brick began to scream as I dug deeper, attempting to pull both of his eyes out of his head. Brick backed up in blindness and started to thrust me into the wall as I wrapped my legs tightly around his waist. But with each thrust I felt my spine cracking as I began to lose my grip from his eyes but still managed to hold onto his neck.

"Stoppit'," Bailey cried. "You punk bitch," she screamed louder as she pulled out the can of mace that she always kept on her and started spraying Brick in his injured eyes. Unfortunately, when she sprayed him in his eyes he went crazy and he began to thrust me against the wall even harder. He then turned around with me still on his back and began to walk toward Bailey, slapping her with the back of his hand with every step that he took until she fell backwards onto the bed.

By this time, I had slid off his back and onto the floor. I turned my head, looked over and saw that Ice was still out cold. I turned my head in the other direction, looked under the bed and I saw the billy club that I kept there for protection. I then looked up to see Brick on top of Bailey allowing his anger to direct every punch and every slap he inflicted upon her. I crawled over and reached under the bed to grab the billy club. I pulled myself up and found the strength to start wailing on Bricks back and upside his head like it was no tomorrow.

Brick turned his attention from Bailey and towards me and all I could see was his blood angry eyes. He grabbed hold of the billy club and snatched it out of my hand in mid flight. And with the other hand he picked me up by my neck and began to squeeze. I was helpless as I frantically kicked my feet in a desperate attempt to free myself.

The room began to spin as I gasp for air. Everything started to go black as Brick proceeded to choke all of the life out of me. I began to see the faces of Speed, Lola, Ice, and Javier as I saw my life like a motion picture pass before me. And then I heard the voice of my father. Speed was calling out to me as I saw myself hanging from a cliff reaching out for him to grab onto my hand and pull me up as I was slipping. I pleaded with him to grab me because I could no longer hold on. But before I completely let go I heard a loud sound. It was the sound of firecrackers and then… Speed disappeared.

I started to regain consciousness as I struggled to take air into my lungs. The noise got everyone's attention as the room became silent and the drama ceased. Brick slowly released his grip from my throat, my feet touching down on the floor, and I became grounded.

Brick looked down in amazement to see a hole as big as a nickel right below his heart. He then looked at me, fell to his knees, and then fell face down on the floor. Bailey and Art got up and looked over to see Ice holding a revolver with smoke coming out of its barrel. It was clear at that point that the sound I heard did not come from a firecracker.

In minutes, the police, the paramedics, and Big Tommy arrived and Brick was pronounced dead at the scene. They witnessed the bruises and contusions on all of us and said that they had to take us all down to the police station for questioning. And Even though it was self defense, Ice was taken into custody, and with no money to make bail, he spent the next four months behind bars awaiting his trial date.

Chapter Twenty-Three

Needless to say, that was the longest four months of my entire life. I went to visit Ice at least once a week until his trial. I was having a very difficult time facing him. It took all of four days for the jury to try and convict Ice of second degree murder. The jury established that due to the nature of the incident they found probable cause in an attempt to kill or inflict bodily harm to another person, which was absolutely bull shit but he was found guilty anyway.

It didn't matter to them that Brick brought harm to all of us and we had the visible injuries to prove it; or the fact that he was in the process of literally choking the life out of me. None of that seemed to matter at all.

Uncle Blaze was also at the trial everyday for that entire week. Ice's attorney was horrible. He was definitely a poor excuse of a lawyer. I could have done a better job defending him myself. I don't even know why the courts even bothered to appoint an attorney. It was all a big joke.

Ice had to wait for the courts to schedule a hearing for sentencing the following week after the guilty verdict. He was given thirteen to forty two years. My little brother would be at least thirty by the time he would be eligible for parole. I thought the worst thing out of all of that was the fact that Ice was paying a debt that didn't belong to him. Fair or not - like many of us, it is sometimes the circumstances of others that dictate the outcome of our lives. And my life and my circumstances dictated his, like my mothers dictated mine.

At twelve fifteen in the afternoon the officers of the court removed Ice from the court room on that day. I felt as if the entire building had come down on me. I couldn't believe what had happened. It's strange how some families never experience tragedy and then there are other families who have their full of it. At the very moment that the Judge called out his sentencing I knew that we had to be cursed.

It was different when Javier died. It was different because I still knew that I had somebody out here that loved me. I still had a sense of purpose in life no matter how pathetic my existence was. I still had hope. I still had a reason to live. But that was all over now. They had taken my brother away from me. And they might as well had taken me along with him because I knew that I would be lost without him.

After the hearing I sat outside the courthouse until nightfall, staring up at the building that held my brother captive. At around nine thirty that evening a foot beat officer walked pass and asked me to kindly leave the area because there was no loitering allowed. And so I left. But where would I go? Without Ice I didn't have a home anymore. At least when I was working, although I spent a lot of time away from home, I still looked forward to having a Ice and a home to go to.

I left from outside of the court house and went into town to the all night theater; feelin' about as low as I could get. I was crazy that I wasn't able to shed a tear when I lost Javier. The tears did come but they wouldn't fall. But the day that they sentenced my brother I cried like a baby. And I cried day and night for the weeks that followed.

It was almost six months since Ice killed Brick. I needed to cop and I needed to cop bad. I went over to Dudley street first to see

Bailey. I hadn't been over there since that dreadful day. But I needed to feel connected to something; to somebody. Since Brick was dead I needed someone new to cop from. For the past four months Bailey had been hookin' me up out of her own stash but I needed a new supplier and I needed him like yesterday.

Bailey knew people and people knew Bailey. And whatever you needed Bailey was resourceful enough to lead you to it. She led me to this girl named Raleigh who worked the strip and hustled dope on the side. She was smarter than any of the girls that worked it. She was straight about business. She kept all the money that she made strippin' and made a enormous profit sellin' dope. But the kicker was that she didn't even get high. That was unusual for a girl on the strip. Everybody that I came in contact with got high off of something.

So I admired her for that. That's what made her smarter than the rest of us. She was clean. She operated solely and independently. She didn't have anybody to answer to. She knew a couple of people that didn't mind taking care of her just because they liked her and they thought she was cool. She was also in the counterfeit business and could get you any kinda license or identification that you needed.

I didn't understand why she stripped when she had so much money from her other resources. But she explained to me one day that it was just business. She said that she had goals to meet and a time frame and strippin' was just a means for meeting her goals that much quicker. And that by the time she reached thirty she would be out the game for good; retired at thirty.

So I met up with Raleigh to score. I was feeling lower than I had ever felt in my life and I let her know that I wanted her to give me something that would get me high and keep my high because life was just too painful for me to face. And that's when she introduced me to a different kind of monster; smack. I had never used heroine before that day. I never believed in it. But at that particular time in my life I didn't believe in anything.

It was clear that I would not be an intravenous user because the idea of using needles absolutely creeped me out. Raleigh handed me the crystalin alkaloid prepared from morphine that was packaged in two blue paper wrappings with the words TNT on them.

"You want me to show you?" she asked because she knew that it would be my first time.

"Yeah," I said eagerly. And so we went inside an abandoned building that was at the corner of the block and she demonstrated for me.

"If you're smokin', the surface you use is very important." She instructed me like she had used before. "You want the surface to be able to heat quickly and cool quickly or else the vapors will be lost and there goes your product and your high. You feel me?" she explained.

I shook my head signaling that I understood.

"Aluminum foil would be your best bet," she suggested as she pulled out some aluminum foil from her pocket book. "You place the crystals on top of the aluminum and then you place the flame directly underneath the aluminum until it begins to boil. You use a tool that would allow you to inhale the vapors, preferably a glass tube or a plastic tube" she explains. "Even a toilet paper tube is good to use because the width of the tube is large enough that you are likely to lose very little smoke. You I'ite wit dat?" she asked.

"I'm cool," I said.

"Okay then. I guess I'll be seeing you another time," and she left me there.

I came out of the abandoned building and decided not to cop right then and there. I went to the corner store and brought two cans of colt 45 and placed them in my pocket book. I'd watched Lola years back and one thing she taught was never leave the house without a pocket book; a large pocket book. Lola wore dresses most of the time, but whenever she did wear pants she would wear slacks. I could count the amount of times on one hand that I'd seen her in a pair of jeans or sneakers. I guess that's why I didn't care too much for jeans.

Once I got inside the movie theater I went into the bathroom to cop. I went into every stall looking for an empty roll of toilet tissue until I found one. I did just like Raleigh told me and it worked like a charm. The product began to give off the vapors and I began to inhale as much and as quick as possible. And within seconds I began to feel its consequence. As the drug took on a very ecstatic and analgesic effect I began to experience an intense feeling of well being as I entered into a dreamlike state. My anxieties completely disappeared as I surrendered them to the universe.

I was paralyzed and wasn't able to move for sometime while my body adjusted to its new analgesic friend. After about twenty minutes in a sleep like condition, I vaguely remember finding my way into the theater. The movie was already playin'.

I remember that it was The Chronicles of Riddic. I know that I was in and out of consciousness and couldn't remember a whole lot. But after about four hours later I felt something strange crawling down my back and woke to find some strange guy trying to maneuver my pocket book from around my neck and under my arm. That's how Lola always wore hers. I jumped up and snatched my pocket book. I turned and looked directly in the eyes of that culprit and without saying a word I got up slowly and walked away.

It was three thirty in the morning and I finally decided to go back to the place where I lived. I hadn't been home since Ice was sentenced. I stayed everywhere accept home. Home is not where I wanted to be. I placed the key in the door and turned the lock. Once the door opened the first thing that I saw was the welcome home banner that was draped across the living room. The house was decorated with Ice's favorite color - blue.

I walked in and with a solemn face and a sense of doom I began to tear everything down piece by piece. I came to a halt when I ran across a picture of Ice and me. Ice was seven and I was eleven. I was reminded that life for the two of us had never been easy. It was always him and I against the world. And we had seen some pretty bad days. But this was one of the worst days of all. I collapsed onto the sofa and remained there until the following day.

I woke up the next afternoon and called Bailey. I didn't feel like going out and so I asked her if she could go score for me. And like the true friend that she always had been, she did it. Bailey knew my struggles and I knew hers and so we helped each other by bearing one another's burdens. It was life and death for the both of us and we knew it and we took it at face value.

She brought a package to me about a half hour later. I already had a six pack in the refrigerator that I started on as soon as I woke up. I pulled out a video of Ice graduating from middle school. I watched it over and over again. I cried and I wept and I would never be able to understand any of it.

I felt myself becoming reclusive again. Pedra would come by periodically to check on me. She always referred to me as Javier's wife even in knowing how I was livin'; his whole family did. I sometimes got down with Javier's cousin who had been a base head for about ten years. We spent a lot of time reminiscing about Javier and the best of times. I respected the fact that Javier's family never judged me. They knew that I was hurting. And outside of love if they felt anything for me, it was sorry. Pedra mentioned rehab to me once or twice but I wasn't having it. Javier's family knew that I didn't really have anyone family members in my life that I could go to except Uncle Blaze and Bailey and so they tried to stay in close contact.

I saw Bailey about three times a week when she would drop my stash off. I still had my hook up with Raleigh but Bailey took care of it for me most of the time. She knew that I was slowly trying to kill myself. But she was too messed up in her own head to really help me do anything about it.

She threatened to cut me off a few times but then I would just go out and cop on my own and she really didn't want me doing that because it would always be a more detrimental result. There was an incident last spring where I was dropped off on my door step after three days with nothing on but a sheet; bleeding from my vagina. And all I could remember was that it hurt like hell.

I thought about going to the police and making a report but I didn't know what to tell them because I couldn't remember a damn thing. I don't know if I was a willing participant or not. And if I wasn't, I wouldn't know the person or persons on the street even if I passed them by.

Chapter Twenty-Four

Uncle Blaze came by one Tuesday afternoon like he did most Tuesdays. He came by like clockwork to check up on me. There were times when he would knock and I would refuse to answer the door. I was getting annoyed with my Uncle intruding on my life; coming by whenever he felt like it. But I could tell by his facial expression that he was hurt to the bone about how things were turning out for Ice and me. He would frequently call me by my mother's name by accident.

"I'm not leaving till' you open this door," he yelled from outside and began to bang harder until I just couldn't take it anymore.

He came in and I could barely hold my face up to look at him.

"So, how you been?" he asked a question that he already knew the answer to."
"I'm good,"

We both sat down and he stared at me for about a minute, trying to find the words I guess. And then he reached over and placed his hand on mine.

"You know, although Lola was ten minutes older than me she took pride in being my big sister. And she would stand up for me to anybody. She would never let no body mess with me; and she would get in your face, if you know what I mean.

She was working all kinds of odd jobs to save up money so that she could put herself through school because that was her goal. Our Mother never had much and after your Grandfather took off she could barely keep food on the table or shoes on our feet. Your Nana was a great provider. She couldn't give us everything we wanted but she gave us everything we needed. We didn't have money but she gave us a lot of love.

Early on when your Mother and I was about twenty-two or so, I got into some trouble with some really bad people. Your Mother took all the money that she was saving for school and got me out of it. That's just how she was. And it's something I'll never forget.

And you're so much like your mother," he said with his puppy brown eyes. "You have the same spirit and love for your family. But you've always had an advantage. You're stronger than she is. What you've done with Ice – you've done a wonderful job. You're my sister's daughter," he said as he pulled me in and hugged me. "And I love you. And I want you to know that from time to time we all need help when life seems to be getting the better of us. And I've come over here today to ask if you could do me one big favor. I want you to consider going down to that new center they just built over there on the Avenue.

"Come on Uncle Blaze."

"No Uni. I'm not going anywhere until you agree to go down to that center so that you can get some help. I mean it; right now; today."

"How many times do I have to tell you? I don't need no help Uncle Blaze, I'm fine," I argued.

"Listen to me. You're not fine. Okay. You've got everything in this world to live for. It might not seem like it today. But in time you'll see that. Now I went over there and I talked to a Miss Yolanda about getting' you in. They got a detox program over there that they havin' a lot a success wit'. She said if I bring you over there today by six she can get you a bed. You don't need to bring nothin' but some ID. It's four thirty now so it's not too late.

"I don't need no got damn help don't you understand?" I cried out. I'm fine.

"Look you have to stop fightin' me on this. Do you realize it's been over six months since you've seen your brother? He's worried about you Uni. I'm worried about you. He keeps askin' me what's goin' on and I'm not gonna' be able to keep covering for you much longer.

You've got to hear me on this one. If anything happens to you out here there won't be a need for him to appeal the court's decision. Right now he has a chance because he's a first offender. But he will give up fighting if he knows that he doesn't have you out here fighting with him. Do you understand? He will give up on his life. Do you hear what I'm saying to you? Is that what you want, huh Uni? Do you want this boy to give up on his life? Because that is exactly what will happen if you don't get yourself together.

Giving up is not an option for you. Now either you gonna' come peaceably with me over to that center or you gonna' go by force. It really dutn' matter to me. But you're going one way or the other. Now where is your ID? He grabbed my pocket book and started going through it lookin' for some form of identification. I had never seen my Uncle like this before. He looked for about five minutes and then he came across my non-driver's license ID.

"Now come on," he said as he leaned in and pulled me out of the chair. I reluctantly began to walk to the door.

"Come on. These are the first steps toward a new life," he said with great anticipation.

We arrived at the rehab center about twenty minutes later. I was terrified. Uncle Blaze wanted so bad for me to get clean. But I wasn't really sure if it was what I wanted. I knew that I was really out there. But gettin' high was the only thing that I had to look forward to everyday. I knew the drug and the drug knew me. We had a relationship and an understanding and I could count on it. Sure the falsehood of the drug was less considerable then the truth of my reality but the thought of living without it was even worst.

How could I make Uncle Blaze understand that I knew who and what I was and I didn't mind it. How could I make him see that right now in my life this was the only way that I would be able to keep living. For the first time I accepted the fact that I was indeed my mother's child. The thoughts that continued to ravage my mind were more than I could bear to stand. And so I began to freak out internally.

What was I doing here? I knew that I was there for Ice. And I could see the love in my Uncles eyes. They were the same eyes that had stared down at me when I was just a child. He and my Aunt Mika loved both Ice and me. And I knew that it was a legitimate love. But the truth is that Ice and I never even really had a chance at all.

I heard some old lady on the bus the other day tell a man about thirty years of age that the sins of his father would fall upon him and I baffled as to what that meant. At the time that I heard her say it I wasn't really sure. But then it became very clear to me what she meant. She meant that sometimes a child may suffer in his or her life for the bad things that their parents had done.

And if that was the case then I guess my parents had done some pretty horrible shit because me and my brother's life was a clear indication of that.

"Next," the voice of a husky woman called out. "Who's next?" she screamed.

"Uh, uh, right here," Uncle Blaze responded.

"Well, step up. I don't have all day. Name?" she asked.

"Unique", I answered.

"Speak up sweetie, I can't hear you", she said.

"Unique Jefferson," I spoke louder.

"Age?"

"Twenty-one"

"When's the last time you used?"

"Last night"

"Drug of choice?" she asked

"Drug of choice?" she asked again when I didn't respond.

I looked over at Uncle Blaze and then looked down before I answered. "Heroine," I said as I spoke softly in embarrassment.

"Excuse me ma'am, is it necessary for you to make her business public knowledge like that"? Uncle Blaze asked the lady behind the desk when he saw that I was uncomfortable.

"There's no need to get bent out of shape sir, everybody's here for the same reason", she explained.

"What about her rights to privacy", he asked.

"Oh, she gave that up when she walked through those doors. I can understand your concern, but look around you. Does it really look like anybody cares about her business? Here's a cup. She can use the bathroom around that corner to fill it.

I took the cup and went to the bathroom to fill it. And then I brought it back to the counter when I was finished.

"Dump out the contents of your purse on the counter please", she said.

She removed the aspirin and volume that I had in my purse. Then she handed me a hospital gown, some footies with the rubber grips on the bottom, and a ticket with a number on it.

"That's your room number. Go there, get undressed, and someone will be with you shortly", she said.

Uncle Blaze walked me down the corridor until we reached my room. It was a dull, dingy, and colorless room with a granite floor and no windows. It had a bed, a night stand, a chair, and a small dresser. Uncle Blaze stood outside until I was finish changing. I opened the door to let him know that I was done and that he could come in. I sat on the side of the bed and he sat in the chair.

He took off his hat and held it between both his hands nervously turning it clock wise. He looked up at me and began to speak.

"You know", he said and paused. "I can remember when you were about five years old and your dad came home with this Trivia Pursuit game. He and your mom invited me and the family over for dinner. We were sharing a couple of drinks and a couple of laughs, when all of a sudden your father goes into the next room and brings out this game. We were so competitive about everything and your Mom and your Aunt "T" hated it because your father and I would go all night trynna' beat each other out.

Well this particular night we had the game tied up and it was your dad's turn. If he made the next point he would win. And if he didn't, of course I would win. The women most definitely were not goin' let us play another game because it was already about two o'clock in the morning and your Aunt "T" and the children were tired and ready to go home and go to bed.

Your father was havin' a hard time trynna' come up with the answer. So he picked you up and then he whispered something in your ear and you pointed and said something that only he could hear. Next thing I knew, he gave the right answer and he won the game. He swore up and down that you didn't give him that answer because after all you were only five years old.

He spent about a half an hour trynna' convince me that you couldn't have possibly given him the answer. But I thought about all the games we played up until then and I realized that your father always had you near by. He believed that you were smarter than all the other kids; that you were special and that you were his good luck charm.

And as I watched you over the years, the report cards, the awards......even through hard times you somehow excelled. You are an extremely intelligent and gifted girl. And it comes natural to you. I saw how you looked after your mother when she was home and how you literally raised your brother.

I understand how painful it must've been dealing with the Javier thing. And I can't pretend I know why any of these things happened, because I don't. God knows I've asked myself that a thousand times. But I want you to know that I love you like a father loves a daughter in spite of whatever it is that you've been doing. I've learned that instead of lookin' at what a person does, I think it more important to know why they do it. I just wish that I could've been there for you and your brother more. And I'd like you to know that any father would be proud to have you as a daughter.

You've taken care of a lot of people in the short time that you've been in this world. But now it's time for you to let somebody take care of you."

At that moment, there was a knock at the door.

"Hi my name is Ernestine. And I'll be your counselor during your stay here. I have with me a list of all the rules and regulations," she went on to explain as she handed me a piece of paper. Lights out at ten, no phone calls for the first week, no leaving the premises under any circumstances unless it's cleared with a supervisor; no visitors without written permission and your visitors would have to be placed on the list prior to the request. There will be no fighting, no narcotic use, and no fraternization. Violations of any kind will result in an automatic and immediate dismissal. Are there any questions?" she asked.

"No", I responded.

"Good. Please sign this and check the box stating that you agree to the terms of this contract,"

I signed the paper.

"Here is something to help relax you if you can't get to sleep. If you need anything at all just push the button above your bed and that will signal the nurse's desk and someone will be in shortly. Do you have any questions?"

"No ma'am," I said.

"I wanna' congratulate you on the decision that you've made today. I know how hard this is for you. I'd like you to know that my door is always open," she said. "I'll be back around eleven to see how you are doing.

Ernestine seemed sincere enough. But I knew that I wasn't prepared for what was about to take place and I knew that I needed more than aspiration to get me through this. I've heard people talk about a higher power and of God. I even think I prayed to him once or twice. But he doesn't seem to listen to the prayers of a person like me.

"She seemed pretty nice, don't you think?" Uncle Blaze asked me after Miss Ernestine left.

"I guess," I responded.

"Well I guess I better be goin' now so you can get settled in," he said as he gently hugged me. "Just remember that you can do this. And I'll be waitin' for you to call to let me know when I can come visit. I'm goin' up to see your brother tomorrow. I'll make sure I tell him how good you're doing. I can't wait for him to see you. You goin' be alright?" he assured me.

I shook my head yes.

"Okay then. I love you," he said.

"Me too." I replied.

Uncle Blaze left and then I was alone. When he closed the door behind him it resembled the sound of prison gates closing and I was on the other side of them. I had known loneliness in different stages in my life. It was almost a part of me. But never had it been so cold. Uncle Blaze had done the best that he could. He did more than any Uncle would be expected to do. And Ice had done his part as well. He sacrificed his freedom for me and our family. He gave his life.

And as I lay there alone in that room thinking over the events of my life, there was a multitude of emotions that began to stir. The anxiety caused the onset of hyperventilation as my throat began to close making it very difficult for me to breath. The voices in my head became loud as they overpowered my thoughts. It was clear that I was losing control as the walls started to close in on me. Thoughts of failure and defeat had swallowed me whole.

"I can't do this," I thought to myself. It was now nine o'clock and I was beginning to lose my mind already. I reached over and picked up the pill that Miss Ernestine left. I took the pill along with the water that was left for me. I waited for about an hour for the pill to kick in but I felt absolutely nothing. I rang the buzzard that was beside my bed.

"Yes, can I help you," a voice came over the intercom.

"Can you please come to my room?" I requested.

"Some one will be there shortly," the voice told me.

Then some lady showed up.

"You needed something?" the lady with big hair and name tag that said Charmayne asked.

"What took you so long?" I asked as I became irritated.

"It's only been three minutes since you called," Charmayne said.

"Well it seemed a whole lot longer than that."

"What can I do for you," she changed the subject.

"Yes, um, I paused. I'm not feeling well at all. I took the pill that was left here for me over an hour ago and it is not helping me to relax at all. Is there something else I could take?" I asked.

"It takes longer for some than it does for others." She said.

I began to scratch the itch on my neck and rub the creepy crawling sensation that ran up my arms.

"You wanna' give it a little more time?" she asked me.

"No, not really," I told her without tryna' sound desperate. "I need something now,"

"Give it about another half hour and if nothin' happens we'll see what we can do," she said unconvincingly.

A half hour came and went. And finally she returned.

"Any change?" she asked.

"No," I told her.

"Here, this is all I can give you right now," she stated.

"What's this?" I asked as I became irritated.

"It's a muscle relaxant. It should relax you enough so that you can get to sleep," she said.

"A muscle relaxant?" I asked with intense disappointment. "I need something stronger than that," I said almost with anger.

"It may be that you have a very high tolerance for whatever we'll give to you. And it's not our intention to get you off of one substance only to have you become addicted to another. You've only been here a few hours and I don't think that you're really giving yourself a chance," she said.

Panic started to set in.

"Miss, I need something just to get me through the night. I thought you were here to help me."

"Unique, the first few days are always the hardest. If you could just manage to hold on…just for a little while, I promise it will get better."

"Don't call me by my first name because you're not my friend," I became irate. "I told you that I was not feeling well. I didn't ask for you to come in here to lecture me about being patient. You don't feel what I feel and don't you dare try and pretend like you understand me, ok. Now could you please get me something stronger please?" my tone became desperate.

"I'll see what I can do," she said as she left the room.

The thought of whatever tomorrow would bring mortified me. I was stricken with fear.

"I'm not ready for this," I said to myself. "I can't do this, not now," I convinced myself.

I wanted to get clean. But the drugs had a hold on me for sure. And I wasn't prepared to face tomorrow without them. In a span of five minutes I had talked myself out of that contract and convinced myself that this wasn't the right time for me to do this. And so I got dressed and retrieved my things from the drawer and made a "B" line for the door. The halls were clear and there was my opportunity.

I moved as swiftly down the halls and to the exit without being detected. My first and only thought was to go cop as soon as I got out of that place. But I had no cash. I was broke. But that never stopped me before.

I had to get to a phone 'cause I could definitely use a ride. My mind was racing a mile a minute. The adrenalin had my heart pumping so fast I could feel my heart protruding from my chest.

Awl man, I needed to calm it down. Oh snap, I needed to get in contact with Bailey. My hands were shaky and I was sweatin' like I was being interrogated by homicide detectives.

Since I had no car fare and no ride I had no choice but to start walking. I was at third St. and I had to get to Twenty-Ninth St. So I started walking without thinking about the distance. I needed the exercise anyway, I told myself. I began to walk…and walk…and walk. I walked until my calves began to throb and my thighs began to burn as I reached Fifteenth St… Sixteenth St…Twenty Second St…and Twenty Fourth St.

All of a sudden I was startled as I looked over and saw Uncle Blaze and Aunt Tamika coming out of the Save-A-Lot on Fenkell and Twenty Fifth. I was stopped dead in my tracks just a few feet short of them. Damn! What a coincidence. I quickly turned and ducked inside a building four doors from the Save-A-Lot before they had a chance to see me.

"Whew! That was crazy," I thought.

My heart fluttered as I thought of how Uncle Blaze would have felt had he seen me. I remembered what he said to me just hours before. I recalled the hope that he had in his eyes when he spoke to me and the expectations and optimism that he had for my life. It was all so undeniably comforting to know that he believed in me. But I let him down. My hands rested up against the door as I felt a chill in my spirit. I softly rested my tired head upon the backs of my hands as my face became flustered and the ducts in my eyes filled with warm tears.

CHAPTER TWENTY-FIVE

For some reason I became faint and my legs felt like rubber. I automatically had thoughts of my Nana Ruth; Lola and Uncle Blaze's Mom. She was always so lively, full of songs, homemade remedies, and the truth.

Although I never could relate to any of the songs that she sang back then I can remember that they were as sweet as lullabies. Almost as sweet as my Nana's famous blueberry cobbler and all the other mouth watering treats that she made and that I longed for when I was not in her company.

Blueberries were never my favorite but it seemed like I loved everything that she made regardless of that fact. It was something about the way that she took her time with everything; how she rolled and sculpted the crust; and how she added admiration to the salt and the butter as she sifted plenty of affection in with the flour and baking soda.

She seemed to enjoy pouring in a little ecstasy with the orange juice and folding in bliss with the sugar and fresh blueberries that she'd picked early that morning. She did it all with so much love. I'd never seen a person who enjoyed cooking so much in all my life. How could she put so much love into baking a pie?

See for Nana it wasn't just simply about the pie. That pie was a representation of something more important. It represented devotion and harmony. It represented love and unity. It represented our struggles, past and present. And it reminded her of how far we had come as a people; as a family.

No, my Nana didn't have much and it always behooved me how she could go through life with a smile on her face as though she had it all; enjoying only the simple things and appreciating the small things despite the hand that she was dealt.

So there I was hiding out from Uncle Blaze waiting for the coast to become clear. I felt extreme pressure in my chest as I thought about all the people in my life. My heart was beating two times its normal rate. My face still fever flustered as I just became exhausted. The ducts in my eyes tried to expel the tears that wanted to pour like rain but then I listened as I heard voices.

I thirstily drank the soulfulness of unfamiliar voices that belted out Yolanda Adams' "What about the Children". I took in the words as they fed me. All I could hear was my Nana saying, "go head and cry baby. Cryin' cleanses the soul. We all gotta' cry sometimes."

I turned slowly and began to follow in the direction from which the music came. I found my way into a room that looked like a sanctuary and found a pew to sit down in as I stared out into emptiness. I began to reflect on the few good times that I could remember in my life as a tear drop fell onto my hand that lay on my thigh.

"Cryin' never helped nothin' anyway," I said to myself.

So why couldn't I stop my tears from falling? I sat there and I grieved. I grieved for the life that had my name on it.

I was so consumed with grief that I didn't notice the body that slid into the pew right next to me. There was an arm that extended across my shoulder in an attempt to comfort me. And without even looking up I spoke;

"I'm so alone," I confessed. "And I'm so tired." I said.

"That's where you're wrong," a familiar voice said. "You are never alone.

It was Jackson. But what was he doing there? I sat still for a moment and tried to embrace the irony of it all. And then a strange woman came over to where we were sittin'.

"Is everything ok?" the woman asked.

"Yes, thank you Sheila," Jackson responded.

"I'll be across the hall if you need me," she said.

"Thank you," Jackson responded.

"Everybody's gone, Jackson." I confided. "They all left me."

"I heard about your brother and how that went down. I was really sorry to hear that. It just don't seem right, I know. But if I could just have a moment to share something with you," he said as he continued. "My Dad died right before my family and I came up to Detroit to live. My Mom never really had a job outside the house and so she stayed at home to care for me, my brother and two sisters while my dad went out to work.

My Dad was a big fan of baseball. And so one Saturday afternoon during a baseball game my Dad was hit in the temple by a fly ball and he collapsed. He never regained consciousness and he died the very next day. It was just like that and he was gone. Everything was moving in slow motion.

My family and I began to pack everything up and about a month following his funeral we moved up here. We were devastated at our lost. It was just something that you could never prepare yourself for. So for the first time in my Mother's life she was faced with having to go out into the world by herself.

She went on a job interview almost every day. She looked for almost six months while we were on welfare. It was a very hard time for all of us. And at twelve years old I was the oldest. My brother was ten and my sisters were four and five. We never knew what being hungry was until then. We moved to a much smaller place because it was all that we could afford. All of us kids were in one room and my Mom was in the other. We were on top of each other. My Mom was really having a hard time with everything and I could see that. And it hurt me.

When my Dad died I decided to take on the role of being the man of the house. It wasn't anything my Mom put on me. It was just something I wanted to do on my own. I felt like it was what I was supposed to do. It wasn't until seventeen months after my Dad's death that my Mom found a cleaning job over on the South side. And so she depended on me to make sure that my brother and sisters got home from school safe, got their homework done, ate and took their baths. It was a lot on me but I wanted my Mom to know that she could trust and depend on me.

My Mom found a second job about five months after that, but even with two jobs we still had a tough time tryin' to make ends meet. I got so tired of seeing how tired she was all the time and I wanted to help. So I started bagging groceries down at Wilson's a couple of blocks from my house. I made a few dollars a day. It was something but it wasn't enough to make a real difference. Sometimes when I would come in from work I could hear my mother crying in the other room and I felt helpless.

One day after baggin' this lady's groceries she said that she would give me a couple of extra dollars if I carried her groceries all the way to her house. So I did, you know. She lived in an apartment building right off of Thirteenth St. and Dicks Ave. I'll never forget it. She lived on the fifth floor. Of course the elevator was busted so we hadda take the stairs. When we got to her door she opened it and went in.

"Come on in and shut the door behind you," she said.

So I came in and stood there waitin' to get paid. She went back to the kitchen where it was a couple of guys sitting at this table. It looked like they were counting money and puttin' this white powdery substance in these little plastic bags.

"What you looking at young blood?" a voice from the kitchen sounded.

"Joe leave that boy alone and pay him for carrying these groceries here from the store. Something your ass shoulda did," she sounded off.

"You see me here takin' care of bidness," he told her. "I can only do one thing at a time."

"Come here," he called out to me.

"I'm talkin' to you young blood, come here."

I stood there a minute thinking before I started to walk back.

"Are you deaf?" he asked. "I said come here."

I slowly walked over and stood in the doorway of the kitchen.

"You ain't too bright are you?" he asked me. "What's your name?"

"Nate," I said.

"Nate what? He asked.

"Nate Jackson," I responded.

"Well here you go Nate Jackson," he said as he handed me five dollars.

I had never gotten a whole five dollars before for carrying no groceries up the street. So I was happy.

"Where you live Nate?" he asked.
"On Toronto St.," I answered.
"You know lil' Keith and Robo and them?" he asked.
"No," I answered.
"So you bag groceries everyday?" he asked.
"Yes," I answered.
"How much you makin' baggin'?" he asked.
"About three or four dollars a day," I responded.
"You want a job?" he came right out and asked.
"Another job?" I asked.
"No, not another job, a real job," he answered.
"Doing what?" I asked.
"Instead of baggin' and delivering for Wilson's you'll be baggin' and delivering for me. Same job different employer," he said.
"Baggin' and delivering what?" I asked.
"Don't worry about that right now. I'll start you out with thirty a day til' I see how you work out. And then maybe we can talk about a raise."
"Sure," I said.

I started off making a hundred and fifty dollars a week. That was a lot of money for a kid my age. I delivered my first package that very night. A hand full of cocaine packets delivered to one of Joe's business associates. I would stop pass Joe's to get my assignment everyday. Joe would send me to the back alley ways, bars, strip joints, and even abandoned buildings to make deliveries. I would deliver the package and I would bring Joe back the cash. He never had me deliver more than a handful because it was just too dangerous.

My mother didn't have a clue as to what I was doing. She thought I got promoted at Wilson's because I still worked there as a cover and so she never really knew the difference. She would question me from time to time when she got suspicious because of how much money I was spending. But I just told her I was buying stuff hot and that I caught lots of deals. She would have died had she known how I really made my money and the dangers that I placed myself and my family in. But I convinced myself that I was doing it for the family and so it was ok.

I was fourteen years old and running dope. I made more in one month than my Mom made all year. I stashed most of the money so she wouldn't get suspicious. I brought my brother and sisters things that she couldn't afford to get them.

I had my Mom goin' for a while until people in the street started talkin'. People are always goin' talk. They were going to my Mother and accussin' me of all kinds of things and most of em' were true. But that was beside the point.

After a while she came right to me and asked if I was doing anything illegal. She started going through my things. She looked in my drawers and under my mattress. And then she looked in my tennis shoes and she found a wad of money. I had at least four thousand dollars. I guess it wasn't normal for a fifteen year old to have four thousand dollars stuffed in his tennis shoes.

She caught me red handed and I couldn't even lie about it. I thought surely she would put me out in the streets but she didn't. She didn't like what I was doing but the way she looked at it; I was still her son and she loved me. She sat me down and she talked to me about it. And I listened. But she didn't convince me to stop. A few months later we moved to a bigger place and everything was good.

If running dope wasn't bad enough, I had to pick up one of the worst habits there was – gambling. Being out in the street a lot, I took a liking to card games and dice and spiraled out of control. The cops were always watching me and I was in and out of jail on misdemeanors for about four years before the feds got me on drug trafficking.

I spent two and a half years in prison. Six months in I got word that my brother Tyrone had picked up where I left off. He had a beef with a couple of guys from one of the nearby gangs over some territory thing. And so one night when he didn't come home my Mother went to the police to report him missing. The police didn't budge. They knew what Tyrone was into and they knew he was my brother so they didn't even bother to look for him. Two weeks later he was found in an abandoned house two blocks over from where we lived. He was twenty years old"

Jackson paused as he remembered what had to have been a difficult time in his life. By this time I had stopped crying about the tragedies of my life and gave my undivided attention to him. Listening to his story and all that he went through, allowed me to take the focus off of the mess that my life was in and what I was feeling inside and begin to imagine what Jackson must have gone through during that time in his life. But why was he tellin' me all of this I wondered?

"My mother was devastated to say the least," Jackson continued. She never came right out and blamed me out loud but I knew how she felt in her heart and that she believed it was all my fault. I always thought that she didn't wanna' really place all of the blame on me because somehow she would have to blame herself as well for maybe not puttin' a stop to my activities when she first found out.

But it was nothing that she could've done. My brother and I chose our own paths. But losing him changed her. And she was never really the same towards me afterwards. And what hurt me most was that I wasn't even allowed to come out to go to his funeral. I didn't even get a chance to say good-bye. My Mom basically stopped visiting me after that. And it didn't matter if she blamed me or not because I blamed myself. Tyrone was dead because of me.

Anyway, after I got out everything had changed. My Mom just shut down completely. She practically stopped livin' and there was nothin' I knew to do about it. All she talked about was Tyrone. The memory of my brother haunted me and all I could hear my Dad saying to me was, "how could you let this happen?"

So I began to take on a criminal element just because I felt worthless. And when you feel worthless you do worthless things. So me and my crew started sticking up people. We would snatch a purse here and there. Every penny we scored would be spent on having a good time – a real good time; drugs - chicks.

This went on every night for months. We'd go out and rob or even beat down some innocent passerby. I was angry all the time and all I knew to do was to take my frustrations out on society and I felt justified in doing so.

I couldn't find work. Nobody wanted to hire an ex-con. My brother was dead. My Father was dead. My mother didn't want to live and my sisters were out there. They were way out there. They became very promiscuous and so my Mom didn't know what else to do with them besides send them back down South to stay with my Grandma. My Grandma had a way of straightening things out.

When I looked around and saw the condition of my family I felt like I had let them down. I felt like a failure because when I fell by the way side they were right behind me. It was like a domino effect.

Shortly after my sister's left, I remember it was a winter day. It was one of the coldest nights of the year and it was around two in the morning and me and the crew were out lookin' for some get high. We started scramblin' through our pockets for change but everybody was comin' up with nothin' but lent. We started to get anxious because we hadn't gotten high enough and we wanted to keep the party goin'.

We were getting' real anxious when we heard somebody say, "somebody's comin'" and so we quieted down. It was some man who looked to be about fifty or so I guess. He had on a suit, tie, hat, and a brief case in his hand strollin' about humming some tune I'd never heard of. Me and my boyz looked at each other like, what is this corny nigga' humming for? We all wanted to burst out laughing but he would hear us.

We followed him all the way to his house. We wanted to get him bad because in our minds he was just too damn happy. And he looked like he had some money on him and we wanted it. So, once we got to his house we watched him as he put his key in the lock. He opened the door and started inside. And that's when we bum rushed him. It was dark. There was a big scuffle. The man proved to be more than we bargained for - a lot more.

We barely got outta' there alive. The man beat my friends unmercifully. Everybody had run off but somehow I was still in this man's house tryna' find my way out. All of a sudden I stopped in my tracks when heard the click of a gun behind me. I turned around slowly to see a revolver pointed directly at my head. That was something I wasn't expecting at all. I was caught off guard and was paralyzed by my fear. I knew I wasn't ready to die but I couldn't move my feet.

"I should blow your head right off of your goddamn shoulders. That's what I should do you piss ant lil' bastard," he said. "And I would be well within' my rights to do so."

"Yes sir," I stuttered.

I could barely speak. And when he saw that I was so scared that I defecated on myself he lowered the gun slightly from my head.

"I'll spare your life this time," he said. "But you're gonna' owe me. Everything that I have I've earned it. And I'll be damned if I let you and your thugged out friends take it from me. You ever worked hard for anything in your life?" he asked but didn't wait for me to answer. "As long as you live the one thing you never do is take what don't belong to you. You got that?" he asked

"Yes sir," I managed to say in terror.

He pulled out a card and told me to report to the address that was on the card the next day. He didn't know me from a can of paint. What even made him think that he would ever see me again? But to make a long story short, he did see me again. After he let me go I went home and cleaned myself up. I couldn't believe that I had crapped my pants. It's amazing how your body can just let go of all its fluids like that. I had never been so scared in my life.

When I got home I lay there all night thinking about all the innocent people that I took from. I thought about how hard my mother and father worked and what if someone took from them. I thought about how angry I was and how I will never underestimate anybody again. I took a glimpse at the type of person I had become and I didn't like what I saw.

I didn't like him at all. So the next day believe it or not I show up. I didn't know where I was going or what to expect when I got there and my stomach was full of knots. The name that was on the card that he gave me was Abraham Childs of The House of Job. I came here everyday for about six months, feeding the homeless, cleanin', cookin', and prayin' for people."

"Prayin'?" I asked.

"Yes prayin'? Nobody could have been more surprised than me – believe me when I tell you. But I was happy to be here. I was happy that God placed something in that man's heart that he could see somethin' in me worth savin'. 'Cause I was on my way to a quick grave and I couldn't see it. But once I began to help others, getting' to know them, and becoming familiar with their circumstances I realized that we were the same. We all had some of the same struggles. Some people struggled more than others, but we all struggled with life. I was victimizing people whose lives were really no different than my own. And I wanted to be better. It took me to step back and away from myself in order for me to be able to see that clearly. And so I began to rebuild my life.

"But why would God let such things happen?" I asked in confusion.

"What I got from the whole experience is that there are always a reason why everything happens. And God and his infinite wisdom knows and understands things a lot better than we ever could. And so most of the time you don't learn what those reasons are until much later on down the road when you see it all unfolding. It's like a process. You know you can't get to "c" unless you go through "a" and "b first" he said.

"But what does that mean?" I asked.

"It means that I couldn't have become who I am today unless all of those things happened to me yesterday. And you can't run from the course that has been mapped out for you. We can't run from ourselves. You did some things in your life like we all have; some good and some not so good. But you started out doing them for all the right reasons. You took on the responsibilities of an adult before you had a chance to be a child. And whenever things are taken out of its natural order you can rest assure that there's gonna' be chaos.

But you have nothin' to be ashamed about or feel guilty about. We're not judged by our actions. We're judged by our hearts. You took the resources that you had and made a way to take care of you and your brother the best way you knew how. You sacrificed yourself for him and that is commendable. And he in turn did the same for you. But If you really wanna' help him you have got to start takin' care of yourself."

"But I let him down though," I began to sob.

"I know he doesn't see it that way. He did what he saw you doing for him all those years. It's called love. Now you do owe it to him to get better because he needs you. This Missionary has been standing for seventy five years. We get volunteers from all over the world. We have a program that sponsors people like you to go over seas to volunteer helping other countries build hospitals, schools, and churches. I think it would be a good opportunity for you. As a matter of fact they have a group that leaves in two day," he said.

"Where are they going?" I asked.

"Nairobi," he answered.

"Nairobi as in Africa?" I asked.

"That's the one."

"But what would I do in Africa?" I asked.

"Find yourself. It was a gift that was given to me, and now I want to give it to you, if you are willing to except it.

"So I just go over there and…where would I stay?" I asked.

"Look, all of that will be explained to you. You'll be in good hands. I promise. There will be a group of seven going. Everything will be taken care of. You need this," Jackson emphasized. "Come with me. Let me show you where you would be staying until your departure."

I didn't say yes or no or anything after that. I mean, I heard everything that he said and it was compelling – but Africa? That was just a little over my head. I just didn't know if I could even do it. Would it even be possible? I knew that there was an urgency in my life but I didn't know if I would survive let alone be so far away from everything that I've ever known in my life; Ice, Bailey, my Uncle and Aunt…and my get high. And how could Jackson and these people manage to get all the paper work and pass ports and things like that ready for me in two days? But I followed him anyway, upstairs to the room where he said I would be staying.

"I do have somewhere to stay you know," I told him. "I have a house."

"I know, but I think it best if you stay here. You need a support system around you right now," he explained.

"How long will I be gone?" I asked curiously.

"I think you'll be gone about eighteen months,"

"Shew, eighteen months?" I questioned almost with an uneasiness. That's an eternity I thought to myself. I started to panic within and deliberated for a moment about even the remote possibility that I could pull this off. Although I felt that I would eventually need to get high in the near future, I didn't feel the need to at that very moment because I was preoccupied with a possible alternative.

The desire to give in to my vice had temporarily faded. I felt almost the same way I felt the night that Javier came to me after I had been hospitalized and pleaded with me to let him help me change my life. It was the fact that I saw how much more he cared for me than I even cared for myself. And it is the same fact that holds true right now in this moment.

"I'll need to stop by my house to get some personal things," I informed Jackson.

"Oh okay. Just give me a few minutes and I'll take you," he told me.

So a few minutes later we were in the car and on our way to pick up some things from house. We were there a little longer than I expected.

"I'll be out here if you need me," Jackson assured me as I exited the car.

I got out the car and went up the stairs leading to my residence and went in after a small pause. A strange eerie feeling had come over me. I wasn't sure of what I was doing or what was happening I just knew that everything was moving at warp speed. I knew that my heart was over taken by sorrow; sorrow of things past and the uncertainty of things to come. I wasn't sure of anything at that moment but I knew for the first time in my life that I needed to let go of all the grief that consumed me. I realized that if I could somehow manage to release all the pain and all the agony from the dark place deep within me then I might very well have a chance. But to do that would almost feel like a betrayal to all those that I love. Because my grief and my pain was as a symbol of my undying love for them and I vowed never to forget it.

I went into my room and pulled out a box from underneath my bed. The box was no ordinary box. It was a box that entombed bits and pieces of my broken life. In it I had placed the things that were dear to me. There was the locket that Javier had given to me on our first anniversary in which I later placed a picture of the two of us. There was a Teddy Bear that Speed had given me the year he died. I reached in and pulled out a picture of Speed and Lola during happier times and one of Ice and me sitting with Speed on his motorcycle. And there were all the medals that Ice had won at his basketball tournaments, reminding me painfully of his scholarship and the possibility of playing pro ball among the many other opportunities that had been lost.

I placed these items in a drawstring bag, got my duffle from the closet, and began to collect other personal items from the house. Jackson did inform me that I would not be needing to take too many things with me, just the necessities. But I had to take as many of my things as possible. I needed to be with them and they needed to be with me.

I started grabbing things; a dozen pair of panties, half dozen bra's, half dozen jeans, some bathroom supplies, about fifteen tops, a few pairs of pajamas, a robe, four pairs of flip flops, a pair of shoes, a sweater, a light jacket, a slightly heavier jacket, twelve boxes of soap, I always stocked up on soap, three bath cloths and two towels, deodorant, hair supplies, and moisturizers.

I didn't know if it was hot all year round in Africa or not. So I didn't want to take any chances. I cleaned the kitchen real quick, swept and damped mopped the floors. The house hadn't been cleaned in months. I looked around for what seemed like the last time I would ever walk through those doors. I left and locked up behind me, and quickly ran down the steps and jumped into the car. Jackson was asleep.

"What's gonna' happen to my place?" I asked Jackson.

"Don't worry about a thing. I'll take care of it," he told me. "You up on the rent?" he asked.

"I don't pay rent. I own my house."

"Well, smart girl," Jackson responded. "That makes it that much easier then doesn't it." Maybe we can find someone to rent it out to just until you get back. That way you can generate some income while you're gone."

"Ok," I shook my head."

"Just leave me the keys and I'll come by in a few days and box everything up and put it in storage for you. Once you get to your destination you'll get a stipend that will come to you every month from the Missions Fund. You definitely won't need to spend it all. Nobody ever does. So I would suggest you save as much of it as you can for when you get back. Once you get back you'll have enough to hold you over until you find a job.

"Okay," I responded.

When I got back to The House of Job I went straight to the room where I would be staying for the next couple of nights. I opened

my duffle bag and got out my pajamas, a pair of panties, a pair of
flip flops, a bar of soap and a wash cloth and went down the hall to
where the bathroom was. I was very particular about my wash cloth
and soap.

I went inside the bathroom and looked around. I opened a
closet that was over by the window and found fresh linen for the
bed, towels, and bath cloths. I showered, dried off with one of
the towels in the closet, put on my pajamas, and went back to my
room. Before this night I hadn't showered in about a week or two.
I couldn't really remember. I moisturized, made the bed, kicked off
my flip flops, pulled back the sheets and blanket and crawled in. It
was only seven o'clock.

I lay there listening to absolutely nothing. I'd never heard a quiet
like that before. There was no television, no phones, no anything.
I held my arm out and began to study my hand. My hand was as
steady as a rock and I could hear my heart beat. I looked around the
room and watched the reflections of the car lights that shined on the
walls of my room like strobe lights and the mist that accumulated on
the window as the clouds began to cry. The stillness of the night, the
silence of headlights, moving cars upon the asphalt, and the sound of
the rain tapping on my window all seemed so relaxing as my eyelids
became very heavy and I drifted off into a sound sleep.

CHAPTER TWENTY-SIX

It was early the next morning when I awoke to a knock at my door. It was Jackson.

"Unique, are you awake?" he called to me through the door as he softly tapped against the wooden frame. "Unique," he called again, while opening the door slightly and peeking in.

"Unique," he said once again before I responded.

"Yeees," I replied groggily.

"Breakfast will be ready in ten minutes."

"Okay," I said as I rolled back over and placed the pillow over my head.

I couldn't believe it was already morning. I hadn't slept that good since Javier was alive. It was a peaceful non drug induced sleep that had me feeling absolutely rested. No ghost chased me or haunted me in my dreams and no sluggish mornings.

I got up, brushed my teeth, washed my face, and slipped on a pair of jeans and a top and went down the back steps that led to the kitchen. There stood Jackson, Miss Sheila, a round elderly man wearing a pair of school boy reading glasses whose muffin top draped over his belted pants. And right next to him was an equally rounded elderly woman with pinned up silver streaked hair and an apron on.

The table was set and decorated with french toast, pancakes, grits, sausage, bacon, buttermilk biscuits, steak, scrapple, ham, eggs, home fries, orange juice, milk, and maple syrup.

"Hi, I'm Gladys," the strange and bubbly woman with the pinned up silver streaked hair said as she introduced herself. "And this is my husband, Abraham," she said. "It's a pleasure to meet you young lady. We've heard so much about you. Why don't you have a seat?"

I sat down as I experienced a sense of bashfulness.

"Welcome," Gladys said.

"Do you eat like this everyday?" I had to asked.

"Oh no dear," Abraham answered with a short chuckle. "If we ate like this everyday we would be as wide as all out doors," he said as everyone broke out into a light laughter. "No ma'am. This is a special breakfast."

"What's the occasion?" I asked.

"You are," Gladys responded.

I was taken for a loop when she said that. These people didn't know me from a can of paint. Who were they and who was I to them and why were they all being so nice to me?

"What's the matter?" Gladys asked as she witnessed the look of confusion on my face.

"You do know that you're special, don't you?" Abraham jumped in.

I just couldn't bring myself to respond to that because I didn't know how to.

"Well let me answer that one for you. Yes you are," Abraham continued.

"But you don't even know me," I said.

"We don't have to know you to know that you're special. Every child of God is special. And this is our way of saying that it is our pleasure to meet you, that's all." Gladys replied.

"I don't know what to say," I responded.

"You don't have to say anything. Just believe it," Abraham said.

"Yes," Jackson co-signed.

I picked up my glass of orange juice and brought it up to my lips when Sheila reached over and lightly touched my arm signaling me not to drink just yet.

"There is always something to be thankful for," Gladys said as she began a prayer;

Thank you gracious Father for waking us up this morning and for the food that you have given to us this day to nourish our bodies...for life, love, and second chances. And thank you oh God... for Unique. Amen.

I swallowed the frog that was deep in my throat as everyone replied *Amen*. Immediately everyone picked up their forks and began to dig in. I looked around, held my head down, and softly mumbled, Amen, and began to eat. For the next fifteen minutes or so there was complete silence except for the clanging of the forks and knives against the stoneware plates. I couldn't remember ever having such a glorious breakfast. Every morsel that fell upon my anxious tongue melted like butter. My soul was truly satisfied.

"Can I ask a question?"

"Sure," Abraham and Gladys responded jointly.

"Why is your missions called The House of Job? Does your organization find people jobs."

"No," Abraham said as they all smiled. Job is pronounced with a long "O" sound. It is a person's name. Job was a faithful servant of God who had many trials in his life. Sorta like the trials we all have today. But despite all of his trials, he never gave up his faith in God. And so when Gladys and I brought this building there were so many people that flocked here; the homeless, the abandoned, the hungry, and the weary at heart – all seeking refuge from their trials. And so we thought it only befitting to name our missionary "The House Of Job".

"Oh, okay. I understand," I said.

Well, after we were all finished eating everyone got up from the table. Gladys went over to the sink and began to run the dish water. Jackson began to remove the trash bags from the cans. Sheila began to clear the table and put away the milk, juice, and leftovers into the refrigerator. Everyone was doing something.

As I witnessed this strange mutual collaboration of team work I was immediately compelled to join in. I went over to where Gladys had just finished washing up a number of plates. I looked around and saw that there was a drying cloth hanging near the sink. I picked it up and began to dry and put away the dishes that were in the drainer.

"We'll finish up here and then I'll walk you down to the auditorium. There is an orientation that you'll need to sit in on," Gladys stated.

"Afterwards, will I be considered a missionary?" I asked.

"You'll be considered whatever you want to be considered. We try not to get too caught up on labels. Most people categorize us as being missionaries. But we are just people who try and lend a helping hand to those in need the best way we can. It's simple and it's plain," she said.

"Oh," I responded.

There were about seven or eight of us in the orientation. It lasted about five hours give or take a half hour or so. It really didn't seem that long though I guess because I was interested in what was being said.

There were two people from the Global Volunteer Development Association (GVDA)who were there to speak to us about many things. They discussed the water shortage in Africa, the heat index, the dangers of dehydration, the different animals and insects, the infectious diseases that were associated with people and live stock living in such close proximity, and the culture of the people of Africa in general.

They spoke on Africa's economy and on their political powers and legislation. They spoke on the health and welfare of their residents and the national health care system that was in place and living conditions. They talked about their trading policies, exporting and importing. Then they began to speak specifically about the trip that we would be taking. They briefly touched down on departure times, the length of the flight which really had me concerned because I had never been on an airplane before and was a bit fearful but excited. And they basically discussed what we should expect once we got over there.

It was almost like being in a class room but better. I didn't know what to expect and I was initially apprehensive because I knew that something inside of me wanted to at least give the whole thing a try. It had been two days since I coped and I was looking forward to a

third day. The spokes persons for The Global Volunteer Development
Association ended the orientation at about a quarter to two.

"I'd like to see Unique Jefferson and Marcia Cabbott up front
please," one of the associates said at the end of orientation.

When the two of us got up front there was a folder for each of
us with paper work in it that we were expected to fill out and sign. I
was informed that they were expediting an application on my behalf
in two days that normally took two months. I was told that my visa
and passport would be ready in twenty-four hours.

"I want the two of you to step over here in front of the screen
while I take a photo," the receptionist instructed.

Marcia and I were also informed that it was mandatory that we
have certain inoculations for overseas travel. So Abraham had his
private doctor there ready to inoculate us. I was never good at taking
shots and so it took me a good minute to decide if I was gonna' let
them stick me with those three big needles. Oh my God!

We were given a travel bag complete with insect repellent,
tooth brushes, hand sanitizer, soap, thermometers, mint body wash,
sunglasses, head visors, first aid kits, sun screen, towels, bath cloths,
shampoo, peppermint lozenges, deodorant, and a bible. The girls
were also given a special packages containing supplies for females
only than contained sanitary napkins, tampons, and wipes.

There was so much stuff in the travel kit that it was unbelievable.
It was past lunch time. I wasn't that hungry because of the huge
breakfast that I had, but I could still eat a little something. There was
a sandwich tray sent over by Sheppard's Delicatessen and they were
outrageously delicious. Just as I finished up my corn beef special and
dill pickle, I looked up to see Sheila coming towards me.

"Excuse me ladies. The six o'clock service is about to begin," she informed us.

"I said to myself," service? "What do I need to go to service for?

We gathered up all of the copies of the paper work we had signed, our information packet and travel bag, stuffed it all into the back pack that we were given, and proceeded to the sanctuary. There, I saw the people who were in the orientation and what looked to be their family members and possible friends. At this time Jackson found his way to the aisle in which I occupied a seat and sat right next to me. I thought that it was nice of him.

We all stood and people began to pray for a safe departure, safe return, and the success of the mission that we were about to embark upon. There were a lot of "yes Lords" and "Amen's" filling the room as we held hands and sang songs. It was different than anything I was used to. But I think I liked it.

The night progressed quickly. I didn't get to sleep until about two o'clock in the morning. I was a bundle of nerves. I'd never been so nervous in all my life. The last time that nerves got the better of me was when I was waiting for the Judge to hand down the verdict at my brother's trial. But this was different. This wasn't a feeling of dread or fright. This was refreshing. I knew that this was a chance for a new beginning. I had a chance to turn everything that had worked against me into something that would work for me. And although I still had second thoughts about how fast everything was happening and I questioned whether I really had time to think all of this through. I didn't know if I would be able to pull this off or not, but I entertained myself with the notion that I would be.

It was the end of another day. The service was over and everyone had gone. Once again I found myself alone in my room thinking about tomorrow and what was about to take place. I knew that it wasn't too late to change my mind but I tried not to think about that. But before I fell off to sleep for a second night in a row without any stimulants I managed to write three letters; one to Ice, one to Uncle Blaze, and the other to Bailey.

By the time you receive this letter I will be long gone; on my way to a better me. There will be many, many miles between us but we will never, ever be apart from one another. I suspect this journey will be good for me and so ultimately it will be good for us all.

I miss you already and will think about you every day until I see you again. I would like to thank you for always being there for me. I know that without your love and support I would have never had the courage to take such a leap. I hope that when you receive this letter everything will be fine with you. I will carry you in my heart and in my thoughts... never forgetting ...always remembering our bond and just how much you truly mean to me. I love you and will write again soon.

Forever.........Uni

I put an identical letter in each envelope with their names on it because the letter described my feeling for each of them. They were the three most important people in my life. They were all I had. They had been there since the beginning. I put on my favorite lipstick and sealed each envelope with a kiss. I lay awake for hours just thinking about the transformation my life was about to undertake and I wondered how it came to be that I stumbled into this place while trying to run away.

The next morning I woke at about six o'clock with only three hours of sleep. I got dressed and started to gather and pack my things and was ready to go. I couldn't believe that I was about to do this. All of the volunteers met outside The House of Job waiting for the van that would arrive shortly to pick us all up and take us to the airport; Marcia, the other females, three guys, two coordinators, and myself.

I looked around wondering if my legs would actually move once the van arrived. I held on tight to the three letters that I was hoping to give to Jackson to deliver for me but he was nowhere to be found. Everyone had at least one person there with them to see them off; everyone accept me. About ten minutes later I felt a tap on my shoulder from behind; it was Jackson. I almost wanted to smile.

"How you doing Peaches? You ready to go?" he asked.

"I guess so," I responded.

"I want you to take this. This is my contact information and a few extra dollars for you just in case. If you ever need to talk to me about anything I want you to use this number. Don't hesitate day or night. I'm here for you. And don't worry," he said. "Everything is gonna' be just fine. You'll see."

I looked into the envelope before I responded and saw that there was a few hundred dollars in there at least. I was speechless. My emotions compelled me to hug him.

"Could you deliver these for me?" I asked as I handed him the envelopes.

He looked through the envelopes. "Bailey?" he questioned.

"Yes, she's my best friend," I replied.

"I see," he stated. "She any relation to Claudette and Junnie from over there on Rhawnhurst?" he asked.

"She's their niece," I responded.

"I know exactly who she is," he said with conviction. "I'll make sure she gets it. I'll make sure to deliver them all," he confirmed.

"Thank you Jackson," I said.

"Everybody have your papers out and your picture ID," one of the coordinators announced as the van pulled up curbside.

"You be good now," Jackson stated as he put his arm around me and kissed my hair; almost like a father would do.

I reluctantly shook my head as I turned to the coordinator and showed my papers. I had so many mixed feelings. I realized that this was all about to become a reality. I told myself that if I was gonna' change my mind I knew that I had better do it sooner rather than later.

I was pretty calm up until that moment. Then I realized that I was surrounded by complete strangers. I boarded the van as my stomach did cart wheels and summersaults. The door to the van closed slowly. Right before we pulled off one of the coordinators began to pray;

Father, in the name of Jesus; thank you for this wonderful opportunity. Bless us as we journey across the waters that divide us from our homeland, our family and our friends. Give us traveling mercies and protect us and shield us as we do the work that you have set before us. Amen.

And with that the driver began to pull off slowly. Everyone began waving good bye to their friends and loved ones. I saw that Jackson had started to walk along side the van waving at me with a smile on his face. I raised my hand and cautiously began to wave back. I wondered if he could detect the look of fear and uncertainty on my face.

The ride to the airport wasn't so bad. I was alone but so was the other six people I was traveling with. We arrived at the airport about forty five minutes later. It was my first time ever being in an airport. The last couple of days were full of first times.

The airport was huge. There were people everywhere. We approached the arrow that directed us to the check in line. We all had only one duffle bag that we could carry on with us free of charge. We were scheduled to be on the ten o'clock flight to Nairobi.

"Come this way guys. Our flight departs from gate seventeen 'B" and leaves in half an hour," the coordinator said.

Upon hearing the coordinator announce that we all began to move quicker. As I walked the corridor I saw signs and arrows leading to flights headed for Botswanna, Tanzania, South Africa, and Zanzibar. Those flights were headed to places that you would only dream and read about. And I stood there in awe while I read all the different destination names. "Oh wow! This is really about to go down," I thought to myself as my heart began to flutter and my hands began to tremble.

As I walked through the airport I looked into the faces of people from all over the world and wondered if they could tell just how terrified I was by looking at me. The group continued to walk until we saw Gulf Airlines, the number seventeen with the letter "B" and the word NAIROBI overhead.

It occurred to me that I'd never really thought about flying before. I had never even been outside of Detroit. I began to think about Ice, Javier, and Uncle Blaze, and how proud they would be if they could see me now. I thought about Bailey and how I wanted so much to be successful at this so that it would give me hope that some great force could actually cause her to change her life too.

As far as I was concerned, the bond that Bailey and I had went far beyond any drug I had ever let influence me. It went far beyond any John that I had ever let crawl up inside of me. Bailey is the only one who actually knew first hand how I felt about the short comings in my life since we both had the women from whose wombs we emerged, turn their backs on us as though we never mattered .

Bailey and I are comrades. We are allies. We are ride or die friends to the end. Nothing could come between us not even seven thousand, seven hundred, and fifty five miles.

CHAPTER TWENTY-SEVEN

The coordinator gave each one of us a ticket with which to board the plane. We got in the line, and one by one, we gave our tickets, showed our ID to the flight attendants, and walked through the portal to board the plane.

The plane was humongous. I noticed as I boarded that there were three aisles. My seat was to the far right side of the plane, the second seat from the window. Everyone in our row was either small or average in size and so we had enough leg and arm room between us.

To the left of me sat a guy who was in our group. He was the only one in my row that I recognized. The rest of the group was scattered about the plane. The Stewardess gave instructions and a quick demonstration of what to do in case of an emergency. The take off was smooth. You could hardly feel the plane leave the ground.

Once we were up in the air the stewardess offered us beverages and snacks; at a price of course. There was even a movie for us to watch. My mind really wasn't on the movie as I gazed out of the window, trying to see everything that I could see. I was amazed at the fact that something so big could rise to such height and float quietly above the clouds.

As we glided high into the atmosphere I looked onto the clouds and imagined that my Dad and Javier were up there with me. I was hoping against all odds that I would see them up there somewhere.

"This your first time?" I was asked by guy who sat next to me.

"My first time what?" I questioned

"Flying?" he asked.

"Does it show?" I asked.

"Uh,…maybe a little. Would you like to sit here near the window so that you can see better?" he generously offered.

"No, thank you," I responded.

"It won't be any trouble at all," he assured me.

"Well," I thought. "Okay thank you; if you're sure it won't be an inconvenience," I said as I took notice of my speech.

"Not at all," he promised.

And so we stood up slightly and criss crossed into each others seat.

"By the way, I'm Aaron," he introduced himself.

"I'm Unique."

"Okay, that's different," he said while I smiled and nodded my head in agreement.

The movie had played and went off but I couldn't quite remember what the movie was about because I was more focused on the window and the sky. We were about three hours into the flight when I began to doze off. It was three o'clock eastern time and we still had about twelve hours to go before arriving at our destination. Three hours and fifty minutes later I woke up just in time for the landing.

"Are we there already?" I asked Aaron..

"No, we had to stop for a while. This is what you call a layover," he said.

"A layover?" I questioned

"Yes, a layover," he said. We'll probably be here for a while and then most likely we will have to change planes because this one has gone as far as it can go. It works for me. We get a chance to get off, stretch our legs and maybe take in a few sites close by.

"Where is here?" I asked.

"Looks like we're in Amsterdam," he replied.

"Amsterdam?" I said in disbelief.

"Yes, Amsterdam," he answered. "You know where that is?

I almost caught an attitude with him for asking me such a question. But then I had to slow my role and consider the fact that maybe he didn't mean anything by it. Maybe he wasn't trying to be insulting. After all, there were a lot people where I came from who didn't care much about Geography and didn't know where other countries and continents were located.

As a matter of fact, most of the people that I grew up with weren't really concerned with anywhere outside of where they were. But I guess I get offended when people assume the same things about me. I mean just because I've never been on a plane before or even been outside of the Detroit area for that matter, doesn't mean that I haven't studied maps and read books about far away places. It doesn't mean that I haven't visited those places in my mind and in my dreams.

"Holland, right?" I took a stab at it.

"Right," he confirmed with a look of astonishment on his face. "You're familiar with the Netherlands are you?" he asked.

"History was one of my favorite subjects in school," I responded softly. "So we're in Europe?" I asked him, even when I already knew the answer to the question. I just wanted to let him know that I knew.

"Yes we are," he answered. "We're just North of Belgium."

"So Germany would be...I raised my hand to point my finger in the correct direction but was unsure. And so Aaron took my finger and pointed East.

"It would be East," he answered.

"Precisely," I said in amazement at the fact that I just used the word precisely as I tried to sound intelligent.

It was like I never had a reason to use the word before and now I did. I was grateful that I paid attention in class to all the different words and its usages when I was in school. Most of the kids that I went to school with never really appreciated word usage, grammar, or the need for an education. They felt that school taught them things that weren't related to their lives or their daily living and so aside from reading, writing, and arithmetic, why did they need to learn any of it? Most of them could never see beyond the streets of Detroit and never believed they would ever have the opportunity to. But look at me. You never know where life may take you.

Our coordinator, Max, came over to inform us that since we had a three hour layover, some of our crew would be heading over to the Anne Frank House that was nearby. He told us that we didn't have to go but that we could if we wanted.

I found me a seat in the airport and all I wanted to do was sit, rest, and watch the people and the hustle and bustle of the airport. Even though I had slept about three hours on the plane I was still pretty drowsy. It must have been the jet lag thing that I've heard people talk about.

"What are you doing? Come on let's go," Aaron demanded.

"Go where? No, you go head," I encouraged him. "I just wanna' sit that's all."

"We have over eight hours of flight left. You can rest after we resume flying," he pressed. "You don't come all this way and not take in a bit of history. I thought history was one of your favorites? he asked with sarcasm.

"That's not right," I said with a smile on my face.

"You coming or what? How many times have you been to Europe?" he asked.

"Okay," I said. "Okay. You have a point. Lead the way."

We walked for an unknown amount of kilometers when we arrived at the house where they say Anne Frank lived. It looked like a museum. There were pages of her diary shown on exhibit along with her biography and other known or unknown facts that I began to examine when Aaron came over and decided to enlighten me.

"What a story huh? It's unbelievable that Anne Frank was one of the one point five million Jewish children and five million adults who died of starvation, disease, or execution during the genocide attempt of the European Jews during the second World War," he said.

"Yes I know," I responded.

And Aaron went on about Anne Frank's parents, Otto Frank and Edith Hollander who were married and gave birth to Anne on December sixth, nineteen hundred and twenty nine. He began to recount history as though he himself actually lived through it all as he continued to relent.

"It was a critical time for all Jewish owned businesses because they were boycotted once Hitler took office as Chancellor of the German Government. The Germans destroyed all of the synagogues, shops, and homes, and banned all Jews from marrying," he continued.

"Why are you so quite?" Aaron asked because I was listening attentively without really responding.

"Well, I just think you covered it all. There's nothing left to say," I responded. "It was an absolute tragedy."

By the look on his face I could tell that he wanted me to be more engaged in the conversation.

"Am I boring you? I'm sure I'm not telling you anything that you don't know," he said.

I walked over to one of the displays and looked into the eyes of the girl in the picture; the girl they called Anne Franke. She looked so ordinary but it was clear that her circumstances were not. I didn't know Anne but I knew what it was like to be judged merely because you're thought of to be different.

Like Anne, I too came from a place where my ancestors had been persecuted because of how others perceived them. Many things hold true for both mine and Anne's ancestors. But one of the differences between the two struggles is that her persecution is over and mine is still a reality. It still exists.

What a sad world we live in when one group of people can look at another group of people and within their own consciousness define the other group based on their own ignorant preconceived notions. And the very notion that God himself has given anyone the authority to decide such things is simply tragic.

Well, I was taken back for a moment as I tapped into a reserve of feelings that this moment allowed to resurface. Everything that Ms. Malone had taught me was still within me. And for that, I was grateful.

"You okay?" Aaron asked as he saw me drift off to an unknown place.

"Yeah, I'm fine," I came back.

"Where did you go?" he asked.

"I don't know. I guess I went back home," I said as I was deep in thought."

Just then, we heard a voice come over the intercom. "All Peace Corps, Missionary Trainees, and Volunteers report back to the terminal. We have fifteen minutes till departure.

"That's us," Aaron said as he looked over at me.

"Yeah, guess we better go," I added.

I took one last look around at the pieces of Anne's life before we made our way back to the terminal.

"Hey we still have time. You wanna' get a bite to eat before we board,"Aaron suggested.

"Sure," I responded.

We found a restaurant on the upper level of departure two, where there was also a Burger King in the Amsterdam's Schiphal, which is Dutch for "Airport." The food was priced between eleven and twenty dollars.

Although it was four o'clock in the afternoon in the US, it was seven o'clock in the evening in Amsterdam. I looked over the menu about a half a dozen times and decided to order a Uitsmijter Spek En Kaas, or how we say it in America, bacon with fried eggs and cheese.

Aaron saw what I was getting' and decided to order the same. Nothin' else on the menu really looked appetizing. We took our twelve dollar and fifty cents bacon egg and cheese meal and found two available seats.

"I would like to just say that I'm very familiar with the history of your people," I began to speak candidly. But I want to ask you how familiar you are with mine?" I asked as I looked him in the eye.

Aaron looked at me with suspecting eyes, paused, and then he responded.

"Uh, I believe I am pretty familiar," he answered.

"Well, have you ever heard of a woman by the name of Mary Turner?" I asked.

"Uh, I can't, um, say that I have," he hesitantly replied."

"Well, she was a black woman," I went on to explain, "maybe about my complexion. She was born in the late eighteen hundreds, approximately eighteen ninety eight. In the year nineteen eighteen, when she about twenty years of age, she was eight months pregnant with her first child when her husband was lynched. It happened Sunday, May 19th in Brooks County Georgia. You can imagine how she felt knowing that her unborn child would be fatherless.

And so she was so devastated that she started to publicly object to the murder of the love of her life. She was so grief stricken that she had the audacity to swear out warrants for all those who were responsible, which was unheard of at that time.

The more she sought justice, the more threats were placed upon her life and the lives of her family members. The threats were so that she thought it best that she leave her family and her home and run for her life and the life of her unborn child.

But I guess she didn't run fast enough because they caught her. And then they took her to a place they named Folsoms Bridge. There was a mob of people waiting to witness the horrific agony that they were about to inflict upon her.

They tied her about the ankles, turned her upside down and hung her from a tree and then they proceeded to burn her alive. They cut her from her chest to her vagina. And her fully developed baby fell screaming from her body as it hit the ground and they proceeded to stomp it to death. And if that wasn't enough, some felt as though she wasn't quite dead enough and so they began to shoot her body full of holes. Mary Turner and her baby were buried that very night by family members just a few feet away from the very spot where they were murdered.

As Aaron held his sandwich in his hand he looked at me with bewilderment in his eyes as he visualized the graphic description that I had just painted for him. He placed his sandwich back onto his plate and threw his napkin down. Maybe I should have waited until we were finished eating. I guess that would have been the proper thing to do. But I felt it was as good as time as any.

"Why did you tell me that story?" he asked.

"If you don't mind me asking, what is your last name?"

"Excuse me?" he asked in surprise.

"Your last name, what is it? I asked.

He looked at me and paused.

"Diecther," he said.

"That's Jewish isn't it?" I asked.

"Yes. And where are you going with this?" he questioned.

"Oh! Nowhere that I haven't been before," I responded.

"And what does that mean?" he asked.

"It means that I find that Black History is defined in just a few lines written in America's history books and that the Black experience defined in America always seems to be down played as a shared concept amongst many of the other cultures in the United States and around the world.

"Okay, I get that," Aaron responded when he saw my anguish.

"It's just that it's important that people be reminded that many injustices are still being played out right now in today's society," I said. "While I can hardly dismiss the travesties against your people; we are still living ours.

Some of you were able to escape who you were by relocating and changing your names or even your nationalities because the color of your skin allowed you to be able to blend in wherever you could get in without being detected. But there was no escape for us. We never had that option."

It was obvious that Aaron didn't know how to respond to what I was saying. The truth is that I didn't want him to respond. I just wanted him to listen and understand that whenever any group of people suffers by the hands or laws of another group; that we all suffer. But I wondered if he really got that or did he just think I was just another angry black person trying to blame her problems on her oppressor. Sure, it might have been better if I hadn't said anything at all. But then that wouldn't have been as interesting.

I got up and was on my way back to the airplane and Aaron got up and followed me. We boarded the plane and I sat in my seat near the window. Once the plane took off and we were in the air flying high above the white cottony billows I gazed out my window at the surreal view. We were settled in for about an hour when the stewardess came by.

"Would you like anything?" Aaron asked me.
"No thank you," I responded. And so the stewardess left.

Aaron leaned over close to me while my head was turned towards the window and spoke softly;

"I'm sorry about what has happened and what is still happing to your people. I can't pretend to know how that feels, but I can imagine. And you're right, nobody should have to endure such atrocities. I only want to help. That's why I'm here. That's what this trip means to me.

I turned slowly towards him and looked into the eyes behind the square framed glasses.

"Thank you. And I'm sorry for what happened to yours," I stated. "If I came off bitter or angry, I'm sorry. I really didn't intend to come off like that.

"And forgive me if I was at all insensitive. I'd really like for us to be friends," he said.

"So would I," I responded.

"You know what? I'm starving," he said.

"Me too," I laughed. And so we called the stewardess back over and ordered a couple of million dollar sandwiches.

"I bet you were the smartest person in your class," he said.

"I could've done a lot better," I replied.

Aaron smiled without saying a word. The rest of the flight went pretty smooth. After we ate we passed the time away playing trivia word games. It was a good time.

CHAPTER TWENTY-EIGHT

Nearing the Eighteenth hour of the flight I heard a voice come over the intercom an make an announcement.

"Ladies and gentlemen we have been cleared for landing at this time. In approximately thirteen minutes we will arrive at the terminal gate. We'd like for everyone to remain seated for the duration of this flight. Please make one last attempt to check and secure your seat belts. If you are seated next to an emergency exit, please read carefully the instructions located by your seat.

At this time we request all cell phones and radios be turned off as these items may cause interference with our navigational equipment on this aircraft. We remind you that all flights are non smoking. Tampering with, disabling, or destroying the lavatory smoke detectors are prohibited by law. We thank you again for flying Gulf Airways."

"We are finally there. We were actually in Nairobi, Kenya," I had to keep saying to myself as the plane began to descend.

I became very anxious. My stomach felt like there was a colony of frogs living inside it. My neck began to stiffen and my arm pits became moist. I could barely feel the plane touching down at the Jomo Kenyatta International Airport, named after Kenya's first president. As the plane began to descend we were in awe of the splendid view that was in front of us.

Yes, I did say splendid didn't I? And Ms. Malone would be tickled to know that I did. But it was truly the only way to describe what I was seeing. The runway's surface wasn't as smooth as the flight but it was alright. The Congo River was a sight to behold as the moisture and heat gave off a misty steam that rose from its jungle. The river was massive in all of its two thousand seven hundred and twenty miles. I remember reading that it was the second longest river in Africa, second to the Nile River. It is seen as the biggest source of transportation in Central Africa. The endless African Amazons were breath taking.

After exiting the plane the coordinators gathered us all and briefed us on a few things having to do with the flight. The airport JKIA was in definite need of a face lift as it was quite different from the airport in Detroit. It was in the worst condition; quite dirty, very hot, and smelly. There was only one working sink in the bathroom and most all the toilets were soiled. The staff was not very helpful at all. I was very cautious as I approached them.

There was no decent food or beverage available. We were there for about an hour when night fall began to approach. And just as our passports were being inspected, we were overcome by complete darkness when all the lights went out and a feeling of terror came upon me. The first thing that I had a mind to do was grab hold of my bags and pull them close to my body with my arms wrapped tightly around them. The money that Jackson had given me was secured in my bra and so I had everything under control.

We were assured by the attendants that everything would be okay and that there was nothing to worry about. Apparently, that sort of thing happened all the time. Shortly thereafter, a van showed up and we were on our way to our next destination.

We went from the airport directly to the training site in Nairobi. There were two groups of volunteers that arrived in Nairobi yearly. One group came in November and the other came in June and you stayed between six and eighteen months. My group was in the second part of the year and was joined with the Community Health and Development Volunteers.

Nairobi bordered on the North by Ethiopia and Somalia and on the South by Tanzania. Shockingly and unfortunately, twenty four percent of all Nairobi people live with the HIV virus, tuberculosis, and numerous parasites.

Chapter Twenty-Nine

The next day there was a pre-service training that was mandatory for all new recruits to take. We were told that it would be an extensive and rigorous eight week course. We would have to train for five days a week eight hours a day with our coordinators, the six people that accompanied me from The House Of Job, and another group of people who came from London. I felt like the orientation that we received before we arrived here was sufficient enough but I guess the training would make it all a reality.

Once the training started I embraced everything that I was being taught. But I wasn't really sure if I would be able to apply what I was being taught to a natural setting. I was assigned to a small, orange bricked, oval shaped, one room living establishment. It had a blue door, a straw sap roof and was furnished with a bed, a small sized two burner gas stove, a table, a dresser, and two chairs.

I had to walk a pretty good distance to get water from a community tap. There was a latrine facility separate from our living quarters; I was surprised that there was electricity in our lodging. I refused to use that bathroom. It would be two days before I was actually forced by nature to go.

My first week there, I had an overwhelming urge to get high

because I was beginning to feel very anxious. I had been clean for nine days at this point but now the urges were strong and coming for me. I looked around at my surrounding and what was expected of me and I began to panic. How could I help others in their struggles when I was in a struggle all of my own? Who would help me?

I began to wish that I was home. I now thought of my house as a mansion compared to the housing that I was assigned. How would I be able to manage? I never knew I could miss Detroit so bad. How would I survive this jungle? I don't know what happened to me between the time I got off that plane and now? But I began to freak out.

I wished I could wrap my arms around my brother and tell him how very proud I was of him and how much I loved him with everything in me. I wondered what Bailey was doing. By this time the both of them would have received the letters I left for them. I wondered what they were thinking. Were they missing me as much as I was missing them or did they hate me for leaving? All of a sudden I began to think about having just one bite of KFC, a biscuit or two with some butter and jam, some Welch's Grape Soda, and some fries. But there was no KFC to be found. I hadn't been there a week and already I was craving American food.

Chase was my immediate supervisor and guidance counselor. I guess he suspected that I was having a problem because he kept a close eye on me. When we first arrived we were told that out of every group of volunteers there was always at least one person who would have a hard time adjusting. And so I guess I was that one person out of our group. Chase did speak to me briefly before I made the decision to take this trip and asked about the circumstances that brought me to that decision. I did discuss some things with him but not everything. I told him that I had a lot of personal problems and that my little brother was incarcerated and I missed him. I told him that I was scheduled to go into rehab a week ago but hadn't had the urge to use any type of drug the entire week - not until now.

By this time I think he realized that my state of mind was a bit fragile. And he knew that it was important for me to adjust quickly because if not, there would be a good chance that he would have to make arrangements for me to go back to the states.

We were in the second week of training and I had already managed to miss the first few days because I just couldn't focus on anything. I couldn't even remember what I was being taught from one day to the next and so I decided not to attend any more classes at that time.

Chase met with me daily in hopes that he could help me through that transition successfully. He would give me one more week to adjust before deciding whether to send me back. I refined myself to my quarters for a few days; isolating myself from everyone, wanting only to be alone with my thoughts. But at the end of the second week I heard a knock on my door. It was Aaron and the girl named Marcia from our group. I went to the door and opened it.

"Hey Aaron."

"Hi,"Aaron started. "Um you know Marcia"

"Hey," I said.

"Hey," she responded back,

"Uh, we were just on our way over to the bank to exchange some money. We didn't know if you needed to go over or not. So you wanna' come along?" he asked.

"No," I shook my head, "I'm cool. You go ahead," I said as I proceeded to close the door.

"Um, are you sure? Because we really think you should come out with us, you know, just to get some air. Um, I insist," he said hesitantly as he placed his foot in the door as I tried to close it.

"Yes, I am sure Aaron. Is there anything else?" I asked, trying to be polite. "I'm kinda busy right now.

"I see…uh…wow! What's that you're listening to?" he continued, referring to the music that I was playing on my battery operated radio.

"It's R & B. You wouldn't know anything about that," I responded.

"Why, because I'm Jewish? It's Mary J right?" he shot back. "It sounds good. What's the name of it?" he asked.

"Look, I don't mean to be rude but I gotta' go," I responded.

"See that's your problem right there. You need to listen to something a little more up beat," he said.

"Aaron, I'm really not in the mood," I said after I figured he was just trynna' make small talk.

"What are you doing, huh?" he asked.

"I don't know what you mean."

"You do know what I mean. You're trying to ruin this whole thing aren't you?"

"What did you say?"

"You heard me. You haven't even given yourself a chance and already you're trying to find a way to get out of it," he said.

"You don't know what you're talking about. Listen, just because we spent a couple of hours together on a plane ride doesn't give you the right, ok. You don't know shit about me. You don't know what I'm up against.

"And I don't doubt for one minute that you aren't up against a lot." Aaron jumped in. "But what are you gonna' do about it, you wanna' go back and do what? You came here for a purpose I thought. We all did. Although, all of our circumstances are different. We're all here because of something bigger than us. You think you have it bad? You probably do. But look around you. What do you see? Look, I'm here for you. Whatever you need, I'm here for you," he said.

"Right now what I need is for you to remove your foot from my door," I said adamantly.

Aaron looked me in disbelief and then slowly removed his foot. I slammed the door as hard as I could. My mind was racing and I began to explode.

"Who in the hell do you think you are? You don't know me," I cried out at the door. You don't know anything about my life, Ok. Why can't you mind your own damn business and leave...me...the hell....alone," I screamed as I began to pick up things and throw it at the door and about the room.

Meantime, Aaron and Marcia remained outside listening and knocking at the door.

"Oh God, you should have not said those things," Marcia said to Aaron.

"She'll be fine," he said. "She needed for somebody to tell her. It's Ok. We'll wait here until she calms down.

"I hate it here," I screamed. "Do you hear me? I hate it here and I want to go home," I wanna' go home, I began to cry.

I didn't understand why I was so angry at Aaron. All I wanted to be left alone. I was just beside myself. I mean, I guess I was mad at him because I thought that it was very inappropriate for him to say those things to me when he just met me. You can't just judge people like that. It's not right. Yeah, I was mad at Aaron. But I guess the real reason I was mad at him was because I knew deep down inside that he was right. "Damn him." I thought out loud. He was right.

I collapsed onto the bed. I reached over to grab hold of my teddy bear and the picture of Javier, Ice, and me. I held the picture tightly near my heart while I cried inconsolably into my teddy bear until I drifted off to sleep. A couple of hours had gone by and I was awakened by yet another knock at the door.

"Unique, Open the door Unique," Aaron called out. "Unique."

I dragged myself off the bed and walked over to the door and opened it.

"Are you still here?" "What do you want?" I asked.

"Are you Ok?" he asked.

"Yes, I'm alright," I said in a much calmer tone. "I'm sorry Aaron," I'm just….

"Don't give it another thought," he cut me off. "All that matters is that you're Ok."

"Well I guess it's too late for us to go over to the bank now huh?" I asked.

"Yeah, you think?" he said, as we both snickered.

"Well some of the guys are getting together right now to go over to Casablanca" said Marcia.

"Do you feel up to it?' Aaron asked me. "If not, we can just hang around here.

"No. It sounds like fun. Why not?" I surrendered. "Why not?"

We met up with one of Marcia's friends, Ethan, and we all chipped in to take a cab over to Club Casablanca, which was about an hour away. The club was a lot different than I pictured it in my head. First of all, I had never been to a real club before anyway, so I really didn't have anything to compare it to. But I just didn't think it would be so modern.

It was really nice. The building was round with a glass front and trimmed with the color raspberry. It was two stories high with swing panel doors and a balcony on each floor. Each floor also had its own bar, bathrooms, and sitting areas. There was Moroccan style furnishings and a casual style dress code. The lights were dim as they played music by African singers such as; Lucky Dube who was famous for his mature reggae sounds and other artist like the renowned Youssou N'Dour, a singer and composer from Senegal who was highly respected in this country for shaping the mbalax music style.

We came in and found a table on the upstairs balcony. The atmosphere was mellow. There was a pretty good crowd and everyone seemed to be having a good time. I sat and watched the different colored outfits and shoes that all the women had on. Shoes were one of my favorite things to buy and look at.

"Anybody want anything to drink?" Ethan asked. "I'm goin' up to the bar to order a couple of beers.

"I guess I'll go with you. I could use a cold one," said Aaron.

"Just get me anything fruity," Marcia said.

"Unique, you want anything?" Aaron asked.

"No, nothing for me, thanks," I responded. "I need to find a bathroom though," I said as I got up from the table to take a look around. "But I'll take something to eat," I said.

"Something like what?" Aaron asked.

"I don't know. Something good," I responded.

"Alright," Aaron said.

So, Aaron and Ethan worked their way through the crowd and up to the bar. I went looking for a bathroom and Marcia stayed at the table. I looked around and finally saw a bathroom sign posted and I followed the arrow. I went in to the bathroom which I found to be fairly clean. I did what I had to do and was on my way back to our table when I notice a strange looking man lurking in the hall outside of the ladies bathroom.

"Good evening," he said with some sort of an accent while staring at me as I passed him in the hall."

I studied him out of the corner of my eye and quickly moved on without saying a word. As I passed him I looked back one time before I sat down and sure 'nough, he was still looking.

"What's the matter with you?" Marcia asked.

"Some strange freaky guy was waiting outside the ladies bathroom when I came out staring at me like he was a crazed pervert.

"Which guy?" Marcia asked.

I sat down and turned around to point him out to Marcia, but when I turned around to look, the stranger was gone.

"Good, he's gone," I said.

And just then, Ethan and Aaron came back to our table with the drinks and some golden fried "Prawns." I was in heaven. The meat was sweet and flavorful and practically melted in my mouth. I had never had Prawns before but they were more than tasty. We ate and laughed and laughed and ate and it was one of the best times that I'd had in a good while. It was almost as if the incident that had taken place just an hour or so ago had never even happened. I was calm, reassured, and very happy that I decided to come.

CHAPTER THIRTY

Later that night when I went back to my little one room house that somehow looked different to me then it had before I left— warmer even. I had time to rethink all of my reasons for wanting to leave this place and go home and decided to let the very same reasons that I wanted to leave count for why I needed to stay.

I would be back home before I knew it anyway; back to a place where things didn't always make sense but it was what I was used to. There was a vague difference between this world and the world that I left. Children didn't have to go hungry in America and they rarely did.

I recalled the metal clothe bins back home on various sidewalks and parking lots filled with clothes and shoes that people gave away simply because they no longer wanted them anymore; or maybe they had so much in their closets that they needed to make room for new things. There are shelters that provide housing for those who were not fortunate enough to have a home.

I found it extraordinary that the Nairobian people had very little but still had a spirit and belief in hope. The volunteers and I lived in the Kibera slums in Nairobi – Africa's largest slum. Most of its people live in extreme poverty making less than one dollar per day. There were few schools and most of the locals couldn't afford an education for their children. But ironically, about 95% of all Kenyans were owners of a cell phone.

There were very few households that could afford such luxuries as a television or even a daily newspaper. But most times you could find a newspaper or two in the workplace. In thinking about the people of Nairobi and the conditions in which they lived I made a conscious decision to stop crying over spilled milk and to stop feeling sorry for myself and put my game face on.

I decided that I wanted to try and stay on, not so much for the people of Nairobi, but for me. I needed to stay to find out what my purpose for being here was. I believed in my heart that I could learn from the locals more than I could teach them.

Here was a people that was in a serious struggle; a struggle of survival. And here I was whining about what? I didn't have a clue. I just knew that I needed to be there in hopes that some of their survival techniques would wear off on me. I needed to learn how to become stronger and this was without a doubt a strong people. I knew that my life's misfortunes were more than some would ever see or ever know. But I had a feeling that this was a people who knew all that. And it was for the sake of my brother that I needed to learn how to go on.

I looked around my small temporary home and I began to allow myself to gracefully embrace it. The weekend had come and gone and Monday was already here again. But this time I was prepared for a day of intense training and my expectations did not let me down. And for the next seven weeks I was consumed with learning everything I could about the history of Nairobi and its wonderful culture.

My group spent most of our days in the field. We participated in group lectures, field trips, and hands on practical tasks. We would spend one to two days out of each week at the training center or in one of the schools engaging in deep discussions that prepared us for the next assignment. We attended essential cross-cultural, health, safety, and integration sessions that were amazing.

During the integration sessions we spent time with some of the other volunteers from different groups. One particular group was from England and that's where I came into contact with the strange guy from the club. At first I wasn't really sure if that was him or not because it was pretty dark that night in the club. But the way that he kept looking at me convinced me that it was him. And just like the first time; I saw him and then he was gone.

My group was trained by Kenyan Nationals. They provided a bi-national perspective to bridge the transition from life in America to a life in Nairobi, Kenya. The Kenyan Nationals gave us a crash course on the general environment of Kenya and their political and economic situations within certain frame works.

Kenyan language classes were four days a week and were necessary if we wanted to successfully be incorporated into our host families. We learned only basic words like; yes, no, hello, thank you, and good-bye. The temperature in Nairobi was a lot like that of California, at least that's what I've been told, since I had never been to California.

In the days to follow, I received a letter from Jackson and was very anxious to see what he had to say. We had mail call once a day and it was a very exciting time for everyone. When I opened the envelope I saw that there was not only one, but two letters inside. One letter was from Jackson and the other was from Ice. I took my letters back to my humble abode and sat on my bed and began to read:

"Dear Unique. It's been a little over a month since you left; one month down and seventeen to go. I hope and I pray that all is well with you and that when this letter finds you everything will be in

order. I know how difficult it must be for you to be so far from home; away from everything that you know. So I hope that you are adjusting well.

I went pass your Uncle's house to take him the letter that you wrote to him. I took it to him two days after you left. We sat and talked for a good minute, reminiscing about the old days. He spoke on the subject of how he couldn't really believe in his mind that you were actually in Africa. I must admit, it would be difficult for anyone to believe.

He told me that before you left he was completely consumed with worry about you and how relieved he is now. He asked me three times to explain to him how it happened that you were over there. And each time I explained it to him he had a smile on his face that went from ear to ear. I gave him the P.O. Box number to where he could write to you because he indicated that he wanted to send you a care package. The meeting with him went well. The news really made him happy.

I also went over to Bailey's house to deliver the letter for her but her mother said that she hadn't seen her in some time. I heard it through the grapevine that she was hanging out at the Cave and so I tried my luck there and was successful. She didn't look quite like how I last remembered her from a couple of years ago. It seemed that life was takin' a tremendous toll on her.

Anyway, she took the letter and said thank you. And then I put your brother's letter in the mail along with a letter that I wrote to him explaining how I knew you because I knew that as your brother, he would have some questions about that. And a couple of weeks later he wrote me back and thanked me. I recently sent him another letter asking him if it would be alright for me to visit him from time to time.

I went over to your house and pack everything up just like I said I would. I stored all of your belongings in the basement of the House Of Job. It will be safe there until your return. Oh! By the way, I think I found someone who is interested in renting your place out for the months that you will be away. I'll let you know how that works out.

Be mindful that if things ever get a lil' tough over there for you, I want you to remember just how far you have come. And be reminded of the many blessings that are ahead of you. You have to believe. Take care of yourself. You know how to reach me if you need me.

"Jackson"

With a smile on my face I carefully folded Jackson's letter and placed it back into the envelope. Then I took out the letter that was written by Ice, opened it and began to read:

"Hey big sista. I can't believe that this letter is gonna' have to travel thousands of miles before it reaches you. I've been trying everyday to write you since I got your letter but I just couldn't get my words and my thoughts together. You know that expressing myself has never really been my strong point, but here goes.

When I received the letter that you wrote me I didn't know what to think. I didn't wanna' believe that you would just up and leave the country like that. I mean, I just didn't believe it in a million years, given your demons and everything that had taken place in our lives. What would be the possibility of that?

But Jackson broke it down for me real simple like when he wrote me. I don't know him but he seems like a good dude. I can't judge him. He even took the time to come up and visit me the one time and I respected him for that. When I saw him he explained to me how it all went down. And I was really able to see it clear for myself that this was your destiny.

You've always been real. You've always been the truth and I'm happy for you. And I want you to be happy for you 'cause I know how your mind works. You've always had a hard time excepting good things when they happen to you. But except this because nobody coulda' pulled dis' off but you.

I know how hurt you were when I got sent up. And I'm sorry that it went down like dat'. I know that you know that, that's not what I intended to happen. But if I had to do it all over again, I know without a shadow of a doubt, the result would be the same. Because I'm convinced that it all had to be played out just like it did because of fate. Dis' had to happen and I hope you can see dat'. Look, you're off the streets now. You're clean and you're in Africa doing great things. You can't tell me that this isn't what was supposed to happen.

The first night that I was able to really sleep comfortably was the night after Jackson visited me. The same way you feel about me being in here was the same way I felt about you being out there without me to look after you; like you looked after for me all these years. And I love you for dat'. But I can chill now 'cause I know you're alright and I don't have to worry.

And on my end – I got dis'. This ain't nothin'. I'm not goin' let this time do me. I'm goin' do this time and I'm goin' do it on my own terms. I'm goin' make this time count for somethin' good. It already has. So don't worry about me. I've got a lot a time on my hands and I plan to make the best of it. Who knows - I might even write a book or somethin' huh?

Your Brother "Ice"

The tears flowed as I finished reading. I blew my nose and wiped my face. I fell back on the bed, kissed the letter and placed it directly on my heart as I closed my eyes and let myself go and envision another time. It was a time when my brother and I would be together again and everything......everything would alright.

CHAPTER THIRTY-ONE

The next day I walked over to Benevolence Orphanage where I was assigned to work. I can't say that I was particularly fond of the assignment that I was given because I knew nothing about kids and I really didn't care to know. I was taken to an area on the orphanage grounds where they were beginning to lay the foundation for a small library. As I got closer to the project site I saw a couple of familiar faces. One of those faces was Aarons.

"Hey you. What are you doing here?" he called out to me.

"Yeah, I'm askin' myself the same question." I responded. I've been assigned here."

"Well it looks like we're gonna' be working together. I've been assigned here as well," said Aaron.

"I just can't get rid of you, huh?" I said with a smile.

"Stuck to you like glue," he said.

"So this is going to be the new library huh? Cool," I said.

"Yeah, it is pretty cool, isn't it?" he commented.

"I see everyone here has a partner. So who's your partner?" I asked.

"You are," he answered.

"Why am I not surprised? How many people did they assign to this project?" I questioned.

"I believe it's about eight people," Aaron replied. You wanna' hand me a couple of those two by fours?" he smirked.

For about three hours we were sweating, hammering, and measuring when a little girl about the age of seven came over to where we were working and just stood there and watched us. After about an hour or so the little girl spoke out in an unknown language. I had no idea what she said and so I proceeded to continue working. And then she said it again, and again. I became frustrated at the fact that I couldn't understand a thing she was saying. Then she began pointing to her hair saying the word "hair".

"Hair?" I questioned while the little girl stood there expressionless. And then she repeated the word hair again.

"I think she wants you to do her hair," Aaron said.

"I think so too," I agreed. "Hair?" I asked. "You want me to do your hair?"

The little girl gave a nod like she understood me. I didn't know what to say at first. I did see that the little girl's hair was a bit matted and needed something done to it. But I didn't want to be the one to do it. Besides, I knew very little about doing anybody's hair. I could barely keep up with my own hair.

The little girl stared at me with huge, brown eyes, with beautiful lashes that must have been at least two or three inches long. They were so long that they almost didn't look real. Once she got my attention with those eyes I found it difficult to say no to her.

"Tomorrow," I said. "Come back tomorrow and I will do your hair – tomorrow," I said.

The little girl with the big brown eyes stood there for a few seconds until a voice rang out.

"Fathiya – come," one of the food preparers called out. And in a flash she was gone.

When the next day came I was prepared for the little girl. I had my hair bag that held everything I needed to make the little girl's hair special. I had my shampoo and conditioner, my hair butter, coconut oil, and hair accessories.

After about an hour or two had passed the little girl they called "Fathiya" showed up again. I wasn't really sure if she understood me yesterday or not when I told her to come back, but obviously she did. It was clear that she understood English and could even pronounce some words. I put down my hammer and nails and began to walk towards the outside showers. I looked back at the little girl and signaled her with my hand to come with me.

"Come," I said. And she began to follow me.

I took her into the shower, removed her cotton, shirt like dress so that it wouldn't get wet. She immediately knew to bend over and place her head under the water. I pulled out my shampoo, poured it onto her hair and began to massage her scalp. I was happy to know that she wasn't afraid of the water getting into her eyes.

After I finished shampooing her hair I gave her a deep conditioning which she seemed to enjoy a lot. We found a quiet place to sit outside and I began to gently comb the kinks out of her naturally curly locks. It took me all of an hour just to comb and oil her scalp; and then another hour to braid her hair. And when I was finished I pulled out a small mirror from my hair bag and held it up in front of her. She gazed at herself, looking at her head from different angles, touching and feeling her braids in amazement.

"You like?" I asked.

And without any notice, she smiled and took off running. About an hour later she came back.

"Eat," she said to me.
"It's lunch time, she wants you to eat with her," Aaron stated.
"Okay, okay, let's eat," I said.

We went into the central area of the orphanage that housed thirty or so abused, abandoned, underprivileged, needy, orphaned children. There were two long wooden tables that were in the dining hall. There were sick children stricken with various diseases, some of the same diseases that claimed the lives of many of their parents, grandparents, and siblings, who were quarantined in a separate area of the orphanage so as not to contaminate others or because of their need of medical attention. And so they had their meals brought to them. The orphanage was surprisingly maintained despite the lack of funding.

I entered into the dining area and laid eyes on some of the most beautiful children I had ever seen and in all their innocence. I sat at the table barley eating as I studied their curious faces, their movements, and how they interacted with one another. They looked at Aaron and me with curiosity and we were equally curious with the mere site of them.

I experienced a feeling of pride as I sat next to Fathiya, observing her as she played with the locket that was around my neck. In looking at her I realized that I saw some things in myself that made me rather ashamed. I saw that all of those mother and fatherless children were smiling and they seemed to be happy even though they had to be unsure about what their futures would hold for them. I ate small bites of the beans and bread as I tried to imagine all of what those children must have suffered in their short lived lives.

The last two weeks had slowly defused my anger and made me sensitive to the people and things around me; at times almost bringing me to tears. When I got home that night I went to bed early. I was anxious to awaken to a new day and a new chance to help make the lives of the orphans just a little bit easier than the day before.

One day I took a break from work and introduced some of the children to a couple of games that I used to play when I was a very young child. Red light green light and dodge ball were two favorites and mine. It warmed my heart to see them chuckle and laugh in their amusement of the newly introduced games.

It was the end of the day when everyone was saying their goodbye's and see you tomorrow's, when I heard the voice of the English speaking stranger echoing from behind me.

"You're great with them you know."

I turned around and there he was again. "Are you a teacher?" he asked. I was non- responsive.

"Excuse me. How rude of me. Allow me to introduce myself. My name is Dylan."

I remained non responsive.

"I see you're not much of a talker," he concluded. "Well neither am I," he said.

"Really?" I mumbled beneath my breath. "I didn't get that," I said sarcastically.

"Ahhh. So you can talk. And I see that you have a bit of a sense of humor. Tell me, do you also have a name?" he asked.

"Unique," Aaron called out to me right at the moment when he saw the strange man trying to hold a conversation with me.

The stranger and I looked awkwardly at one another and then without a word I turned and walked away.

"Is everything alright? Was he bothering you?" Aaron asked.

"No, everything is fine," I said. And then I began to help Aaron finish clean and tidy up the area.

Aaron looked over and saw Dylan standing in the doorway of the orphanage.

"Did he say who he was?" he asked me.

"No," I said.

"Did he tell you what he wanted?" Aaron grilled me.

"No," I answered.

"Well what was saying to you over there?" he asked with curiosity.

"Nothing really," I replied.

"Oh Okay," Aaron said unconvinced. "It sure looked as if he was saying something.

Maybe I was just imagining things," he said sarcastically.

CHAPTER THIRTY-TWO

When I got home I showered, got cleaned up, and then I settled in for the night. I lay there taking in the events of the day. It wasn't at all how I initially anticipated it to be. I looked over at the picture of my family like I did every night. I missed them so much. I wondered how Bailey was makin' it and what was the deal with her mother and her rapist boyfriend?

Every night my last thoughts before I went to sleep would be of my brother. I still couldn't believe that I was in Africa and that Ice was thousands of miles away in a Detroit prison for murder. Up until now I had not been able to bring myself to think or say the words Ice and murder in the same sentence because it was just too painful.

Today was the first time in a very long time that I felt like I had done something that was really worthwhile. Even though I did what I had to do to make sure that my brother and I stayed out of foster care and that Ice grew up having his needs met, I knew that there were a lot of things that he needed that he didn't have or couldn't give him; things that money couldn't buy. So I began to wonder what was it all for? Everything that I was afraid would happen, has happened. My brother and I were separated and I was the cause of him being placed in the very jail that I fought so hard to keep him out of. I didn't understand how we got to this place and I didn't know how to make it right. But as dark as it all seemed, something inside of me was allowing me to press on. So I began to write a letter. I addressed the first letter to Bailey.

Dear Bailey,

It's been close to two months since I've seen you. Life here is so different than the one back home. It's hard to believe that I'm away from you all. And it's even harder to believe that I've been clean and sober this whole time. I haven't coped in two months and it feels pretty good. I find that I'm able to think clearer now and see things differently.

I keep waiting for you to burst through that door at any moment now and tell me to get up and get myself together. I wake everyday in disbelief that it's really going down like this, but guess it is. I only wish that you and Ice were here with me. But I know that we will all be together again real soon.

When I first got here all I wanted to do was to come home. I missed everyone so terribly. But I'll be home before you know it and we will catch up on everything and it will be like old times, but better.

I want to ask if you could do me a favor. I want you to think about getting clean. Not because I did it, but because it is time to. I had a lot of time to think about how we've been living our lives and I know now that there's a better way.

I want you to know that I was never a slave to the drugs or that life style although it may have seemed that way. And neither are you. I know now that it was never about that. But it was always about the pain; yours and mine. I see that now. I know that there were a lot of things that I did because I felt like I had no other options. And that may have been true at that time. But it doesn't hold true for me now and it doesn't have to hold true for you either. We have to learn how to manage our lives without masking it. I owe this second chance that I've been given to everybody in my life who believed in me. I owe it to Ice and Uncle Blaze, I owe it to Jackson and I owe it to you because you looked after me. You always made sure that I was okay. And I will never forget that. Now it's time for me to give back to you what you gave to me. I know it won't be easy, but I want you to think about it. I love you and I'll see you soon.

Love Unique.

I placed the letter into an envelope and sealed it, and then I gathered my thoughts once again before I started the next letter.

Dear Brother,

I have so much to say to you, but there's just not enough time in a day and where do I begin. The last image that I had of you being handcuffed and taken away from me was an image that burned clear through to my soul. It's been very hard to say the least, being away from you. And I'm not going to say that I have come to terms with any of this because I haven't and I never will.

The adjustment has been vicious, almost cruel even. I did get your letter a couple of weeks ago and I'm just now feeling strong enough to write you back. I have so much inside of me that I can't even explain the pressure that builds in my heart sometimes just thinking about you, where you are, and how you got there. I can almost explode.

I've been so use to taking care of you and making sure that you were straight even if I wasn't. But somewhere along the way you grew up and you started taking care of me. I can't seem to figure out when all of that happened. But all I know is that I'm proud of you. I've always been proud of you. You're the reason that I'm alive today and you are the only reason that I even want to live. And I want you to know that you are not alone in there because I am right there with you. Your pain is my pain and your struggle is my struggle and it will always and forever be that way.

I promise that I'm going to make sure that none of what happened, happened in vain. And I'm going to count the days until we're together as a family again. My spirit won't rest until that day comes. And I'm going to make sure that every move that I make while we're apart counts for something worthy. And my word is my bond. I love you brother and I will see you soon.

Your Sista Forever,

Unique

After I sealed the envelope I laid there and I kissed the envelope and caressed the locket that was around my neck. I thought about Javier and I knew I couldn't let his death be in vain either. I wanted more than anything to make them both proud of me. I owed them that. I kissed the picture of Lola, Ice, and myself. I looked at Speed's obituary for the millionth time and then I turned out my night light and went to sleep.

CHAPTER THIRTY-THREE

It was Saturday, my favorite day of the week. I didn't realize how wiped out I was from the vigorous work schedule. I met up with Aaron and we had lunch. We hung out together for most of the afternoon and then we came across a flyer that advertised an eventful night with a circus, bonfire, and other activities over at the Kenton School that sat alongside a small secluded beach. So we decided to travel the two hours it took to get there in order to take part in the festivities.

By now it was two o'clock and the ride was long, hot, and sweaty. Once we got there we ran into Ethan and Marcia. It was always good to see familiar faces in a foreign place. Ethan and Marcia were sent to work at the same site as Aaron and me, but just North of the Benevolence Orphanage. I was glad to be in the company of people who were from my group.

We all hooked up and decided to hang out together for the evening. There was plenty to do and see. There were fire jugglers, and candy floss machines, clowns, and acrobats. I had never been to a circus before and so it was thrilling. The sky became an insignia of oranges, reds, and yellows, and streams of blues and greens as the sun began to rest and the fireworks came alive. People started to gather around as the drums played a symphony of erotic beats. A large fire was lit and thin branches were passed out amongst the hundred or so people who were encamped around it for the marshmallow roast.

Everyone sat along the small beach as they maneuvered the sand between their fingers and toes as they sang songs and chanted hymns. It was the first time that I'd ever been on a beach or roasted marshmallows. It was a nice experience. It was new and exciting for me and one I would remember for a long time to come. I laughed and giggled just long enough for me to lose myself, and with it, all the details of my sorted life.

Some who gathered felt comfortable enough to begin to share stories about their experiences of living in Africa in the short months that they'd been there. For some, it had been their second or even third trip to Africa, and so for them, Africa had become a way of life. Some of their stories were funny and some were not so funny.

The temperature had steadily dropped slightly below sixty two degrees, and the cool breeze that was blowing off of the water made it feel even cooler. There was a huge crate filled with shawls and maasai blankets sitting about twenty feet in back of us along the boarders of the school. And so I got up and proceeded to go and get a couple of blankets from the crate. But as I walked several feet I noticed that I was approaching a shadow right before me whose silhouette had reached into the crate ahead of me, pulled out a blanket, opened it and held it up, and welcomed me to come inside. As I approached the shadowed silhouette I recognized the defined body structure.

"A rather cool night isn't it?" Dylan stated as he offered to place the blanket around my shoulders.

"Are you following me?" I asked in an inquiring tone.

"I was about to ask you the same thing," he countered.

"What are you doing lurking around here in the dark?" I asked.

"I don't lurk. I was simply watching; admiring the view. Is there any law against that?"

"No, It's just creepy is all. You're creepin' me out," I responded.

"Well that is definitely not my intention. I offer my apology." He said in a very proper tone.

"Don't apologize," I instructed. "Just stop doin' it." I said as I began to walk back to the marshmallow roast.

"You mind if I come along?" he asked.

"Do what you like. I'm not the boss of you," I answered.

"You are from America, correct?" he asked.

"Correct," I responded quickly.

"So what brings you all the way over to Africa?" he asked.

"You could say it was a last minute decision," I said.

"How does one manage to make a last minute decision to travel thousands of miles away from their homeland?" he questioned.

"I don't know. Things happen. You never made a last minute decision to do something that you'd never thought you'd do?" I asked.

"I have," he replied.

At that moment we stopped walking as we realized that we were back amongst those gathered around the fire. I searched the faces in the crowd for Aaron, Ethan, and Marcia. Once I found them I made my way back into the circle, snug and warm inside my blanket and seated myself next to Aaron. Dylan followed and seated himself next to me on the opposite side. And in a state of confusion, Aaron looked at me.

"Where'd you find him?" he asked me.

"He was just back there, I don't know," I answered as I shrugged my shoulders and shook my head.

"He was just back there?" Aaron questioned. "Well, is he bothering you?

"No. I guess he's ok," I answered.

"How do you guess that?" "It seems like this guy is stalking you," Aaron insisted.

Dylan heard some of what Aaron was relaying to me, when he reached pass me with an extended hand to Aaron.

"Hi, I don't think we've had a proper introduction. I'm Dylan," he said.

Aaron shook his hand but he nixed any sort of introduction.

"It's getting pretty late," Aaron said. The last bus will be leaving soon. We'd better make our way over to the bus depot if we want to get a good seat.

"Well I'm driving if you want to stay a while longer. I can take us all back later if you want," Dylan suggested.

"No, we're fine thank you," Aaron quickly dismissed Dylan and spoke for the both of us as he stood, signaling me to gather my things as though he were my father.

"It's been a pleasure, Unique," Dylan said as he made eye contact with me. "I hope to see again soon.

I responded with my eyes because at that point I didn't know how to respond with my mouth. Unsure of whether I even cared if I saw him again or not. And so I said nothing. Ethan and Marcia noticed our attempted departure and came over.

"You guys leaving already?" Marcia asked.

"Yea, we're gonna' be on our way," I said.

The truth was, I really was having a good time up until then and I wanted to stay a while longer. And I would have preferred the car instead of the bus, but Aaron was acting rather strange and I didn't want to make a scene. So I went along with what he insisted upon.

"Well, we're gonna' hang out here for a little while longer and hitch a ride back to the site," Ethan honed in.

"Ok. Maybe we'll see you tomorrow then," Aaron said.

"Ok then," Ethan said as he and Aaron shook hands and Marcia and I said our good-byes.

Aaron and I left for the depot before everyone else and arrived in plenty of time to catch the last bus. I slept most of the ride back, confused about Aaron and his reaction to Dylan. Did Aaron see something suspicious in Dylan that warranted his behavior or was it something more?

Chapter Thirty-Four

The next day when I awoke I took a cold shower and had a bowl of hot cereal for breakfast. It was a typical Sunday. I spent the day washing clothes, reflecting on the week's events, and recording my experiences in my journal. I enjoyed recording my daily events because I knew that if there would ever be a time in my life when my mind would fail me and I would question whether or not I was truly here; I needed for the words in this book to speak to me and remind me that I was.

Monday came again and I got up early and headed straight over to Benevolence. Fathiya was there waiting for me like she had been every morning since the day I met her.

"Come," she said.

"You know what sweetie, I won't be able to come inside with you today. I promised Aaron that I would be more focused on my work today. He feels like I've been slacking in my duties. He gets a little grumpy at times. But not to worry, it's a man's thing. Men are like children. If you don't give them enough of your time they'll become irritable and throw tantrums. But you'll have plenty of time to find out about that," I said with a snicker. "So I'll be out here for the most part of the day. But I'll come in and check on you later on okay?"

Fathiya looked at me puzzled about what I had just said to her. I think she understood most of it and that's what counts.

"I'll be in later for lunch okay, lunch," I emphasized on the word lunch.

She nodded and backed up away from me with disappointing eyes. I began to look forward to seeing her everyday just as much as she looked forward to seeing me. I worked very hard that day and the next, in temperatures that soared well above one hundred; only breaking to go inside to have lunch with Fathiya and then returning back to work.

That Wednesday I noticed that Fathiya was not there to greet me when I came in to work. I went inside the orphanage to question the staff of her whereabouts. Nobody really seemed to know at first or even care for that matter. But after about a half hour or so I was approached by a lady who said that Fathiya was in with the nurse. Shortly thereafter, the nurse appeared.

"Fathiya is not herself today," she said. "My name is Zena Ghir and I'm the nurse here at Benevolence. Fathiya has a virus. We are afraid that she may be contagious and so she will be confined to her quarters until her condition changes," she said in a matter of fact way.

"Can you show me where she is at least?" I asked.

"I don't think it would be wise for her to have any visitors at this time until we are sure that the virus is no longer contagious," she sternly stated.

"Okay, but I am willing to take my chances. I just want to see her for a second," I almost pleaded.

I don't know why I felt the urgency to see Fathiya when I had only known her for a short time. But I was really concerned for her.

"I do understand your concern," nurse Ghir said, "but I have the well being of not just Fathiya to consider, but of yours as well. I'm sure you can understand. But if you check back later, perhaps tomorrow, I will give you an update on her condition," she said.

I walked away for a brief moment to reshape my thoughts. "Okay", I said, speaking to myself. "I guess I have to find out where she is on my own." I began to wander around the orphanage discreetly, quickly checking every room that I came across. I didn't realize the size of the orphanage before then. It was larger inside than it looked to be from the outside. And after about fifteen minutes, I found her. There was an attendant watching over the twenty or so children in that area. My heart melted as I gazed across the room at all the vulnerable little people who were confined to that room. I walked over to her bed and I pulled up a seat, hoping in the back of my mind that I wouldn't catch anything. And with my back turned I heard footsteps coming towards me.

"Excuse me miss, this is an unauthorized area," the voice behind me said.
"It's Okay I have authorization," I said.
"Authorization by whom ma'am?" the attendant asked.

I ignored her question while I fixed my eyes on Fathyia as she lay there sleeping.

"Hey, I missed you this morning. You're not feeling so good today huh?"

"Ma'am," the attendant persisted. "Authorization by whom?" she asked again but this time louder.

And again I ignored her until she became frustrated and walked away. I reached for the dry rag that hung above her bed post. I went to the sink that was in the room, wet the rag with cold water, and placed the compress upon her feverish forehead. I began to gently rub her hand. And then in a moments time, Fathiya opened her eyes and tried to turn on her side to face me when began to whimper.

"It hurts Fathiya?" I asked. "Where does it hurt precious? Here?" I questioned as I gently touched her side. She was burning up with fever.

Without a word she painfully nodded, yes.

"Excuse me, what did you say was wrong with her?" I called out.

"The attendant came over. "It appears that she has a bacterial virus," she responded.

"I'm sorry. But somebody that I am really close to had the same symptoms before, and it turned out to be the appendix," I said. "What are you giving her for this fever?"

The attendant came over to me and began to speak.

"There were four other children admitted when this child was admitted, all having the similar symptoms; symptoms that this child also displays. And so I think that diagnosing should be left to the doctors miss.

"I'm sorry. I don't know what those other children have, but I know what these symptoms look like. My brother had the same symptoms when he was about her age and I think you should at least consider the possibility that it could be her appendix. Can I please speak to a doctor," I asked.

"The doctor will be in on Friday," she responded.

"That's two days from now. Her appendix could burst by then," I relayed.

"Miss, Miss, I understand," she said.

"No, I don't think you do," I became agitated as she attempted to dismiss me.

"Miss there is only one doctor for this entire region and so he comes here once a week. The nurses here are more than equipped to handle these things until his return.

"What seems to be the problem Nyaguthii?" a familiar voice asked the attendant. And to my dismay, it was Dylan.

"I'll tell you what the problem is," I answered before the attendant had a chance.

"Fathiya needs a doctor. She has a fever and she's in a great deal of pain on her right side and this attendant is tellin' me that she has a virus. Let me show you. Here, place your hand gently right here," I said as I gently guided his hand to the right side of her body a couple of inches past her waist. Fathiya cried out in pain. "Does that sound like a virus to you?" I said convincingly.

"Okay, how do you know this?" he asked.

"Let's just say I've had experience with it, that's all you need to know," I responded sarcastically. He looked at me with suspicious eyes.

When I saw the expression on his face I realized that it was not his fault and that I shouldn't take it out on him.

"Okay," I said as I calmed down. Let me rephrase that. My brother had these exact symptoms and he almost died. Please! She needs I doctor," I expressed to the attendant and Dylan both.

"Alright, Dylan said. "My truck is around the back. I'll bring it around front and then we'll go. The Nairobi Hospital is about forty miles away.

"But Mr. Dylan," Nyaguthii said, I do not think it wise to move the girl, please Sir, the virus will pass."

"It'll be fine Nyagutgii," Dylan assured her. I'll take full responsibility for her," he said.

And he left to go get his truck. He was back within minutes. He reached over and covered Fathiya with a blanket before picking her up, and ever so gently carrying her out to the truck where he had several other blankets laid in the back seat already prepared for her. He jumped in on the driver's side and I climbed in the back with Fathiya. Aaron saw that there was something going on and ran over to the truck.

"Where are you going? What's going on?" he called out.

"She's sick Aaron, she needs a doctor," I said.

"Well, do you want me to come along with you?" he asked. "Just let me put this stuff away," he said.

And before I had a chance to respond, Dylan sped off.

The drive seemed longer than it really was as I tried to make Fathiya as comfortable as possibly in the back of the truck. I mean, she was really burning up as the beads of sweat escaped through the pores of her tiny little body.

I remembered how I felt on my way to the hospital with Ice. The fear that comes over you is just ridiculous. Why was I getting involved with this little girl? Why did it even matter to me? My mind took me back to all the walls that I ran into while trying to keep the Department of Children's Services from finding out that Lola had

abandoned Ice and Me. I was terrified that they would find out and
come and remove me and my brother from our home. I was scared
that they would separate us. It seemed like yesterday.

"We're here," Dylan called out.

Once we came to a complete stop Dylan got out and came to
the back of the truck, opened the door and lifted Fathiya out of my
arms. He headed toward the hospital door and I jumped out quickly
and followed closely behind him.

"Excuse me," I called out. "Can somebody help us?" I asked
almost in a state of panic but still trying to remain calm. "Excuse
me, we have a sick little girl here that needs attention," I called out
as Dylan stood by and waited as I sought help.

"Excuse me," I spoke louder as I approached the desk. "Can
somebody please help us? We have a very sick child here," I said in
a more disturbed voice.

"Can I help you Miss," a lady behind the counter asked.

"Yes, yes you can," I said as I lowered the tone in my voice. "We
have a child here that needs medical attention right away.

"What seems to be the problem?" the lady asked.

"She's burning up with fever and she has severe pain on her lower
right side," I said.

"What kind of medical coverage will you be using today?" the
lady behind the desk asked.

"She is a resident of the Benevolence Orphanage," I
emphasized.

"Well all orphans from Benevolence will have to be taken over to
the Kakuma Camp's Hospital to be seen. The International Rescue
Committee has to issue an admittance document before we are able
to see her here."

"Well how far away is it?" I questioned.

"That would about seventy kilometers South," she answered.

"Uhhhh," Fathiya moaned.

"Seventy kilometers? Miss, that's forty miles out, I responded.

I was about to let them see the Detroit side of me come out because it was knocking at my door and I didn't know how much longer I could contain it.

"She needs a doctor and you're standing here talking about insurance and politics to me when this little girl could be dying? Are you kidding me?" I asked as I felt myself becoming hostile.

"Look, my name is Dylan Buel and it is vital that this little girl be admitted immediately," Dylan intervened. "I will take full responsibility," he said.

"Mr. Dylan, of course sir. I'll see to it right away," she responded to him with a changed tone and attitude after taking another look at him.

Was it the fact that I wasn't from around here or that I was a woman. I don't know what it was. But whatever it was, the lady at the front desk got on the phone and called somebody and within minutes a bed was brought out and Fathiya was admitted. They wheeled her back through a set of double doors and into an area where they cared for trauma patients. And it was there that a Doctor emerged.

"Mr. Buel, so sorry for any misunderstanding. My name is Dr. Absko, Chief of Pediatrics, and I will be handling this case personally. If you would allow me to examine the child it would be most helpful.

"Absolutely," Dylan said. "We'll be right out here waiting," he said.

Dylan and I stepped into the hall in a small waiting area where we sat quietly for about an half hour until the Doctor returned.

"Everything is gonna be alright," Dylan said as he looked over at me. He disappeared for a few minutes and came back with a cup of soup and some hot tea.

"Here," he said. "You need to put something into your stomach."

"I'm not hungry," I said.

"You need to eat," he insisted.

I took his advice and ate the soup. I remember that it was Sweet and Sour. But I couldn't really remember how it tasted because I was thinking only of Fathiya. I remember I was half way through with my tea when Dr. Absko returned. Dylan and I immediately stood up.

"We gave her something to bring down the fever. I'm afraid that there is a blockage at the opening of the appendix into the cecum which is causing a severe infection at the wall of the appendix. The body has launched an attack on the body in an attempt to kill the bacteria, but has been unsuccessful in subduing the massive build up of inflammation. The infection is spreading quickly through the wall and could rupture at any moment. If it ruptures and spreads through to the stomach, I'm afraid her chances will not be good.

"So what do we do?" Dylan asked.

"We have but only one option. We have to do an emergency Appendectomy. It's the only chance that she has.

"Okay," Dylan stated as I remained quiet and listened for the first time all day.

Three hours had passed when Dr. Absko returned yet again with an update on Fathiya's condition.

"The surgery went well as far as we can tell. We're having trouble right now regulating her blood pressure. It'll be a while before we can tell how her body is responding to the surgery. The next several hours will be crucial," Dr. Absko said before he walked off.

Upon hearing that, I felt the need to get some air. I left out of the waiting room, walked through the emergency room waiting area, and right out the exit. Once I got outside I took in a deep breath, trying to fill my lungs with all the air I possibly could in an attempt to rid myself of the overpowering feeling of suffocation that came over me. Dylan came out after me.

"Are you Okay?" he asked. "I know that it sounds bad, but I know that everything's gonna' be fine.

"You do? And how do you know that? In the real world stuff happens and everything doesn't always have a happy ending," I snapped.

He paused for a minute as he tried to figure out a way to respond to my statement.

"Yes, in some instances they don't. But in this case it will," he said.

"What makes you so sure?

"My faith. My faith is what makes me sure of that," he said.

I shook my head, refusing to listen to Jackson's words coming out of Dylan's mouth.

"Your faith?" I questioned.

"Yes, my faith," he firmly repeated.

"I'm so confused. How does that work?" I asked.

"It's essential to the very presence of life," he continued. "Faith is what you believe and know in your heart to be true. And right now that little girl needs for us to believe.

He turned and began to walk back into the hospital.

"Are you coming?" he asked.

I turned slowly and followed him back inside the hospital. We went straight to the intensive care unit where Fathiya was resting. I stood there next to her bed as she lay there so peaceful and unaware of her life and death predicament. I wondered if she had any brothers or sisters; any family at all out there. I knew that I couldn't afford to get emotionally attached to this little girl. Already, the pain of even knowing her proved to be more than I was capable of handling at this point. Why did I let myself even get involved with her? Why did I let myself care?

Dylan bowed his head and closed his eyes as if he were meditating.

"Excuse me Mr. Buel," a voice said.

"Yes," he answered.

"She probably won't wake until tomorrow. If you wish to leave and come back in the morning we would know something for sure by then," A nurse explained to him.

Dylan saw how concerned I was and he knew that I really didn't want to leave her. It was six o'clock in the evening.

"If its okay, we'd like to stay with her," he responded.

"That will be fine," the nurse explained.

About one o'clock in the morning we were both fast asleep when Fathiya began to fidget. She coughed and then she opened her eyes. Dylan woke before me and witnessed Fathiya coming around. He gently rubbed my back to awaken me.

"Hey. She's awake," he said.

I awoke to also witness the first sign of hope from a little girl who truly had a rough night.

"I'll go get the Dr," Dylan said before he left the room.

"U(nick)," she said my name for the first time. She couldn't pronounce my name properly so she called me, Unick.

"Hi sweetie. How are you feeling?" She reached for her side, suggesting that she knew something was wrong there.

"No, No, don't touch. It has to heal ok. You had a bad infection. But the Doctors went in and cleaned it all out. And so it's gonna be sore for a few days but it will heal in no time, Okay precious," I promised her.

Just then Dylan returned with the Doctor. The Doctor began to examine Fathiya.

"Her vital signs are good. It seems that the fever has broken. We're gonna have to keep her here for a few days you understand; just as a precaution.

"Yes we understand," I responded.

"It was touch and go for a moment there but it looks like she pulled through nicely," The Doctor confirmed. "There are some additional papers that we neglected to have you sign when she was first brought in. They are waiting for your signatures at the front desk," Dr Absko said. "Visiting hours are from ten to six. I'll be in to check on her about six o'clock unless something unforeseen happens that will call for my attention before then," The Doctor explained.

"Thank you Doctor," Dylan said.

"We're gonna' be leaving now, but we'll back in a few hours to see you," I leaned over and whispered to Fathiya, and then I kissed her forehead.

"You get some sleep now," Dylan said to her as he held her hand.

We went to the front desk to fill out the admittance forms and some contact information sheets and then we left. When we got outside, Dylan opened the passenger side door to his jeep for me and I got in. As we buckled up, I felt Dylan staring at me.

"You saved her life you know," he said. "You knew what it was and you acted on it. If it weren't for you," he stopped himself from finishing the sentence.

"I didn't do anything," I responded.

"No. Yes you did," he insisted. "You cared enough to demand that somebody take notice. You should be proud of yourself," he said as we drove off.

Dylan dropped me off at home. I was so relieved that Fathiya was alright, but I had so many mixed feelings about everything. I went inside and sat down at the table and stared up at the ceiling for about five minutes when suddenly a sense of fear came over me. I thought about Fathiya and how unexpectedly I became involved with this little girl and what it would have done to me if anything would have happened to her.

CHAPTER THIRTY-FIVE

The next day when I woke I didn't feel any better than I did the night before. I realized that as much as I wanted to see Fathiya, it would be best if I kept my distance. I just couldn't risk getting close to anybody else at this time in my life. I didn't want to be responsible for that type of relationship.

The next day I left my home early and went into town to work on the Library Project. The project was a couple of months shy of being completed. I also assisted some other volunteers with giving out literature on the HIV virus and other diseases that threatened the existence of the Kenyan people and all Africans across that Continent. I made sure to keep myself very busy.

Every evening for the next six days, I would arrive home around seven. And every evening upon my arrival I would find a note that Dylan had taped to my front door. The note would always tell me how Fathiya was coming along and that she missed me. I would read the note and then discard the note. But on the sixth day I left my home at about a quarter of eight in the morning. And when I stepped outside my door there was yet another letter affixed to the door that read;

Unique, I will pick you up tomorrow morning at
nine o'clock so that we can go and visit Fathiya.
She asks about you every day and I am running out
of excuses as to why you have not been to visit her.
Whatever your reasons, I think Fathiya
deserves to hear it from you.

Dylan

And just like with the letters I received the five days that preceded it, I removed the letter from my door and disposed of it. On the seventh day, I stepped back outside in another attempt to leave early so that I wouldn't run the risk of running into Dylan. But as I turned to close and secure my front door, he startled me as he approached me from behind.

"Do you ever plan on coming back or is that what you do run away?" he asked

"What do you want from me? I don't owe you or anybody else anything." I said without even looking at him.

"Well just in case it means anything to you at all; she was released yesterday. If it meant nothing to you then why didn't you just leave her there at the orphanage to die? Why?

"That's not fair. Why would you ask something like that? " I responded.

"You sure about that?" he asked.

"She's okay now. And so I just think we need to put some space in between us."

"Just like that huh?" he said cynically.

"Look, she won't even remember me when I'm gone," I expressed.

"Is that really what you think?" Because I thought you would be smarter than that. She will remember you just as she remembers everyone else whom she's loved and lost," he expressed.

"It's not my problem. What do you know about lost loves or abandonment? You don't come across as somebody who knows anything about it. So don't stand here and try and make me feel guilty about something you don't understand

"Well explain it to me." He demanded.

"You people. You do this because you're bored. You don't have a clue about real life issues. You don't know anything about what it's like to go without anything do you; food, money, clothing, the bare necessities, do you?"

"You people?" he questioned. You know I would have never pegged you for being a racist?" he said.

"Don't you dare try and make this out to be about race. You know that has nothing to do with anything," I made clear. This is about those who have versus those who have not. This is not about color," I snapped. "I'm just calling it like I see it."

"Well from where I'm standing I don't believe you can see too much of anything," he said.

"Why because you think just because you come over here, volunteer a few months out of your life to help some poor, misfortunate children that it makes you some kind of great humanitarian? You think it makes you a better person? Uh? And then what? You go back to your little cushiony home after you've done you're good deed and sit around with the friends and have a couple of drinks and a good laugh?" I know all about your kind," I finished as I began to walk away angrily.

"You really think you know so much, do you? Well you don't," he came back at me. You think you have this whole thing all figured out and you're not even close. But you won't have to worry about me bothering you anymore because I can take a hint. I know that you have more important things to do and I wish you well in doing them. And I hope that one day when you're able to see things clearly enough, you'll see fit to remove whatever it is you have lodged up your ass because it reeks something awful." he said.

Well needless to say I was dumbstruck. I stood there speechless wondering to myself what the hell just happened. I went into town that very day and proceeded to give out literature on Hepatitis and Aids. I tried to pretend that the conversation I had with Dylan never took place; that it didn't matter, but I couldn't get Fathiya or the things that he said to me out of my mind.

I had the entire day and all that evening to think about everything. The next day I managed to get up the nerve to go and visit Fathiya who had been sent home two days ago and was resting comfortably at the orphanage. I got to the door of the room where she lay resting. She lay on her side staring out of the window. I knocked lightly on the door before I entered. She rolled over slightly to see who was knocking. When she saw that it was me, she rolled back over and continued to stare out the window as if I wasn't there. It felt like my heart dropped into my stomach.

"Hey," I said as I continued into the room. "I see somebody is feeling a whole lot better."

I saw that it would be difficult now for her to trust me. She had put a wall up and was determined to shut me out. It was a scene that I was all too familiar with. So I sat in the chair that was directly next to her bed. I sat there about ten minutes thinking of how to approach the situation. All I could do was ask for forgiveness.

"I'm sorry I haven't been to see you," I said.

She continued to stare out of the window. I put my head down in defeat when I realized how much I had hurt her. I only wish I could make her understand that I didn't mean it. Just then Dylan appeared.

"How is the most beautiful girl in the world doing today?" He asked Fathiya.

She gave him a smile that was as big as the room. But only the bottom row of her teeth where exposed because her top row had fallen out. I thought it made her look all the more cute.

"Hi," Dylan spoke to me. "Look who's here," he said to Fathiya. Did you say hi to Unique?" he asked.

Fathiya remained quiet.

"I don't' think she wants me here," I said.
"Sure she does. She just doesn't know it yet."
"No, she doesn't. Maybe I should go and come back another time."
"I would agree with you if I thought it would be easier the next time. But unfortunately, it would only be worse. So I'll leave now and give the both of you time to get reacquainted. I'll be back later," Dylan said.

Fathiya remained silent and Dylan left. I got up and walked over to the other side of the bed where she was facing. I sat down and then I began to talk.

"I missed you."
"You lie," Fathiya responded with clear English as she caught me off guard.
"I know I hurt you and I'm sorry. But I mean it when I say that

I missed you. It's just that I….I was afraid, Fathiya," I came out and admitted to her. "You may not understand this but you and I have a lot in common. Like you, I know what it feels like to lose someone that you really love. And I guess I was just afraid of it happening again. I got scared when you got sick and I didn't know what to do and I didn't want to be around to see what came next because I thought it would be bad," I explained.

"You didn't say good-bye.

"Yes, I know and I'm so sorry for that. But if you would give me one more chance, I promise that I'll never leave again without saying good-bye. Look, I have something for you," I said as I reached into my back pack and pulled out the Teddy Bear that my dad had given me when I was about Fathiya's age.

"Mine?" she asked.
"Yes, yours," I replied.

Fathiya began to hug the Teddy Bear with all of her might. I sat in the chair and I scooted up closer to bed. I reached in my back pack and pulled out a story book that I had just purchased and I began to read. Midway through the story, Fathiya fell off to sleep. I pulled the sheet up over her. I took a moment to watch her cradle the Teddy that meant more to me than she could ever know. I zippered up the back pack and left Fathiya to dreams that I hoped were sweet. I came outside and walked over to where Aaron was working.

"Wow! it's really starting to come together," I said as I observed Aaron climb down from the roof.

"Yeah, we should be able to start painting in a week or so," he said and then he paused. "Is everything Ok with you now?"

"I'm fine," I responded.

"Because if you're not….you know you can talk to me," he said.

"I know," I answered.

"Well are you going to stand around all day or are you going to give me a hand?" he asked.

We both looked at each other and smiled as I reached for the extra tool belt. Before I knew it, Aaron and I were back to working diligently on the library. Dylan kept his distance but always seemed to be somewhere close by. Fathiya was up and about by the following week. We were back to having our lunches, playing dodge ball and enjoying each other's company. I made sure that her hair was done most times and I tried to keep my mind off of the day when I would have to leave; the day when I would have to say good-bye to Fathiya - forever.

Chapter Thirty-Six

Several weeks later I received a letter from Jackson. He told me that he remained in contact with Bailey and how well she looked the last time that he saw her. He had just visited Ice a few days before I received the letter and he said that Ice remained in good spirits and was about to file for an appeal for a lighter sentence. Nobody could imagine how good that news did my heart.

The Benevolence Library would have its grand opening in about two weeks. And everyone was just thrilled about it. The skies were sad that day. The drab and dreariness made you want to just stay inside. There was a brownish green mass that hovered over the orphanage like a plane that was about to land. My ears began to pop as the wind howled and the dust blew a million small particles into my eyes, blinding me.

"We'd better get inside until the winds die down," Aarons voice spiraled above the high pitched whistling of the wind that was now up to about forty miles per hour.

And so we began to gather all of our belongings as quickly as possible. Aaron had his hands full with tools and paint cans.

"Come on," he called out to me.

"I'm right behind you," I bellowed back.

As I began to make my way inside I saw a small shaded outline of a person through the dust and debris coming toward me with an object in hand.

"Oh my God! It's Fathiya," I said to myself as I slowly made out her face through the drifting rain that had begun to fall.

"Fathiya no, go back," I warned her as she walked towards me clinching Teddy close to her body. Go Back Fathiya," I cried out. "Go Back."

The winds started to double in speed and strength in a matter of minutes as the rain began to blow in buckets. Without notice, the wind began to pick up nice size objects from the site and hurl them viciously through the air. I looked around and became frantic as I observed the columns of the library literally being uprooted from the ground.

"Unique," I heard a small voice call out to me.

All I could think of at that moment was that Fathiya needed me.

"Fathiya?" I screeched in a panic. "Fathiya? I cried out, terrified that she would be next to be hurled by the winds of the angry sky. "Where are you?" I called.

Mechanically, I dropped everything that I had in my hands as my vision became obscured. I held my hands out in front of me but was no longer able to see them. I continued to reach out with my hands, hoping to grab a hold of Fathiya's small frame.

All at once, a portion of the roof to the library had been torn from the nearly completed structure. As I tried to look on I saw a dark image coming toward me in a speed that was as fast as lightning. My reflexes caused me to throw up my hands in front of my face defensively. I remember hearing someone calling my name. And then……. everything went dark.

"Help me, somebody," I vaguely heard a voice. "Help me get her inside."

And then my memory went blank until I woke up three days later to see Aaron standing at the foot of my bed and Dylan was at the head. I couldn't completely make out their faces because my vision was fuzzy. But what I couldn't see with my eyes I was able to feel with my heart, and I knew who they were.

I made out everyone face except Fathiya's. My head was throbbing like something I'd never experienced in my life. And although my vision was impaired I could see well enough to realize that Fathiya was not there. I tried to sit up as the room began to spin and I became queasy as my breathing became irregular. My head felt as heavy as a ton of bricks as I gave an extra effort towards lifting it.

"Fathiya," I mumbled.

"No, No, you lay still now. Fathiya is just fine," Dylan responded as he held my hand to calm me. She's fine.

"She's fine," I repeated his words. "She's fine."

"Yes she is. It's eleven o'clock pm. Fathiya is asleep," Aaron responded.

"Asleep?" I asked in my semi lethargic state.

"Yes, asleep," Aaron confirmed.

With that my head fell back onto the pillow. Marcia, who was there also, informed me that I was in and out of consciousness for the next three days. I had sustained a severe head injury that left me completed incapacitated. When I was finally able to stay conscious for longer than five minutes I was absolutely famished. I hadn't had anything but an intravenous for food for almost a week. The doctor said that it was a good sign that I was hungry.

I was lavished with food by Ethan, Marcia, Aaron, everyone from the House of Job, and Dylan. Everyone was so caring and supportive. I was really glad to see everyone. I was told by Aaron that Dylan never left my side and that he was really afraid for me.

"You and Fathiya are going to be the death of me," Dylan said to me as he assisted me in sitting up.

He picked up a bowl of soup from the table stand beside the bed and began to feed me. And ever so softly he dabbed the corners of my mouth after each spoonful. I looked over at Fathiya as she sat silently watching.

"She stopped talking you know…when you got hurt," Dylan said.

I took my hand and patted the bed, signaling Fathiya to climb up onto the bed with me.

"How is my little Princess today?" I asked her as I cradled her in my arms. I was convinced of her strength; being reminded how much trauma she had already witnessed in such a short time which would explain why she hadn't spoken since my injury.

"Fathiya, it's time to eat now," a caretaker said as she entered into the room. "Come, you can return later after lunch," the caretaker said. Fathiya looked at me for approval to leave.

"Go ahead, I'll be right here when you come back," I promise. "Go on now," I instructed her.

"Dare I say, someone is getting quite close to you," Dylan suggested. "You know when you are feeling more like yourself, I think it would be only appropriate, given all that has happened in the last couple of weeks, that we go out for an evening of relaxation - you know – to try and unwind. I know a great restaurant"

I looked on without knowing quite what to say.

"There's no rush," he established. "Whenever you feel up to it."

CHAPTER THIRTY-SEVEN

It was two days later and I was resting comfortably at home. Dylan and Aaron saw to it that I had everything that I needed. I wasn't use to so much attention. I was feeling almost a hundred percent better. My vision was almost back to normal. My headache was practically gone and I was no longer dizzy. I observed Dylan surveying the room and the pictures of me and my family. He picked up the picture and then he looked at me.

"I'd like to say that this will be the last night that you two will be spending the night here. I'm fine now and I appreciate everything that you've done. But now it's time for the both of you to get back to your lives. I'll be fine.

"I've got to meet up with Ethan in a half hour. I'll check back with you when I get back later," Aaron said.

Dylan hung around and fixed me a cup of Chamomile and Lavender Tea. It was the best cup of tea that I ever drank.

"What do you say to me taking you to that restaurant I mentioned," he said. "Tomorrow would be just as good a time as any. How about I pick you up at six?"

"I don't know if I'll be up to it. I'm still not quite myself," I said.

279

"You'll be fine," he said. "And I won't take no for an answer."

I found it hard to oppose him in his persistence. And so I humbled myself and graciously accepted. Needless to say the next day he was very prompt. He was there at five forty-five with a bouquet of white roses in hand. They were beautiful. When I agreed to go out with him I didn't really feel like it would be a date, date. But I believed in Dylan's heart it was a for sure date.

"White Roses? Where did you get them?" I asked.

"In Karen," he responded.

"Karen?" I questioned.

"Yes, there's a greenhouse on the out skirts of Karen, a suburb of Nairobi. By the way, you look lovely this evening," he said.

"Thanks," I replied.

"How are you feeling today?" he asked.

"I'm feeling a lot better, thank you," I replied.

"Shall we?" he asked as he held the door open for me.

Why were we acting so formal? Why did he have to be such a gentleman? I remember Javier being just as gentleman like. I could see that there was a big difference though. Javier knew everything about me. He knew my past and he still loved me in spite of it. Dylan didn't have a clue as to who I was or where I came from and I really couldn't trust myself to get too close to him. He didn't know anything about my life before Africa. And I didn't want him to know. My culture was so different from what he was accustomed to. Yes, I do believe that there were some mutual feelings there. But what could really come of them? I mean, we had a few things in common, yes. But we were worlds apart.

We drove for about one hour before we reached our destination; Le Rustique. It was a truly magical place located in a remote area.

Once we got inside I noticed that there were candle lit tables, some were shaded by large umbrellas and some were not. The patio was elegant, lit by fire place, and offered a most spectacular view of the city. Who would imagine there would even be places like this in Africa?

The menu was delicious. It listed mouth watering fruit filled crepes, delicate soufflés, and entrees ranging from specialty waffles and fresh seafood to prime beef and rack of lamb. You could have breakfast and dinner all at the same time. They offered every kind of soup that you could imagine.

They had an assortment of pastries and ice creams and an array of delectable quiches, soufflés, crepes, and quiches; who would have ever thought that they would have restaurants this beautiful in this area. We had the perfect table. We were seated in a quiet corner away from everyone. I was a bit uncomfortable with the intimacy of the location of our table. But I didn't let my feelings show.

I ordered a blueberry filled crepe, a bowl of crab bisque, and a cup of rosehips tea. I'd never had these things in my life but they sounded like something that I would enjoy. Dylan ordered the waffles stuffed with cream cheese and boysenberry syrup and when the waiter came we ordered two glasses of chilled Chablis. Suddenly, I felt awkward as Javier and Ice entered my mind. A sadness grabbed hold of my heart. The love of my life had been murdered and my brother, who had been closer than a son was sentenced to prison. And here I was with the audacity to be out and about having a good time.

"Is there something wrong?" Dylan asked as he witnessed my expression change.

"No, I shook my head.

"Is that headache coming back?" he asked.

"No, I'm good," I tried to play it off.

"Tell me," he went on. "The picture on the bureau in your home, is that your family?

"Yes," I said.

"You look like you all are pretty close?"

"I'm close with my brother, yes," I responded.

"So the woman in the picture, is she your mother?" he asked. "The resemblance is amazing.

"I cleared my throat and then took one sip of the glass of Chablis. And then I drank until the whole glass was gone.

"Please excuse me for a moment," I said as proper as I knew how.

I left the table and went to the bathroom. I have no idea how long I was in there but I must have been in there for at least a half hour. Every time someone came into the bathroom or went out, I could hear Dylan calling for me.

"Unique." He called out in a whisper, but loud enough to hear.

I was inside one of the stalls, leaning up against one of the walls thinking about what Dylan had asked me and why it threw me like it did. I don't know if I would ever be prepared to talk about my mother in a social setting because there was nothing social about that subject. Just the mention of her name opened up so many wounds that would probably never heal. It was so easy when I was with Javier because he knew about the things that tainted my life and he never judged me for it. He understood what it was like for me and I could be me around him.

Although Javier didn't experience what I did in my life, we were both from a place where most kids had never been on a plane or even gone to summer camp. We couldn't relate to higher education or even how we could accomplish it with all the responsibilities and obligations that we had. We came from a place where there was death and destruction on all four sides and where mother's sold their babies for crack on a regular.

I can't really speak to where Dylan came from because I didn't know anything about him. But in my heart I imagined he was from a different place. I imagined he was from a place where fathers didn't get murdered everyday and mother's didn't do drugs and abandon their children. I imagined he came from a place where mother's prepared breakfast for their children and packed brown bag lunches for them every day before they sent them off to school. And I imagined that he probably knew what it was like to celebrate his birthdays and Christmas' on the very day they fell on and not a week, or a month later.

Dylan obviously thought that I was somebody worth his time. But what will happen when he finds out that I'm not? I didn't ask for any of this and I didn't want it. I felt like I wanted to run far, far away. But it seems I had gone all the way across the world and it still wasn't far enough.

Finally, I got the courage to come out of the bathroom and face him. I had things on my chest that I had to get off and I knew that I owed him some type of explanation. But how would I even begin. Dylan was out in the hall sitting patiently across from the bathroom. He immediately stood up when he saw that I was coming out. I walked towards him and sat down calmly. He sat down after me.

"I apologize if I said anything to upset you," he began to try and rectify whatever he thought he may have done wrong.

"No," I interrupted. "I'm sorry, I began to explain. The lady in the picture is my Mother," I just began to empty myself. "My life growing up was anything but easy. My Father was murdered when I was seven years old. The police never found out who did it; and my Mother was never the same because of it.

She turned to the streets and eventually abandoned my brother and me. We managed for a while but with no money, no food, or any of the bare necessities, It became impossible. And so, at thirteen I was left with the responsibility of taking care for my brother and keeping a roof over our heads.

There wasn't much that I could do at thirteen years old, and so I had to do a lot of things that I'm not proud of in order to take care of us and keep us together. I met someone really special; my soul mate, Javier. And we would be married now, but he was murdered on our prom night. I never knew that I could care so deeply for another human being.

And to top it all off, in an attempt to rescue me from destroying myself, my little brother accidentally took the life of someone who was exploiting me and trying to hurt me. And so at seventeen years of age the courts convicted my brother, the only person that I have in this whole wide world, for a crime that would've never taken place had it not been for the choices that I've made in life.

So you see, everyone that I've ever cared for has been taken away from me in one way or another. I came to Africa to try to make some sense out of my life. I came because I owed it to the people who I let down .

I don't know who you think I am and I wouldn't expect you to understand anything that I've just shared with you. But I told you all of this because I want you to take a good look at me. Don't you see? I am insignificant. I am of no consequence and I don't matter.

I thank you though for your kindness and if I have mislead you in any way, I am truly sorry. But this is all clearly a mistake. So if you could please take me home now –please?" I pleaded.

And with that I got up and left Dylan sitting at the table with a lot to digest. A few minutes later he followed me out to find me sitting in the jeep he left unlocked. I knew that I had just given him a mouthful. I don't know why I felt compelled to tell him my whole life story in a span of three minutes. But I was glad. He had to be told so that he would stop pursuing me because I did not want to be pursued.

It was dejaveau all over again as the ride back home was a quiet one. We were about a half hour into the ride home when Dylan stopped suddenly along the side of the road.

"Why are we stopping?" I questioned.

"Come on, I'd like to show you something," he said.

As I stepped out of the jeep I noticed the sun had began to fall but there was still a glimmer of sun light that was shone through the promising darkness that was about to surpass the sky.

I looked across the field and I saw a house that seemed to stand alone illuminated with outdoor post lights. We stood there for several moments as I waited for him to explain.

"My best friend's family resides in that house. His name is Kaleb. He won a full Rugby scholarship to a University in Welsh, England; the same college that I also attended. We were roommates and it wasn't long before we became friends. It was almost instant. Kaleb played everything and he was good at it; rugby, football, lacrosse. He was such a comedian. Oh! How he made me laugh.

He would be the first in his family to go to college and so it was a really big deal to his family that he was graduating. They put all their hopes and their dreams in Kaleb. Kaleb worked two jobs in order to send money back to his family because his father was no longer able to work his construction job because his knees were bad, and so Kaleb felt it was his duty as the eldest son to provide for the family. There were four of his siblings left at home and there were days when there was barely enough for them to eat.

Well, one day before a big game I came up with the brilliant idea that it would be most entertaining if we were to borrow the other teams' Mascot. Kaleb was totally against it from the start but I always had a way of talking him into things that he was dead set against, and so he buckled.

We had everything planned out to the tee. We made our way into the other team's dorm quarters and managed to retrieve the mascot without any interference. We found our way in quite easily but we ran into difficulties getting out. The security guards began making their rounds and started locking all the doors – so we had to find another way out.

We found a second floor window that was opened and it had a small platform outside on the ledge. It was our only way out and so we would have to jump from where we were to the other side. I went first. I made the jump but I realized it was a lot harder than it looked. I made a clean landing without so much of a scratch on me.

But then it was Kaleb's turn. Kaleb was afraid of heights and so it was very difficult to coax him into that jump. He kept saying he wanted to give up and confess to the guards what we had done. But I wouldn't have it. So he came out onto the ledge…and he jumped. He missed the landing by a few inches and came down on a fence that surrounded the walk way. The fence caught him in right underneath his chin and it practically severed his head.

The school had a small insurance policy on all its players. His family had a small home a few kilometers from Benevolence. And after Kaleb's death his parents used the insurance money to purchase the moderate home that you see before you.

Contrary to what you might believe about me, I didn't come to Africa to be anybody's savior. I came because I wanted to be close to what Kaleb was close to. I wanted to be near his family and his roots and the things that he loved. So I guess you could say his causes have become my causes."

There was a brief moment of silence. I was speechless. I didn't know quite how to respond to it. And so rather than comment on it, I attempted to change the tone of the evening.

"So do you ever intend on finishing college?" I asked.

" I hadn't really thought about it. Maybe I will one day," he replied as we slowly walked back towards the jeep.

On the way home I thought about how crazy of a night it had been. I didn't know what to say or what to expect next. I didn't know how much of what we told one another would affect our views of each other and cause us to see each other differently.

I do believe I saw him in a different light. I guess nobody's excluded from the tragedies of this life. It was obvious that he was on his mission and I was on mine. It seemed both of us were looking for some type of redemption.

"I'll see you tomorrow?" he posed the question as I my made my exit from the jeep.

"I guess so," I replied.

"I just want you to know," he said. "Your past is in the past and it can only define your future if you let it," he said.

I kept walking towards my house and dare not turn around; when I heard the jeep's door slam behind me.

"Oh my God!" I thought. "No he didn't just get out."

"It's what humbles us," he yelled out.

I stopped and stood still for just a moment with my back still turned.

"What is?" I asked.

"Our past," he said. "It's what keeps us grounded; reminding us of what we want and what we don't want in our lives. It prompts us to recall where we used to be and where we are now. I could never ask you to forget your journey and what is behind you because it is what has brought you here to this point today. All I ask is that you just take a moment to look and see what is before you."

And then he did it. I was so hoping that he would turn around and go back to the jeep and just drive away – just drive; without attempting to make any kind gestures towards me because that would not be good. But he moved in and he took my hand.

"Oh Lord! I felt the warm blood running through the veins in his strong hand.

"Dylan, please," I said. "I'm not gonna' do this now. Go back."

"No, I want you to stop running, listen and hear me out. I want to know how I can get to know you? I want to know everything about you; your likes and your dislike; your favorite color and your favorite foods. I want to know your dreams.

And I want you to know that I have taken a very good look at you and you are anything but insignificant; but a magnificent and dynamic creature of life. And you matter to me. And if you're looking for an easy way out I'm here to tell you that there is none."

I was definitely running out of ways to deter this man. And I was determined not to let my guard down. I wouldn't allow myself.

"I'm sorry Dylan. I can't do this. This is simply not gonna' work," I said.

"Why? You tell me why? How could you come to such a conclusion?" he demanded to know.

"Look at us," I said. We are literally night and day."

"Look at what? Is this about skin color?" Is that really the issue here," he questioned. I see that we're the same where it matters. It's apparent to me that between the two of us we've been up against much larger obstacles," he said with conviction.

"It's not just that. I've got enough stuff going on in my life. And I just can't be in a relationship right now. I don't want you in my life.

"I don't believe you." he said.

"Well I don't care what you believe. That's how I feel." I made clear.

"So, you can look at me and tell me that you don't feel anything for me?" he asked

"Yes," I said as I looked at him.

"I want you to say the words," he said.

"Say what words?" I asked as I became agitated.

"Tell me that you don't feel anything for me," he persisted.

"No, I won't play this game with you," I refused.

"Game? Is that what you think this is?" he asked. If you feel nothing for me at all, then tell me. Say the words," he pressed.

I tried, but for some reason I couldn't bring myself to say the words.

"I can't afford to lose one more person in my life. I can't," I expressed

"And you won't," he assured me.

"And how will I ever know?" I cried out.

"Know what?" he asked.

"If I'm not just some charity case; some good deed thing that you needed to do so you could feel better about yourself. How will I know…….?"

And before I could say another word, Dylan walked towards me and I backed up trying to elude him but there was no where left for me to go. I fell back against the door as he leaned in with his body, his lips against mine and began to ravenously conquer them. I fought him off for about three seconds before I succumbed to the passion that ignited in us both.

Five seconds into the forbidden, illicit, fervor, Dylan slowed down. He began to gently nibble at my left ear lobe.

"You can't possibly think that's who I am. How will you know?" he questioned. "You will know every time you look into my eyes, and every time I place my hands on your backside, or kiss your inner thigh. You will feel it in every fiber of your existence that I am smitten with the very essence of you and everything about you just by the mere touch of my hand against your cheek. And you will see that I am intrigued with how you look, the shape of your lips, your smile, how you move, and how you have a way about you that demands respect from anyone that crosses your path? And so I need to know right now if you feel anything for me. I need to know now," he demanded.

Damn. Why did he have to say all of that? He was so confident and sure of himself. I just wish that I could've felt just as confident. But I didn't. I became paralyzed. I thought that I was finally making him understand but it was clear that I was not. But I recognized that it was the other way around. Everything that he said to me sounded like sheer poetry. I had never been spoken to in such a manner. But I couldn't forget – I would never forget about Javier and how he loved me. I could never abandon his memory.

"Do you care for me, Unique?" he demanded an answer in the most persuasive tone.

I opened my mouth in an attempt to speak and once again there were no words; nothing came out. And then out of nowhere, a single tear escaped my right eye and trickled warmly down the side of my face. Dylan paused as he looked at me with eyes that pierced my heart and he proceeded to gently kiss the tear on my cheek. He leaned in and lay his forehead up against mine and breathed a big sigh of relief.

"It's Ok. You don't have to say anything."

I reached up and gently felt his face to make sure that he was real and to let him know that I felt the same way.

"I should go in now," I said. "It's getting late."

"Yeah, I guess it is. But will I see you tomorrow?" he asked.

"Yes," you will see me tomorrow," I responded.

Chapter Thirty-Eight

The next day wasn't as awkward as I imagined it would be. As a matter of fact I felt no pressure at all. I did question myself as to whether or not I should have let myself become vulnerable and if I would live to regret it. But at that moment there were no doubts and there were no regrets. And I couldn't deny the fact that I felt free. I felt free enough to be myself around Dylan with no pretenses. And I hadn't felt so liberated since the day that Javier told me he loved me. I never thought that my heart would ever allow me to care for another man.

I began the day in the usual manner. Once I got to the site, both Dylan and Aaron were close by. Aaron was obviously aware that the relation between Dylan and me had changed somewhat in light of the gestures and smiles that Dylan and I shared that morning.

Aaron had been working with several organizers in the community for weeks now trying to develop new plans for the reconstruction of a new library. It hurt so bad to think of how the storm had destroyed almost the entire library and all the months of hard work that went into building it. Aaron took it the hardest.

We were in great need of building materials, supplies, and

funding if we were gonna' have any chance of erecting a new Library, at least by the New Year. And it was clear that we would have to make its foundation a tab bit stronger than the one that was destroyed.

Aaron was great at motivating people to give and to donate time and money to worthy causes. He was a natural politician. He believed that he could change the world one library and one school at a time. He almost became discouraged because there were no promising leads and the money trail had dried up...so everyone thought. But on this particular day and without any warning, a cashier's check for ten thousand dollars arrived at the orphanage with no name attached or no clue of where it came from. Everyone was ecstatic, especially Aaron. And right before it was time to break for lunch Aaron approached me. He waited until Dylan had gone inside before he came over.

"So is it serious?" Aaron came right out and asked.

"I don't know what it is right now. It's new," I responded.

"Well, I'm worried about you," he said. "You're vulnerable right now."

"Don't be. I'm fine," I replied.

"Have you asked yourself what do you really know about this guy? I mean he came out of nowhere and now he's everywhere. Don't you think you should give yourself some time until you find out more about him?" he questioned.

"No, I don't. Why are you acting like a jealous boyfriend? You act like you like me or something,"

"Maybe I do," Aaron got serious.

Well needless to say, that wasn't the response that I was looking for. Oh! Lord. I didn't see that coming. But maybe I should have paid more attention to him. I feel like I should have known.

"I know you care about me," I smoothed over quickly. "And I'm so lucky to have someone like you in my life who cares about my welfare," I responded sincerely.

He looked down to the ground for a moment…looked back up and said….

"Well if for any reason this doesn't work out for you…you can come to me. I'll always be here for you," he said. "I just want you to be happy."

"I am happy. Right now at this moment I am happy," I said as I placed his hands in my hands and softly kissed him on the lips. "Thank you."

We looked at one another for a second or two and wrapped our arms around each other. Somehow I knew that Aaron would always be in my life. After our embrace, I turned to see Dylan looking over at Aaron and me. I made sure that Aaron and I were still cool and then I walked over to where Dylan was standing.

"Is everything alright?" he asked.

"Yeah," I answered as I looked back at Aaron. "Everything is fine."

"Now that we know that you're alright – how about him; is he alright?" Dylan asked referring to Aaron.

"I believe he's fine," I answered

"I just had a great idea," he said with excitement. "Let's go get Fathiya and maybe go for a ride and get a bite to eat," he suggested.

"Can we just take her like that?" I questioned. "Don't we have to get special permission or something?" I asked.

"No, they trust me."

"Oh yea," I said mockingly. "Why does the orphanage trust you so much that they just allow you to take the children off the premises whenever you feel like it?"

"It's not like that. I guess I'm just a trust worthy guy like that?" he said with a smirk on his face.

"Okay, I guess I'm supposed to believe that, huh?" Like you have it like that huh?" I asked with a raised brow.

"Have it like that? Yeah, well I guess I do," he said.

"Mmmmm huh," I said suspiciously.

"No, I am responsible in that way," he said.

"Okay,"

"I can't help that I'm charming and charismatic," he gloated.

"Umm huh. You left out big headed," I smiled and he laughed.

"Oh I'm not charming?" he asked. "I'm charming and you know it," he said as he grabbed me and put his arm around me like he knew he could do that. Needless to say, he was right.

So we went inside and got Fathiya and was on our way. We had an amazing time. We laughed and joked the entire time. We stopped off at Jolly Rogers Theme Park and Restaurant where we experienced an awesome time.

Dylan picked up Fathiya and started to carry her up on his shoulders. She stayed up there for a great deal of the time and Fathiya enjoyed every moment of it. I thought it was special how Dylan handled her. He flipped her and tossed her into the air and she would laugh. And to hear her laugh for the first time was something I'll never forget. Her laughing caused me to laugh. It was definitely contagious and so I wanted her to continue to laugh as much as possible and of course I got much enjoyment out of it. And the moment was captured in my heart forever.

The staff at Jolly Rogers was very child-friendly. They had a play area where they supervised all the children so the adults could relax and enjoy some time together. And so Dylan and I sat and looked on as Fathiya had the time of her life. But then the smile on my face slowly disappeared as a horrible thought entered my mind.

"I hadn't thought about the fact that I will be leaving in five months. I'll have to say good-bye to her? I won't know how to do that," I expressed to Dylan.

"Then don't do it" Dylan took a serious tone. "You can always stay here,"

"I can't stay here. I have my brother and a very close friend that I need to see about.

"Yeah, I know. You're right," Dylan said

"I know you're not going home, are you?" I said.

"I visit home from time to time. But there is so much to be done here," he said.

"But what about your family and friends, don't you miss them?"

"I do. Yes, I do, but they understand that these people need me more," he explained.

I observed a look of apprehension on his face. I couldn't tell what he was thinking, but I had a good idea.

"You know he would understand if you ever decided to leave here and go back and make a real life for yourself," I said to him.

He looked at me, stunned at the words that had just come out of my mouth.

"Who will understand?" he knew but he asked me anyway.

"Kaleb," I answered. "He'll understand.

"You don't consider this a real life I see?" he became sensitive.

"Yeah, I do. I didn't mean it that way at all,"

I knew I had to watch my tone and the words that I used; trying to be careful about what I said next as I took his feelings into consideration.

"I just know that if it ever came a time when you wanted to leave, I know by what you've told me about him, that he would understand. How long has it been?" I asked caringly.

"Seven years," he answered.

"Do you have any idea how long you might be over here?"

"No," he said. The spirit of God will let me know when and if I should leave."

"I know that you've been in a lot of pain over what happened, but when and how are you going to be able to move pass the pain long enough to start living your life without guilt?" I asked.

"I'm working on it. It's not something that I can very easily do, at least not in my own strength. And I have sense enough to know that. And so I've spent many a nights praying for courage, strength, and the permission to forgive myself in hopes that Kaleb forgives me. And in my mind I know that everything happens for a reason. But I'd just wish that my mind would tell it to my heart.

"What possible reason could there be for a senseless death?" I asked, trying to understand .

"See that's just it. I'm just starting to realize that no death is senseless. The act may seem senseless, but there is always a purpose in everything. Although we may not know what the purpose is- there's a purpose none the less.

As horrible as his death was, it did cause me to change my life," he went on. "I was literally forced to take a good look at myself and the life I was living. It made me see that I was selfish and irresponsible. Kaleb was the responsible one. He was the voice of reason. And my callousness and negative influence is what caused his life to be cut short.

As a result something inside of me was awakened and I knew that his death had caused me to want to be a better person. So no, his death was not in vain and it was far from senseless because it made me care about others and it led me to you.

"And the spirit of God is what did all of that?" I asked. "How does that work?"

His spirit is everywhere," Dylan explained. "And he'll chip away at the walls and the shields that we put up in order to keep him out of our hearts. And eventually, if we let him, he will break through them. But he'll only do it if we want him to. He wants it to be something that we want and not something that he has forced upon us.

And yes, we will always experience pain and loss as a part of life. But as every life leaves this world a new one comes in like a flower that is born into a season of spring and departs quickly as winter approaches. But even in its departure, it will forever be connected to the soil of the land and will be reborn as it will bloom again in a new season of spring. Is any of this making sense to you at all?" he asked. "I know that it may sound crazy.

"No, it doesn't sound crazy," I responded.

Right then, a staff member brought Fathiya over to us just as we were finishing up with that conversation.

"Oh! my goodness. What happened?" I asked Fathyia in alarm as I observed her scrapped knee and dirt smudged shirt and shorts.

"Push me," she said with a somber look on her face."

"Somebody pushed you down?" I repeated sympathetically. "Well, I'm sure they didn't mean it," I said. "How about an ice cream? Would that make you feel better?" I asked.

"Un huh," she replied.

"Ok then, let's go and get you an ice cream," I said.

And so we all got up and went for ice cream. Nothing could really compare to the intensity and anticipation of that day besides the day in the park when Javier proposed to me. From that day on, Dylan, Fathiya, and I went out a couple of times a week for the next few months; if only for a drive or a walk. It was a magical time.

Jackson wrote me yet again and told me that he couldn't wait to see me. He said that he could tell by the letters that I wrote that I was different in my spirit. He said that he couldn't wait for my return and that he had a surprise for me when I got back. I couldn't imagine what it could be.

CHAPTER THIRTY-NINE

Two months had gone by and my feelings for Dylan and Fathiya were stronger than ever. I opened myself like a door to both of them and was unsure if I would ever be able to close it. We did everything together like real family's do. Like Javier, Ice, and me used to do. We had been to the Safari, taking in the wonderful sights and the beautiful animals. I had been to the Detroit Zoo once or twice in my life time but the animals in the zoo back home couldn't hold a candle to the animals in the Safari. There was a clear distinction between the enslaved animals in the zoo back home and those in the Safari that were able to roam more freely.

One evening after we had taken Fathiya back to the orphanage Dylan and I sat outside my residence and we talked. There were so many things that I didn't know about Dylan because he didn't really talk much about himself. I realized that we would probably never get to know everything about each other because it would take a life time. I had been waiting for him to invite me to his home but he never did. I didn't know what to make of it and I wasn't sure that I wanted to make anything of it. But I just couldn't resist.

"When will I get a chance to see that bachelor pad of yours?" I brought up casually.

"It's nowhere interesting. Nowhere I think you would wanna' be," he responded.

"Well, shouldn't you let me be the judge of where I wanna' be? You would be surprised at what I find interesting," I remarked.

"Well, I guess when I make it a little more presentable I will have to have you over,"

"I'm afraid I'm gonna' have to hold you to that," I said with a smile on my face.

Dylan nonchalantly changed the subject.

"What are you most looking forward to when you return home?"

"All I can think about is seeing my brother. That's all I ever think about. And I've had a lot of time to think since I've been here.

"I can imagine," said Dylan.

"You have any brothers or sisters?" I asked.

"I have an older sister," he responded.

'Oh," I said.

"I've been thinking about going back to school once I get home and settled. This thing with my brother has got me thinking about law school. I could become my brother's lawyer. I owe him that. He doesn't belong in that place no more than those animals belong caged up in that zoo. If I could trade his life for mine I would do it today.

"He really means a lot to you, huh?" Dylan questioned

"He means everything to me. He's all I have and I'm all he's got. That's just the way it's been.

"Well hopefully one day real soon you'll be able to fit me into that equation," he responded.

I heard him but I looked away when he said it and continued to speak on my brother.

"Yeah, he's a good kid. I know you'd like him. Who knows, maybe one day you'll get a chance to meet him. Stranger things have happened."

We continued to talk as he pulled me in close to him and I laid my head gently on his shoulder. Night fall was approaching but neither one of us wanted the evening to end.

It was four nights later when Dylan came to my house in the middle of the night. The knocks at the door were startling and seemed urgent. I quickly hurried to answer it. It was Dylan.

"I'm sorry to be here at this late hour but there's been an emergency back home," he said. "My mother has sent word for me to return as soon as possible."

I definitely saw his lips moving and I heard the words "have to return home as soon as possible", but I was deaf to everything else that he said after that. It all seemed so dream like.

"I will contact you as soon as I am able. I can't believe this is happening. I don't want to leave you," he went on.

"You have to do what you have to do," I told him.

"Will you kiss Fathiya for me?" he insisted. "And let her know that I will be back."

I hesitated before I answered.

"I will," I said.

"I love you," he blurted out.

It was the first time that he had actually said the words. He had said lots of things to me but not that. And although I believed I felt the same thing for him I could not bring myself to say it. I had a horrible feeling right in the very pit of my stomach. It was a feeling of dread that made me question if that would be the very last time that I would ever see him. I smiled a painful smile and nodded as we embraced for about seven seconds until I pulled away and wished him a safe trip. He stared into my eyes as he turned and went back out into the night. I closed the door behind him.

I held onto the door knob for a few seconds before I turned around and fell back against the door with one hand over my heart and the other hand over my mouth, trying to hold back my tears. Then I became angry. My efforts to try and turn my life around seemed to be in vain. I felt myself wanting to destroy something, anything. At this time I felt exhausted. I was tired of this life and all of the pain and the unhappiness that it had brought me. I thought about what Dylan said and how he believed that everything happened for a reason and with purpose. And for the first time in my life I fell to my knees and looked up to where heaven was suppose to be and softly cried out;

"If you can hear me, please tell me what I need to do? I'm so tired. Please tell me that you didn't bring me all this way just to do this to me again?

I don't understand."

I remained on my knees for the rest of the night trying to understand the purpose of living. I woke the next morning still on the floor from the night before hoping that last night was all just a dream. I even found myself waiting for Dylan to come by and pick me up to take me to the orphanage as he had done everyday for the past two months. But he didn't.

I took a duck bath and got dressed despite how I felt and walked over to the orphanage. I wasn't sure how long Dylan would be gone or if he was ever coming back. But in two short months I too, would be leaving. I would have to figure out a way to say good-bye to Fathiya. I wish I could have found a way out of that dilemma but I couldn't. I wished I could stay here with her but Ice needed me and I needed him. Or better yet, I wished I could take her home with me. But that wasn't an option.

I started to question the reason why I was even there. And then I began thinking about all the extraordinary things I had experienced. Whether I wanted to or not, I had to admit that coming here had changed my life. Jackson was right. It helped me to learn how to cope with and in life without engaging in artificial and temporary fixes. It was just sixteen months ago that I would have easily gone out to cop a fix if I ever felt that life was getting the best of me. And although my heart was aching, I wasn't sure if I could even think of a world without ever coming to know Dylan and Fathiya. I knew that I could never return to my old life and my old ways because I had a chance to see that there was so much more to life.

During my last month in Africa I spent some time with Aaron, Ethan, and Marcia. We all talked about our experiences in Africa and agreed that it greatly impacted all of our lives and wondered what it would be like going back to the states after this type of experience.

Fathiya would ask constantly ask about Dylan. She reminded me of Ice and how he would question me about Lola and would never want me to leave him to go to the store or anywhere because he was afraid that I wouldn't come back. I reassured her the best way that I could that he would be back. I tried to convince her and I tried to convince myself of it.

There were three mail deliveries that month and not one letter came from Dylan. Ice wrote me and spoke about how exited he was that I would be coming home in less than a month's time. I had written Bailey several times in the last few months. I believe I sent both Ice and Bailey one letter for every month that I was away. Ice wrote me back for every letter that I sent him. But I'd only heard from Bailey twice. But I knew that she was never good at expressing herself.

Now it was less than a week before I would be boarding a plane back to Detroit. I had mixed feeling about it. On one hand I was happy because I did miss everyone, Uncle Blaze, Ice, Bailey, and Jackson. But on the other hand I would be leaving an entire experience behind and people that I've grown close to.

Starting a new life once I got home would probably prove not to be complicated. I was able to save quite a bit of the money while I was away since I was renting my house out. I thought about finding me a small apartment when I got back because Ice was away and I would be living alone now and would no longer needed a big house anymore. But I wanted to be back in my home, Ices' home, the home that we shared together. The tenant was already aware of the date and time that I would be back next week and agreed to be gone when I got there.

Those last few days were harder than I ever imagined they would be. Every night I stared at the photo of Dylan, Fathiya, and myself. I had one picture of Fathiya that I was particularly found of. There was a dress that I had purchased for her some months back from a dress maker in the city. The dress was too big for Fathiya and so I had to have it taken in. It was a very pretty dress that reminded me of autumn in Detroit.

The dress was streamed with oranges, browns, and golds; beaming with sunlight and the anticipation of the birth of new things. I placed her hair into two half corn rowed afro puffs. I was the only one that she would allow to do her hair. I didn't really spend money on much of anything. But when I did spend it, I spent it mostly on Fathiya and some of the other orphans.

I loved buying them things, especially jewelry. I loved to buy them hair accessories and footwear too. I loved to buy them whatever I felt would put a smile on their faces and make them feel like the princesses they are.

Fathiya was sweet as cotton candy. She had a smile that twinkled as bright as the brightest star, with a glow that radiated from her chocolate kissed skin that rendered anyone that looked upon her beauty helpless and she would win their hearts.

Her tongue was always peeping through the space that was left between her bottom row teeth as she waited for the missing teeth to be replaced by her second set that would grow in any time now. With only a few days left, I knew that it was time for me to have the conversation with her that I had been dreading ever since I laid eyes on her.

Fathiya, like most of the children of Nairobi had seen and experienced enough misfortune and calamity in their lives to last them ten life times. It was at the age of two that she lost her nine year old sister to sleeping sickness; a disease whose host is usually a domestic animal and whose symptoms are characterized by fever, lethargy, and anemia which borders on Jaundice; attacking the liver and the spleen.

Three years ago, Fathiya's Mother and Father took Fathiya and her baby sister and brother to a nearby church where they thought they would be safe from all those who disputed the up and coming election at that time and were intimidating the citizens who lived in the surrounding villages.

But while they were there, angry supporters of their rival candidate set fire to the church where they sought refuge, burning it to the ground; killing men, women, and children. Those who escaped the fire were hunted down like dogs, captured and hacked to death. Fathiya's misfortune came as she witnessed the slaughter of her family while she hid among the dead bodies. She was the only one in that village to survive the attack.

My heart just ached when Dylan told me her story. How horrible for a child to have witnessed such a thing. Like me, Fathiya was use to life's disappointments and almost expected them to happen and to be a permanent fixture in her life.

Two days before I was scheduled to leave I placed the picture of Dylan, Fathiya, and me into my backpack. I would be leaving for America the next day. Needless to say, I slept late that day and I still hadn't told Fathiya yet. I still hadn't found the words or the nerve. I went over to the orphanage around noon. Right after lunch Fathiya and I played lots of Patty Cake. I read Fathiya and some of the other children a story, like I did on most days. Except now we have story time inside the new library instead of outside. We went over the alphabet and numbers. Most of the children knew pretty good English.

At the end of our story and game time the other children went off to play independently and so it was now or never. I reached for her hand.

"What beautiful hands you have," I said with a smile as I looked into her dreamy eyes as she smiled a picturesque smile. "You remember how I always speak of my home back in America?" I asked her.

"Yes," she answered.

"And you remember how we've talked about me having to go back to America one day?" I asked.

"Yes," she nodded.

"Well…It's time for me to go back to America. I'm gonna have to be leaving for America tomorrow afternoon to check on some people that I left behind; people that I had to leave in order to be able to come over here and meet you. Do you understand?" I asked.

"Will you be back?" she asked with her head down.

I looked in her eyes and meant everything that I was about to say.

"Yes, I will be back to see about you, Okay?" "Do you believe me?" I asked her.

"When will you be back?" she asked.

"I'm not really sure about that. But I'll write you and I'll send you some of your favorite things," I assured her.

"From America?" she asked.

"Yes, from America," I replied. And hey, look what I have," I said as I pulled from my back pack the picture of the Fathiya, Dylan, and me. "Do you think you could hold on to this and take care of it for me until I am able to come back and get it?" I asked her.

With water filled eyes she nodded her head yes.

"Come give me a big hug," I said as we wrapped our arms around each other tightly.

"Okay now," I said as I slowly pulled away from her. "You make sure you do your studies everyday," I said. "And I'll see you later Okay."

I got up, turned around, and began to walk off. I turned back to wave one last time. Fathiya just stood there holding Teddy in one hand and the picture in the other. I turned and began to walk faster and faster.

"Unique, wait up," Aaron called out as he ran to catch up to me.

When he finally caught up to me he looked over to see the tears streaming down my face. He wrapped his arm around me and began to rub my shoulder.

"You've grown to love her haven't you?"

With both my hands I cupped my mouth and he knew what the answer to that question was. Aaron and I hung out with Ethan and Marcia one last time before we went state side the next day. We vowed to always write one another, visit, remain close, and never forget the experience that brought us all together to form a life time friendship.

CHAPTER FORTY

The flight back home was dismal. Yeah, sure, I couldn't wait to take a hot bubble bath in my own tub, or buy a package of Swedish Fish and a bag of Ranch Flavored Doritos. I couldn't wait to spend time with my girl Bailey and to see Jackson again. I couldn't wait to get a couple of tight tracks laid in my head, and get me a fresh pedi and manicure. I couldn't wait. I had to catch up on all the movies and T.V. shows that played for the last eighteen months. But most of all, I couldn't wait to wrap my arms around Ice. There had been so many times that I have traced his face in my mind. Oh! I had so much to tell him.

Aaron and I sat almost in the same exact seats on the plane going back as we did when were coming over. It was crazy. All I could do was reflect on everything that had taken place in the last eighteen months. As my mind sped up I realized I had a lot to recapture and a great deal to absorb I thought to myself as I stared out of the window during take off as the plane began to rise up above clouds that resembled mounds of hand churned vanilla bean ice cream that sat atop the cones that Dylan, Fathiya, and I shared at the park.

I smiled as I reminisced about how Fathiya managed to get ice cream on her nose and chin as she tunneled her way down into the come with her tongue. I smiled as I committed to memory the moments where we played tag or hide and seek and Dylan would always win. I wondered what Dylan and Fathiya were doing at that very precise moment and if they were thinking of me in the same manner as I thought of them. My heart throbbed a familiar twinge that extended clear down to the marrow in my bones.

The haze was thick as we stepped off the plane on that September day when we landed back on US soil. I noticed that I couldn't help but pay attention to the details that were all around me. I witnessed the families that were reuniting in the airport – the hugs and joyous smiles in particular. I paid specific attention to every little girl I saw that was around Fathiya's age, especially the ones who were snag-a-tooth. I saw white folks in a totally different light. My heart towards them had softened. I realized that they weren't all out to oppress me, depress me, and suppress me.

Their blue eyes were no longer a representation of the hell that was home for a lot of blacks in this society. But now when I think of blue eyes I'll think of oceans and blue skies. I'll think of sunny days and new beginnings. I'll think of bon fires, sandy brown hair, and a cleft chin. I'll think of Dylan.

There were conversations going on all around and about me but I could still hear someone calling me.

"Unique," I heard a muffled sound bringing me back from my thoughts. "You want me to get your bag or are you ok with it?" Aaron asked.

For some reason I was searching for Dylan's face in the crowd and so I was unable to respond to Aaron's question right away.

"Unique," Aarons' voice became stronger. "Look it's Mr. Jackson," he said as he attempted to retrieve my bags from the conveyor belt.

Aaron's words finally registered and my eyes began to focus.

"Well, if you're not a sight for sore eyes," Jackson said as he walked straight towards me. "All of you," he said, "All of you look absolutely wonderful. Come here," he said to everyone from The House Of Job . "Let me look at you. I guess you're too big for a hug huh?" he asked.

I smiled at him and moved in for my hug. It was one of the best hugs that I'd ever received.

"Yep," Jackson said. "You've got the bug. I can see the rivers of Nairobi flowing through those eyes. How you doin' little sista?"
"I'm great now that I see you," I flattered him.

We hugged one last time before we proceeded to go home.

The drive from the airport was peculiar. The streets and the old neighborhood were exactly as I had left them. And out of nowhere I experienced a feeling of separation anxiety that subdued me; a feeling of disconnection. I became uneasy. I felt like I had consumed an entire bowl of cooking grease that lay in the pit of my stomach as I became nauseated.

As we drove past Dudley Street I felt like something prickly had run up my back as I caught a glimpse of the hotel. I closed my eyes and took a deep breath as I revisited thoughts on the things that went on in those rooms. It seemed like such a very long time ago. But it had been just eighteen short months ago that my life resembled something so dark and so ugly that I couldn't recognize myself in it. And so I chose to turn my head and look in another direction, trying to focus on a more positive scenery.

It was within minutes that we arrived at the House of Job. There was quite a welcoming party that awaited our arrival. There was a great big welcome home sign hanging outside of the missionary. Everyone exited the van and removed their bags before going inside. Once we were inside there were many people there to celebrate our return. All the volunteers had family and friends there waiting for them. Most of the faces I didn't recognize but was still happy to see them. Truly I was.

I looked out into the crowd and all of a sudden my heart felt warm as my eyes scaled the room and landed on Bailey. We screamed and hollered and jumped up and down as we ran into each other's embrace. Jackson just stood there and looked on with anticipation and this huge smile on his face as everyone exchanged hugs and kisses. And then I saw Jackson's eyes gaze across the room mysteriously. I thought to myself, "what is he looking at?" as I tried to follow his eyes with mine.

And then for one split second I thought I saw someone who remotely resembled Lola. Oh my God! It was Lola.

"What the..?" I asked myself as Lola stood there and watched me watching her. She looked at me as if she was waiting for some sort of reaction from me as I stood there in shock, completely still until Jackson realized how awkward the moment was for the both of us and stepped in.

"Well," Jackson started. "Aren't you two gonna' say anything?" he asked me.

I didn't know what to say or how to respond or even if I was supposed to. I only wanted to know why. "Why was she here? And what did she want from me?" Because whenever Lola came around she always wanted or needed something from me; she was always a taker and never a giver. But at this moment in my life I didn't have anything to give her and I refused to allow myself to live through anymore of her drama. My heart just wouldn't be able to bear it.

"Let me just take your bags upstairs. You'll be staying in the room you stayed in before you left," Jackson said to me. "Your tenant asked for a few more days. So you'll be moving back home on Monday.

I was still in a fog and my mind went completely blank.

"There's a huge welcome back celebration going on in the dining hall," Jackson said. "Go on in and relax and enjoy yourself. I'll see you both there in a few minutes," he stated as he looked at both Lola and me.

So Bailey, Lola, and me, walked down and around the corner to the dining hall. I walked ahead of the two of them and found some empty seats and sat down. Lola and Bailey followed. It was strange because I hadn't seen Lola in four years. And a lot had happened in that time.

I had actually thought about what this day would be like. I think it is only natural for a child to go over in their mind what they might say or do if they ever got the chance to confront the parent that abandoned them, and how the conversation might possibly go. I imagined her showing up one day out of nowhere. And I always wondered what she would say to me and Ice. I would always dream of how happy a day that would be.

Well, that day had finally come and it was nothing like I had imagined. I didn't feel happy. Maybe it had something to do with the fact that when she left us I was just a child but now I am a woman. And as children, my brother and I have had to endure a number of life and death situations while we tried to come to terms with the reality that everything that happened to us was all because of her.

I never realized up until now how much contempt I had for my Mother. I didn't want to own it but it seemed to have owned me. I knew that her spirit was weak and that she seemed not to be able to help who she was, at least that's what I kept tellin' myself all of these years because I was a child who desperately needed to be wanted by her mother. And it was for that reason that I did not hate her.

But spending time with Dylan and Fathiya changed something in me. My time with them reminded me that I had never really known what it was like to be a child because I never had the opportunity to be one. I thought of all the other little girls and boys that were just like Ice, Fathiya, and me and who had to live lives that looked like ours.

I knew in my heart that even if I never saw Dylan again I believe that he saw something in me right from the very start just as Javier had. He knew that I had come to Africa for answers. He knew that I was looking for a purpose in life; my purpose, because I didn't know who I was or what to do with my existence. I was searching for something that would give me a reason to live; something that would cause me to feel significant because I was broken.

Growing up I was told by most of my teachers that I possessed a gift, a gift of learning. And while most kids had to work hard at it, it was something that came natural to me and I liked it. But I know now that it really doesn't matter what other people see in you if you can't see it in yourself.

And after laying eyes on Lola again after all this time I suddenly decided for sure that I did want that Law Degree and I was clear on what I wanted to do with it. I wanted to dedicate my life to helping runaways and displaced juveniles like I once was. I wanted to start programs and help pass laws that would keep siblings in those types of situations together instead of apart if for any reason the courts had to remove them from their homes. I wanted to do whatever I could to help those children feel significant because they mattered too. And so first thing Monday morning I knew that I would be registering in somebody's college for the next semester.

"So how have you been?" Lola's voice interrupted my thoughts.

"Huh?" I asked.

"How have you been? You've become quite a young lady," she said. "You look good."

"So do you," I responded with small talk.

"I've been clean for two months now," she said.

"Two months?" I questioned. "Wow, good for you," I replied.

I thought to myself how ironic it was that it was just two months ago when I said good-bye to Dylan.

"So what finally made you decide to get clean?" I asked.

"Well, that's a long story. But to make it short I was in Pop-Eyes on twenty-third street one evening and Jackson came in I guess to place an order. He saw me there and told me he had something he wanted to show me. I thought he was gonna' start preachin' to me like he always did and so I tried to brush him off and decided I would get something to eat later and I turned to leave," she went on to replay the events like it was yesterday and I found myself feeling like I was right there with her and Jackson when it all went down.

"Hey Lola," Jackson called out to me as I got near the door, Lola described.

"I would um, stop and talk to you but I forgot uh, I have to be somewhere in about fifteen minutes. But it was great seeing you anyway," I said to him.

"This won't take but a minute," Jackson replied as he jumped in front of me. "Just sit down," he said with a little force; "just for a minute. Please."

So we sat down in one of the booths.

"Uh, excuse me. Do you still want that order Miss," the cashier called out to me. You can't sit in here without ordering sumpthin'," she stated.

"Ok, yeah," Jackson responded. She still wants that order and I'll have the same thing that she's having, he said.

"Jackson opened his jacket, reached inside it and pulled from his pocket all the letters that you had written him. He was just carrying them around hoping for the opportunity to see me one day so that he could show them to me. The thought of that just blew me away. So I sat there and read one or two letters and looked at every picture that you sent. They were beautiful.

It was hard for me to believe that a child of mine was actually in Africa. Then Jackson began to tell me everything. He told me about Ice and how he had been visiting him. I mean I did know that he was locked up. I believe I heard something about it a while ago but I couldn't recall the details.

It really didn't surprise me when I heard Ice was locked up. I knew that he would probably end up in jail or dead anyway considering that's what usually happens to most of the guys where we come from," Lola went on.

"No, that's not just what happens," I jumped in. Ice is a good kid. He always has been but you wouldn't know anything about that. He would've never ended up in that place if it hadn't of been for me. I'm the reason he's there. He sacrificed his life for mine because he loved me and because he was afraid that I would end up like you. You don't know anything about that kind of love and you don't know anything about him. And so unless you have something worthwhile and positive to say about my brother, I would appreciate if you kept his name out of your mouth.

Jackson came over right in time to calm the storm that was building between Lola and me.

"Look," I continued. "I'm happy for you and the fact that you're clean now. And I hope everything works out for you. But I can't look at you right now" I said as I got up and walked away. Bailey quickly got up and left with me.

"Unique," Jackson called out to me. "Come on back here and sit down. You haven't even eaten yet.

"Thanks Jackson." I called back to him. "I'm not hungry," I said with the quickness. "But I'll see you later," I

CHAPTER FORTY-ONE

Bailey and I found our way upstairs to my room. As soon as we walked in I took a quick glance and my heart smiled when I saw the cross that hung over the bed, the mirror that hung over the bureau, and the spherical rug that covered one fourth of the floor. I couldn't wait to take a warm shower. Bailey sat on the bed while I began to unpack.

"Girl, I can't tell you how good it is to see you. You look so well put together. I've never seen you like this before. Africa really changed you huh?" Bailey asked.

"Yeah," I had to agree. It has. But I don't want to talk about that right now. I want to hear all about what's been going on with you. I see something different about you too. I hear you have a job now," I inquired in disbelief. "How did that happen?" I said in a sarcastically, joking manner.

"Yeah, can you really believe that? Jackson hooked me up," Bailey answered.

"I see Jackson was real busy while I was away," I stated referring to Lola.

"Yeah, he got me a gig working at this nursing home," she smiled as she looked down at the bed as she explained.

"A nursing home Bailey, are you kidding me?" I asked.

"I kid you not. I've already quit about three times. But seriously speaking, it feels good to get a pay check, you known. And it's legit. I'm renting a room over at the Winbush and so I need that money every week just so I can pay the rent," she explained. "I know that I could get that money a number of other ways, but I feel better about myself getting' it this way. It's not like I make a whole lot but I'm making it."

"Girl, you're staying at the Winbush? That is crazy. Oh my God Bailey. Oh – my - God."

"I know," she said as we both became emotional and hugged for the umpteenth time.

"It's just a studio apartment. It's not a big deal," she added.

"What? It's twenty steps up from the Dudley. Don't you dare downplay that. This is major."

Bailey began to nod her head in agreement.

"Right, right," she said.

"You damn straight I'm right," I confirmed. I continued to unpack when I noticed a distant look that came over Bailey's face and all of a sudden she was quiet.

"Hello," I said to get her attention.

"Huh?" she asked.

"What you freezin' up on me now for?" I asked.

"No, no. I was just thinking about something. 'That's all."

"Thinkin' about what?' I asked.

"Well, you know how Jackson is a terrific person right?" Bailey asked suspiciously.

"Yeah, I know. He's great." I said.

"Ok, when I first met him it was really strange because I wasn't use to anybody except for you who really had a legitimate concern for me. You know what I mean?"

"Yeah, I think I do," I responded. "I went through that with him too, but I think it was easier for me to accept his help because he knew my family. I mean he knew both my parents and he helped me to put a lot of things in perspective, so I really do know how you feel about not being used to someone who legitimately cares," I explained.

Again Bailey became quiet. And it really wasn't a good kind of quiet. I could see that she had something on her mind and she was trying to lead up to it. And I admit that I was almost afraid to find out what it was.

"I was just so appreciating the fact that Jackson was taking time out to be nice to me and he seemed to really care about me. He just made me feel like things could really be different for me. And so I......," she started.

"You what?" I asked curiously but she didn't answer. "You what?" I asked again as I stopped unpacking and sat down and gave Bailey my full undivided attention. "What did you do?" I asked

"Well, I kinda came on to him," she said.

"You what?" I asked again as if I didn't hear her the first time.

"He was just so nice to me. I know it was stupid. But he would come around to see me, you know, to see if I was okay. And we'd begin talking about things, you and Africa and he would tell me how my life could change if I really wanted it to and how he would help me and everything. And finally, I started to believe it.

Jackson took me over to the rehab center where I stayed for three weeks. Uni, he was so attentive. He helped me through all of it. And then when I got out of rehab, that's when he helped me find this job at the Nursing Home. He even helped me with the down payment to get into the Winbush. No man ever did those type of things for me before. He treated me like I was somebody, you know.

So, one night after going to this service they had at The House Of Job, Jackson drove me back to the Winbush. I was having trouble setting up this new DVD player that I had just brought and Jackson said that he would take a look at it. So he came up to my apartment. And while he was trying to fix the DVD, he had his back turned, and I don't know what happened. Before I knew it, I got undressed," she described.

"Bailey you didn't," I somberly stated.

"I did," she said. "Unique," the look in that man's eyes when he turned around; I'll never forget it. I never had a man reject me before. It was just so awkward. He looked at me in sheer shock and then he told me to put my clothes back on.

"Everything has value," he said to me, "including you. You are a treasure. But you have to start treating yourself as such. Do you understand?" he asked.

I stood there in shame and shook my head yes. I was so humiliated.

"We all make mistakes. Mistakes are made so that we can learn from them and move on," he said. So, as far as I'm concerned this never happened and so we can move on okay.

"Okay," I said.

"Alright then. Your DVD player seems to be working fine now, "he switched the subject. "Give me a call if you have any problem with it. I'll see you tomorrow," he said as he was leaving.

I was so embarrassed. I couldn't say anything. And after he left, I felt like crap. Out of all the times I've taken my clothes off in front of a man, it was the first time that I'd ever really felt naked. I didn't know how I would be able to face him after that.

But the next time we saw each other he treated me the same as he always did. I knew that he saw that I was acting differently and he didn't want me to feel bad about what I had done. So he pulled me to the side and told me that I should always hold my head up even when it was hard to. And that I had to learn how to let things go and leave them in the past. He told me that I would always be a rose. And then he hugged me. The very next day I went out to find the CD, with that song that Aretha Franklin sings about being a rose. I played that song for an entire week. And then everything was back to normal.

"And so everybody's straight now?" I asked.

"Yeah. "It's as if it never happened," Bailey said.

"Well, that's all that really matters," I responded.

"So what's up with your Mom and Jackson?" Bailey asked. "It really tripped me out when I first saw those two together. I mean it's really obvious that Jackson feels strongly about her. But I wonder if they are a couple or is he just helping her like he helped us?"

"You askin' me?" I asked. "I should be askin' you that very same question. I just got here. I don't know what's going on. I just hope that Jackson knows what he is getting into.

"Look, if he helped you and he helped me," Bailey started, "then you have to believe that he can help your mom too. He already has. Look at her. I thought you would be happy that she was back in your life and that she's clean."

"I did too. But the truth is I don't know how I feel about her right now. I'm happy that she's clean. Don't get me wrong. But so much time has passed. I'm different now and she seems to be different. We're practically strangers. I don't know who she is. And I just have a bad feeling that she's just gonna' end up hurting Jackson. Something tells me that's what she's gonna' do.

"Well maybe not," Bailey responded as she tried to change my mind. I feel what you're saying though. But all you can do is just give her a chance and hope for the best. Don't trip on it. Everything is cool. Jackson is a big boy. He can take care of himself, believe me. So let's not talk about that anymore. Let's finish talkin' about Africa," she suggested. "I want you to tell me everything about it. You were over there for a year and a half and you didn't meet anybody. There wasn't one strong African King over there that caught your eye?"

"No," I responded hesitantly.

"What? Girl you were swimming in a sea of never ending hunks of glistening chocolate and you mean to tell me you didn't see anything over there that you wanted to taste? I would've been swinging from all types of Mandingo African vines," she said.

"Yeah, I know that's right. That's cuz you nasty," I said as we both began to laugh.

"Well whatever. Anyway, what are you planning on doing tonight?" Bailey asked. They gotta' new spot over there next to the Radison. They say it's hot. You wanna' go check it out?" she asked.

"I don't know. I kinda feel like stayin' in tonight," I said. "You know, catch up on some zzzz's."

"Girl, if you don't stop playing wit' me. What you domesticated now?" Baily reacted.

"Noooo, it's not that. I just……," I tried to explain.

"You just nothin'. We are going out. You ain't been home in over a year. Ok. We're going out and that's it.

"Alright," have it your way. "Give me about an hour and I'll meet you over there," I said.

"Alright now. That's all I wanted to hear," she responded.

CHAPTER FORTY-TWO

It was two hours later when I met Bailey over at the club. It took all of twenty minutes before I began to feel out of place. So to take the edge off I ordered a wine spritzer.

"I didn't know that you still drank. I thought you gave all that up?" Bailey asked.

"I have an occasional glass of wine. Drinking was never really a problem for me. Neither were the drugs. I used them both to help me to conceal what was really wrong in my life," I responded.

"Well I'm happy for you girl. I'm glad that you finally figured it all out. I'm right behind you too. I'm getting there. Slowly but surely I'm getting' there. My counselor suggested to me not to ever drink again. She says that drinkin' would trigger and prompt me to want to do all sorts of destructive things," Bailey relayed.

"Yeah well, everybody's different. And everything is not for everybody. And what works for me may not work for you. If it makes you uncomfortable that I'm drinking then I won't because I don't have to" I assured her.

"Oh no," she said. "I'm cool. It doesn't bother me" And with that we both smiled; she with her sparkling seltzer and me with my spritzer as we tapped the rims of our glasses together with a toast.

"To us. Can't nobody turn us around," Bailey toasted.
"To us," I confirmed.

That night Bailey and I were out until about five in the morning discussing our alter egos and the lives that they lead and why. I was just so grateful for having Bailey in my life and to know that we were growing together instead of apart. I really had a feeling that we were gonna' be alright.

We talked about everything from losing weight to our dream occupations. And never once did I mention Dylan or Fathiya, not once. I could never remember a time when Bailey and I both were sober at the same time and without drama in our lives. And it felt good.

"Look at us. Look at you Uni. Look at your life. Everything is just comin' around full circle for you. You know I often think about my mom and the relationship that I wished we coulda' had. She never had a co-dependant problem or anything like that. Maybe if she did, I would've understood her better. But her problem was always men. They were always her drug of choice. She always scraped the bottom of the barrel when it came to her men; always bringing home the ones that nobody else wanted because that's all she thought she was good enough to have. It came natural to her to sacrifice me and my brothers in the process. But you have a chance Uni; a real chance at having a relationship with your mom," Bailey said.

"What are you saying?" I responded.

"I'm saying that I know you're relationship with your mom is not perfect by a long shot. And she has definitely done some pretty bad things. But it's just the fact that she's willing to be right here up in your face, right now; I'm just saying," she finished.

"Everything has always been on her terms, forever. I'm not even sure if I want her in my life. It was always for Ice. He missed her most. But he's not here now is he. Once upon a time I did need her desperately in my life. But I don't need her anymore."

Bailey didn't want our night to end on a sour note so she kindly got off of the subject of Lola.

"Well, everything will happen when and if it is supposed to. We are not going to end this evening on a sad note. We're supposed to be celebrating.

"Okay, well I'm good. Come on let's get out of here," I said.

As we were leaving, we ran into a guy who obviously knew our alter egos.

"Running any specials today? How's about two for one?" he called out to Bailey and me.

"Excuse me, Bailey questioned. What the hell is a two for one?"

"You know what it is," he sarcastically responded.

"Come on," I said to Bailey. "He's not even worth it."

"You jackass," Bailey shouted. "I got your two for one bitch," she hollered as I pulled her out the door.

"Come on. We are having a great time. We are not gonna' let him ruin it." I told her.

"I guess people ain't goin' never let us forget are they?" Bailey questioned.

"Maybe not," I answered back.

First thing Monday morning I took myself down to the
community college and registered at the admissions office as a full-
time student. I had just made the deadline for registration. Classes
would begin in one week. I was told by the admissions office that I
qualified for their work study program and would be given a part-
time job in the mail room. I knew that I would not be able to pay all
of my bills with the hours that I would be getting through the work
study program and so I picked up a few extra hours as a billing clerk
to supplement my income. That was the worst job ever.

I was glad to be back in my own house. In a month's time, I
managed to register for college and land me two jobs. And now
there was still one more thing that I had yet to do. I had to go see
about my brother. So I made my way up to DMSP, The Detroit
Michigan's State Penitentiary, to see Ice. I wondered in what state
I would find him. From the letters that I had received from him, it
seemed that he was in very good spirits. In the letters that he wrote
me, he never once complained about anything. But I needed to see
him for myself. I needed to look him in the eyes and talk to him to
make sure he was okay.

When I first arrived at the facility, the guards buzzed me through
some serious metal gates and asked me for proof of identification. I
was given a small locker to put all of my personable belongings in
because I wasn't allowed to carry anything into the waiting area. I
wasn't even allowed to keep my pocket book with me. They made
me put my pocket book into a locker that I had to put a dollar
twenty-five in.

Then I was taken into a small room and thoroughly frisked by
one of the female correctional officers. I was so humiliated when
she asked me to strip all the way down to my underwear. And after
I was violated I was then asked to get dressed and have a seat in the
waiting room.

I waited there for about an hour and a half before he came

out. When I first laid eyes on him it was obvious that he had been spending a lot of time pumping iron. He was big all over. And when he walked his arms swung outward, away from his body. His neck was an inch or two thicker, his chest sat out noticeably and the size of his biceps were just ridiculous. He started blushing as he came towards me.

"Oh my God," I said as I wrapped my arms around all of that muscle. "Look at my little brother, Oh my God, I repeated. "Look at you. I don't care how big you get you'll still always be my little brother. Wow, you look good," I said. "Real good."

"So do you," he replied with a great big cheese smile on his face. "You look a lot different from the last time I saw you," he said as we sat down.

"I don't know if that's a good thing or a bad thing," I said.

"Oh! it's most definitely a good thing," he assured me. "Your complexion, your hair, everything about you is good."

"Well I'm glad that you approve.

"I do," he said. "So how was your flight coming back over, different I bet?

"Yea, it was different then when I went over. But coming and going, they were both good.

"So how are you? I mean, you're holdin' up pretty good huh?"

"Oh! Yea. You know that," he responded.

"Yeah, I know. But I just needed to come see for myself," I said.

"See what?" Ice asked.

"See that you were really alright," I said.

"Shoood, I learned from the strongest person I know that you're never suppose to let your situation get the best you. And no matter how many times you fall down, the important thing is that you always get back up. You taught me that. I'm not goin' say that I don't have an occasional bad day, because I do. But then I read one of the letters you wrote me and I know that everything is well with my soul," he said.

My visit with Ice was more than I even expected. He had grown into such a fine young man with a mind that those bars could never imprison. But after about an hour, the guard came over and told us that it was time to end the visit. I couldn't bring myself to mention Lola to him until I got to the bottom of it. I didn't know how he would react. And I didn't want him to get his hopes up until I knew what her motives were.

In the last few minutes of our visit we embraced and we almost didn't want to let one another go. But right before I left, Ice candidly said to me;

"May God continue to bless you and keep you." he said.
"You didn't go and get religious on me now did you?" I asked.
"I wouldn't say all of that," he responded. I'm just sayin' that we need to recognize is all."
"Yes we do," I agreed.

I looked at Ice that day and realized that in a lot of ways he was so much smarter than I ever was.

"God willing, I'll see you soon," he said.
"God willing," I repeated back.

CHAPTER FORTY-THREE

Several weeks had gone by and I was well into the semester at school. I enjoyed my classes but still found it hard to believe at times that I was really a college student. Two years ago I would've never thought that college would have been in my future. I started my work study job in the mail room and I began tutoring two days out of the week, in addition to my billing job.

My schedule was full and I barely had any time to breathe. But I had to admit that it was very fulfilling at the same time, especially the tutoring. I tutored a GED preparatory class for people eighteen years and up. The youngest person in my class was eighteen and the oldest was sixty nine. I just thought that was so cool to want to better yourself no matter what your age.

Getting reacquainted with the classroom was stimulating and working inside a mailroom couldn't compare to building a library, but it was satisfying. I remembered the drilling, pounding of nails, pushing wheel barrels, lifting and merging the countless two by fours I had become accustomed to while in Africa.

In would remember Ms. Malone, my tenth, eleventh, and twelfth grade math teacher who was often on my mind. I often wondered if she had any idea how much she had impacted my life and I'm sure, the lives of others she had taught. I could never forget her. It was on my mind to visit her as soon as possible.

At a little pass three o'clock on a Friday afternoon, about two weeks later. One of my classes had been canceled for the afternoon and so I thought it would be the perfect time to visit Ms. Malone. I knew that school let out at three fifteen sharp and I had just arrived in time for school dismissal. As I approached the steps of the school building the bell rang.

I waited for all the children to exit and then I went into the building, passed the office, and went straight up to room two hundred and seven. And sure enough, there she was giving one of her famous speeches to someone, no doubt, that she saw great potential in. The great thing about Ms. Malone is that she had a tendency to see something in all of her students. I'm sure that there were different degrees of that something, depending on the individual student, but there is something just the same.

I stood outside of her door and eaves dropped for a minute with a smile on my face as I listened to the speech that I knew all too well, to the point where I had it memorized word for word. And when the meeting was over and the student had gone home I softly tapped on the door and walked in.

"Ms. Malone," I said. "Hi."

She stared in awe at me for about two seconds, put her pen down and stood up and walked towards me.

"Well, Miss Jefferson, what an end to a perfect day. What a lovely surprise," she said as we walked towards one another with arms open wide. "I see life is treating you with a bit more respect," she said in that special way that she says things.

"Respect that I had to start demanding for myself," I responded in a way that showed her that life had taught me some lessons.

"There you go," she said. "You're finally getting it like I knew one day you would. So tell me about your travels. I was told that you were involved in a peace corps operation in our Mother land."

"Yes, I did an eighteen month tour with The House Of Job," I replied.

"What an eye opener that must have been," she said. I want to hear all about it."

"Well, the experience itself gave me an overall sense of humanity in discovering that we are all in some sort of a struggle; some worse than others.

"My, my," she said.

"It had so much of an impact on me that it caused me to want to go back to school. So, I'm enrolled at Community College right now. Being in Africa helped me to, in a lot of ways, find my passion. So when I finish at Community, most likely I'll be enrolling in a four year University; hopefully with a major in Law and a minor in Psychology.

"Look at you, look at you," she said with a look and a smile of approval. "There ain't no stopping her now. So your visit to Africa was a life changing experience for you?" she asked while already knowing the answer.

"In so many ways I can't tell it all," I responded. "I met some of the most wonderful people there; some will be in my life forever I know, and some will just remain in my heart. But the point is that the person that went over there is not the same person that came back. She may not be completely whole, as she hopes one day she will be, but she definitely isn't completely broken like she once was," I spoke of myself in the third person.

"And it shows Miss Jefferson," Ms. Malone confirmed for me. My soul rejoices at just the thought of you in all of your brilliance, knowing that you have come into your own. And in knowing that…all things are possible. Life is your foot stool. You stand on top of it and never let it find its way atop of you," she said with so much feeling and so much purpose and intent just as she always did.

"I just wanted to come by to let you know that I'm alright and to say thank you. Thank you for taking the time out to really teach me, and for seeing something in me that I didn't see in myself. I want you to know that I carried your teachings, your words of encouragement and love with me over to Africa. Needless to say, both our eyes were filled with tears.

"Are you trying to make me cry girl? Because I just put this mascara on," she said as we both smiled and hugged. Well it looks like you've arrived and I'm so happy for you. If anyone deserves the very best that life has to offer, it's you. And I'm so glad that you decided to come by here today. I hope this won't be your last visit. You know, standing here before me you remind me of why it is I get up every day to come in here and do what I do. Thank you," she said as we walked out together. "And you must invite me to your graduation. I would be honored.

"Oh you know I will. You don't have to say it twice," I laughed. "I will."

My visit with Ms. Malone was all so inspiring. It's funny how you get around people who you admire and respect and how you are conscious of the way you speak around them, being mindful of your grammar and word phrases. I thought it was deep how she continued to thank me when all I ever wanted to do was thank her. I guess we all needed a purpose, a reason to get up in the morning. And I believed that her students were hers.

CHAPTER FORTY-FOUR

It was two weeks before the end of my first semester and I had been back in the states for about three and a half months now. Dylan, Fathiya, and Africa were well behind me now. I wasn't even sure at that point if the memory of Africa even belonged to me. It was as if I had dreamt it all.

It didn't take long before Popeyes Chicken and biscuits had become an important part of my diet. But on this particular day I decided I wanted to eat something different; something more wholesome. I had grown tired of the greasy foods and the indigestion. And so I plugged up my Forman Grill and placed on it a couple of pieces of seasoned tilapia with lemon and herbs. I steamed some broccoli sprinkled with parmasean, and made me a small pot of wild rice. And I was just about to sit down and sink my teeth into it when the door bell rang. It was Lola and Jackson.

"You got time for a little company?" Jackson asked.

"Sure, why not. I just made some talapia, broccoli, and rice. Have some?" I asked cordially.

"No thank you, we just ate," Lola replied.

"We just stopped by to see what you were up to; see how everything is coming along?" Jackson asked.

"Everything is coming along just fine. I take my finals in a couple of weeks and then I go on break" I answered.

'That's great," he said. "The semester is almost over huh, that quick?" he asked.

"Yep, it's almost over," I replied. "I'm already looking at the classes that I'm going to take next semester."

"Good, good," he said.

It was obvious that the two of them were pretty tight. But looking at them I noticed that they seemed a bit fidgety. I still had a slight problem with their relationship and I think that Lola knew that. Because most of the time when Lola and Jackson came to visit, Lola would never say much. I found myself always having a conversation with Jackson while Lola basically sat there and listened. It got to be very uncomfortable at times. But we muddled through.

But on this particular day I was more uneasy than the previous times. I had a hard time even enjoying my meal because it was something about the nature of the visit that just didn't feel right. Something was going on and I knew it.

"So what's going on?" I inquired."Why are y'all so quiet?

The both of them looked at each other and then looked at me.

"Nothing," they both said unconvincingly.

I dropped my fork into my plate and sat back and asked again, but this time I looked them both in their eyes.

"What is going on?" I asked in a more serious tone.

"Okay, we wanted to come by today to get your opinion on something," Lola said.

"I'm listening."

"How would you feel about being my brides' maid?" Lola asked.

This was a shock. I knew that my mom and Jackson were kinda' seeing each other but I never saw this coming. I slowly got up without a word when I was suddenly struck by a sea of emotions that I thought I had under control. I felt them rising up in me like a flood so I knew I had to remove myself from the room before I said something that I would not be able take back. I had a sudden urge to do the dishes. And so I cleared the table and head for the kitchen.

Lola attempted to follow me but Jackson interceded and insisted that she stay put until he had the opportunity to talk to me. And so there we both were in the kitchen as I unknowingly began to splash water everywhere in an attempt to clean the dishes.

"You feel like talkin' about it?" he asked.

"Talk about what?" I played dumb.

"Whatever is on your mind, Unique. It really matters to me and your Mother what you think about all of this," he said.

"Well, my opinion never mattered much any other time and I don't see how it could matter now. She has never cared about what anybody thought.

"Look," he started. I don't want to stand here and talk to you about love as if you knew nothing about it, because you know everything about it. You know what it's like to care deeply for someone. And you know that those feelings just don't go away just because you want them to.

I've cared for your Mother for many years and I had given up on any possibility of her and I a long time ago. I gave up on the notion of ever being with her; not because I stopped loving her, but because life just didn't seem to give us an opportunity. But when I look at you, Bailey, your mother, and even myself, I know that anything is possible through the power of God," he stated.

"I hear what you're saying Jackson," I cut him off. "But you don't know her. You don't know what she's capable of. So it's easy to swallow whatever it is she's feeding you because she's good like that. But let me tell you it's not real. I know you love her. But the question is can she love you back? Is she even capable of loving anyone back? I've spent my entire life wondering that about her and that's something that no child should ever have to wonder about their mother, not ever.

What you did for me; you changed my life and I am so grateful to you for that. I know what it's like to love her. But I also know what it's like to have her turn her back on you like she never even knew you at all.

I don't want that for you Jackson. I don't wanna' see your heart get broke. But that's exactly what's gonna' happen if you go through with this marriage. She's selfish, inconsiderate, insensitive, and unkind. You can't change something like that.

"Unique listen," Jackson started to defend her.

"No Jackson, she's right," Lola came in and interrupted. I was all of those things and I'm sorry. I'm sorry that I wasn't there for you and your brother. Believe it or not I thought the same things about myself that you think about me. I thought I was useless. I thought I was no good to you. I thought that the two of you would be better off without me," she said.

"What kind of Mother abandons her own children?" I screamed out. "What kind of human being leaves her own flesh and blood behind to be preyed upon by the elements of this world? You left us alone with no food or money. You left us alone to die. Didn't you know that? Didn't you care enough to fix whatever it was wrong with you so you could be there for us? I was just a kid – a kid Lola," my voice escalated," "You cost me everything. My father is gone because of you, my brother is gone, and Javier is gone. They're all gone because of you."

And in that very instance my mind took me back to revisit all that pain of my childhood; the nights Ice and I went hungry. I remembered the times when the electric and gas were turned off and we had no running water and no heat. I went back to the night when I lost my virginity and the exact point when I could smell every man that had ever climb on top of me. And before I could realize what I was doing, I had jumped on my Mother like she was somebody on the street and I tried to do serious harm to her.

Blow after blow I struck her over and over again until Jackson was able to restrain me about a half dozen punches in.

"Unique stop!" Jackson said as he pulled me off of her. Unique no!"

Both Lola and I both began to cry uncontrollably. Jackson was so disheveled and out of sorts he was trembling and you could see the pain in his eyes.

"I'm sorry," Lola kept repeating. "I am so sorry."

My heart was beating a thousand miles an hour as I left the kitchen and made my way into my bedroom where I closed my door and collapsed on my bed in grief. I felt like I had just got finish running a marathon. I was out of breath and exhausted. I couldn't believe what had just happened. And I never even saw it coming. I laid there cried for my childhood. I cried for Ice, Javier, Bailey, Dylan, and Fathiya. I cried until my head hurt and then I fell asleep.

Hours later, I heard a knock at my door. Lola had never left. The one time I wanted her to leave she decided to stay. Why?

"You awake? Can I come in," Lola asked as she let herself into my bedroom. She came over and sat on the edge of my bed.

"You're right about everything, you know. You have every right to feel the way you do. What kind of mother does those things? I've asked myself the same questions for years. I tried to get the courage to come back and every day that passed it became harder and harder to even bring myself to face you knowing what I had done. See I felt like I was nothing and so it was easy for me to convince myself that it was better that I stayed away from both of you. I thought that I was doing you a favor. I wish I could blame it all on the drugs and the streets but the truth is even the drugs and the streets have to have something to feed on. And so it fed off of my coward behavior and self pity. It ate away at me until there was nothin' left.

I let a lot of people down, I know. My husband was taken from me and I lost the respect of my children. I wasn't there for my father when he was dying because I was too high to even be there for him and I broken my mother's heart. Til' this day, she never recovered. She's sick right now because of me. And my brother whom I shared our Mother's womb, even he has given up on me too. You think this is how I wanted it? I would have rather been dead. You and your brother were the only things in this world that I was proud of.

But I didn't come back to disrupt your life or cause you any more pain. That was not my intention. I just got tired of running and I had nowhere else to go. And I knew that if I didn't change my life soon I would die out there in 'dem streets. And I didn't want to die out there alone.

And then when I saw Jackson and he showed me the pictures and the letters from you I thought it was a sign. I thought it was a sign from God that it wasn't too late. And it gave me the courage to at least come back to try and face you guys.

I know I'll never be able to change anything that has happened. And I will understand it if you don't ever want me in your life. I'm just glad to have been able to see you doing well in spite of everything that has happened to you and your brother because of me. And if it's gonna' cause you that much pain, I won't marry Jackson. And the kind of man that he is, he will understand.

You've got your father's strength and I'm proud to have you as a daughter. I know that I don't have the right to ask anything of you. And I know I don't deserve to be called your mother. But if you could, I would like to have a couple days to try and smooth this over with Jackson. You're right. I'll probably find a way to mess his life up too," she said.

And then I heard the door open and closed.

CHAPTER FORTY-FIVE

I woke the next morning, unfortunately to find Lola asleep on my couch and Jackson asleep in the chair. I got myself together and went into the kitchen and started to prepare breakfast. The aroma of the eggs, bacon, grits, pancakes, french toast, home fries, and biscuits woke up the dead. Lola staggered into the bathroom, came out and began to set the table. It was strange to have the mother that I had been longing for my whole entire life standing right next to me in my own kitchen helping me prepare breakfast. I was all messed up inside. I couldn't even think. I hated it but I liked it. I realized that I was angry and that underneath the anger was hurt. But underneath the hurt was love.

"Well did you guys set a date?" I asked.

" Not really," Lola responded with a sigh of relief. "A couple of weeks maybe."

"Yeah, a couple of weeks sounds just fine," Jackson sounded off.

So, the following month, Jackson and Lola were married. I still had my reservations about all of it but I wouldn't allow it to consume me. I wouldn't allow the ill feelings that I had towards Lola get in the way of any new found relationships that were being built amongst all of us. And so I hoped that the hatred that I felt for Lola in my heart would leave me because I didn't want to become a slave to it.

The wedding was pretty nice. They both seem to be happy. So who was I to stand in the way of that? Jackson deserved to be happy and that was for certain. And Lola in all of her mess, even she seemed sincere in her love for Jackson; but only time would really tell. Jackson and Lola left for the island of St Thomas the morning after they took their vows. It was the first time that Lola had been anywhere besides Detroit and so it made for an exciting time for her. A week later they were back. They immediately moved into a quaint little home on the other side of town.

We all agreed that we needed to tell Ice about Lola and the wedding that had taken place between her and Jackson. And so it was decided that we would all go up to the prison together and tell Ice in person; as a "family."

When we got up to the prison and entered the room where Ice was waiting, his eyes lit up just like before when he saw me walking towards him. He was quite happy to see Jackson as well. But when Lola stepped out from behind the two of us, Ice's expression of happiness became an expression of disbelief. I guess he thought that his eyes were playing tricks on him. He looked on and slightly shook his head no, in denial as he looked at Lola and Lola looked at him.

"Hi," Lola said. "Would it be alright if I hugged you?" she asked.

Ice stood there non-responsive as Lola came in for a hug anyway. Ice kept his hands in his pockets.

"So what is all of this? So what you back now?" he questioned Lola.

"Yeah," she responded. "I'm back."

"For how long?" he asked.

"For good this time," she responded.

"Let's everybody have a seat," Jackson suggested. So we all sat down. Ice took out a cigarette and lit it up.

"How long you been back?" he directed all of his questions towards Lola.

"A few months now," she answered.

"A few months?" he asked shockingly.

"So why didn't nobody tell me?" he asked.

"It was basically my decision," I jumped in. "We didn't know how you would react to all of this and I didn't know if she was gonna' stay around or what. So I wanted to be sure before we told you."

"I wanted to come up here myself and tell you that I've remarried," Lola interrupted.

"Is that right?" Ice mocked in an irritated tone. "When did all of this take place?"

"About two weeks ago," Lola answered.

"Wow, who's the lucky guy?" Ice remained sarcastic.

I know my brother. And in that moment I knew that he was hurting. His sarcasm was just his way of covering his true feelings.

"I am," Jackson answered for Lola.

"Wow! I should have known. Y'all came up here to drop a bomb on me," he responded as he looked at all of us.

"It's not like that Ice, it's not," I tried to convince him with that ridiculous line.

"Don't even worry about it. It's all good," I've gotten use to all the saga. But hey", Ice replied as he reached out his hand to Jackson. "Congratulations! You're a good dude and I hope it works out for you" he said to Jackson.

"Here, I have some pictures of the wedding and the honeymoon," Lola said as she pulled the pictures from her purse and held them out to Ice, totally dismissing his comments.

"Sure why not," Ice said as he removed the pictures from her hand.

Ice sat there and looked through all the pictures of the wedding. I even caught him smiling a couple of times. And that's when I knew it was gonna' be alright because it was evident that Ice was much more forgiving than I could ever be. But I knew that his family meant a lot to him and so he would want it all to work out. Maybe it would because he didn't see what I saw or hadn't endured all of what I had endured. But however it went, I did what I needed to do to keep the peace as I tried to hold on to whatever small portion of normalcy there was within this shattered family.

The visit with Ice went better than I had expected. And for the next two months we all took turns visiting Ice. Jackson and Lola would always go together every other Sunday. And I would visit him on my own usually every other Saturday on the weeks that Jackson and Lola didn't visit. And I liked it that way.

CHAPTER FORTY-SIX

I really felt in tune with most of my professors. I guess my love for learning may have had something to do with that. And besides, school took my mind off of the here and now. And whatever present evil that tried to invade my space lost all of its power as long as I was preoccupied basking in knowledge.

And so it was a hot Saturday morning and I thought I would beat the heat and get an early start; and with no classes I didn't have to work. So I figured I would work on my final class paper for my Sociology class that was due at the end of the week.

I got up and made me a bowl of hot wheat with butter and honey. I got the last bottle of cranberry juice from the fridge and took my school books, pad and pen, onto the porch where it was cooler. I always was able to think better while taking in the fresh air and listening to the sounds of nature around me.

As a very young child, when my father was alive, he would often take me to the park where I would just be still and listen to all the different sounds that were around me. I could close my eyes and was able to separate every sound one from the other. I could hear a bird chirping and bicycle wheels turning amidst barking dogs, the laughter of children on the sliding board and swing; or the kids who were on the skate board ramp.

The block that I currently lived on was a quiet block because most of my neighbors were of retirement age and I was the youngest. There were no sounds of children screaming and running up and down the street at all times of the night and no sounds of domestic violence. The absence of those command sounds allowed me to hear more clearly, the sounds that were more subtly; the leaves blowing, wind blowing softly, and the pitter patter of a squirrels feet hurrying up a tree.

I was just finishing up the opening paragraph to the assignment that I was preparing to turn in on the "Tuskegee Experiment"; a very interesting clinical study that was conducted between 1932 and1972 by the US Public Health Service in Tuskegee, Alabama that was initiated to study the natural progression of untreated syphilis.

The Public Health Service along with the Tuskegee Institute began the study in 1932. Investigators enrolled in the study 399 impoverished black sharecroppers from Macon County, Alabama and intentionally infected them with syphilis. That's what I said, "intentionally."

According to the Centers for Disease Control, the men were only told that they were being treated for "bad blood," a local term used to describe several illnesses, including syphilis, anemia, and fatigue. And as a reward for participating in the study, the men were given free medical exams, free meals and free burial insurance. These men were never told that they had been infected with the syphilis virus, nor were they ever treated for it.

I found myself trying to visualize a time such as that and what it must have been like to live in a place in that moment where someone could have even considered doing something so unspeakable to another human being. Even reading about this study raised a strong reaction in me and the thought of being deceived and betrayed in the most unscrupulous way by your own Local Government and feeling

that they valued the lives of their own dogs far more than they did
the lives of black people was most heartening.

And it was for that reason that I knew it was necessary that I
write from a perspective that could only resembled those from whom
the experiment was done. And so I began to write and describe one
of saddest eras in the history of Alabama. Engulfed in thought and
deliberation, I was seven minutes into my paper when I heard a
car door slam. The sound almost instantly directed me to exit my
thoughts and to take notice.

There was a white limousine that pulled up in front of Mrs.
Barksdale's house, a widow who lived directly across the street from
where I lived. I looked up just in time to see the driver walk up and
knock on Mrs. Barksdale's door. Two or three minutes later Mrs.
Barksdale came to the door and spoke to the driver for about ten
minutes. At one point I noticed Mrs. Barksdale pointing over in the
direction of my next door neighbor's house. From what I could gather
that the driver was at the wrong house. And I began to ask myself
what he could possibly want with my neighbor, Mr. Holister.

Mr. Holister was a quaint older man about seventy years of
age. I don't think he ever married and I knew definitely that he was
without children. He was a kind man, at least from what I could tell.
And he pretty much kept to himself. He didn't like people much.
He even had all of his groceries delivered to his house once a week
because he hated the super market. Just last month he asked me if
he could give me a key to his home in case of an emergency. I was
flattered that he even had that much trust in me.

I put my book down and slowly stood up and looked on as the
driver went back over to his car for a moment. And just as I folded
my arms in an attempt to be patient I watched the car door open and
the driver once again point in my direction I continued to look on.
For some reason I didn't like what was taking place as it felt a little
intrusive on my part and so I decided to go inside.

I backed up with an extended arm reaching for the door behind me. I tried to direct my hand to the knob of the door but was having difficulty. On the third time, I turned to look back as I reached for the knob and managed to open the door and went inside. Once I was inside I went to the window and peeked out. I saw the car but I couldn't see the driver any longer. Two minutes later there was a knock at my door.

"I know this man is not knocking at my door." I said to myself.

I couldn't imagine what he could have possibly wanted from me. And so I stayed inside hoping he would go away. But then there was another knock, and another.

"What in the hell did this man want from me?" I asked myself as I started to get really agitated.

I didn't know anything really about the neighbors and I preferred to mind my own business. And besides, I didn't want to know anything. All of a sudden I heard what I thought was my front door open and close. I just knew good and damn well this man didn't just walk up into my house. Calmly, I went for my bat that was behind the chair that I was sitting in and positioned myself as I prepared to take his head off. And right when I heard footsteps that came from out of the vestibule get louder, I heard a voice say;

"I see nothing's changed. You're still just as feisty and beautiful as I remember," he said.

I remained in my self defense mode and couldn't find the words. I slowly released my grip from the bat and sat down in the chair behind me and was dumb founded as he walked further into the house and found a seat right across from me.

"I've missed you," Dylan confessed.

I didn't know anything at that moment and was completely taken by surprise. I just sat there and stared at him. Somewhere in my heart I knew that I did love him. But I never thought that it would amount to anything outside of Africa. But in my deepest imagination I dreamed of it but would always wake up.

"Please say something," he said as I sat there in silence.
"I need for you to leave, "I finally said.
"Leave?, he questioned. Listen, I came back to the village the very day that you left, but you had gone," he responded.
"I would like to be alone now," is all I could say.
"I tried to contact you. There wasn't a day that passed that I didn't think about you. I dreamed of you constantly. I had so much to tell you but I wanted to talk to you face to face.

"There was no need for you to come here. There is nothing here for you," I said.

I didn't know why I was even saying those things to the man I loved. I had thought about that moment for so long and now it was here and I didn't know what to do with it.

"You want me to leave?" he asked in disbelief.
"That is what I said," I responded.
"I can imagine what is going through your head right now and why you're being so cold and uncaring. But that's not who you are. I'm sorry that it took me so long to find you. I never

meant for that to happen. You have to believe that," he tried to explain.

"I don't care about anything that you're saying right now. I just want to be left alone."

"I know that you don't mean that?" he stuttered. "You really want me to believe that you don't care that I'm here right now? And so, what are you gonna' just pretend like Africa never happened? – Like we never happened?" he asked.

"I told you from the beginning that this was a bad idea and that it would never work. I'm sorry if you thought it was more," I explained.

"No, it did work. It was working. Listen, my father had taken ill and I was needed at home to tie up some lose ends," he said.

"You don't have to explain anything to me," I interrupted.

"Obviously I do. I never for one second…"

"You don't have to explain," I cut him off again.

"I never for a second forgot about you or stopped loving you.

"Just stop. I don't want to hear it," I said.

"The whole time I was away from you I thought about what it would take for me to be happy – I mean truly happy. I had been so distant from my family and uncertain about my life in general that I never even considered happiness; not for me. Because I didn't feel I deserved it. And then you came along and remained the only constant thing on my mind. And I realized that the happiest days that I've had have been with you. You… are what make me happy."

"It's been seven months, Dylan. Do you realize that? It's been seven months without so much as a word from you. You left me no other choice. My life had already experienced so much of the worst. But I'm in school now. I have a job. I know where I'm headed. And I'm here trying to salvage whatever my life is.

I can't deny the fact that I really did enjoy the time that I spent with you. But this is the real world now. And whatever we had was just….

"Just what?" he cut me short. "All of that was just what? C'mon, I need to hear you say it. Because I know that what we had was real. It was real then and it's real now. And don't you dare try and down play that. Do you love me?" he blurted.

"None of that has anything to do with anything. Why can't you understand that?" I blurted back.

"Because you're wrong. Love has everything to do with everything. And you know that. But you can't admit that the real reason behind why you are acting this way is the fact that you're afraid and that's why you're trying to shut me out."

"You're damn right I'm shutting you out. You're the one that left; no address and no phone number. I didn't know if I'd every see you again. And I'm not gonna' give you that opportunity again."

"Ok, I know. I know that it never should have happened like that. But I'm here now and I promise that it will never happen again. Do – you – love me?" he asked me again.

There was another knock at the door.

"I'm sorry Sir, we have a bit of a bathroom emergency," the driver said to Dylan.

"You brought a driver all the way from England?" I asked in confusion.

"In a minute Lionel," Dylan responded.

"Dylan it's alright, he can use the bathroom." I calmed down. "Come on in sir, you are more than welcomed to use the bathroom.

"Just a minute Lionel," Dylan insisted. "Unique, do you love me?"

"Dylan, I can't talk about this anymore. Would you just let the man use the bathroom," I insisted. "Sir please, come in and use the bathroom," I practically demanded.

"No ma'am, it's not me," Lionel replied.

"I don't understand," I said as I went to the door to see for myself what he meant.

Once I got to the door, I looked, took a deep gasp and threw my hand up to mouth.

"Hi Uni," Fathiya said in the sweetest voice I ever heard as she stood on the porch with Mr. Bear in her arms and a picture of the three of us in her hand. I couldn't pick her up and hug her fast enough.

"Oh my God. Oh my God," I repeated. "Hi sweetie pie. What are you doing here?" I said as tears rolled down the side of my face.

"Are you sad?" Fathiya asked.

"No precious."

"But you're crying," she said.

"I know," I answered. Sometimes people cry when they're happy," I responded.

"Are you happy?" Fathiya asked.

"Yes. Yes I am very happy to see you, I said as I looked over to see Dylan looking over at the two of us. "Come on now," I said to her, let's get you to the bathroom. Would you like to leave Mr. Bear and the picture down here with Dylan until we come back?" I asked her.

"No," she shook her head.

"It's Okay. You don't have to," I said.

So up the stairs we went to the bathroom as all kinds of thoughts rushed through my mind like undefined waters, with no color, no odor, and no taste. I didn't know anything at that moment. I couldn't seem to wrap my head around all of what was just happened in those few minutes. I was totally blown away. How was he able to pull this off? " I asked myself. "Oh God, what am I gonna' do now?

"Are you hungry?" I asked Fathiya. "Would you like something to eat?"

"Yes," she said.

"Okay then," I said.

We washed our hands and went downstairs. Once I got downstairs I immediately went into the kitchen. Fathiya followed me.

"Would you like to help me?" I asked her.

"Yes, she replied.

We fixed pancakes, eggs, bacon, hominy grits, sausage, and biscuits. I was glad that I had some fresh orange juice in the fridge and some milk. Once Fathiya and I finished cooking Dylan washed his hands and joined us and said grace. And then we ate…and ate… and ate. There was no conversation at all between Dylan and me. We both only spoke to Fathiya.

Once we were finished, I wiped Fathiya's face and hands and took her into the living room where I sat her up in the couch and turned the television to the nickelodeon station. She was so excited to see all the different animated characters on that channel. I turned and walked back into the dinning room where Dylan was still sitting and I began to clear the table still without a word.

"Aren't you gonna' say anything?" he asked.

"When there's something to say, I guess I'll say it," I responded.

"I thought you would be happy to see us," he said.

"I am. I'm happy to see Fathiya. How did you do it? How did you manage all of this and why?" I asked.

"I was going to explain all of it to you when I got back to the orphanage. But you were gone. But that trip wasn't a lost trip at all because I got to see Fathiya. When I got there I immediately went to her and she would not respond to me. And for the entire week that I was there she refused to speak or anything," he said. "And it was then that I knew."

"You knew what?" I asked.

"I knew that I couldn't leave her there, not without you. The time that we spent together - the three of us, was magical. It was the nourishment in our lives that we all needed. And I know you felt the same way. It didn't have to end there," he said.

"What are you saying?" I asked

"I'm saying that it could be like it was for always. I want us to be a family. Look, I have the papers here. All we have to do is sign them," he said.

"Wait a minute. What are you talkin' about?" I questioned him as I took the papers from his hand.

"She can be ours if we want her. That's what I'm doing here. That's what I've come all this way to tell you. That's one of the reasons that I was away so long. I had to have the proper paper work for Fathiya, a passport and medical records before the government officials of Nairobi would release her to me."

"You've adopted Fathiya?" I questioned.

"It's not official until the papers are signed and returned. And if you will have me, then we could begin our lives together as a family – the three of us" Dylan said.

"I don't understand. They, they just let you take her, just like that without signed papers? That just doesn't sound right. I didn't know that they just let people do that?" I stuttered. "What is really going on?"

"There are so many things that I didn't get a chance to tell you about me. There just wasn't time," he went on.

"Tell me what? Tell me now then, I insisted.

"The reason that I was able to get custody of Fathiya in such a short time is because I'm kinda' like the founder of the orphanage," he disclosed.

"Founder, like in owner?" Is that what you're telling me?" I asked in disbelief.

"Well, my family owns the orphanage," he responded. "I wanted to tell you from the very beginning but I didn't see that it would matter. And I didn't want you to pre-judge me on that aspect. I wanted you to know me for me. I wanted you to treat me as an equal," he said.

"Are you standing in my face trying to justify how you mislead me? You are kidding aren't you? This whole time you had me thinking that you were a worker, a volunteer like I was….unbelievable."

"Look, we have plenty of time to discuss these things," he tried to change the subject.

"No. I would like to discuss them now. What other kinds of things does your family own, Dylan?"

"Look, what does it even matter?" he asked.

"It matters a lot and I want to know," I demanded.

"My family is in the manufacturing business. We own quite a few things."

"So, you're rich?" I asked.

"No, my Father's rich. It is his money" Dylan said modestly.

"It's the same thing and you know it. Don't play word games with me," I said as I turned away from him and became very emotional. "You came all the way here to tell me this. And you what, want me to marry you? I'm just curious. Have you told your parents about me? Have you? Have you told them that I'm black?"

"Not yet, but I plan on telling them as soon as we got back"

"After we got back? Alright, stop. Just stop. You know what, this is all a bit much to take in. I mean, this would be too much for anyone." I stated hysterically.

"And I know this," he said. "And that's why I didn't want to tell you right away until after we got to know each other because I didn't want you to concentrate just on any of the other stuff. How was I supposed to know that I would love you and love Fathiya?"

At that point I completely shut down. I was literally unable to hear anymore. My brain had taken in all that it was capable of at one time.

"Really?" I questioned. "I can't think about any of this right now. I need for you to go. And I'm not gonna say it again"

Dylan dropped his head in defeat, lifted it again, and looked me in my eyes.

"What about Fathiya?" he asked.

"I wanna' stay Uni," Fathiya cried out as she listened to the whole conversation.

"She'll be fine. She'll stay here with me," I said with a sternness.

Dylan reached into his pocket and pulled out a generous amount of money and placed it on the table.

"Whatever you need, just call me. This is where you can reach me," Dylan stated, handing me a card that said "MGM Grand Detroit, at1777, 3rd St, Detroit, Michigan, 48226. "No matter the hour just call me," he finished.

He kissed me softly on my neck, picked Fathiya up and hugged her and told her that she could call him whenever she wanted. And Fathiya and I watched Dylan as he left.

The days that followed were pretty awkward. It was hard to explain to everyone who Fathiya was and how did I come to have her. After hearing the story, Jackson and Uncle Blaze believed that everything would work itself out for the good of all those involved. But it was difficult to explain it to Lola. When she heard that Dylan was well off she just couldn't understand my dilemma. But she would never understand the discord of my relationship with Dylan and what it would have to undergo if we were to be together just because of our backgrounds alone. She just didn't get it.

It had been a week since Dylan and Fathiya arrived. Dylan called my house day and night for an entire week but I couldn't bring myself to answer any of his calls. He sent a number of flower bouquets. I knew that we all had a past and I believe that real freedom lies within the connection between the state of reality and the imagination. And my imagination at times had allowed me to escape my reality; but only for a little while. Dylan was becoming impatient and I knew I would have to face him sooner rather than later. And soon would come shortly after the second week.

Dylan had become bored with sending the flowers and calling a dozen times a day. I guess he just couldn't wait any longer. So he decided to come over and camp outside my door. He made camp on my porch and refused to leave until he got a response from me. He was out there three days and two nights before I finally opened my door. I came out onto the porch and sat there with him. We sat in silence for about three minutes and then he spoke.

"If it's my family you're worried about – don't," he suggested. "My Father is ill. My Mother is difficult at times. They are a very traditional people. But I am their only son and while we don't agree on everything, ultimately, they only want what makes me happy," he said..

"I can imagine. I mean, anybody can see that our differences will not make it easy for us. I don't know how we would begin to make something so complicated work. You would be taking on a great deal of responsibility. I am a damaged soul and I know it. It would be very challenging for you take on someone with my background and a child who is equally as challenged. I just wonder if you've really given it a lot of thought.

"It's all I've been thinking about. Taking on you and Fathiya as my family will not be something that I would consider a challenge but a privilege. You two have added to my life everything. I was lost until I met you. I was searching and looking for something to make me feel whole. You made me want to come out from hiding. Loving you is has been the easiest thing that I've ever done. I blamed myself for a lot of things that I know I can't change. But you made me see that it was alright to forgive myself. You helped me find a desire to live without guilt"

Just then Lola and Jackson pulled up. They got out of their car and walked up onto the porch.

"Hi, I'm Lola, Unique's Mother," Lola introduced herself.

"And I'm Jackson, Unique's step dad," Jackson said.

"I'm Dylan. It's a pleasure to make your acquaintance," Dylan said as he kissed the back side of Lola's hand. "Now I see where Unique gets her beauty from.

"Ohh, my an Englishman. What a kind thing to say," Lola blushed.

"How long are in town for?" Jackson asked.

"That would be up to Unique," Dylan replied as he looked over at me.

"Well, we just came by to see Fathiya. We stopped by market and picked up some of those chicken fingers that she loves so much. Where is she?" Lola asked.

"She's in there where she's been for the last week glued to the television," I answered.

"Okay, we didn't mean to intrude. You two keep right on talking. We'll be inside with Fathiya if you need us. Nice meeting you Dylan," Lola said.

"It's been an honor," Dylan replied as Jackson and Lola entered the house. "I'm glad to see that everything is good with you and your family now," Dylan said to me.

"I wouldn't say everything is good." I stated. "I'd say that everyone seems to be trying and I'd just leave it at that," I said with clarity.

"Well I know that I am willing to do whatever it is that you need me to do. Just tell me what it is. I have something for you," he said as he reached into his pocket and handed me a piece of paper. I took it from his hand and opened it and I began to read. I looked up at Dylan in awe and then looked back down at the paper as I had to readjust my eyes to make sure that I was not misreading the words that was on that paper.

"Am I reading this right? This says that Ice is being considered for a pardon. But how can that be" I asked

"Yes," Dylan answered as he looked on anticipating my reaction. I sat there for a moment and I began to sob.

"What is going on out here? Unique, what's wrong?" Jackson asked when he came to the door.

"Unique, what happened? What's the matter with her?" Lola questioned.

I gathered myself and found my composure and handed the letter to Jackson.

"Is this for real?" Jackson asked. "This says that Ice is gonna' be getting' out of jail."

"Yes sir, it is for real," Dylan assured Jackson.

"Who are you that you could make something like this happen?"

"It wasn't me sir. I can't take the credit for this. My father holds a rather important position in the British Embassy and he called in a favor. He did this to please me," Dylan said as he held my hand and looked kindly into my eyes.

"And you did this to please me?" I asked.

"I would do anything for you. Don't you know that?" he assured me.

"How can I ever pay you back?" I asked.

"Your happiness is payment enough," he said. But I would like an answer to a question that I've been asking you for some time now. Do – you – love me?" he asked as he gently stroked my hair.

I could no longer deny my feelings for this man that did this thing for me.

"Yes, I do," I answered as Dylan pulled me up from where I was sitting and placed his hands on my hips and pulled me in close.

"Will you be my wife?" he asked.

"Yes, I will," I responded.

Dylan began to give me small warm kisses about my face until his lips reached mine. We engaged in a fiery kiss that lasted about a minutes or so.

"Let's go take our daughter out for some ice cream," he said.

"Ok. But I have something to do first," I answered as I leaned in starved for yet another kiss.

I remember that day well. I remember the clouds began to merge and the scent of the air was summer rain. Dylan's lips were soft and his breath sweet with a tint of peppermint patty. Loving him was more than I could have ever imagined. And him loving me was more than I could have ever dreamed. I always knew in my heart that I would see my brother walk free one day. But never in a million years would I have thought it would have happened like this.

Dylan and I went inside to get Fathiya. While I was inside I went into my room for just a moment to take care of something.

I stared in the mirror as I messaged the locket that was around my neck; the locket that I had worn since Javier died. I knew that I would never be able to hold Javier in my arms again but that I would always hold him in my heart.

But I realized that God had placed favor upon me as he restored my family and sent me a man after his own wishes. There was no other explanation. He had assured me that I could loosen up my grip and let go of a past that I felt had robbed me of things that would cause me pain for the rest of my life if I allowed it to. I knew that I would never see my father or Javier ever again but I would never forget them or the love that we shared.

"Rest in peace baby. I'll see you on the other side," I said as I took the locket from around my neck, opened it, kissed it, placed it in a safe space inside my draw and inside my heart. And I quietly left the room.

The End

THE BACK OF THE BOOK

The ordeals that came to test Unique Jefferson only mirrored the magnitude of strength that she possessed within her. Because no matter how difficult the trials that she would have to face, they could never outweigh more than she would be able to handle. But that was something that she needed to find out for herself. Her story is a clear testament that the significance of life is relevant in the existence of every living thing no matter the size or the circumstance. And even when all the world has failed you and your back is against the wall and there is nowhere else you can turn, the power of God will sustain you and overcome it all.

The End